Knight
of
Rapture

"A thrilling and emotionally evocative tale filled with adventure, love and hope. Casie's weaved an exciting medieval fantasy romance series that I can't get enough of."

...Eliza Knight, USA Today bestselling author

Praise for

Knight
of
Runes

"... full of, 'on the edge of your seat' suspense, mind-boggling drama and a forever-after romance."

...Romance Junkies

"... the plot builds steadily through dangers and discoveries that affect the hero and heroine, leading to a powerful conclusion that precedes the next highly anticipated follow-up book."

...Single Title

Ruth A.
Casie

Knight
of
Rapture

Ruth A. Casie (signature)

Timeless Scribes
Publishing

Timeless Scribes Publishing LLC
Print
ISBN-10: 0-9862464-4-9
ISBN-13: 978-0-9862464-4-9

Digital
ISBN-10: 0-9862464-3-2
ISBN-13: 978-0-9862464-3-2

Cover created by Alchemy Book Covers and Design
Edited by Mallory Braus
Copy Edited by Michael Mandarano

This edition published by arrangement with Timeless Scribes Publishing LLC.

www.TimelessScribes.com

Dedicated to ~

This is for all the readers who waited patiently for the next chapter in Arik and Rebeka's story. I hope you love it as much as I do!

Paul, my husband, who keeps me, enraptured with his magic all the time—I love you.

Mallory Braus, my editor, for encouraging me, for talking me off the cliff—multiple times.

Knight

of

Rapture

CHAPTER ONE

September 22, 1605 — Early Morning

Visions of his warm bed and even warmer wife lit Lord Arik's face. A deep, rich chuckle rumbled in his chest at the vivid images of how he'd wake Rebeka.

Who would have thought the great druid Grand Master was a besotted bridegroom? The summer had been warm and all the sweeter with Rebeka by his side.

He stood on the open terrace at the back of the manor, surveyed his domain and swelled with pride. Fayne Manor was a thriving estate that had been the family home for eleven centuries and it would stand for eleven more.

While he waited for the sun to rise, he prepared for the ritual. He took off his linen shirt and braced himself for the crisp September air. The morning breeze stirred, sending the red and orange leaves racing across the garden, twisting and tumbling like rowdy children at play.

Out of the corner of his eye he sensed movement but nothing was there. It sobered him. The Shade, an otherworldly thing, was an old acquaintance begging for an audience. Like an old woman with aches and pains predicting bad weather, the Shade's shadow warned him of trouble. What did it bring this time? He had learned long ago to listen to it. The warning was accurate, most of the time. He glanced at the manor door. A little longer. He wanted more time to love her before he began her training. Dark Magick. *Faith*. She wouldn't be the same when they were done. He didn't want any changes. She was fine the way she was.

He placed his shirt on the stone railing as the sky brightened. Any moment the small sliver of golden sun would crest the rim of the hill then he would ask the Great Mother to grant his people a good day.

His nostrils flared. The trace of a sweet, pungent metallic smell sobered him. He tried to push it aside but it remained at the edge of his mind, stealing the last of his pleasure. Lightning. The smile slid off his face. For everyone's safety he needed to take action—he recognized the signature.

Bran.

He cleared his mind for the ritual and thoughts of Bran faded—for the moment.

"Hail and welcome," he declared to the east as fingers of sunlight stretched over the hill. His body warmed as the tattooed runes draped across his back and chest, thrummed and brightened. They were a sign of his station as the druid Grand Master. Each rune strengthened his power and had been earned as he progressed in the Order from druid to Master to the ultimate title of Grand Master. "Thank you, Great Mother for giving us another day, a day of peace…"

And, he murmured, *for giving me Rebeka.*

The lingering mist faded with the morning sun. Like a cozy down blanket pulled from a bed, the retreating haze revealed the thriving village and farms.

Soon the quiet valley would come to life. Farmers would set off on their daily chores, the villagers would open their shops, and his soldiers would take to the practice fields. His chest swelled. Was it a sin to be proud of what he, together his people, had accomplished? He'd do anything for them, anything to protect their hearths and homes.

He closed his eyes for the morning blessing. "*As above, so below. As within, so*—." He took a deep breath and caught the faint scent of lavender and roses. The teasing fragrance announced Rebeka was near. Her morning appearance, with his tankard of watered ale, had become part of his ritual. "*...so without,*" he continued the rite. "May guidance and love mark our way. And bring success for our clan today. So mote it be." He opened his eyes.

"The day appears promising." Rebeka's voice brought a smile to his lips. She tugged her shawl closer around her shoulders. "M'lord." Soft puffs of breath surrounded her mouth. There was indeed a chill in the morning air. She gave him his discarded shirt and waited while he shrugged into it before handing him his ale.

She had little on beneath her great shawl. It made his mind wander. "Yes. It will be a good day." It was always a good day when it began with her at his side. "Almost as good as last night." They drove each other mad with their verbal banter and soft touches yesterday until she surrendered to him. His reward was to tease her until she yielded last night. Who knew who would yield today? Either way they both won.

Her gaze slid from his chest to his face. Her searing expression brought back the warmth of their passionate evening. Her flushed skin was her silent response.

He returned his gaze to the valley pretending to be interested in the smoke now rising from a distant chimney. He turned his attention back to her.

Faith, how he loved sparring with her.

Out of the corner of his eye he caught her blank stare. But the challenge was given and he understood it had been accepted. With a long pull on his ale he returned his attention to the curling smudge in the sky and like a game of chess waited for her to make the next move.

She rose on tiptoes and bathed his ear with her soft breath. "But not as good as tonight will be," she whispered. "We celebrate Samhain tonight."

He didn't try to hide his arousal. He set the tankard on the wide stone railing before the ale sloshed over its rim.

"Happy thoughts for the day, husband." She laid her hand on his chest and bent to kiss his cheek.

He caught her around her waist and brought her face to his. How he adored the passion in her violet eyes. They asked for more. He answered with a searing kiss and teased her mouth open with his tongue. She didn't protest. Instead she moved closer, molding her body into his. Encouraged, his tongue swept her mouth and he reveled at the sweet taste. When he released her she stood in the crook of his arm, her head on his chest with his cheek resting on her hair. Quiet and content, he savored the last few moments while the sun rose over the edge of the hill.

"Wife, you surprise me with the...thoughts you put in my mind." His blood heated at the mere idea of his musings.

"I didn't..."

"Yes, I know... But if you did mind-touch and put thoughts in my head I know what they would be." Mind-touching was a special skill. No druid would trespass another's mind. It was a grave violation. She would never abuse her ability.

The sound of footsteps from the Great Hall interrupted them. "Arik? Ah, here you are." Logan, his younger brother, peeked out the terrace door. "Are you ready to leave? The sun rose hours ago. I thought we'd breakfast with the men and start maneuvers today."

Logan gave Rebeka a devilish nod. He casually filched Arik's forgotten tankard and took a deep swallow.

Arik observed the bottom of the sun clear the eastern hill. "Hours?" He shook his head and let out a snort. He threaded his fingers through Rebeka's and gave them a tender squeeze. He had wanted more time with her. He always wanted more time with her. But for now their game was over, at least until tonight.

"Hours," Arik muttered while he released her then took the tankard out of Logan's hand. "And get your own ale. Better yet, get yourself a wife to bring it to you," he told Logan in feigned aggravation before he drained the tankard dry.

"Ah, but where will I find one like Rebeka?" Another nod for his sister-in-law. Rebeka bobbed a quick curtsy and tried not to laugh.

Find one like Rebeka, indeed. There was no one like her, but good sense told him Logan would find a love of his own. He earned that. A cool morning breeze stirred the bottom of Rebeka's thin nightdress and she shivered.

"Go get something warmer on before you catch your death," Arik whispered in her ear. She nodded and scooted into the house.

"Maneuvers today?" Arik glanced at Logan and observed his pleasure turn to concern. "The winter's coming. We should make sure the farms are prepared, there's enough food stored and the necessary repairs have been made before the snow." He had hoped the calm that his valiant soldiers fought to achieve in August would last longer. "There's still more to teach Rebeka. She's not ready to face Bran."

"She came through the portal to return to you. She's strong. We need her skills to defeat Bran. We can't do it without her." Logan didn't hide his impatience. "Yet you haven't taught her about Dark Magick. Instead you hide it from her. And I know why." Arik almost sneered at Logan. This was an old argument. Logan would have had him start her training after their wedding night.

"You're afraid she won't be able to control it, that she'll become like Bran. Don't you see she's made of stronger stuff?" Arik waved him off. He stepped away to put space between them. But space wouldn't help.

Who did he fool? Certainly not Logan. Arik glanced at his brother and recognized his silent strength. The only fool here was him. He couldn't continue with this idyllic illusion. Logan was right. He had been delaying teaching her. He knew Dark Magick would test her, change her. And he wanted her just the way she was.

"After years of being battle ready the men have earned more than a two month furlough," Arik said in one last effort to put off Logan. The air was alive with Logan's unspoken objection. He was losing this battle. *Faith*, he didn't want anything to change. He knew she would agree with Logan. He was lost. He couldn't fight them both. "We'll recall the men."

"I put out the word. Many of the men arrived last night. I've told them to meet us at the garrison this morning." It was Logan's turn to find the smoke from the distant chimney interesting.

"You haven't forgotten about the portal," Logan said. Rebeka returned in her morning dress and shawl.

Ah, this was the crux of the matter. Maximillian's last time-travel portal still existed. Arik had sealed all of the others except this one in order to leave Rebeka one opportunity to go back to the twenty-first century. She valued her independence and ability to determine her own destiny. It challenged him but he loved her for it. He couldn't seal it, trap her here. It had to be her choice.

"We've spoken about closing the portal on Samhain," Logan said. Magick was strongest on the first day of spring, with its balance of light and dark. He needed that magick to finish the former Grand Master's work.

"I agree with Logan. Seal the portal and begin my training." Arik stood next to Rebeka; she had no idea what she asked.

He brought her around to face him and peered into her eyes. "I can't undo the magick once it's done. You must be sure." Would she regret not returning? He *needed* her to be certain.

"My father took me to the future to protect me. All my life I've been searching for something without knowing what it was. When I came to Fayne Manor, your Fayne Manor, I knew I had found what I had been searching for." She held him close. "You. Here is where I belong. Why would I want to be anywhere else? Seal the portal now, forever, before anything happens."

"She's right. Seal the portal before Bran finds a way to use it," Logan echoed before he took to the terrace steps on his way toward the manor gate.

"Wait," Arik called after him. "I'll go to the garrison with you." He trotted down the steps and caught up with Logan.

"So, you recalled the men. You were certain I'd agree." He had considered calling the men after Samhain. A few days earlier were fine with him. But he hadn't wanted to start Rebeka's training. He glanced back at her standing on the terrace. Logan was right. They needed his sorceress wife's strength.

"Of course you would agree. Once you reviewed the situation from every angle. Besides, you've sensed the Shade, too. We both know it's time."

Arik threw his arm around Logan's shoulder. When had the adoring younger brother become a knowledgeable man, a good friend and soldier? "I thought I heard them gathering when I prepared for the morning ritual. While you organize the men I'll see to the portal. I'll meet you at the practice field when I'm done."

Rebeka watched the brothers leave through the garden gate and marveled at their similarities. People moved out of their way to let them pass. Their self-confidence and air of authority was obvious to everyone. Arik gave the appearance of one who demanded instant obedience. Logan was quick to learn the skill. From the back they were difficult to tell apart. But she would recognize Arik anywhere. He moved with a smoothness and grace that excited her.

She took the empty tankard then entered the Great Hall ready for breakfast. Maybe later, when she finished harvesting herbs, she'd take the trail from the meadow that passed by the practice field. She pursed her lips at the idea. It was more than watching her sweaty husband half-undressed practicing with his men.

No. She set a wicked smile on her face.

It was all about watching her sweaty husband half-undressed.

"Are you going to gather herbs in the meadow?" Skylar asked while she spread jam on her morning bread. "If you don't need help, I thought I'd cheer the soldiers on while they practiced."

"And how did you know the men would gather today? You shouldn't eavesdrop." Skylar's scarlet blush flashed up her neck to her checks. Rebeka bit her lip to keep from smiling while she took her seat at the table. Skylar's embarrassment told her she was right.

Cheer on the men? Rebeka was more inclined to believe that Skylar meant to cheer on her Robert. And how different was that from her watching her Arik?

"Rebeka," Aubrey, the younger of the two girls,

interrupted, oblivious to her sister's discomfort. "I can go with you. I'm sure Elfrida wouldn't mind."

Elfrida, the oldest person in the village, lived alone in a large house on the path to the lake. She had been Skylar and Aubrey's nurse, and even Rebeka's nurse. Some said the woman was so ancient that she had been the nurse for the Ancients who lived in the Otherworld.

Her nurse. She hadn't remembered Elfrida when she returned. She hadn't remembered anyone. When her father took her to the twenty-first century to protect her from Bran and his Dark Magick he clouded her memory with an enchantment.

Skylar's head rose. "It's not that I don't want to go with you." The bread in Skylar's fingers was poised in midair. The pleading expression on her face melted Rebeka. It was obvious to her that Skylar wanted to do both but who could compete with the handsome Robert? The boy searched for any opportunity to spend time at the manor house.

Young love.

Rebeka laughed. "Go ahead to the practice field but don't stay too long. Jeannie and the other women will need help with the tables and food." Skylar popped the last of the toast into her mouth then got to her feet. "How do I look?" She brushed imaginary crumbs and wrinkles from her skirt.

"Don't shine too much or you'll blind Robert." Rebeka shook her head then realized that being older and in love wasn't much different.

"I'll be back in plenty of time." Skylar rushed from the room.

Rebeka's gaze slid to Aubrey. "What wouldn't Elfrida mind?"

"We're making sachets for the festival. I can tell her I'm coming later." A frown settled on Aubrey's face. "I do like helping her. She always tells old stories about the family." Aubrey licked the jam from her fingers. "Skylar likes to listen to them, too. She pretends she's grown up but you should see her when Elfrida starts. Her face gets all dreamy." She wiped her hands on her napkin.

Elfrida, a born storyteller, held everyone's attention with her tales of the different families. She'd been a source for Rebeka, helping her fill in some of the spaces to recall the past once the enchantment was broken. "I'm helping in the village when I'm finished in the meadow. You make your sachets with Elfrida. When you're finished meet me by the baker. We can volunteer to sample the meat pies."

Aubrey's face broke into a broad smile. Rebeka was glad to see the young girl happy and animated. It had been a few months ago that cousin Katherine had bullied and harassed her. A distant cousin of Arik's, Katherine arrived for a visit and stayed on after Arik's sister Leticia's death. Without a woman in the house, Katherine had taken on more and more household control until she ran Fayne Manor.

But Katherine was gone.

Now Aubrey's face was bright and she chatted almost as much as her sister, if that was possible. The change had been startling. She had been withdrawn and almost never spoke. Everyone in the manor and the village had been concerned. Katherine had found Aubrey's vulnerable spot, Leticia. The more Aubrey tried to hold on to her mother's memory, the more Katherine bullied her.

Katherine, the witch. The very idea of the woman made her blood boil. Katherine had tried to keep Arik under her power and isolate him from everyone.

It wasn't all Katherine's fault—it was Bran's. It had taken little for him to manipulate the woman's already jealous and spiteful mind—giving her the tools to plot against her family. When she realized Arik would never be a part of her twisted dream, to be the true mistress of Fayne Manor, she used the tools Bran gave her for her own purposes. With murder in her heart she was determined to see her dreams fulfilled.

Memories of what happened at the standing stones and portal filled her mind. She had been caught in the magick gateway. Arik had been intent to get her out. He didn't see Katherine attacking him from behind. But she did.

She threw her dirk and hit her mark. Arik got her out of the portal. But while Katherine lay wounded, she taunted them. She admitted she had killed Leticia. The pain that had crossed Arik's face had broken her heart. The woman had kept on laughing until Arik swung his sword and silenced her forever.

Rebeka glanced at Aubrey finishing her meal. No regrets. She'd do it again to save those she loved. But when would Arik understand the man behind everything, Bran, was beyond saving?

There was no way he could turn back.

She understood the devastation that Bran suffered when his wife, Cay, died but that was a long-overused excuse. Bran knew the consequences of using Dark Magick before he began. Everything had consequences and some couldn't be avoided. Arik knew that better than most in his capacity as Grand Master and lord of Fayne Manor.

"Rebeka, is something wrong?" Aubrey asked.

"Nothing's wrong. Reminiscing." She pushed Bran out of her mind and concentrated on her breakfast.

"You'd better hurry and get over to Elfrida," Jeannie told Aubrey when she came in from the kitchen, carrying an empty tray. "I left some scraps of material in a basket by the garden door. You can take those with you to make your sachets. And don't forget the flower petals you gathered."

"I won't." Aubrey dusted the toast crumbs off her

hands and rose. She leaned over to Rebeka. "I'll meet you in the baker's as soon as I'm done." She hurried off through the kitchen.

Jeannie set the tray on the table and collected the dishes. "And you'd better hurry, too. I'll need those herbs. I'm making the herb goat cheese you're fond of." Jeannie gave her a sideways glance.

Rebeka licked her lips thinking about the creamy cheese. It was a recipe she'd made for Jeannie, one she learned in the twenty-first century. "Yes, ma'am," she said as she, too, left the room.

The day was bright and mild, a good day for a festival. Not a cloud in the sky. A breeze carried the hint of cooler days to come. After the hot summer, it was a perfect relief.

The aroma of fresh-baked bread wafted up to the manor and drew Rebeka into the village. Happy and content, she leaned against a table in the market square, eating the last bite of the warm, crusty bread slathered with sweet, creamy butter.

"You approve?" Mary's voice grabbed her attention. "You told me you were eager to see everyone." Rebeka had a special place in her heart for Mary.

"This is perfect. The aroma of the hot bread," she lifted hers in salute, "is better than any alarm bell. My mouth watered as soon as I stepped outside the gate." She leaned her head toward Mary. "And I'd already eaten."

Rebeka glanced past Mary at the crowd milling around the table and the clutches of chattering neighbors who had been hard at work with the harvesting and preparing for winter. It reminded her of the twenty-first-century coffee wagon.

"The loaves were set out to cool when Lord Arik rode through the village with Doward. I gave them a large slab for their ride." Mary pulled Rebeka around to face her. "Is it true he goes to seal the last portal? You're not going back?"

"Yes. This is where I belong and where I want to be." All those early concerns about how she had arrived at the manor. The irony was laughable. The Lord Knight of Fayne Manor was the druid Grand Master—the ultimate magician. And she'd worried his people wouldn't be able to accept that she'd traveled through time. Yet when he'd tried to explain his magick she considered him to be primitive. How absurd and narrow-minded.

"Mary." One of the other women waved her over to another table.

"I'll be right there," she called out. She turned back to Rebeka. "Wait until you see what we've planned. I know I shouldn't say anything but it's your first fall festival as lady of the manor and we have a surprise for you." The woman was so excited she couldn't stand still, but hopped from one foot to the other.

Rebeka laughed. "You don't have to do anything special. Not because I'm lady of the house."

Mary took Rebeka's hands. "You're right, but being lady of the house isn't why everyone wanted to do something special for you. You are an inspiration. You lead by example. You're smart, fair-minded and, yes, maybe a bit strong-willed. To me, you're my valued friend."

Rebeka paused. "You know you mean as much to me." Mary was the first in the village to befriend her, an outsider. All her life she shied away from attachments with a sense of not belonging. But she didn't retreat from Mary.

"Mary." The woman's call grew more insistent.

"Coming," Mary shouted. She squeezed Rebeka's hands. "Of course I do. And understand I am not the only one who recognizes the good and caring person you are. Everyone does." One final squeeze and she hurried off. Rebeka stared after her.

In the twenty-first century she and her father, an authority on Celtic history, lived near a rural college campus. It was only the two of them. She surmised that her parents must have been very much in love. He never spoke about her mother nor did he have any pictures of her. She asked questions but got short, unsatisfying answers. Over time, she stopped asking. They kept to themselves most of the time. He died when she was a freshman in college and she believed she had no family and belonged nowhere until she discovered her place and her people. She only had to travel back in time four centuries to find them.

"They need more bread." Marcus, Arik's captain, stood next to her. "Skylar and the older girls set a table by the practice field to serve the men. She mentioned the villagers were gathering here. I came to see. Was this," he motioned to the people in the square, "your idea?" He nodded his thanks to the young boy who handed him a tankard.

"No, the morning gathering was Mary's idea." Her eyes moved from one group of people to the next. The villagers greeted the arriving tenants and their families with shouts and laughter. The small children ran about while the older ones chatted, the boys on one side and the girls on the other. More bread came out of the ovens and barrels of ale from the brewer.

Marcus's gaze scanned the crowd. His satisfaction and approval was apparent from the broad grin on his face. "Most of the men have arrived. The practice field is filled to capacity." He brought his tankard to his lips but before he took a sip he gave her a teasing smile. "Lord Arik will be wrestling later. You may want to watch." He drained his tankard.

How did Marcus know she enjoyed watching Arik?

"Don't look surprised. Your secret is safe with me." He had a pleased expression on his face. Marcus, too, was a good friend. He was the second, after Logan, to pledge himself to her after she married Arik. "My soldiers have found their ale and are taking a few kegs for the field." He nodded toward a knot of men hefting barrels on their shoulders. "If you'll excuse me, I have to get back. This was a fine idea. Everyone's looking forward to the banquet tonight. I hope you and Arik will sing for us. You were the highlight of the summer celebration. What was the song you sang?"

She reflected for a moment. "Row, Row, Row Your Boat." She had taught Arik, Logan and the girls to sing the song in a round one evening after dinner. They taught the song to the villagers at the summer bonfire. She saw a different side of him at the festival. Not the warrior, but the man. That was when she realized she loved him. "I'm certain if you ask him he won't say no." Marcus titled his head in salute then followed his men. She observed him exchange his empty tankard for a piece of bread when he passed the last table.

She glanced around and absorbed the warmth and closeness of family and friends and her love for Arik. How could he think she would ever want to leave? She slipped on her empty backpack and took her staff. If she hurried, she could harvest the herbs then watch Arik on the field. That would still leave her time to meet Aubrey by the baker.

Chapter Two

Arik and Doward rode along to the rhythmic clinking of the horses' metal tack and the clop of their hooves across the stone-strewn path at a gentle pace. The magick thickened as they neared the stones. Unable to ride any closer to the sacred spot, they dismounted and left their horses at the outer edge of the glen. They crossed the last hundred yards to the megaliths. This was a special place—a magical place.

Arik knew how impressive the stones were to the outsider but to the initiated, the standing stones hummed a soft tone with magick in the late-morning mist. The faint iridescent glow added to their mystical appearance. Ringed by a lush forest, the tall trees stood like silent sentinels that protected the perimeter.

It was good to be here and to be traveling with Doward. He couldn't remember a time without him. His good friend and druid mentor was at his side when he became Grand Master until Logan was ready and assumed the responsibility. Now Doward crisscrossed the countryside with his tinker wagon selling old wares and carrying news.

It was Doward who found a disoriented Rebeka on the trail after she came through the portal and brought her to him. Neither one of them was prepared for her return. Faith, neither one of them knew who she was. He saw her every day but recognized nothing. He shook his head in disbelief. Maximillian had considered everything when he took her into the future. She had no memory of home and, when she returned, no one recognized her. He had protected her well. It wasn't until Arik found his mark on her neck, the one he gave her at their betrothal, that he was able to see past the enchantment. But she still didn't have her memories. It was after the battle with Katherine, when he and Rebeka touched her staff together, that she remembered her past and him.

"You're preoccupied this morning," Doward said. "Not very good company."

Arik filled his lungs with the sweet air. "Reminiscing. What would you like to speak about?" They continued on at a casual pace.

"The last portal to seal. I'm glad." Doward glanced at Arik. "You told me you didn't want to seal it. Why the change?" The calm air stirred, the breeze ruffled Doward's long white hair and tugged at his clothes.

"The portal has served its purpose. It brought Rebeka back. It has no other use." The undercurrent of searching for something outside his grasp that had driven him for years was gone. He was content. It was a new feeling for him. "She wants to stay and not to return to her time—"

"Her time? This is her place, her home. You must recognize that." Doward's vigorous outburst startled him. Hadn't the old druid learned anything about Rebeka? About him? She had to want to stay, to be his wife. He would never force her.

Of course this was her time. This was her home. Lost to them for fifteen years, four months ago she, in fact, fell out of the twenty-first century into his seventeenth-century arms. The very idea made him grin.

Nineteen, he had been nineteen when he returned from his druid training and Maximillian announced he would be the next Grand Master. He saw the excitement and pride in his father's eyes and felt the love in his mother's touch. Bran and Cay were married at the end of the year and he and Rebeka were betrothed. They exchanged runes. He wore her mark over his heart and she wore his on the nape of her neck. They were happy then and looked forward to the future.

But the following year when Cay caught the fever, Bran was distraught. Ellyn, Rebeka's mother, was a great sorceress and healer. She tried everything to help Cay but she got worse. That's when Bran experimented with Dark Magick. But nothing saved Cay. Bran struck out at everyone and threatened Rebeka. Fearing for her life, Maximillian took her away.

Maximillian told him they would be back in four years. But four years had come and gone. No Maximillian. No Rebeka. He waited. Six more years and still no word, all the time his memories of her fading until she became a shadow to him. Five more years would pass until she returned.

"Still reminiscing?" Doward questioned.

She was here now and wanted to stay. No need to go over the past. He took a deep breath. The scent of lavender and roses floated on the air. Yes, his wife's home was here with him. "A little."

The specter of the Shade moved beside him and warnings flashed in his head. He was on high alert. Something was out of place. Doward must've sensed it, too. They stopped and turned in all directions, scrutinizing the area, searching for the oddity.

"There," shouted Doward. Off in the distance a small whirlwind spun among the stones. How was that possible? Dark clouds rushed toward them until they enveloped the two druids. Arik shielded his eyes against the swirling debris kicked about by the wind. A sweet, pungent metallic odor swirled around him but it was the whirling wind that held him transfixed.

"The portal's open," Doward yelled over the din. "I. Can't. Move."

"Don't struggle." Arik bent into the wind.

"But how?" Doward's surprised expression matched his own.

Arik turned to him. "Bran." Bile rose in his throat. He wanted to kick himself for not having seen the danger.

The scent of lavender and rose assaulted him again and cold sweat trickled down his back. Rebeka was near.

He opened his mind but found no trace of her. The wind tore at him. He bowed his head against its force. He pushed forward. He had to find her.

Rebeka, her staff in hand, trekked the worn forest path toward the meadow. Patches of sunlight filtered through the trees, creating small pools of warmth in the cool woodland. She slowed her pace and took a deep breath, enjoying the rich, earthy fragrance of the damp ground and delighting in the bright leaves that littered the forest floor. She continued on to where the trees thinned and the trail widened.

A loud boom shook the trees and sent the birds squawking and fluttering away. Startled, she searched the sky for the threat but saw nothing. *Oh please, not a thunder storm. Let the rain hold off.*

Everyone would be disappointed. They had been planning the celebration for weeks. If it rained, Jeannie and the women would need everyone's help to move things indoors. Perhaps she should gather the herbs another time. She glanced ahead. She was already here and if she made quick work of it she could still get back in time to help the others.

She rushed up the trail into the meadow then skidded to a stop. Her heart skipped a beat.

Arik leaned against the stone signpost. He straightened when he spotted her, a sensual smile spreading across his face beckoning her toward him.

"Love, come quickly," he called in his deep, melodic voice that both chilled and heated her. He must have finished with the portal sooner than he expected.

"I'm coming." Eager for his touch, his kiss, she rushed toward him. Perhaps she'd teased too much this morning. Should she admit she had been disappointed when Logan appeared? She rushed toward her husband, the man she loved and trusted beyond all others.

A hint of wind brushed across her face. "Hurry, there isn't much time," he shouted over his shoulder while he moved deeper into the meadow toward the oak tree. He was a few steps ahead. Why didn't he wait for her? She took another step and past the stone marker.

The air chilled and the sky turned an array of colors. Everything around her began to swirl. She realized her mistake too late. The portal—she was in the portal.

Arik. Close to him now, she reached for him but her hand passed through the form. She examined her hand, turning it over, then spotted the shadow of the man.

An illusion?

The shadow turned toward her. She watched as the wind washed over his face and it changed. "Bran," she whispered in disbelief. Her head swiveled while she searched for something, anything to grab on to. The portal had one use and she had no intention of leaving.

Get out, her brain shouted.

His lips twisted into a cynical sneer. He tilted his head in jaunty satisfaction, snapped his fingers and vanished.

"No," she yelled. "*Arik*," she closed her eyes and screamed in her head, trying to mind-touch him while the wind tore at her.

"Beka," he boomed.

Her eyes snapped open. She shielded them from the dust and debris and stared at Arik on the other side of the opening. He stood at the high plateau, miles away. His hands were braced on the opening's edges, which were nothing more than solid streams of whirling wind. He struggled to keep the portal from closing.

"Come." His voice didn't allow for any argument.

The wind whipped at her, pushed her back. She tried again. "I can't. The wind. Keeps. Pushing. Me. Away." She shoved her staff in front of her and anchored it in the ground. Against the gusting wind, pulled herself toward him.

"A little more, Beka." He gripped the edge of the portal with one hand and stretched the other out to her. She shoved her hand toward him as far as she could. The tips of their fingers brushed. In a burst of effort he caught the top of her hand, a precarious hold. With a tight grasp she wrapped her fingers around his thumb.

Safe. She wasn't far now.

She concentrated on his face. The corners of his mouth turned up as he pulled her toward safety. The wind grew stronger, buffeting around them, then changed its path.

Before she could brace herself for the new direction, the gust blasted them. Without a firm grip, her hand began to slip. She pushed through the building panic. His smile slipped. The expression on his face turned to determination. Again her hand slipped until he held her by her fingertips.

He held them fast—crushing them, but that didn't matter. He had to hold on to her. Every muscle strained. Inch by inch he brought her closer to him. She tried to help him the best way she could. Anchored to the edge of the portal, Arik encouraged her on. But his alternatives were limited. The closer she got to him, the stronger the gale blew. Just a little closer, that's all she needed for Arik to grab her and get her out of the portal.

The wind exploded from another direction.

The blasting gale pushed her staff away from the opening, across the dirt, cutting an ugly scar in the ground and dragging her away with her staff.

Away from Arik.

Their bond snapped, Arik fell backward, out of the portal. The wind kept them pinned where they were as cold air swooped around the entrance. When at last the wind eased, they stared in horror at the thick sheet of ice that sealed the portal between them.

They fought their way to the frozen sheet. Rebeka's hands on one side, Arik's on the other. In desperation they searched for a weakness.

Time was slipping away.

Arik took out his sword and slashed at the ice but he didn't make any progress. He sheathed his sword and pounded on the ice with his fists.

Rebeka pummeled the ice with her staff. Chunks flew off but nothing weakened it.

Desperate, they hammered away at the icy barrier.

She took notice as Arik moved his hands over the ice. She did the same. His lips moved but she was unable to hear him. He raised his hands in demand. What was he doing?

Lightning struck the ice and turned it fiery hot.

In horror, she stared at the agony etched on his

face. She stood by and watched, unable to help him. He pummeled the icy surface with his fists, his knuckles raw and bleeding. She fixed her stare on the runes on his chest. They pulsated in rhythm with his fists.

Small cracks in the ice appeared and his fists flew faster. He flashed her an encouraging glance but all she saw were the deep cuts in his flesh. His blood was everywhere.

Tears slipped down Rebeka's cheeks. Helpless, his runes kept flashing faster and his heartbeat raced to keep time. She was certain his heart would burst.

She leaned closer to the barrier, her eyes begging him. *Stop*, she called to him in her mind. He kept on going. She spread her hands on the shield. "Stop," she screamed, her voice raw with her effort. The vibration and low-pitch moan of the surface made her flinch. She pulled her hands away.

Unsure, she touched the shield again. It was still. The scream, she was certain it caused the tremor. She searched Arik's face. He wasn't aware of it. The beat echoing in her head was almost a steady tone. Fear twisted around her heart. His blood stained the barrier. She was certain he would die if he kept this pace. She couldn't wait.

She gathered her strength and with lightning speed built the chant inside her. When she couldn't hold it back any longer she let it loose in a grief-stricken scream.

Everything stopped. The wind. His pounding.

They stood facing each other.

"No, Beka. No," he screamed, his arms spread out across the barrier. She watched the glazed look of despair spread across his face.

A small portion of the shield fractured, then another, and another. The tiny explosions gathered momentum until they built into a frenzy and every inch of the shield was cracked.

Then silence.

She hesitated but at last placed her hand on the shield. Arik did the same. Their hands separated by the splintered magick. The fractured shield trembled, small pieces tumbled around them. For a brief moment their hands touched and she felt his warmth and love.

A great force pulled them apart as if they were puppets at the will of a puppeteer. They struggled to their feet and ran to each other but before they could get to the opening the portal snapped closed and vanished.

His roar echoed through the mountains. "I will find you."

"I love you," she sobbed as the portal took her away.

Away from him.

CHAPTER THREE

Present Day

Breath by breath, she pulled herself out of the haze, Arik's pained expression fixed in her mind. The warmth of his hand lingered on hers. She flexed her fingers but her hand was held tight.

Arik? Her eyes flew open. She yanked her hand out of someone's grasp. Blood—his blood stained her hand. The nightmare was real. *Arik, I love you*, she screamed silently to him. Nothing.

"Arik," she whispered, unable to smother the sob that escaped. She didn't try.

"Dr. Tyler?" A calm female voice broke through the fog. "Dr. Tyler. I'm trying to find where you're bleeding." She stared at the woman. Standing in the middle of the small circle of stones, she still grasped her staff. Her hand slipped along the smooth hawthorn pole as she sank to the ground. Slumped against the cool damp stone, she stared into a familiar face but couldn't place the woman. Her knees raised, she lowered her pounding head between them.

"Where am I?" Did she even care? Deep inside, she knew that wherever she was, he wasn't with her.

The woman slipped an arm around her and

anchored her to the spot. "You're in Avebury. By the stones. Take a deep breath."

She didn't want to breathe ever again.

"Would you like some water?" Rebeka studied the woman's face, struggling to put it in its proper place, and took the offered bottle. Where had she met this woman? She drank as if she hadn't had water for days and so fast that the water trickled down her chin.

Her rescuer patted down her pockets then glanced at the blood-stained cloth she held. "This is all I have," the woman apologized and dabbed at Rebeka's chin. "I've called Mr. Hughes. He's on his way and should be here any minute." The woman glanced over her shoulder. When she turned back, Rebeka glimpsed her rescuer's growing concern.

Like an engine catching after several miss-starts, recognition hit her. "I know who you are." She straightened her back against the stone. More of the fog cleared from her mind. "The tour guide." That got a smile from the woman—or was it relief that brightened her face? She tilted her head back against the stone and closed her eyes. "Is this part of your tour?"

Pictures of Bran and Arik flashed in her mind. Panic left her breathing hard, threatening to crush her chest. Bran. She was useless to Arik here.

A gentle hand touched her shoulder. "Yes, I'm Agnes from the tour group and no, this isn't part of the service but I'd rather you stay awake right now."

She opened her eyes. The woman was familiar with first aid. "What happened?"

"There was a clap of thunder. We were concerned there'd be an electric storm, which didn't seem at all feasible with the clear sky. We had everyone leave the area as a precaution. Well, there weren't any additional thunderclaps so we allowed the visitors back into the site again. One of them found you a bit despondent chanting by the Cove Stone. He came and got me. By the time I got here you were wiping your hand—"

"Rebeka!"

She lifted her head to see who'd called her. Not far away, behind a rope, curiosity seekers stretched their necks to get a glimpse at what was happening. Pain washed over her as reality hit her again. She was back in the twenty-first century.

Alone.

Out of the corner of her eye she watched a couple duck under the makeshift barricade and rush toward her. "Rebeka." The man knelt in front of her. "Thank you, Agnes." He gave the woman a relieved smile. "We'll take her back to the manor."

The familiar voice caught her attention. "George?" Her shoulders relaxed. He squeezed her hand. The small gesture relieved her.

"Yes, Rebeka." He gave her his full attention. "We're here."

"We?" She tried to get her feet under her but couldn't get them to work. That didn't matter; somehow Arik had found her. She shaded her eyes, expecting her husband to be standing over her. Instead, a woman stood next to George. Frantic, Rebeka scanned the area.

"Rebeka." She focused on George. "This is Cora, my sister." A stabbing ache in her chest caught her breath.

Arik wasn't there. The swell of hope plummeted to despair that made her ache even deeper. Of course he wasn't. It was too much to think that this nightmare would be over so fast.

"Let's get her back to the manor." Cora bent toward her and extended her hand. "Can you walk? The car's not far."

Once on her feet, she stuffed the blood-stained cloth into her pocket and took her staff. She turned back to the stones but knew the portal was gone.

"That way is closed." Rebeka faced George's sister. Her anxiety level ratcheted up. What did they know? And who were they?

Agnes hurried off and disbursed the small crowd while George and Cora got Rebeka into their car. With everyone settled and strapped in, George pulled out onto the road for the ride to Fayne Manor.

Rebeka slumped in the back and stared out the window. She replayed things in her head. Why didn't she recognize that it was Bran and that it was a ruse? She was certain Arik had been standing at the signpost. She should've known that there was no way he could've closed the portal and gotten to Oak Meadow before she arrived.

They made their way from Avebury to the M4. The green countryside that flashed by hadn't changed much in four hundred years. This was not the time for withdrawing and feeling sorry for herself. No, she had to use her wits and figure out how to get back. But she had no idea what to do next.

"Rebeka." She turned away from the landscape at George's gentle tone. "Where do I start?" He kept his eyes on the road.

"Perhaps at the beginning with who you are." He hadn't told her everything when she'd met him four months ago. She'd believed he was a barrister out to complete his client, Lady Emily's, last request, to find her heir. His law firm had the highest credentials.

He pulled onto the M4 and glanced at Cora next to him. "Our family has a long history. The family business has been active for hundreds of years."

"Yes. Your law office has quite a long history." She knew that. She wanted to know the rest.

"Our family goes back almost as far as yours." She was a historian. There were a great many people in England who could trace their families back for centuries. This was not a revelation.

She stared at the back of his head. Who could she trust in this century? George? Cora? She'd have to figure that out fast. Every instinct told her she was safe—but she'd believed she'd been safe at the meadow…

"I should've told you when we first met but I believed you needed to learn about Arik's family. I assumed we had more time. When the National Trust suggested making Fayne Manor a reenactment site we jumped at the chance to re-create the seventeenth-century manor." His expression shifted to one of sadness. "We believed we had more time."

"Time?" She let out a deep breath and returned her gaze to the window. Bran must be up to something to get her out of the way. But what?

"There's no need to evade the issue now." Cora turned in her seat to face her. Rebeka appreciated the woman's directness. "Our family is from a long line of druids. George and I were going to explain everything to you the first night you were here but you disappeared." Had they expected her to reappear? She wasn't as naive now. Whose side of the family were they on? Arik's or Bran's?

"Go on, tell her the rest," he urged her.

"No, let me," Rebeka said. "My father brought me here from the seventeenth century because of a threat, a threat from Bran. I was supposed to return and marry Arik. But that was prevented, by Bran. How am I doing so far?"

"Just fine." She noted George's approving nod. "How did you leave us four months ago?" There was a note of concern in his voice that eased her.

She made a quick decision to confide in them on some level. Getting back to Arik was her goal. If Cora was right and she couldn't go back using the portal she'd arrived in, she'd need help. She had no idea where to start except with them. And they were druids. She'd have to be cautious but she needed to start somewhere.

"Figuring that out took me a while but I put the pieces together. I joined the Avebury tour, where I met Agnes. I listened to the chant on the audio tour, sang along word for word." The rhythmic beat of the chant echoed in her head. "When I got to the Cove Stone the portal opened and I was caught inside." Her heart pounded as the beat built quickly to a crescendo, then as quickly as is began, it stopped.

"I had no memory of my previous time in that century when I was here and still none when I met Arik. It took…a lot to remember." Painful would be a better description. "But I did. Arik and I married." Her chin quivered. She took a deep breath to steady herself. "I've never been happier." Her voice was a choked whisper.

Cora turned and looked into the backseat to face her. "Then why did you come back?" She searched the woman's face. Did she think she wanted to return? No, she had no idea.

"I didn't have an option." Her voice was lifeless. "I hadn't planned to come back." The bitterness rose in her throat. "Bran, on the other hand, had a different idea." She fisted her hands, her nails biting into her palms. She blew out a breath and the acrid taste of fury rose. "But is he in for a surprise." She tried to keep her voice controlled but even she detected its hateful tone.

September 22, 1605 — Midday

Arik slouched in his saddle. Doward rode at his side. The two men plodded their way back to the manor in silence. Their horses' heads hung low, mirroring their own.

Dark Magick. That's what had held Rebeka in the portal.

He needed time to think but the image of her pained expression filled his mind.

The cadence of the horse's hoofs beat out his chant, *I will find you, I will find you.*

He sent the message, but she was beyond his reach. How did Bran time it so well? He was at the end of the chant, a few words away from completing it, when Rebeka screamed. He let out a bitter grunt. He had done an excellent job of destroying the portal. His own words doomed her and he couldn't reverse them. The portal was gone forever and so was she.

Rain was pelting them by the time they arrived at the manor valley. The storm must have moved in fast. Most of the tables in the square were covered. Some wares lay soaked and forgotten. The streets couldn't handle the quick torrent and had become rivers with small rapids flowing over the cobbles. The village was battened down for a storm. For him, the tempest would last until Rebeka was safe at home.

Arik, his head bowed against the rain, moved on to the manor. At the barn he threw the reins to the groom and left Doward without a word. He hurried to the library, gathered a few select books then went to his tower room, leaving instructions he wasn't to be disturbed. He needed time to read and think.

From time to time soft footfalls stopped outside his door. He ignored them. He kept reading and working well into the evening.

"Arik." Logan pounded on the door.

"Come." Arik's quill scratched on the parchment. He glanced at the door as it opened and tried to disguise his annoyance. He believed he made it clear he didn't want to be disturbed.

"You've been here for hours." Logan glanced at the books and scrolls scattered on the table. "Doward told us what happened. Everyone's troubled." Arik glared at Logan as he took a seat across from him. The laugh lines that marked his brother's face were replaced with deep creases of worry. He didn't have time to see to Logan's concerns, nor explain his actions.

Arik put down his quill. He pinched the bridge of his nose, hoping to relieve the stress. "There is a way to find her. At least that's what I keep telling myself. I'll not accept anything else."

"Doward and I rode back to the stones as well as to the meadow." Logan leafed through a book as if he had all the time in the world. Arik watched to see which books he reviewed. There were several he'd rather Logan didn't notice.

Why hadn't Logan and Doward told him where they were going? His temper rose but he doused it before it boiled over. He told them not to disturb him. "The meadow? I hadn't considered where she was, only that she was gone." He took the quill and made a note on one of the parchments.

"Yes, she planned to harvest herbs. We found hints of the portal in both places." Logan closed the book. "Along with traces of Dark Magick."

He recognized the dread in Logan's eyes. "He knew I was going to close the portal. He got her inside then barricaded the opening. Rebeka broke the enchantment."

"Broke the enchantment?" Logan moved to the edge of the chair. "So Doward was right? He told me he managed to get to you and heard her cry out, that her scream broke the enchantment." The creases on his face moved from worry to alarm. Logan's expression deepened Arik's devastation. So, Logan believed all was lost as well. A dull ache ran through him. What if he couldn't... He left the idea unfinished. So far he hadn't found anything to help him travel through time.

"Yes, but I'd wager she didn't know I was

moments away from freeing her. She was fine until I marked the enchantment—"

"With your blood." Logan winced. On his ride home Arik realized how it must have appeared to Rebeka.

"She must have believed you were in danger," Logan said more to himself. "He took advantage of the portal and used an enchantment to trick Rebeka to use a primal scream. It was a clever ruse."

"I've been reading through the old books. The stones are cold. I sealed them tight. That magick can't be undone. I'll have to find another way." He grabbed a fistful of pages and shook them at Logan. "The answer must be here, but where?" He tossed the papers back onto the table and ran his hand around his neck. He had no idea if he was even searching in the right place. "Bran has gone too far."

"How long are you going to make excuses for him, try to cure him?" Logan's words sent something straight through him. "It's the one thing that stands between us." Logan turned away from Arik. "You should've killed him four months ago. Now look where it's got you."

Guilt swept through Arik. Why did he think he could protect Rebeka from Bran here? Maximillian had taken her to the future to protect her. But kill Bran? Only as a last resort.

"Things have been peaceful since August and all along brother Bran has been watching and waiting." Logan glanced at the scattered papers. He read one then another before he returned them to the table. "You know the danger of Dark Magick." Logan pointed to the parchment. Something in Logan's tone stopped Arik's building anger that threatened to erupt. Logan was worried, and he should be.

"I'm aware of the dangers and I'm just as certain Rebeka wasn't. I was so close to getting her out. If she had waited a heartbeat or two longer." He rose, unable to keep still, and stood by the window. He needed a battle plan and he needed it now. Her face flashed in front of him. "I wasn't able to touch her mind, to tell her. I'll never forget the look on her face before she screamed." He stared at the rain. "I'm certain she didn't know the consequences." He slammed his fist on the sill. "I must find her."

Logan stood beside him. "She has some knowledge of Dark Magick. She's been reading the old books."

Arik spun Logan around. His heart raced. "What? How?"

"She asked you but you put her off. That's when she asked me." Logan held up his hand to stop Arik's interruption. "She knows the consequences of using Dark Magick and how it can corrupt the mind. She doesn't know how to summon it. So set your mind at ease. Together we'll find her. Bran must know you won't sit idle." Logan was either naive or trying to console him. Rebeka would figure out how she broke the enchantment.

Arik let out a lifeless laugh. "I see Bran's scheme too late." He had been so willing to enjoy the quiet, to play the bridegroom with Rebeka. "The summer silence was to make us think we're secure while he plotted and planned."

"Yes, and I think he'll try to keep us occupied so you won't have time to find the answer."

For a moment Arik saw the past, a day when he, Bran and Logan were boys, filching cakes from Jeannie and racing their horses across the fields. They had been close. He had played the great knight to Bran's lord of the manor. Now those memories were so far in the past that he questioned if they ever existed.

"To make her like him," Logan said, breaking his musing.

Like Bran? He wasn't going to let that happen. "She's made of stronger stuff. You said so yourself."

Logan nodded. At least they both agreed on that point.

"Doward has gone to gather what information he can from the other villages. He'll try to reach the druid Council. I'll check the documents in the sanctuary," Logan said, "and bring you what we find." He turned to leave but hesitated. "I'll do anything you need. No questions asked. I'll support you in any way I can. Against anything. We're in this together."

His squire from when they played knight. Logan had sworn his allegiance to him and had never faltered. He grasped Logan's shoulder, grateful for his help. "I know."

A gentle knock on the door drew their attention. "Uncle Arik?"

Logan opened the door. Skylar stood there tall and silent. Overwrought, her hands twisted her handkerchief. Aubrey stood next to her and stabbed away her tears with the back of her hand.

Arik smoothed his face. "Girls?" They rushed at him. Startled, he raised his arms as they grabbed him around his waist. He turned to Logan for support. His brother shrugged his shoulders and appeared to be as uncomfortable as he was.

"It's my fault, Uncle Arik, all my fault." One look at them and his heart fell.

"Hush now." He stroked Skylar's hair. She cuddled closer and her sobs eased. "What's your fault?"

"She asked me to go with her and instead…" Her chin quivered too much for her to speak. "I didn't want to go to the meadow. If I had gone…" Her voice trailed off in a whisper.

Aubrey held her sister's hand. "I should have gone with her, too," she said between sobs.

He held them both close. "Neither of you did

anything wrong. This is not your fault." *Faith.* They hurt as much as he did. "If anyone is at fault it's me for not seeing the danger."

"Bring her back," Aubrey pleaded. Skylar agreed. The girls had such faith in him.

"I will," he said with all his heart.

CHAPTER FOUR

Present Day

Curled up in the large chair in the solar, Rebeka stared at the blood-stained cloth. Her silent tears had turned to mutterings cursing Bran. But that was all a waste of time and energy. She had no doubt Arik had recovered. She was certain she would know if he hadn't.

Over the past four days she'd barricaded herself in her room and became reacquainted with her computer. She spent every minute documenting her time with Arik and what she remembered about the portal. She'd worked without a break and kept the room dark and the coffee strong. After a long discussion with George and Cora she understood that no one had any idea how to reach Arik.

Reach Arik.

It wasn't as if she could search for him on the computer or in some medieval directory. Sarcasm wouldn't help, but the fear that his magick, any magick, wouldn't work here was very real. She needed to study the problem from a different perspective, from every angle. It would take a lot of work and research. Dammit, she was a historical researcher, for God's sake. She bolted out of the chair and threw the small

pillow that had been on her lap across the room.
Breathe. She could do this. He'd be working the
problem from his perspective.

With all her heart she believed Arik would find
her. She had to believe.

She glanced out the open window and got a whiff
of the fragrant garden filled with fall flowers and cut
grass. Breathe. She turned to sit at the desk but she
couldn't type another word. Instead she headed for the
stairs.

"Good day, Miss Rebeka." Charles, the steward,
stood in the downstairs entryway.

"Good day, Charles." She rubbed her temple to
ease the pain. The sides of her head ached from
extracting every fact she could remember.

Faith. What do I do next?

She stopped mid-step on the staircase; her heart
skipped a beat. The corners of her mouth pulled back
at the bittersweet memory of Arik raking his hand
through his hair and muttering his favorite epithet. He
was so much a part of her. She continued down the
stairs and onto the terrace. The sun was high over the
east hill. With her eyes closed the sun warmed her face
and her mind quieted.

"Hail and welcome." She stood at the railing and
scanned the estate. Instead of a thriving village and lush
farms she saw abandoned buildings and barren
parkland. Her friends, her family, her husband... She
missed them all. Her chest tightened at the idea of
never seeing them again. "Great Mother," she vowed,
"I'll do anything to go back. Anything."

"I've put your morning tea and scones in here next
to some papers from Mr. George."

"Thank you, Helen." For days the housekeeper
had kept the house quiet and her coffee cup filled while
she worked.

"My mother swore by this blend. She believed hot

tea was good for what ails you." There was a question in Helen's expression that she seemed hesitant to put into words. Rebeka wasn't ready to encourage questions. But she'd have to think of some explanation for her abrupt disappearance and return.

A noise in the distance made her glance beyond the gatehouse. She imagined she heard the men gathering... No, she had to stop. She was torturing herself. Maybe the terrace wasn't such a good place to be right now. "Tea sounds good." She turned her back on the estate grounds and entered the Great Hall.

"Cream and sugar?" Helen asked, standing at the large table.

"No, thank you." The scent of lavender and mint wafted up from the cup and cleansed her senses. Enticed, she took a seat then a small sip of tea. "It's delicious." Another sip. The anxiety of the past few moments eased. She relaxed in the large chair and glanced around the room. It was much the same now as when she'd breakfasted with Skylar and Aubrey four days ago.

The dais, with its trestle table and chairs, was the same. She spotted the familiar sideboard, although she had never seen the silver plate that gleamed on top. Her historian eye appreciated an old tapestry that hung over the hearth. Four days ago she would have told you swords graced the mantel. The embroidery was faded, making it difficult to see the detail, but she did make out the piece was a good likeness of the manor's facade.

Helen checked the pot and scones. "Charles had the Trust move their boxes out of your cottage to the garden house. If you need anything else I'm close by."

She couldn't stay here in the main house—it was empty without Arik. Besides, the cottage was a few steps across the drive. "Thank you, Helen." The housekeeper slipped out of the room. Another sip.

Maybe it was the warm liquid or the combination of tea leaves but the knots in her stomach eased and the chaos that used her as a lightning rod quieted.

She glanced through the pile of papers Helen left for her and opened the large envelope from George's office. She pulled out Fayne Manor's acceptance into the National Trust. Lady Emily Parsons had been researching the family line, determined to find the surviving heir. After Lady Emily passed, George continued the search. It seemed a lifetime ago that George had contacted her with news that she was the last of the line. She had inherited it all—a family and an estate she knew nothing about.

As a top medieval professor and researcher, the National Trust had asked Rebeka to complete Lady Emily's research regarding the family. She would at least be productive while she waited for Arik. One more sip of tea and she headed to the library, the papers in her hand.

The library was a few steps up the hall. It was a comfortable room. She opened the door and froze.

Her heart plummeted to her feet and slammed back up to her chest. She couldn't pull her eyes away.

Arik stared at her from his portrait over the mantel.

"Arik," she whispered and clutched the papers to her chest. The artist had captured his penetrating blue-green eyes—they burned right through her. She closed her eyes and was bombarded by his pained expression right before the portal closed.

"Rebeka."

Her eyes snapped open and she focused on the face in the picture. Had he called her name? Someone touched her shoulder. Bewildered, she spun and stared at the man behind her.

"Rebeka, it's me, George." His voice was soft. She had to stop thinking Arik was around every corner. A halting breath escaped around the knot in her throat. Would she ever get used to the pain?

"Yes, I know," she muttered. Thank goodness he didn't speak. She had time to collect what wits she still had.

"I'm afraid I'm losing my mind." She gazed at George and realized Cora stood next to him. "Sometimes I have things all together. Then I see his face when the shield broke." She examined the back of her hand and then her palm. "I feel the warmth of his hand, and then nothing." She stepped away from George and stood close to the mantel, staring at Arik's picture. "Then I lose him all over again. Each time the pain is worse until I don't think I can stand it one more second." She struggled to take a breath and keep her composure. "Then I hate him for not being with me. And hate myself more for thinking it."

She lowered herself into a nearby chair. Cora took the papers from her and put them on the desk. "He's my heart." Rebeka searched George's face. How could she expect them to understand? Sometimes she wanted to jump out of her skin from wanting Arik. She inched to the edge of the chair. "You're both druids. Send me back."

"I wish I had that power but I don't." He put his briefcase next to the chair and stood in front of her.

She understood George and Cora wouldn't be able to open the portal but that didn't make the reality any easier to bear. "You must have other magick." She leaned back into the chair. "Do you have a crystal ball?" She let out a choked cackle at her joke.

George took the chair next to her. "No, not a crystal ball. Any magick druids once had has been…" he searched for a word, "dulled in this century. Magick was never meant as an end but only to assist." It must have been the hundredth time he gave that lecture. He'd been drumming that into her head for the past four days.

The bottom fell out of her stomach. She had hoped all they had to do was find the right chant, algorithm or herbs. This was a setback, that's all. *Gather your strength, girl.* She wasn't going to give up.

"But we do have an idea. We've been searching for information about Bran's history. We've found very little. He was orphaned when he was young. Fendrel and Dimia, Arik's parents, took him in and raised him as their own. There's every indication that he was treated and loved by everyone as their natural son."

"Yes, some of my childhood memories have come back." She gaped at the brother and sister. She hadn't tried to look for information about Bran. "Why is there so little information?"

Cora took the chair to the other side of her. "We don't know. George had Lady Emily's family records stored in a vault. He called them out of storage and had them delivered here."

That sounded familiar. She dug a little deeper. "When I signed the inheritance papers, George mentioned he had family documents he wanted me to see. He…" What had he said? At the time it had struck her as odd. "Yes," she said with a burst of memory. "You said they held secrets."

"Right. When they arrived, the documents from 1570 to 1670 were missing." George paced in front of her. "We've been trying to locate them. All we have is Doward's journal—it had been lost among some papers in the library—and Arik's picture." He looked at the portrait over the mantel.

"You have Doward's journal?" She jumped out of the chair. At last, something positive. "What does it say after I left?"

George took the journal out of his briefcase and handed her a battered leather book. "This is what started Emily's quest. It was the single piece of information we had about you. This journal ends about four years after you left with your father. We couldn't find the next one. Everywhere Emily turned led to another dead end." Rebeka sank back into the chair.

"We've been searching for the missing journals. We're afraid they may have been lost among the items that were put up for auction about fifty years ago," Cora said.

"Most often, journals that old are given to a library. I'll make some inquiries and see if I can locate them." She knew of several researchers and libraries that she could contact that dealt with private papers. She went to the desk and jotted down some notes. "I should look into information dealing with auctions. Maybe the Fayne Manor papers were listed in an auction catalogue. That would be nice." She made another notation. She hoped this would put them on the right track.

"I see you found the Trust papers." Cora nodded to the papers she had put on the table.

"I wanted a diversion and had the notion I'd get up to speed on what's been done with the Trust. Do you think my sudden reappearance will pose any issues?"

"No, not at all. I think the Trust will be quite happy. We told them you were on a personal project and they understood." That was a relief. At least she didn't have to explain anything to them.

"I read your notes about your...experience. They're very comprehensive." Of course they were; she was a researcher and knew the value of documentation. She brought her attention back to George. There was a question in George's voice that he seemed hesitant to put into words.

"Is there something you'd like to ask me?" She spent hours documenting every detail. What could she have left out?

"There is one thing." Cora turned to George, who was already closing his briefcase. Rebeka noticed Cora run her trembling hands over her skirt, ridding it of nonexistent creases. George was still warring with himself. She watched and waited. Sooner or later one of them would ask their question.

He snapped closed the clasp on his briefcase and set it on the floor. "Cora and I have gone over everything you wrote about your return. We don't understand how you knew to break the enchantment."

"Enchantment? You mean seal the portal." She glanced from George to Cora. Both gave her a sympathetic look.

"The barrier that separated you from Arik was an enchantment." His tone was matter-of-fact. A chill started at the base of her spine and ran up her back. Enchantments were temporary, even she knew that. Was it that simple, just wait for it to fade? No, it was solid and Arik was as frantic as she was to destroy it.

"Arik and I tried everything to break the barrier. Arik used his sword and I used my staff. Nothing worked." Something at the edge of her mind nagged at her. Cora fidgeted. The chill shifted to a shiver of panic. What had she missed? "When the sword didn't work, Arik pounded it with his fists." Her hands clasped tightly in her lap, her eyes focused four hundred years in the past. She was there, experiencing it again. It was as bad now as it was then. "There was a great deal of blood." She touched her pocket. She still had the cloth. "The runes on his body pulsated with his heartbeat."

"With his heartbeat? How could you be certain?" Cora asked. Rebeka would never forget the constant drumming. Never.

"It echoed in my head. I was sure if he didn't stop…" She was standing at the icy barrier watching, helpless as Arik pounded on it with his hands. The ice was smeared with his blood but he didn't stop. She made out the steady beat once more growing faster and louder as his fists flashed. "I was afraid his heart would burst." She took large gulps of air and searched around her for help but saw nothing. "I had to do something to make him stop."

"Rebeka!" The even control in George's voice brought her back to the present. She focused on where the voice came from but didn't see him past the vision. Her terror began to fade. Cora stood next to her. She gave the woman a weak smile.

"Bran planned this well. There was one way he was able to get into your mind, when your defenses were down. That's when you're most vulnerable. Your protection of Arik was a perfect plan," George said.

Bran? Got into her mind? "No, I called out to Arik but he didn't hear me. The ice quivered under my hand. That's when I understood my scream would shatter the ice." She saw the silent signal that passed between brother and sister. She didn't like where this was going. They knew something that she didn't. Her panic turned to fear. She had made a grave mistake. But what?

"The barrier was an enchantment and temporary. There was no way of knowing if the enchantment would fade before the portal closed with you inside." That was why Arik was working so fast. "However, breaking the enchantment forced the portal to seal over—"

"But it was ice and it shattered. It didn't seal." She stood bent over the desk on fisted hands. "If I hadn't taken action Arik would have died. I'm certain. Don't either of you see that?" Her chin dropped to her chest and her hair cascaded forward, hiding her face.

George grabbed her by her shoulders. "Listen to me." He made her face him. "It wasn't ice. It was an enchantment. The primal scream is a powerful tool. That's what you used." He let her shoulders go.

Distraught, she crossed her arms, held herself tight and turned away.

"What would have happened if I hadn't screamed?" George rose to his full height, a nervous expression on his face. Rebeka glanced at Cora. She was staring at the floor. "What are you not telling me?"

"Arik used a mixture of fire and blood—"

"Lightning struck the ice. I remember the ice feeling hot." She sank into the chair.

"He also used a chant against the ice element. If you hadn't forced the enchantment it would have faded when Arik finished his chant. You would have stepped out of the portal and it would have sealed. When you used the primal scream, the magick came apart and the portal sealed with you inside."

"He would have died if he kept going." The words stuck in her throat. "I couldn't bear to see him hurt. His blood was everywhere." The red smears on the icy film were real. She looked at both of them, her eyes begging them to understand, not wanting to accept the truth. "I saved him."

"I'm sorry. The portal is gone. No one can bring it back." He hesitated. "Not even the Grand Master," George muttered, scrubbing his face with his hand.

Maybe they were wrong. They had to be. She heard Arik's last words—he would find her. He believed it, and so would she. There must be another way.

"Look at me," George demanded. She snapped around. "We're with you in this. Together. We. Will. Find. Another. Way." She was thankful for their help, but one thing swirled in her head. If she had waited...if she hadn't rushed to meet him...if...

Arik, what have I done?

"I've spent the past two days," Rebeka said, sitting with Cora in the library, "making a list of the places we might find information and reconnected with several researchers. They're checking their libraries and archives for the missing journals. I also asked them to research Bran of Fayne Manor. They didn't find anything but said they'd keep searching. I'll start on the secondary list later today." Rebeka read through her notebook, several industry directories and old auction listings she had on the table.

"Do you have any idea why there's so little information about Bran?" Cora helped her organize the papers on the library table.

"It's as if he never existed." That was an interesting notion. "Throughout history, people were erased for the purpose of being forgotten. I remember Bran being a proud boy with a quick sense of humor. Although he was loved by everyone, he struggled for his place in the family. Denied by them would be the worst punishment imaginable." Rebeka stared at the documents on the table.

Arik and Bran had been the ringleaders of all her childhood adventures. She and Leticia, and even Logan, cheered them on playing their supporting role. The pain on Arik's face and hesitancy in his voice when he told her Bran fought against the family set off signals that there was more to the story, but Arik had internal demons he had to conquer before he would tell her. Now she wished she had pressed him for answers.

"Why don't you take a break and come with me to Avebury. I have to drop off some papers at the National Trust's office for George. After I'm through there I thought we'd do a little shopping, have a nice lunch," Cora said.

How could she spend time idling away? Rebeka glanced at her notes. Cora had been a dear over the past days. She was compassionate with a gentle soul.

And was easy to be with and talk to. Spending time with her would be nice, but she had to keep focused on returning to Arik. So far, she'd found nothing that would help her, not even where to look next. She needed…something to give her a direction.

"I know you want to dig in and keep looking but a short break will clear your mind. Besides, we won't be gone long. Promise."

She could use some fresh air. She glanced out the terrace door. Maybe getting away from the manor was what she needed. "Sure. Let me put these books away then we can leave." Rebeka put on her backpack and threaded her staff into the leather straps. She juggled the books in her arms.

"Here, let me help you." Cora pulled several books off the stack and followed her to the back of the library where her personal reference materials had been shelved.

"You can give them to me now." Rebeka spun around to take the books from her. "Cora?" The woman stared at Rebeka's backpack.

"What's wrong?" Rebeka followed Cora's line of sight to see what was behind her.

"Not behind you. You're wearing it." She pointed to Rebeka's staff.

Confused, Rebeka pulled out her staff. Select runes glowed. The only time the runes had glowed was when she and Arik both touched the staff. She searched around; was he near?

"It didn't start until you were close to the bookcase." Rebeka passed her staff in front of the shelves. Like a Geiger counter, the closer it passed to the document drawer the more her staff reacted. Cora opened the drawer, peered inside and rummaged through the items. "It's a carved ball," Cora said, pulling it out of the drawer. "Move it over the ball." Rebeka passed her staff over the ball and the runes grew bright.

"Nothing's happening to the stone. No glowing. No vibrations, nothing at all. Do you know what's causing your staff to light up?" Cora looked into the drawer. Rebeka examined her staff, trying to make sense of what happened. She examined the stone.

"This is an Orkney carved stone ball, unique to Skara Brae. Is there anything else from Orkney in the library?" Rebeka stepped away from the stone. The glowing runes dimmed and died.

"No, I don't see anything else. There're some papers in the drawer. Looks like receipts of some sort." The shuffling of paper filled the silent room as Cora rummaged through them. Rebeka waved her staff over the ball again. The runes brightened, but why.

"It's a wedding invitation." Cora pulled the yellowed document out of the drawer. The old writing was hard to decipher but Cora plowed on. "'Your most royal highness, it is with great happiness and pleasure that I announce my forthcoming wedding to Caylyn of Orkney on May 1, 1590, at Fayne Manor. We hope you will grace our event with your attendance. Your servant, Lord Bran of Orkney.' Well, that's short and sweet." Orkney—of course. Bran was from Orkney, not Fayne Manor.

The invitation was the first mention they found of Bran but the Skara Brae stone held Rebeka's interest. Why did it make her staff glow? She understood why it glowed when Arik touched it but she had no idea why her staff reacted to the Orkney stone. There had to be some connection between the stone and Arik. A sign. She jumped up, electrified by the idea. It had to be a sign. She had a hard time trying to contain her excitement. Now all she had to figure out was what he wanted her to do.

"Has your staff ever glowed like that before?" Cora asked. Rebeka put the stone back into the drawer and closed it. She was giddy knowing she'd be with him soon.

"Only when Arik and I both touch it. We were in the high meadow, after we fought Katherine. We both touched my staff. It lit up and my memories returned." Speaking of it now brought to mind her anxiety when she watched the runes glow. One by one, they lit and marched along her staff, his arm and hers. She glanced at her staff now quiet in her hand. By the time they returned to the manor, memories had tumbled back into place, the closeness of her family and Arik's. And that they loved each other before her father took her away didn't surprise her.

"The runes that glowed?" They both knew which runes glowed on her staff.

"The sigil of my name and Arik's."

"The sigil's believed to have magical powers." Cora paused. "Do you have any idea why only that image lit?"

"I'm not certain whether it's an invitation or a command appearance. Either way, it's a trip to Orkney." Apprehension flashed across Cora's face. Rebeka let out a deep breath. "What else could it mean? Orkney. Our sigil in lights. If that's not an invitation I don't know what is."

"We need to speak to George. I don't think he'll see it your way." Cora was nervous.

Rebeka's chin rose in a blatant challenge. George wasn't making the decision on whether she visited Orkney. Her cheeks burned in frustration. She took a calming breath. George and Cora had worked for a long time trying to find her. Maybe it was their natural order of things, for Cora to defer to him. It wasn't hers.

Her heart skipped a beat. "He sealed all the portals here." She hefted her staff. "He must have found a portal in Orkney." It was so obvious to her. How did Cora not see it? "You don't agree."

"It's not that. I'm a bit skeptical, that's all. I've watched you these past few days go from soaring heights to some deep depression. Nothing would please me more than for you to be reunited with Arik. But let's not take this too fast. Let's think about going to Skara Brae. I'm certain George will know how to interpret this."

She wasn't so certain George would know what to do. If there was any possibility of returning to Arik she was going to investigate it. And that didn't mean remaining in the library. "This is the only lead we have."

"It's not a nice place," came Cora's slow and careful response.

Rebeka glanced at her. "I know. I've been there many times, four hundred years ago. I know exactly how 'nice' is it." She hoped she sounded stronger than she felt. She wanted George to agree with her, even come with her. But in the end, she was going to Orkney with or without his help.

CHAPTER FIVE

October 15, 1605 — Afternoon

Arik held court sitting on the dais in the Great Manor Chair. The old heirloom had been unused for decades. Previous lords of the house had found the massive carved seat intimidating, but not Arik. Its size fit him— as did its significance, the role of deciding his tenant's disputes.

"Was that the last?" He leaned forward, his hands on the chair's carved arms, eager to get back to his tower. He was spending too much time every other Wednesday with these interviews, but it was better than traipsing around the countryside speaking to each tenant. He had little enough time as it was to research the old documents. He glanced out the window, his eyes on the tower. Didn't anyone understand he was losing precious time?

"Yes, for now," Logan said.

Arik bolted out of the chair and was halfway across the room, Logan by his side.

"Everyone seems to be on edge," Logan said as he and Arik left the Great Hall. Arik glanced at his brother from the corner of his eye. Was Logan blaming him for all these disputes?

"What does that mean?" Arik stopped and grabbed Logan's arm, pulling him around.

"What do I mean?" Arik recognized the warring in Logan's eyes. It wasn't like Logan to beg for an argument. "What disputes did you hear today and two weeks ago and two weeks before that?" Logan didn't wait for Arik to answer. "Meaningless, petty arguments and fights. People who have been friends all their lives are arguing over nothing. And why? I'll tell you." The rage that swept through Logan's voice brought Arik up short. He'd never seen Logan in such a fit. "You've been locked in your tower room for weeks. You don't speak to your soldiers, your tenants, the villagers, to say nothing of your family." Logan stepped closer to Arik with each word until Arik could smell Logan's anger.

"You don't understand." Arik moved to push Logan away but his brother caught his hand.

Arik glared at Logan. In a frozen tableau, neither he nor his brother moved. After several heartbeats Logan released Arik's hand.

"You are not the only one who lost Rebeka. We all have. But we have lost more—much more. We've also lost you." Something in Logan's tone made him pull up.

The fight drained out of him like a rupture in a water skin. He studied Logan's face. He looked past his handsome features, boundless devotion and unwavering trust. But his heart was pierced when he recognized his brother's deep disappointment—in him.

He fixed his stare over Logan's shoulder. He couldn't stand to see himself mirrored in his brother's eyes.

"When Leticia died you got us through those dark days." Arik refocused on Logan in spite of his pain. "You kept everyone together, caring for each other, talking, working, moving forward, but we did it together—not only for Skylar and Aubrey, who were so small and orphaned, but me, the tenants, the villagers, our soldiers. You told me together we could face anything." Logan paused. "And we did." His voice low, he added, "This is no different."

They stood for several moments not speaking, Logan's words seeping into his head. He remembered that time, how Letty's death touched everyone. In helping them he had helped himself get through her loss.

"I love her, Logan, and will do whatever needs to be done to get her back. But others shouldn't pay that price." With an unwavering stare, he looked over the terrace railing. He wasn't the only person hurting. Logan was right. "After all my talk to Rebeka about examining a situation from different viewpoints I batter away at one, magick. I don't know where else to search."

Logan was right. He had isolated himself from everyone caring about what Rebeka meant to *him* and not about what she meant to the others. "There is much to do." He gave his brother a sideways glance.

"I'm ready, so are the others. Do you have a plan?" Arik took a deep breath. For the first time in weeks it was clean and sweet.

"The start of one. Would you help—"

"I've been waiting for you to ask. Where do we begin?"

Present Day

"I can't find any druid information here." Rebeka struggled to contain her temper and the urge to throw the books against the wall. "Nothing." She spit out the word and glanced at George, who was not saying a word from his place across the table. He didn't appear to be any happier.

"You're quite right. This is the last of the old texts." George closed the book, his fingers drummed on the leather binding. He stared into space and she questioned what he was searching for. "That leaves one other place, the druid sanctuary," he murmured. He slammed his hand against the old book. The unexpected sound made her jump. "The missing documents must be there. I stand in front of the garrison wall knowing the sanctuary is behind it but none of the chants open it. I was certain you would know how." The accusation in his voice angered her even more.

"I was never there when Arik or Logan opened it." George remained silent but Rebeka noted how he shifted in his seat. At last, he was coming to the same conclusion she had three weeks earlier. "Look, George, neither of us knows how to open the sanctuary. I haven't the time to research what needs to be done. I'm not even certain it's documented. But we're wasting time." She ran her hand through her hair as she paced in front of him. "I can't wait any longer. For weeks we've investigated every inch of the manor and the grounds. We even searched the old mill and Oak Meadow. I've waved my staff around like a madwoman with a divining rod. Nothing." She stopped in front of him. Her patience was running out. They hadn't found an answer because—"Orkney is the answer."

"Not until we have more information about the significance of your staff and the Orkney stone. We're missing something. I can feel it. Orkney is Bran's seat of power. We have no idea what to expect there. Even after all these centuries there may be danger. He threatened your life before you married Arik. We have no idea what he'll do now that you two are married." He was stalling. Perhaps it was a reaction to his vocation. Attorneys always wanted to have all the information before they acted. She, on the other hand, was content with the information they had. Her and Arik's sigil lit up when the staff was passed over the Orkney stones.

She took her staff and ran her hand over the familiar carved runes. "George, I'm going to Orkney. You can come with me or stay here but I'm leaving tomorrow."

George waited without saying a word, challenging her to go through with it. She supposed the scowl he gave her was his best intimidating attorney stare. It didn't faze her.

"I'll have Trudy make reservations on tomorrow's flight. I hope you know what you're doing."

She hoped she did, too.

"All set?" George asked Rebeka. She read a text message as they settled in the rental car at the Kirkwall Airport in Orkney. They had no baggage for the short day trip.

"Cora sent us a message from the Skara Brae archivist. She found some papers we may be interested in seeing. She has them at the information center for us." Rebeka clicked off her phone and stowed it in her pouch.

"As an attorney I've been schooled never to walk into a situation without knowing my opponent and with certainty not when I'm unprepared." His hand hit the steering wheel. "I have no idea what to expect when we arrive." His gaze slid from the windscreen to her face. He took a breath. "I don't know Bran's capabilities, especially with Dark Magick. Nor do I have any idea how to protect you."

She was tired of his challenging stare. She much preferred to distract herself by admiring the wildflowers that carpeted the meadow. "You don't have to. I'm capable of protecting myself." She didn't have to worry about protecting herself. All she had to concern herself with was traveling through the portal. It was uncomfortable but that didn't matter. She'd be with Arik soon.

He didn't say anything. She knew George well enough to know he wasn't easy to scare. If he was concerned, she should be terrified. But she wasn't.

"You think we'll find a portal at Skara Brae." She didn't want anything negative. She wanted him to be positive. Intent, focus and determination—that's what magick needed. She straightened in her seat and put on a poker face that would have made Arik proud. Confidence began with two things: knowing your abilities and a bit of attitude. Right now she was heavy on the attitude and light on the rest. She hoped that would be enough to see her through.

Stay calm, she told herself. *Keep focused.*

"We shouldn't be here. This is a place of Dark Magick." His vehemence caught her off guard until she understood his anxiety had increased as they got closer to Skara Brae. *The world is a duality. Everything has two sides.* It was the first magick lesson Arik had taught her. *So it is with magick, good and dark.*

The air crackled with energy. The gentle breeze of good magick that gave you a rush of energy—the feeling of being one with nature—along with the blustery gusts of Dark Magick with its swirling anger, anxiety and feelings of helplessness, it was all around them. Her instinct to come here was right. This was where the magick gathered. This was where she had to be.

"You think Arik called you here." She disregarded the sarcastic ring in his voice and swallowed hard, trying to keep her anger to herself. Couldn't he feel the energy?

"The glowing runes on my staff were an

interesting invitation. It would be foolish to ignore it. If I can get back and stop this feud, if things can get back to normal, it will all be worth it." His pursed lips indicated he wasn't convinced.

"We'll do nothing until we understand the state of affairs." George's expression was determined and set. He left no room for negotiation. She turned away and stifled a small snort. She would decide for herself what she needed to do.

George glanced at the dashboard clock. "We'll get to the estate a bit ahead of schedule."

They drove a few more minutes before he pulled off the road into a car park. They got out of the car and were pelted with a strong, salty wind. As far as the eye could see there were no trees. In its starkness the barren and desolate landscape had a unique beauty, but only in small doses. Nothing had changed in four hundred years. Even with her family around her this place had been difficult.

She started toward the estate house, carrying her staff.

"Don't you want to get the papers from the archivist? You told me we're to meet her at the information center," George called after her.

"Would you mind getting them? I want to get familiar with the surroundings." She didn't wait for him to answer or to interfere. She continued toward Bran's house. The brisk wind muffled the rhythmic tap of her walking staff on the long flagstone path. Leaning into the wind, she moved on with determination. The tall cotton grass on either side of the walkway swayed with the breeze. Its mop cotton-like flowers dotted the landscape as if a truckload of cotton balls had been scattered across the area. A small crack in her determination surfaced and her step faltered. She had to be right. Her anxiety in check, a soft, rhythmic vibration from her staff encouraged her to keep going.

She was almost there.

She had a clear view of the house now. It was made of fine Orkney red sandstone blocks. From afar the stones had a rosy glow in the fall sun. For her the building had a sad beauty that started at the front door. She hurried forward. But the closer she got to the structure the more she noted its worn, tired appearance. Its warmth had been deceptive. By the time she got to the front gate a sense of dread filled the air. She flicked her hand in the air in defiance, as if she could banish the mood. The staff's slight vibration had grown steadier and with it her eagerness to find the portal.

When she arrived at the doorway she glanced back in time to see George enter the information center. Good. He wouldn't interfere. Straightening her shoulders, she let herself in and closed the door behind her. The damp, musty air tickled her nose but she ignored it. Instead she focused on her staff's delicate throbbing and the knowledge that this was the way back to Arik. She would be with him soon. All she had to do was be quick and find the portal before anybody stopped her. She couldn't let that happen.

Her staff in front of her, she moved it like a probe on a Geiger counter and followed the clicks. The gathering speed of the clicks led her up the stairs and down a dark musty hall to a door in the older section of the house. She hesitated, her heart pounding in her ears. Arik. Her hand was poised above the doorknob. "This is ridiculous. Open the door," she muttered.

The doorknob turned by itself and began to open. She pulled her hand away. Had she pushed it? Uncertain, she remained where she was. "Rebeka, do come in." The door opened wide. In front of her a man stood near a wingback chair by the fireplace. "We've been expecting you."

She remained at the doorway peering through an

iridescent haze. Tilting her head she tried to focus on the man. An acute sense of loss washed over her. It wasn't Arik. She glanced around the room but it was empty. "Who are you?"

He clamped his hand over his heart. "I'm offended. Surely you remember me, dear sister. Come, come. Don't just stand there. Join us and make yourself comfortable." He gestured to a chair near him.

Bran.

Her staff heated. Where was Arik? She crossed the threshold not remembering how she got there. The haze thinned as she came deeper into the room. The door slammed shut behind her. She stopped. Her staff went cold. She drew it close to her chest. There would be no going back now.

A breeze, not stronger than a breath, ran across the room and cleared the haze, giving her a clear view of everything around her. The room was dark with heavy curtains that kept out the sunlight. Large pieces of furniture cluttered the space.

They were not alone. Someone was in the large wingback chair. She turned to Bran. Behind his unkempt appearance, frowning face and threatening presence she sensed a desperate man in deep pain. Why had he brought her here? She focused on the chair in front him.

"Caylyn has been a bit under the weather. I'm sorry my wife is unable to greet you properly." His protective arm rested around the top of the chair. Caylyn was dead. She remembered Arik and Ellyn rushing to Orkney to tend to her. But they had arrived too late to help her.

Her eyes were drawn to the woman seated there. She had an ethereal quality about her. But the woman didn't move or say a word. Could it be Caylyn? What had Bran done?

A muffled noise behind her pulled her attention.

Bran's handsome features morphed into a sneer as his eyes shifted toward the door.

He brought his attention back to her and beckoned with his finger. Her arm holding her staff extended. Beads of sweat broke out on her forehead as she fought for control.

His lips moved but he made no sound as he continued to stare at her staff. Pinned in place like an insect to a board, she was helpless. Her hand trembled but she was determined to stop him. She fought on and, with great difficulty, was able to keep her staff from him.

A smirk lit his face. "I only want to borrow it—for Caylyn. You see, she's not been well. Would you rather help her yourself? Come here." He stepped toward her, grabbed her arm and pulled her toward the chair.

The sound of pounding broke through the haze that clouded her mind. She hesitated and turned toward the door. Yes, that was where the noise was coming from. He pulled her hard and brought her face close to his, so close she saw the dark specks in his amber eyes. So close she saw the haunted, desperate look in his face. So close she knew he would stop at nothing to get what he wanted. Then he touched her mind.

"Heal Caylyn. You're Arik's great sorceress. Heal my wife." Focusing hard, she used all her strength to push him out of her head. She leaned on her staff. Light-headed, she concentrated harder and fought him for control of her mind. But little by little he claimed it.

"Rebeka." Someone screamed from the other side of the door as the pounding turned to the sound of splintering wood.

She glanced back at the chair. The glimmer that had surrounded the woman faded. The woman, her withered hands grasping a faded handkerchief, drew a deep breath from Rebeka. She recognized the dead body of Bran's wife. The handkerchief was her gift to

Cay the day she married Bran.

"Rebeka, I'm almost through," George called as the door splintered.

"Is this why you called me here? For Caylyn?" She stared at the woman and wrinkled her brow. She turned to Bran and searched for any semblance of the boy she remembered but she couldn't reconcile his features. Something—the Dark Magick, she imagined—had erased all remnants of that boy. That's when she understood what he had done. He'd sacrificed everything to bring Caylyn back.

"I can't do anything for her." Her voice was a whisper and his face was awash with tears. "No one can."

"You were my last hope." For a moment his features changed and he was Bran. "I tried everything. There is no other place for me to turn." He slid to the floor and put his head on Cay's lap. His eyes, with a pained expression, searched her face.

She stood next to him. She knew the grief of losing someone you loved. There was nothing she could do.

His body quivered and he bolted up. With his hands fisted at his sides and determination marked on his face, his features appeared to stretch and change.

"Fight it, Bran. Don't let it take hold," she encouraged him. "Let me help you."

"No," he screamed at her. "Don't mind-touch. I don't want to hurt you, Rebeka."

"Don't lock me out." She concentrated and touched his mind at the edges. There wasn't any resistance.

"No. Stop. It's a trap. Don't make me do this. I. Can't. Stop. It." Bran struggled to keep control. "Go, now. Tell Arik I…" Bran closed his eyes. She thought she saw tears. "It wasn't his fault. Leave now," he demanded.

But she hesitated. One more attempt. She was transfixed as his face changed into a maniacal sneer. He grabbed her hair. "I don't need your sympathy. I need my wife." He shoved her away and sent her to the floor, her staff clattering across the room.

In her compassion, her defenses were down. Bran hovered over her like a dark hawk. She tried to retreat, scuttling backward on all fours like a giant crab. She groped for her staff but it was beyond her reach. The sound of her heartbeat was dimmed by something else. Bran. He was invading her mind. She couldn't get him out of her head but she could contain the damage.

Splinters from the smashed door flew past her. She hoped the flying debris would distract Bran long enough for her to get a stronger hold of her mind and push him further out of her head.

"Hold on, Rebeka." She sensed George's touch in her mind before he entered the room. Together, with their minds, they beat back Bran's attack.

Bran winced with her effort and gaped at her. He dropped to his knees, bent over her and let out a sigh. "You fight hard, I will say that. As dogged as Arik. But you'll lose in the end." A moment of doubt flashed across Bran's face. She imagined Bran, the one she knew had returned. Encouraged, she pushed harder. She was gaining ground.

"I dare say you surprised Arik when you used the Dark Magick, but that doesn't matter now." He took a deep breath. "But I'll be kind to you. I'll take away your memories." Her eyes widened. "Oh, don't be concerned. I'll take away the memories of him, none of the others. You won't even miss him. He could pass right by you and you wouldn't recognize him. But Arik will suffer. If he ever finds you he'll watch you and know you remember nothing." He glanced at the door, an uneasy look on his face. "Sorry, I haven't got time to be gentle."

Her hands flew to either side of her head. Her scream started in the depths of her soul.

"Little by little you'll lose your memories. You'll try to hold on to them but you won't be able to. Then one morning you'll wake and they'll be gone." He pulled her to her feet.

The scream raced through her, building, gathering energy. She took no note of it being Dark Magick. Her sole plan was to stop him from taking her memories, taking Arik from her.

"I've been kind to you, Rebeka. You won't remember." He glimpsed at the chair. "I won't ever forget."

She opened her mouth and let out the silent scream.

"Bran," was the whisper that rustled in the room. "Bran." The word got louder.

Bran snapped around and glanced at the chair. "Cay?" He let go of Rebeka, as if holding her had scorched his hand. Standing stoic and still, she watched the confusion touched with fear play across his face. Now was the time to move, while he was distracted. She pushed Bran from her head as George rushed through the shattered door.

"Cay?" Bran ran to his wife, ignoring George.

Rebeka gasped in relief as Bran pulled his mind from hers. Weakened from fighting him off, she stood on unsteady legs and sagged against George. While her eyes were locked on Bran he reached out to his wife with a tender touch. She knew he searched for any sign of life. His love for Cay was so evident that all she saw was a dear friend grieving and for a moment she grieved with him.

George squeezed her shoulder and shook her. "We've got to get out before he comes after us." They made their way to the door.

"Stay here. Don't move." George propped her

against the doorjamb and in desperation searched the floor.

Rebeka looked back at Bran trying to revive his wife. She pitied him but only until she remembered how much havoc and disaster he had caused them.

She grabbed her head. Hundreds of whispers wracked her mind. Was it starting? Was she losing her memories of Arik? Blinded by her tears, she choked at the idea. George was once again at her side carrying her staff. He pulled her from the room. As soon as they got over the threshold the whispers stopped and she collapsed on the floor.

When she woke she was lying in the hallway. George was patting her hand. Arik. She said his name over and over in her mind, imprinting it there so she would never forget it.

"Rebeka." She opened her eyes and noted a slow smile spread across George's face.

"Where?" She tried to rise. George pushed her back with a gentle hand. She was lucky George hadn't left her there after what she had done.

"We're in the estate house, outside the old master suite. How do you feel?" He had covered her with his coat.

"My head hurts. I need to sit up." In a rush, she remembered what had happened. George helped her sit with her back against the wall and gave her a bottle of water.

"Here, drink this."

"Thanks." Confused, she stared at the door in front of her that stood ajar. It was all in one piece. She peered into the room. Sunlight poured through the large, curtainless windows. The room was empty.

"George, the room was filled with old furniture.

The door…" She grabbed George's sleeve. "It was Bran," she whispered.

George put his hand on top of hers. "Yes, it was. You're safe now."

She studied his face. "It wasn't a portal?" She'd been foolish to believe… "There are two of them." She stared off into the distance.

His face was in front of hers. "What do you mean two of them?"

"I saw him." She kept her eyes on the floor. She couldn't look into George's eyes. "The old Bran. The one we all loved. He told me to get out but I stayed. I couldn't leave without trying to help him." He raised her face to his. "I watched as he tried to fight off the Dark Magick. It changed his face. He fought but it took over." She wiped the tears from her cheeks with the back of her hand. "That was who attacked me. I couldn't keep him from touching my mind." She stood on shaky legs with George's help. "It's Caylyn. He asked me to help her but I couldn't." She stumbled trying to make her legs move.

"Slow down, we don't need to rush." He brushed off her singed staff and gave it to her.

She stared at her walking stick. "For a moment I believed it was a bad dream."

"No, it wasn't a dream but it wasn't a portal. I wouldn't have been able to get to you if it were. Even Bran's magick can't create a portal. It was an enchantment. You were there but it was temporary." He put his arm around her and helped her down the hall.

She glanced back at the room. "He said he was taking my memories. I'll lose them little by little until I won't remember…Arik." She started trembling. "I was so sure tonight I would be back with him." She turned to George when they got to the top of the staircase. "Instead, now I'll lose him forever."

CHAPTER SIX

March 20, 1606

"Steady, men," boomed Logan's captain, his voice trumpeted across the field of soldiers.

Arik, at his tower window, watched the men below eager to observe Logan's plan. He scowled at the west. Even at this distance the ground rumbled with the pounding hooves of the advancing horde. In step with Logan's men, he imagined them hefting their swords, others readying their bows, everyone keeping their eyes on the black line of riders rushing toward them and waiting for the order to attack.

"Come on," Arik urged the advancing men. His neck muscles hardened with tension. Logan's second in command raised his arm high, a purple cloth grasped in his hand. His eyes narrowed. Where was the signal? What was the delay? The riders were close.

The purple cloth dropped like a stone.

The left flank sprang into action, crumbling in disarray before his eyes. Arik stood in place trying to make sense out of what he witnessed. In unison, the attacking troop swerved toward the disassembled men and rode for the weakened spot. Horsemen swept up the embankment and clashed with the foot soldiers who tried to maintain a semblance of resistance before their line broke apart. The advancing men and horses thundered past them over the top of the ridge and down into the dry streambed.

He had been driving Logan hard to make certain he was ready for the challenge of taking over for him when he left to bring Rebeka back. But the line shouldn't have collapsed. For weeks his men played war games, neither side besting the other. The tried-and-true tactics were discouraging and Logan had pressed him to try this new maneuver. He couldn't leave Fayne Manor defenseless. Had he pushed too hard? He tossed the notion away. His brother was battle tested.

An arrow, a purple ribbon trailing, soared high in the air and caught his attention. He stretched his neck out the window and searched for the bowman.

On the ground, Logan stood—his spent bow in his hand. The signal understood, in a rush the men on the left flank regrouped, closed the gap, then pressed toward the invaders. The concern that plowed deep furrows into Arik's face smoothed.

Arik's fist pounded the ledge while the exercise continued to unfold, the anticipation building.

Logan wasn't done.

Pursued from behind and seeing the disadvantage of being caught in the bottom of the ditch, the raiders made for high ground on the opposite embankment. As they climbed the rise, a line of Logan's elite forces took their positions on the top of the ridge. Logan's men pressed their advantage and advanced from every direction. Arik roared his encouragement from the tower window. The raiders were surrounded. Victory was Logan's reward for the well-laid trap.

A trumpet blew three staccato bleats. The maneuver was over.

Logan glanced at the tower and gave his brother a

courtly bow. Arik acknowledged his success with a triumphant raised arm. Satisfied in his decision to allow the new maneuver, Arik had not been disappointed.

Arik turned from the window and his soaring spirits sobered. The comforting tower room closed in around him. He scoured the mute walls for an answer, bearing the weight of a pilgrim begging the gods for a cure. The answer wasn't there.

He sank into the chair, resigned, his elbows rested on the writing table. The acute guilt weighed him down like an ox's yoke. "I should have warned her," the damning whisper passed his lips. He slammed his fist on the wooden table, sending his hopes and the parchments flying. Another deep breath, then another. Again. Again, until at last the tempest in his head calmed. "I should have... I should have protected her."

He didn't have to close his eyes to imagine her. She was forever etched in his mind. But his lids slid closed as he sniffed the air like his best hunting dog ferreting out a scent. Last night the fragrance had been lavender and rose. Today, melted wax and spent sulfur.

Faith, the early hours of the morning he had sensed success within his grasp only to have it slip from his fingers. The formula wasn't right. His fists were closed so tight that his fingernails bit into his palm. He was so close he could feel her safe in his arms.

The nights were the worst. She filled his dreams. He felt her touch, heard her voice and tasted her lips only to wake in the morning and lose her all over again.

Enough. This was torture and it wasn't getting him any closer to her. He gave himself a mental shake and forced the images away. No prescription existed for creating a doorway through time, not even for a druid Grand Master. All he had were calculated guesses. "Maximillian had done it," he whispered to himself, staring at the runes on the walls. What did Maximillian have—no, what power was unique to him? The stars.

He rummaged through documents, transcribed arcane symbols and reworked the formulas to align it with the stars. An hour later, he put down the quill and rubbed his eyes, satisfied he had gone over each rune and found where the correction needed to be made. Each druid had a power. Rebeka's magic was still a mystery, but it would be revealed to her. His came from the earth, Logan's from song and Leticia's from plants. He'd been searching in the wrong place.

He stood and stretched to work out the kinks from sitting hunched over the table. He surveyed his tower room. Gone were the beautiful tapestries that had adorned the walls. In their place were hundreds of charcoal markings, runes and formulas that covered every inch of the high walls. He took a piece of charcoal and with precision followed the formula.

"Ninoor nin ah ray," he chanted in a soft whisper that echoed in the room. He went from one symbol to the next. His eyes focused on each rune as he narrowed in on the area he needed. Relief rushed over him when his finger landed on the runes that needed to be altered. He rubbed them out and replaced the section with the new set of runes.

Out of the quiet, while he scrawled the last symbol, the clear voice of another reached his ears. "Ninzure nin ah ray."

Arik went silent. His hand froze.

"Ninzure nin ah ray," the voice chanted with an urgent tone.

A spark of excitement ignited in the pit of his stomach. At last, success was more than a wish and a dream. It was within his grasp. He added his voice to the chant. His heartbeat mimicked the cadence. The runes on his body thrummed with the energy. Where once a lone sash of symbols traced up his back and down his torso to that private place of power, now the markings were embellished with magical sigils and spread across his chest and back like a close-fitting shirt. Each new addition a protection against the consequences of the powerful magick he was invoking.

As the chant crescendoed then faded to silence, so did he. He remained quiet, dizzy from the rush of anticipation. He whispered his thanks to the Great Mother.

Dare he hope for success?

No, no doubts. Magick required intent, focus and determination. He had them all and he would succeed. Now with the corrected formula he was ready to try again.

The gold pentacle that covered the floor between the scrying mirror and the hearth glittered in the firelight. The ancient design of the pentacle was there long before him. Fresh pools of melted wax and smudges of charcoal surrounding the relic confirmed the many times he and Logan had attempted to open the portal. He bent and prepared the area for the last marking. Logan would lend his voice and add the final symbol. He straightened and reviewed his changes one more time.

All was ready.

"Arik," Logan called out from the other side of the door.

His head whipped around. "Come," Arik said. Glad that Logan was with him, he was eager to begin. Today they would succeed.

"I've brought you some bread and cheese. You haven't eaten for two days. I wouldn't want you to waste away." Arik saw the plate but he had no appetite. He had scoured all his books and documents for information, even those with Dark Magick. With great care he drew on select rubrics and had fasted to purify his mind and body.

He welcomed the smile he detected in Logan's voice. The division of work between him, Logan,

Marcus, Jeannie and others had gone well. The result was his tenants were no longer at one another's throats and the estate was running without many problems.

Logan set the plate on a spot he cleared on the table. "You appear rested." Logan tore off a piece of bread and gave it to him.

He gave his brother a penetrating stare. "You're not a very good liar." Holding the bread, he motioned to the window. "The maneuvers went well today, very well." He didn't miss the pride in Logan's eyes. "I had no idea your main battery stood ready behind the ridge. I believed your men were not prepared and that Marcus had the advantage." He clapped Logan on the shoulder. "Your strategy was well planned and executed." He tossed the uneaten bread onto the plate.

"We surprised Marcus—a difficult feat," Logan admitted. A wide grin flashed across his face.

"You should eat something." Logan gave Arik a parchment. "We received a message from Doward before maneuvers."

Arik ignored Logan. *Eat.* He sounded like Jeannie when the girls were small. He blew out a breath. Logan had his best interests in mind. He opened the document. "I was hoping for some word from the Council before I left." As Grand Master they had been in close contact, but since Rebeka left they had been silent.

"He says that they seem to have vanished. He's never seen them go into such deep hiding. There are places he wants to investigate before he returns to Fayne Manor." He handed the document back to Logan. *Faith.* He ran his hand through his hair. He had hoped the Council could help him. No, something smelled and it wasn't pleasant. He knew he had to continue on his own. "Keep watch for him. Tell the Council what has happened and that I've gone to bring Rebeka back." He paused, not wanting to say the words. "And to deal with Bran." He tried to keep his voice even. When he glanced at Logan, he knew he hadn't succeeded.

Logan nodded. Placing the document on the table, he moved to the wall and concentrated on the new markings. "You expanded the air element to include the stars."

"The time portal was Maximillian's design. Including his power may show us the way." He hadn't been this calm in weeks. Was the Great Mother telling him something? Arik examined the formula again. He knew it was right.

Logan nodded and read the rest of the formula. He, too, knew it was correct. "I see you're ready to begin."

"Aye." Arik stood next to Logan. "We made great progress last night. You did well with the change you made to the formula. I finished it."

Logan took some of the scattered papers. Arik leaned over to take them from him but Logan pulled them out of his reach, glancing at them.

"Arik, you needn't resort to this. Dark Magick isn't the answer." Logan shook his paper-filled fist at him. "We spoke about this over and over. We decided. We would not use Dark Magick. Do you think you can control it any better than Bran? Stop it from eating away at you, like it does him?"

Arik had chosen his course. Months ago he was certain of success. Now, each day he faced defeat and he didn't wear it well. How could he explain to Logan that he would rather die trying everything in his power to find her than live without her? He was determined to find her. Now. Not tomorrow or next week.

"Look at the wall." His arm circled the walls around them. "They shout with every attempt we've made." He pulled open his shirt. "I wear the marks of each one. Each time I've tried to locate her, each time I used magick, a new mark was added to strengthen the request. If this attempt fails there is nothing left but Dark Magick. We've avoided it as long as we can. Bran's Dark Magick took her away. It may be the only way to bring her back."

"No, better you use the enchantment than Dark Magick." Logan threw the papers to the floor. Logan didn't try to hide his distaste.

"The results of the enchantment are temporary. Logan, I want her back permanently."

"You must know I do, too. We'll find her and you'll bring her back, but not this way." Logan clapped him on his back.

"Then how? Do you know another way?" Arik asked. The silence stretched for several heartbeats.

"I didn't think so," Arik said, his voice soft. "Enough. There's work to do." Arik opened the large domed topped chest next to the window and rummaged through it. "Today, today we'll find her." He cleared his mind of any doubt that plagued him. "While I adjusted the markings I heard the same chant as last night. It varies a bit from ours." His hands stilled and he beamed at his brother. "Someone works with us."

"Arik," Logan cautioned. His hand stayed his brother's arm. "Do we rush into this too quick?" Quick? They'd been trying for six months. Had they become so accustomed to failure that success was to be avoided? Or was Logan worried about taking his place?

"Sniff the air. Do you smell it?" Arik stood straight and took a deep breath, filling his lungs. "It's success. Don't fear it." He stared at Logan. "Never be fearful of success. Be ready for it." He bent back to rummage in the chest. "I need you to be with me on this. Any doubt weakens our chances for success." Was he trying to convince Logan or himself? "Now let's go over things one more time."

"I will set the wards before we begin." One by one Logan ticked off each task on his fingers. "You'll take your place in the pentagram. I'll not touch you or speak to you. I'll lay the last ward. You'll start the ritual and together we'll chant as we have practiced. And I'll wait for you and help you bring Rebeka back through the portal."

"Good." Arik nodded and picked through his armaments. He'd given Logan a good speech. *Faith.* He didn't know if he was ready? But he died a thousand deaths not knowing if she was safe. No. He had to go. He had no choice.

Logan peered over Arik's shoulder. "You prepare like you're going into battle."

"I've no idea of the consequences we face to bring her home."

"What about the consequences of you traveling there?" Logan asked. Even a druid Grand Master faced consequences using such powerful magick. Any error in the formula or the process and he could be caught between the two times forever. He understood the risks but he wouldn't let them stop him.

Arik raised his eyebrow. "I prepare the best I can to avoid surprises. We both do." He tucked a knife into his waist belt. He removed a small pouch of coins from the chest. He thought to leave them behind then reconsidered and tucked the pouch into his belt as well.

"One thing more." He took off his sword and raised the Sword of Rapture above them. The sword was more than a blade. It sang with the blood of the vanquished and was the glory of his people. It proclaimed its owner its chieftain. He lowered the steel and appreciated the reverence on Logan's face.

"I remember the day Maximillian gave this to me." Arik's voice was filled with respect. "It was too big for me, or rather I wasn't the man to wield such a mighty weapon."

"You grew into it," Logan said, a trace of laughter in his voice.

"Aye, and I've never been without it. The sword doesn't define the man. But the principles it represents—honor, loyalty and trust—do. They are a part of him." Logan had proved he was worthy and able to hold his place while he was gone.

And if he didn't return? A chill passed his shoulders. If he didn't return Logan would carry on.

He swung the blade around and presented the hilt to his brother. By giving Logan his sword he gave him the right to rule. "You've always taken my part when I've gone to court or on campaign," Arik said, his tone solemn. "I leave Fayne Manor in your capable hands."

"There's no need for this." Logan pushed the sword away. Arik recognized a bit of panic in Logan's voice.

Arik put his arm around his brother and drew him close. "You know I go of my own accord. But I don't know how long I'll be gone and I will not leave you at a disadvantage." He took off his chieftain's signet ring and slipped it into Logan's hand. "The sword and signet proclaim your legitimacy to lead." His low-pitched voice rang with authority. "There must be no doubt."

Logan turned the gold ring over in his hand. "It has your sigil." He examined every line in the magick symbol. "I remember watching the goldsmith work the design into the ring. How exacting you were with its creation." He hefted it, testing its weight. "I'd forgotten the energy it carries." He peeked at Arik, a boyish expression on his face. "It hums," Logan added, his tone hushed.

Arik closed Logan's hands around the ring. He was proud of the man Logan had become, a man with great patience and courage beneath a lighthearted exterior. He would miss his company, his counsel and even his sense of humor. He watched Logan fill his lungs with breath.

Logan nodded. "I'll accept them but I'll put them in the druid sanctuary for safekeeping, until you reclaim them."

Arik watched the concern skitter across Logan's face. He knew that look in brother's eyes, the tilt of his shoulders, the dancing from foot to foot. He waited for his request.

"Will you reconsider? I'd rather give *you* my sword arm than take your sword." The hope in Logan's voice was unmistakable.

Arik put his hand on Logan's shoulder. "Your sword arm would be a comfort but it's needed here." It wasn't easy telling him to stay. He removed his hand and closed the chest. "Now, let's begin."

"I'll be ready when you need me. I'll stay here—" Logan swept his arm around the room, "—and wait for you."

"That won't be necessary," Arik said. "With any luck I'll collect Rebeka and we'll both see you tomorrow when we break the morning fast."

The brothers stood by the hearth. "Stay safe," Logan whispered.

Arik nodded his agreement. With nothing else to say, he took his place in the center of the pentagram. The flames from the hearth danced and caressed him in the reflection of the mirror. He turned toward the eastern wall and recited the ritual that asked for a safe journey while Logan responded and set the wards.

"Hail, Guardians of the East. I summon the power of air." His voice echoed through the room.

"By the air in her breath, be with us now," Logan replied.

He turned to the south. "Hail, Guardians of the South. I summon the power of fire."

"By the fire in her spirit, be with us now," came

the reply.

He faced the west. "Hail, Guardians of the West. I summon the power of water."

"By the waters of her womb, be with us now."

Turning north, toward the hearth. "Hail, Guardians of the North. I summon the power of earth."

"By the earth that is her body, be with us now," Logan said.

"As above, so below. As within, so without. Four stars in this place be to open the door of time to me. So mote it be."

"Ninzure nin ah ray." A whisper reached their ears when Logan scribed the final symbol.

Arik repeated the new chant. "Ninzure nin ah ray." *My hearth, my heart.* He waited.

The air stirred, at first rustling Arik's hair then catching his loose-fitting shirt. Yet the papers in the room were still. He renewed his concentration and continued the chant. His scalp tingled with anticipation. Even though he was deep into the ritual he sensed that the room changed.

The flames leaped high in the hearth when the last word was spoken. Soft sounds gathered into whispered words that grew more insistent until a voice called to him, the same one that called him last night, "Arik."

He and Logan searched for the source and turned to the mirror. The smooth surface shifted and swirled. The image of a man materialized holding Rebeka's walking staff covered with the familiar runes and leather strapping. Arik stood rooted to the floor like the great oak in Oak Meadow, excitement rippling through him—he would be with her soon.

He searched the mirror for any sign of his wife but saw nothing. Was she safe? A finger of fear spread across his back. He needed to keep his wits about him. With care, he stepped to the mirror and slipped his hand through the silvery vapor to touch the staff. It was beyond his grasp. He extended his fingers but still fell short of his goal.

He turned to Logan and nodded. Then, showing more confidence than he felt, stepped into the mirror.

CHAPTER SEVEN

Present Day

"Lord Arik." The man's voice was softened by surprise. "*Rebeka.*" He reached out to her with his mind. His eyes never left the staff, Rebeka's staff as the man lowered it. There was no reply. "You're here." The disbelief on the man's face matched the amazement in his voice. He froze for a heartbeat. It took the man another heartbeat before he moved. "I'm George Hughes."

"Hughes?" Arik furrowed his brow and searched the man's face. The George Hughes he knew was his solicitor and an advisor to the druid Council. There was a family resemblance. He'd find out about this Hughes soon enough. He pulled his mind back to Rebeka.

He took in his surroundings, the tower room. He dipped his head toward the staff. She never lets it out of her sight. "That's Rebeka's. Where is she?" He reached out again with his mind and among the debris he located her essence, small and quiet. He didn't like what he found. His hands itched with the impulse to push the man aside but he forced himself to remain calm.

"Your wife is downstairs. But she—"

He took a menacing step toward Hughes. "Is Rebeka harmed? In any danger?" He disguised his fear with the hard shell of ice that clung to every word.

George raised his hand to stop him. Arik held his ground; so did Hughes.

"No. Physically she is well." A new authority colored Hughes's voice.

Finding Rebeka was his immediate goal. He would use anything and anyone to rescue her. He touched the man with his mind but it was guarded well. Arik strengthened his already-tight defenses.

"As for who I am, I'm a descendant of your barrister."

His George Hughes was an advisor to the druid Council when needed. Arik respected the man and trusted him. It remained to be seen if his descendant was as worthy.

"I've maintained the family business on both fronts." A small smile played at the corners of his mouth. "I'm Rebeka's barrister, George Hughes of Hughes, Swift and Lacey." Hughes's brows knitted together.

What was Hughes holding back? He said nothing and waited. There'd be time enough to tear the man apart if anything had happened to Rebeka.

"She has no memory of the four months she spent with you." Hughes's tone was apologetic.

Beads of cold sweat dampened his forehead. His heart hammered in his chest. "What do you mean she has no memory of me?" His voice was soft. George wouldn't recognize the danger it held.

"I have a great deal to tell you." Hughes gestured toward the chairs. "Please, take a seat."

"You'll take me to her, then you'll help with the scrying mirror and we'll return. Now." Less than an arm span in front of the man, he closed the short distance between them and stood in that private space that was intimidating and threatening. His tone allowed no denial.

Hughes didn't budge. "Arik, you must understand some things before you see her, otherwise all may be lost."

Arik dismissed the pleading note in the man's voice with a wave of his hand. "Now, Hughes." He was close to walking over him to get to her. "Do I make myself clear?" Each word shot like a bolt through his clenched teeth. One hand fisted at his side, the muscles beneath his light shirt rippled with tension. "Now." His free hand rested on the knife in his belt, his fingers ready to pull the blade and strike.

"Arik, a few moments, that's all I ask so you know what's happened." Arik softened his stare. The man sounded like Logan pleading his case. He couldn't blunder about. He needed information.

"A few moments. Tell me how she got here and what's happened since. We can discuss the rest at another time." He relaxed enough to listen but was ready to take action.

"She came out of the portal by the Avebury stones. That's where she was when she left us in May." Arik gave George a curt nod to go on.

"My sister, Cora, and I brought her back here. She told us what happened at the portal. Her scream… She had no idea about its power. Cora and I suspect Bran tricked her." He spoke about Bran in a casual tone. He needed to know how much George knew.

"Yes, that's the same thing we believed." Having George substantiate what he suspected didn't make things any better.

"At first she remembered everything and together we determined that Bran was involved." Arik let out a deep breath.

"Cora and I will do anything to help you and Rebeka. We've pledged ourselves to your cause. Bran must be stopped."

"Bran." So he was still a threat in this century—with his Dark Magick. "Take me to her, now."

George hesitated but stepped aside, clearing the way to the door.

Arik glanced over his shoulder at the mirror. He made out Logan's hand pressed against the now-solid surface as the vapor swirled then obliterated him. The portal closed. Something dark and heavy with a sense of foreboding came over him. This way was closed. His plan to return with Rebeka immediately was already changing. He didn't like it when his plans changed unless it was by his design.

Hughes led the way and started for the tower stairs.

"What do you know of Rebeka and her situation?"

"I know she is the daughter of Grand Master Maximillian," George said, "and his wife, the sorceress Ellyn. Rebeka has the powers of both her parents even though they are dormant. Born in your century, she spent a long time in mine. When the time came for her to return to you, something went very wrong. A descendant of yours, Emily Parsons, put the pieces together and before her death charged me to locate her. I searched for years to find her. Maximillian hid her well. When I located her at last, I realized she had no memory of the past. Her father took great pains to keep her hidden from Bran."

"Yes, that was my finding as well." George was telling the truth.

"I'll do all I can to help you both return to your time. But you can't take her back now, without her memory." Arik bristled at being denied. He needed time to think.

No memory of him? He brushed the idea away. Their feelings for each other were deep. Once she saw him she would remember.

They came to the bottom of the tower steps. Seeing nothing amiss, he hurried along the hallway. "Have you...touched her mind to find why she can't remember?" George said nothing. Arik stopped and gave George one of his tell-me-right-now-or-else looks. George's hesitation made him wary.

"Touching minds in this century can have deadly effects." George's words hit him hard—not because of the spoken danger but at what other magick would not function here. "We've learned to keep our minds guarded all the time." The quicker he got her away from here the better.

"Where is she?" he demanded as he marked a quick pace. George followed a few steps behind.

"She's in the ballroom." He stopped abruptly. George slammed into him and lost his grip on Rebeka's staff, sending it tumbling to the floor.

"What ballroom? I don't have a ballroom." The notion never occurred to him that his manor would be changed.

"You do now." George took the staff from the carpeted hall. "You've had one for the last 165 years," George said.

Curious, and with great caution he peered past the top of the grand staircase at a hallway filled with doors that stood like silent sentinels—a hallway he'd never seen before. He turned back to George and gave him his full attention.

"Your descendants renovated the manor several times in the past four hundred years." George brushed the hair out of his eyes. "Some things may be familiar to you but others," he nodded toward the blank doors, "will be very different. I suspect most things will be very different," he muttered in haste. Arik didn't plan to be here long enough to take note. It was as simple as a highland border raid. Go in, get his wife and get out.

"I'll take stock of the improvements later. Tell me

where to find this ballroom." He knew this place. It was his home but now it had a foreign feel, as if he'd never seen it before. He covered his unease by giving George his best intimidating glare.

"Come with me. You'll see Rebeka." George stepped to the other side of the staircase and stood in front of a door tucked neatly in an alcove. "Here, in the minstrel gallery above the ballroom," George said in a conspiratorial tone as he inched the door open a crack. His finger touched his lips for silence before he signaled Arik to enter.

Inside the small room, in the deep shadows, he stood hugging the back wall. Remaining still, he peered out from the small balcony into an almost empty room.

He took a deep breath and amid the musty smell of history he found the scent of lavender and rose—he found Rebeka.

His breath caught at the sight of her standing below him. The ballroom, with its one oversized table, had various documents spread over the floor like giant pieces of a puzzle. Large beveled glass doors bordered the terrace, letting in streams of sunlight that landed in a pool around her.

But Rebeka held his attention.

A quickening beat drummed in his chest and pulsed in his ears. His body ached to crush her against him and hold her close. He wanted to feel her arms around him, her lips touching his—he wanted to bury himself deep inside her and shout his passion to her world and to his. He flexed his fists to control the building tension.

She stood in profile, bent over a large document on the table. Her long dark hair fell loose in a gentle wave, creating a soft drape hiding her face. His fingers itched to feel the silkiness of her tresses once again. His eyes lingered but a moment more then swept down her body.

He stood peering at her, amazed and shaken. He'd expected her clothes would appear different but he hadn't expected them to be so…revealing. Her black breeches molded to her trim hips and long, shapely legs. The lower band of her oversized knitted shirt rested snuggly on her hips. He remembered every inch of her with a longing that was difficult to control. He told himself to relax but his heart kept hammering away.

"My heart," he whispered. Wave after wave of relief washed over him. He was with her at last.

Rebeka glanced at the men. "George. What are you doing there?"

"Showing off Fayne Manor. We'll be right there." George turned, giving Arik a congenial pat on the back. "Are you ready?" At his nod they filed out of the gallery and headed for the stairs.

He had climbed these steps hundreds of times but now the farther he descended the more he moved away from all he knew and loved. He would be foolhardy if he denied his apprehension. Awareness gave him an advantage. He saw things around him others overlooked. He was going someplace new and from what Rebeka had told him all those months ago it would be very exciting. This change in plan was manageable. As soon as he understood the state of things he'd ask George for his assistance to return. This was a small delay.

He straightened his back and continued down the stairs. Each step took him farther away from his century and closer to the new one until near the bottom the twenty-first century closed in around him.

George drove past him. "Let me do the talking." The barrister stood by the ballroom's large carved double doors, his hand on the knob. George straightened his shoulders and settled a comfortable smile on his face then turned to him—was he ready?

Hoping he appeared confident, he gave the barrister a nod. George opened the door and they stepped inside.

"Hello, Rebeka." George placed Rebeka's staff next to the door.

Rebeka turned toward them, a large piece of parchment in her hand. "Hi, George. You'll have to tell me if your theory was correct. I haven't gone into the tower. If you hadn't told me about the runes there I'd never have known."

Her eyes scanned his face. His heart pounded but he kept silent. He was satisfied to be near her—for the moment. She, on the other hand, seemed to be fascinated with his…clothes? She stole another glance at his eyes. He didn't turn away.

"I think my theory's promising. I'm sorry if we're disturbing you." George wandered over toward her.

She laid the parchment back on the table. "That's okay. I need to put everything away and get ready for our guests. They'll be arriving soon."

George turned to him. "To help maintain the manor, it's open to the public, for a fee. We've re-created some historic events throughout the grounds. Rebeka had wonderful ideas about expanding the program to immerse visitors in a total experience. Soon we'll be reopening the entire manor and from the time our guests step inside the gate until they leave, they'll experience life in the seventeenth century. We still have a few things to do but we're moving along quite well."

She cocked her head to the side. "George, are you going to introduce me?" Her eyes were wide and her voice was soft.

"Of course. Rebeka." George grasped Arik's shoulder. "This is Arik…my distant cousin."

He searched her violet eyes he knew so well. He glimpsed a spark of curiosity and maybe even a hint of attraction but shock held him immobile at his acute sense of loss when he realized there was no glimmer of recognition.

"Excuse me. I'm covered with charcoal and grit." She wiped her hands on a rag she grabbed off the table. "Pleased to meet you."

"As am I. George has told me much about you." He gave her a well-practiced nod touched with a devilish smirk. He remembered how she played at being annoyed when he would flash the same smile at her. He didn't miss her quick intake of breath.

"Do I know you? Perhaps at one of George's parties? I can't help but feel we've met." Her brows wrinkled in concentration.

He let out a breath he didn't know he held. "No, not in this lifetime, I assure you." Perhaps there was hope after all.

"Excuse me, Arik. I need to discuss something privately with George."

Arik nodded and stepped toward the table.

She was hesitant to turn away. She noted how Arik's body moved with an easy, commanding grace and she hadn't missed how his massive shoulders filled the light shirt he wore. His fitted pants—no, *breeches*, she corrected herself—emphasized the force of his thighs and the slimness of his hips.

His presence filled the room. He was handsome. His blue-green eyes mesmerizing but there was something else. She couldn't place it other than a need to be close to him.

More than close—in his arms.

For months she'd been detached and uncomfortable. So why now, with this knight—yes that's what he was, she was certain—did she all at once feel…at ease? A knight? How'd that pop into her head? But he wore it like a skin that was part of him. The reenactment must be getting to her. She turned to George and tugged him away.

"Who exactly is he? And what's he wearing? Is he auditioning for one of the reenactment roles?" She took another appraising glance at Arik. A shiver of excitement ran through her. "He looks like he stepped out of a romance novel."

"His home is in the north. He lives a rustic life and doesn't visit here often, a recluse of sorts. But you've given me an idea." He glanced past her at Arik.

"There's something about him." They hadn't exchanged more than a dozen or so words and she was hungry for him. This was so not her. Intelligence and character drew her interest. She never let the physical drive her attraction, so why now? Why him? She stopped trying to figure it out and shrugged her shoulders. "Well, I can't describe it. I'm certain I know him." She saw him handling the document.

"Hey! Don't touch that," she barked, pointing to the parchment in his hand. Rebeka charged across the room but his stare stopped her in her tracks. He was a man who was not to be crossed. Her hesitation lasted one, maybe two heartbeats before she marched to the table. She didn't intimidate easily. With her hand outstretched she requested the document. "This document is rare, hundreds of years old. You can't just pick it up."

"Rebeka…" The trace of panic in George's voice stopped her cold.

"No, Hughes, she's right." Ignoring her hand, he placed the document back on the table. He'd handled the same document yesterday when he'd wrapped it in oilcloth and stored it away.

"Thank you. They're hard enough to translate. The

last thing I need is someone destroying them." The last six months had been difficult but this, the shock of being nothing to her, stabbed at his heart.

"Excuse me, Ms. Rebeka." They all turned toward the voice at the door.

"Yes, Charles?" Rebeka said. From his formal appearance and reverent tone, he assumed the man was the steward.

"Breakfast is served. Mr. George, your office is on the line."

"Ah, at last. I hope they've found the manor papers." George turned to the steward. "I'll take the call in the estate office." He took a step toward the door but hesitated, his hand rubbing his neck. "Arik, don't go anywhere. I'll be back and take you for a tour of the place so you can get reacquainted."

"Charles," Rebeka called to the steward as he was leaving. "Please tell Helen to set another place at the table." She turned to Arik. "You'll join us for breakfast, won't you?"

He hadn't considered food for the past two days and found he had an appetite. A mug of ale, some cheese and bread would taste good. "I'd be pleased to join you," he said with a nod.

After all this time he wasn't about to let her out of his sight.

George left the room shaking his head. A mild panic raced through him. It almost made him laugh. In his own home with his wife and he's…alarmed. But how can she not know him?

"And what does this document contain?" His voice was heavy with indulgence, as if he was inviting a child to repeat their lesson. He had taught her about it and the secrets it held. Could he spark her memory?

"This is a surveyor's document, providing the placement of stones for some reason. These are runes." She pointed to the alphabet on the top of the rolled document. "They're an early form of writing predating Latin found as early as the Bronze Age, about 2900 BCE, and lasting until the Iron Age, about 1200 BCE. Over time, it was…" Her back straightened, the parchment poised in her hand. The knowledge she saw in his eyes gave him away. "You know all this, don't you?"

He watched the slow burn on her face. "Yes—but not from your academic viewpoint." He took the document. She started to protest but he placed it onto the table and pointed to a rune. "This sigil indicates wards for protection. And this," he pointed to another rune, "is the warder's sign." Without thinking, his thumb sought the absent signet on his ring finger. He let that idea go and instead concentrated on Rebeka. He was certain once she saw him she would remember him. He needed to know the how and when she lost her memory before he could figure out how to help her. He was certain Hughes had the answer.

"Are you sure?" The wonder in her voice floated over his shoulder.

Yes, he was certain. He was the warder. He'd created the sigil. He had drawn the map. Rolling the document, he placed it in the carrier and gave it to her. "Oh yes, I'm quite certain." He noted the disbelief that crossed her beautiful features.

"Sigil, a magical sign. Warding! This is an important document." Her scowl reminded him of her first introductions to his world. She'd found his magick difficult to accept then, too. But she had accepted and learned his ways. It was her destiny to be a powerful sorceress. Greater than her mother, Ellyn. Right now he'd have a hard time convincing her of that.

He didn't take his eyes off her as she gathered the other documents and placed them into a waiting box. "Yes, it is."

She stood holding the overflowing box of

documents.

"When the document was created, it was very important." Feeling very much the teacher, he took the box and followed her to the door. "Wards use the energy of the earth to protect something, in this case a place, Fayne Manor."

She took her staff from against the wall and they left the room. They passed the Great Hall and entered the library.

He took a deep breath and smelled the leather of the bound books and oiled parchments. Shelves lined the walls from floor to ceiling. A tall ladder reached high to the upper bookshelves. He scanned the room, pleased to see the library had grown.

It was his library that had brought them together. With one of the best libraries in England, he had believed the king had sent her to do research. After spending a short amount of time with her, he'd suspected James wanted to remove her from court. Her defiant attitude and beauty would make her a conquest for many of the king's courtiers, especially if the king held her in high esteem.

How wrong he had been. She was there to find her way back to the twenty-first century using his vast cache of druid documents. If her spirit was in any room, it was here. How many times over the past six months had he imagined her at this library table?

"I'd like to continue our discussion but I have to get this all straightened before the visitors arrive." She took the box from him, bringing him back to the moment, and placed it in a cabinet. Books lay in disarray on the table. Papers were everywhere.

"You take care of the papers. I'll put these away." He didn't wait for her answer. He took the books and put them on the shelves.

"You can't put them anyplace. I'll never find them again." She retrieved the book he had shelved then stopped. "How did you know where to put this?" she asked with a touch of confusion in her voice. He didn't answer. He'd already stepped through the terrace doors—eager to see his domain.

He stood gazing out at the garden admiring the view. He spotted the garden house with the large flat stone in front. While the house appeared to be familiar, the small house had been enlarged. It must contain several rooms. He was in a foreign place that breathed with familiarity. It was an odd sensation. He tried to distance himself from the changes but in his heart he couldn't. But he'd get by. He'd have to.

"Has the manor changed much since you were last here?" she asked, standing beside him.

Her soft voice sent a ripple of delight through him. He folded his arms across his chest to prevent himself from putting them around her. He sensed more than saw her follow his gaze. "In some ways, yes, and in other ways it's much the same." He kept his eyes straight ahead and tried not to think about the difference.

"Ms. Rebeka, breakfast is served." Charles stood at the terrace door.

"Shall we?" Rebeka asked him.

He nodded and she led the way.

CHAPTER EIGHT

Dishes lay broken, their contents strewn over the floor. Out of the corner of his eye Arik watched George skid to a halt by the breakfast table.

"Forgive me, Trudy, I must ring off," George spoke into the device and slipped it into his breeches. "What's going on?"

Rebeka was on her feet, pushing the wrought-iron chair out from under her with the backs of her knees. She sent the chair scraping along the slate terrace floor. The back legs caught on an uneven stone and tipped over. At the same time she grabbed Arik by the collar with both hands.

He gave her no resistance but flowed with her movements to minimize the impact. He brought his hands up between hers, circled them out and under. The movement forced her to release her grip. He caught her wrists with ease and held her captive.

He took a deep breath to quell the last strains of the berserker pulsing through him. But his purpose was accomplished. "She was going to eat those?" he said to George, nodding at the broken plate on the patio floor.

He didn't know which drove him more, anger or fear.

"What the hell do you think you're doing?"

Rebeka demanded. Her eyes were slits of dark agate and her stance fierce. "He lunged across the table," she said to George, "and swatted the food out of my hand. Then he tossed the plate. Who knows what he would've done if I hadn't stopped him?"

"Both of you relax. I'm sure there's a good explanation." Was the man insane? She was going to eat those, those love apples. If he hadn't been here—he didn't want to think about what would've happened.

He noted George's slight nod and released Rebeka. She flexed her hands and rubbed her wrists. A woman, a servant he suspected, rushed in and busied herself cleaning the mess.

"Even a child knows not to eat poisonous love apples." His clipped speech was coated in a rime of ice. He didn't miss the flash of relief scurry across George's face.

"Ah, I understand. Good show." He pounded Arik's back. "I know I told you we live a seventeenth-century lifestyle here, but for the public, not in private."

He followed George's eyes as they shifted to Rebeka. A sense of unease crept up his spine. The barrister appeared not to be concerned. It was obvious everyone knew some great secret except him and he didn't like it one bit.

"As you can see, this is an ordinary twenty-first-century breakfast: eggs, oatmeal, fresh bread, fruit, coffee and grilled tomatoes." George leaned in and lowered his voiced. "Not love apples, which are *not* poisonous."

"Lord Arik?" He detected the surprised gasp in the voice in front of him.

"Yes?" He scrutinized the servant. "Is there something amiss?" His tone demanded a reply. What else didn't he know? He waited on tenterhooks for what would come next.

The woman's eyes widened in surprise, her speech

stumbled when she tried to speak. "Begging your pardon, sir. You look like the man in the picture hanging in the library. For a moment, with your clothes and all, I thought you were the great lord himself returned these many centuries." His picture? In the library? Where Rebeka spent most of her time. That was interesting. The servant left the room shaking her head, carrying out the broken pottery and spilled food.

Rebeka scrutinized his face as if she were investigating one of her documents. "Come to think of it, Helen's right. That must be why I had the idea that we'd met. He does look like the picture." Something in her eyes told him she was holding back information. What that was, he didn't know, but he'd find out. Finding out things was one of his best skills.

She tossed her head, sending her hair flying around her. "Well, I'm glad that's settled. For a minute, I believed I was going crazy. And, Arik," she said, righting the chair and taking her seat, "you're a good performer. You acted as if you really believed I was about to eat poison. Next time, please don't carry this seventeenth-century idea so far." George gave her a fresh plate filled with eggs. She waved him off when he started to serve her tomatoes.

"Well, I don't know about you but I'm starved." George rubbed his hands together as he took his seat, his own plate brimming with breakfast. "What do you say we finish eating?"

The servant came back with a carafe of fresh hot coffee.

"Helen, a mug of watered ale for Lord Arik. He likes it at room temperature," Rebeka said.

He was startled by her suggestion. The surprise on George's face mirrored his own. Did she remember how he liked his ale? George bent over to Rebeka. "How do you know how he likes his ale?" he whispered.

Her eyes shone with delight. She bent to George's ear. "It's the seventeenth-century beverage of choice." Her playfulness made Arik smile. He recognized her spirit. If she would simply recognize him. He took a deep breath. The besotted Grand Master was in for a challenge. One he was determined not to lose. She faced Arik. "A peace offering, m'lord." She gave him a brilliant smile.

Helen returned and stood next to him. He watched her pour ale. "I hope this is the way you like your ale, m'lord." There was no pretense or falseness in her tone or actions. In his world, his life depended on knowing who was friend or foe. Each new situation called for caution and careful judgment. Here was no different. If anything, not knowing the rules here put him at a definite disadvantage. Where to begin? The way he did when he met new circumstances at home, with caution and staying alert.

She set a plate of scones with clotted cream before George. "Thank you, Helen." George slathered the clotted cream on his scone, a wide smile on the man's face.

"For my champion." Rebeka toasted Arik with her drink.

"M'lady." He raised his ale. "You honor me." He drank in the sight of her along with his ale. The months of not knowing if she was well, not knowing where she was, faded. It wasn't how he expected it would be but at last he was sitting at his table, with his Rebeka.

"Did Trudy have any new information about the Trust?" Rebeka filled her cup.

"At last, she got the court papers and is faxing them here for my review." George popped the last bit of scone into his mouth and licked the clotted cream from his lips. "I'll see to them when I'm done." He turned to Arik. "You don't mind if Rebeka takes you for a tour?" George shot a look to Rebeka. "You have time, don't you?"

"I have some time before my first class." She drained her drink, washing down the last of her toast and raspberry jam.

His eyes were drawn to the single drop of jam that stained her lip. His body thrummed with an overwhelming urge to lick it off but she beat him to it. *Faith*, he needed a distraction. "Class?" He coughed, trying to regain some sense of composure.

"Yes, I'm a professor at Kensington University in the United States. I've established a study center here at Fayne Manor for graduate students in conjunction with Oxford University's Centre for Medieval and Renaissance Studies."

"She won't tell you, but the program is doing quite well," George said. Her humility and success didn't surprise him. It was a deep part of her character.

"And your specialty?" he asked, finishing his ale. He knew all about her teaching. A woman in academia had been new to him and that had been the start. The things she'd told him about the past four centuries were more fantastic than any magick he could show her.

"I prefer the outdoors and flora of the era. My thesis was *Public, Private and Pastoral Practices Employing Herbs in Medieval England*. We found an herb garden behind the old cottage and will be restoring it as part of our plan for the manor."

Starved for the sound of her voice all these months, he made small talk to keep her chatting. Perhaps, by some miracle, she would remember. He observed her objectively, if that was possible. He had never known a woman who was so outspoken, fearless and determined to be self-sufficient.

How she had tested his patience when she first came to his Fayne Manor. They'd seemed to always be on opposing sides of an issue. But there had been a difference after she planted the herb garden and created the herbarium. It must have been her teaching ways. She had shared her knowledge with everyone and endeared herself to his people and family. She had become part of the manor fabric. And before long she had woven herself into the weft and warp of his life.

"I think reviving the herb garden would be a good project for the students. They could stock and manage the herbarium. Besides, it would add to the authenticity of the manor." She was at the table, her fingers around her mug.

"Good, that's settled," George said, reaching for his cup.

"Mr. George." Charles approached the table. "A fax has arrived for you. I've put it in the estate office."

"Thank you, Charles." George ate the last of the scone and stood. "I leave you in good hands," he said to Arik. "If you'll excuse me, I'll meet you as soon as I'm finished." He left the room.

Arik stood and tossed his napkin on the table. "Excuse me," he mumbled as he followed George out of the room.

"George," Arik commanded.

"Lower your voice," George whispered, raising his finger to his lips.

Arik was caught short by George's demand. "I want to know what happened to her memory." Arik followed George toward the estate office.

George stopped in front of the door. "Bran. No memories. I have to go. I'll speak to you when I'm done here." He started to open the door and turned to Arik. "Spend some time with her. Let her show you around. Let her get to know you, again." He entered the estate office and closed the door.

George left him with his mouth gaping open, staring at the closed door. Dismissal was not something he was used to. Perhaps she came out of the portal without her memories. No, he believed it was more serious than that. He returned to the Great Hall. Rebeka was finishing her breakfast.

"If you're ready?" Arik said. It was more a command than a question but she didn't appear to mind.

She was at the door a pace behind him and took her walking stick.

"The etchings appear intricate and well done. Do you take it with you everywhere?" he asked, motioning to her staff.

She studied her staff and turned toward him. "Yes, I do."

"Do you know what it says?" He touched an ornate group of runes. He winced at the icy sensation that stung his hand.

"It is an old prophecy. It's difficult to read. It has something to do with knowledge and strength." He had hoped she'd remember how to unlock the meaning of the runes. Another lesson she would need to relearn.

"The staff fits you."

She lowered it to the ground. "It was my father's. It took a long time to make it my own."

That wasn't what he meant but he didn't comment. Her staff was much more than a walking stick given to her by her father, but she would relearn that, too.

They left the terrace and took the back stairs to the second floor. There they climbed the winding steps to the tower room. Arik stole a quick glance at the mirror that stood across from the cold hearth. He stepped over to the looking glass and put his hand on the smooth silver surface. It was cracked and faded with time but now it was solid.

There was no sign the portal was open or would open. When he was ready to return, Logan would know what to do.

"Well, this is the tower." She flung her arms out and swept them around the room. "From the information George provided it's had many uses, from being a storage room to the favorite room of past residents. Today, it's a storage room." Rebeka wrinkled her nose. "It smells like…sulfur."

"Strange," he said over his shoulder. "I hadn't noticed." He turned toward her.

She stood in the center of the chamber. He watched as her body turned while she scanned the runes on the walls. "They're everywhere. What do you think they mean?"

He stood next to her and followed her gaze. Months of hard work had been dimmed by the passing centuries but he made out every rune. He stood quietly looking at the work he and Logan had done.

"It's a love song."

She whirled around at him. "How can it be a love song? These are runes. There's no documentation runes were used for literary purposes."

He didn't take his eyes off the markings. Each one had been added as his knowledge grew. Each stroke was planned before it became part of the pattern. Each entry brought him closer to her, his love, his wife. It couldn't be anything other than a love song. Logan had added the final touch when he set the words to music. He watched her from the corner of his eye.

"I must be missing something. This is all gibberish," she said.

The exasperation in her tone didn't surprise him. "Gibberish?" These runes were locked just as the runes on her staff. Would his magick open the runes here? He hoped so.

"Yes, nonsense. There aren't any words here. And you think it's a love song. Why?" How did he tell her that he worked every day to find her? How did he tell her that life had been miserable without her? That he woke thinking about her and went to sleep wanting her with him.

"It tells of a lord's quest." He pointed to a portion of the wall and hummed the secret cadence that would unlock the mystery. Her head turned to follow.

"Yes." Her voice was hushed. "I see it now."

"His wife was taken from him and he's determined to find her." He pointed to another section of runes. Even he caught the haunted tone in his voice. He glanced at the scrying mirror. He struggled with himself to not take her in his arms and force the portal to open. All he wanted was to carry her back to his time.

"Did he find her?" Her voice was fragile, as if she was afraid of the answer.

He turned back to the runes. "Eventually." He couldn't take her back, not yet. Not until he knew the extent of the damage Bran had done.

"And did they have their happily-ever-after?" Something in the sound of her voice made his spirits soar. He stood behind her, eager to rest his hands on her shoulders, but instead put them behind his back.

"I haven't gotten to that part of the song yet." His voice was deep and rugged with emotion. "This man is very determined and loves her deeply."

"I hope they did." She turned and faced him. He reveled in the dreamy look in her eyes that matched the soft swell of passion in her voice. Dare he kiss her?

She moved away from him and gave her shoulders a minute shake. "This must be written in an obscure dialect." Sounding stronger and more matter-of-fact, she returned her attention to the runes. "I'll have one of my students do some research." She glanced at him over her shoulder, a satisfied expression on her face. She stole one more look at the walls and they left the tower.

When they got to the bottom, she closed the tower door and followed him down the hall. "We try to keep as much of the original pieces on exhibit." She passed the various rooms with twisted golden ropes hanging across the doorways. "But to keep them safe we've roped off the rooms so guests don't wander in and our priceless pieces don't wander out." He stretched his neck to see into the rooms. He expected to see Jeannie rushing around taking care of the chambers, his nieces in their rooms, Logan in the solar with his flute. He stood between two worlds and his head swam. She continued along the corridor.

"Here we are at the central staircase. The area we've been through is the original section of the house. In 1846 the manor was enlarged. This is the family gallery. It is one of the original rooms." They stood at the doorway peeking into the large room. "It, too, has also had many uses over time, from a convalescent area for soldiers during World War Two, to a ballroom. We've restored it to its original use, the family portrait gallery."

They finished their tour of the upper floor and headed downstairs. How had she coped when she fell through time? She was stronger than he imagined. The travel itself was strenuous but the mental changes, the disorientation, not knowing anyone. She was so much more than she appeared. As they moved along on the older side of the building on the first floor Rebeka hesitated. She stood immobile by the door that led to the old cellar. Her face was ashen.

"Rebeka? Is something amiss?" He had an idea what stopped her but hoped he was wrong.

He placed his hand on her shoulder and she flinched. "This is the door to the cellar. I…I…I can't go down there." She gave him a helpless look. Her voice was a whisper. "I don't know why."

He took her arm and threaded it through his. He felt her thundering pulse when his fingers brushed her wrist. He covered her hand. "That's all right. I've no need to go to the cellar." He churned with guilt. He knew why she couldn't face the cellar.

It led to the dungeon.

He closed his eyes, not wanting to remember that he had left her there for two days thinking she had been in league with Bran. Visions of finding her curled on the cot in the rain-drenched cell tore at him.

Unconscious and near death, he'd fought to bring her back to life. That's when he'd found the mark on the nape of her neck.

His mark.

The one he had put there at their betrothal— before Maximillian took her away and dulled his memory of her. Seeing his mark cleared his mind.

He had almost lost her then. He wouldn't lose her now.

He led her into the safety and comfort of the library—her domain. Searching for a distraction, he let go of her arm and stood by the hearth, under his painting. With his arm on the mantel he mimicked the portrait's pose.

"Do you think the picture looks like me?" He begged an innocent expression. Her eyes slowly, very slowly, swept up his body. He watched her and ached for her touch. When her gaze met his he could almost feel her heart beat faster. She licked her lower lip as if nibbling a tasty confection.

He would bargain with the devil for a taste of that lip.

He stepped away from the hearth and moved toward her. "I feel a draft." He softened his voice, commanding her attention. At her side he leaned close, his mouth by her ear. "Perhaps you should return my clothes, or would you…" he whispered in a teasing voice. He enjoyed her fluster as she stammered and at last let loose a small sigh. He flirted with her shamelessly to recapture some semblance of their closeness. He was satisfied for the small success.

He wasn't a wooer by nature. He left that to the courtiers in James's court. He was a warrior but right now his challenge was fitting in to this new century. That was a new idea. He'd never worried about fitting in before.

"I'm sorry. I was intent on measuring you against our Lord Arik." She gestured to the painting. "I got carried away." She worried her bottom lip again.

He knew she wouldn't deny her actions. She was honest, direct and outspoken. "Did I fare?"

She tore her eyes away from the picture and focused on him. "Yes," she whispered. He held her gaze, unwilling to move.

Remember me, he silently begged her but he knew she didn't hear him. He would have to be content, for now.

The clock on the mantel struck the hour and shattered the spell.

"I didn't realize it was so late." She blinked a few times before she stepped away. "I'm afraid that's all I have time for today." She checked her watch with the mantel clock then reached for a stack of papers. "I have to get over to the gatehouse for my class."

"Gatehouse for classes?" he asked.

"The gatehouse is part of the wall surrounding the manor and along with the gate to the village, houses a military garrison with several large rooms." Yes, yes, he knew what the gatehouse was. "Some rooms function as classrooms and others as a dormitory for students and staff. We use one room as a garrison for our soldiers."

One room for soldiers—how could that be enough to guard the manor and protect the estate? He'd have to review the men and make certain the manor had adequate protection. "Their schedule is much different than anyone else's. We created a program for veterans. When many of them returned to civilian life they couldn't find work. We hire them as soldiers for our reenactment and they take classes toward a college degree."

Rebeka squinted at his portrait then at him.

He followed her eyes to the portrait. "Why is this painting in the library and not in the family gallery?" The corners of his mouth tugged into a smile.

She'd already refocused on the papers and kept her attention there. "The space over the hearth was empty and needed to be filled. This was the only picture that fit." Standing the papers on edge, she tapped them into a pile then she slipped them into her pack. She put on the tattered old backpack, threaded her staff through the convenient leather straps then headed for the terrace doors.

He stood in the middle of the library, his smile sliding off his face. He watched the sway of her hips as she crossed the terrace and knew there was more to her answer.

When she got to the terrace steps she glanced over her shoulder at him. "You care to join me?" She pulled her eyes away from him.

He covered the distance with his long strides and was already ahead of her, leading the way to the garden gate.

"You know where it is? Of course," she muttered loud enough for him to hear. "You've been here before." She hurried to catch up.

They continued on in silence. He was intent on noting the things around him as they traveled along the drive and was relieved that it appeared much the same as when he'd left it this morning.

He opened the gatehouse latch and with a practiced eye took quick stock of the people. It was obvious to him who were students, staff and, if he wasn't mistaken, soldiers. The central room was lived in and in disarray—not to his standards. His garrison appeared to be in good order. The large double doors to the soldier's area—the garrison, she called it—stood ajar. There was one bright spot at the far end of the room, an area that was well organized.

"That's the major. Our most seasoned employee. He's responsible for mustering in the new staff—recruits, as he calls them—getting them settled and oriented. He also hires the soldiers and handles the small military enactments that we put on for the guests. He's retired from Her Majesty's Armed Forces."

Arik approached the man. "Major."

"Sir." The man stood at attention and snapped a salute.

"Don't let me get in your way." He returned the soldier's salute. From the man's manner he knew he was a warrior. From the expression in his eyes Arik suspected he'd seen his share of war.

"Thank you, sir, Dr. Tyler," he acknowledged and continued what he had been doing.

Rebeka bent close to Arik. "Why did he salute you?"

"Old military men know each other even when they've never met." He glanced past the last cot. The druid sanctuary was beyond. The walls appeared to be sound. He could feel the energy of the manor wards and was relieved they were intact. His magick was strongest in the sanctuary. Perhaps he could use it to help Rebeka. She would find it a great historical site. The idea made his heart thump. She'd make it into a museum. He had no intention of corrupting the sanctuary. No, he couldn't allow that. But he had to see its condition.

"I see you're admiring the old stone work. Fayne Manor was very lucky. During World War Two, when the Germans bombed the countryside, Fayne Manor wasn't touched. As a matter of fact, during the war the manor served as a place for convalescing soldiers and a refuge for the surrounding area."

In their quiet time, after lovemaking, she told him things about the previous century. His chest swelled with pride when she spoke of the part Fayne Manor played in the war. He considered the soldiers that she had here now and was pleased she had given them a home.

"Okay, men. We're confirmed for Avebury tomorrow night," the major said.

"Avebury has a facility for blind veterans. Our men go there once a month. They have dinner with the soldiers and they talk 'soldier talk,'" she said.

"Our guests will be arriving soon. Let's suit up," the major said. Arik watched the handful of men halfheartedly make ready. Most didn't change their breeches, only their shirts. Some strapped on swords, others put dirks in their belts. Altogether the result was a mismatched group of disinterested men.

How could these men defend the manor?

"This building hasn't changed much," Rebeka offered. "Like other buildings at the manor, it has been unused for a quite a while. George says it's been used for storage for centuries. The recent renovations to the garden house have been completed. We made it our museum. Some of the exhibits in the new museum were found here."

"What did you include in the museum?" His eyes took in everything around him as they followed the men out into the bailey.

"Almost all of them are farm tools and household items. We found so many original items we had the idea we would put them on display. I have a group of students researching the different pieces so we can note them properly." She checked her watch then glanced toward the manor. "I have to get to my class. I'm certain George will be here soon. Is there any place you'd like to go? I can see if one of the staff—"

"No, that won't be necessary. You go on." The last thing he wanted was to let her out of his sight but he had no choice. Reluctantly, he watched her go off.

A rumbling in the distance grabbed his attention. He spun on his heels to locate the major. The man had to be deaf not to hear the uproar but he and his men took no notice. He peeked through the open gate to investigate the disturbance. A cloud of swirling dust moved up the road. Every so often, when the dust settled, he got a clear view.

A coach without horses. Amazing.

He headed out the gate to get a better look. He turned his head sideways and stared at the machine from a different perspective. From here the long square box gave the appearance of a fallen siege tower.

Rebeka's drawings had been quite accurate. The machine stopped at the far side of the village. George came up behind him. "I can take you for a ride in something smaller a bit later but unless you want to be overrun by an unruly crowd of people we'd best start back."

He nodded and followed George back to the house. "Are there enough men guarding the manor?"

"We don't have the same need for guards as you do. There is a centralized force that we call if needed."

"There is an overlord? Other than the king? My manor was self-sufficient from farming to security."

"No, there isn't an overlord. The Wiltshire magistrate has jurisdiction over Fayne Manor. Our soldiers are here for the reenactment." Arik was relieved. For a moment he believed someone had taken Fayne Manor from the family.

"You didn't appear to be surprised when you saw the coach."

"Rebeka told me about them. She even drew pictures. They're as large as a siege tower. How does it move?"

George smiled. "I'm glad you asked."

An hour later he and George stood in the estate office staring out the terrace windows. His eyes searched the distance for anything that was familiar.

"It's beautiful." George stood next to him, holding a glass of ale.

"Yes, it is." He paused, still looking out at the grounds. "You were right. Many things have changed. The village appears to be shuttered. The crops and the farm houses are gone. It was last week I helped Leo repair his roof." He stared off at the rise where the rutted road wove into the tree-lined drive. He'd learned so much in the short time he'd been here. It was more fascinating than Rebeka had described. But he was ready to bring her back.

"I'm certain this is hard. But we'll get you through it."

He didn't move. "I've found her. Now I have to bring her back."

"It's not that simple. She needs her memories. And to be free of the Dark Magick." He didn't like the delay. "Come. You'll stay with me and Cora at Autumn Chase while we figure this out."

He stiffened but didn't turn. "How do you come to Autumn Chase? It was Stuart's estate."

"Through your niece Skylar. She married Robert."

"Yes." He relaxed. The notion made him smile. "She has a tender heart for Robert, and he for her."

"And one of my ancestors married one of their descendants. I'd like to show you some things. They may seem as wonders to you but I think it will help you fit in. Come with me."

"I'll remain here." It wasn't a challenge. It was a

fact. He glanced across the terrace to the library's glass doors; Rebeka and several students worked at the large table.

George followed his gaze. "She'll be safe. You needn't worry."

"The last time I left her," he turned to George, "she was gone for six months and traveled four hundred years into the future. No, I won't leave her now."

George rubbed the back of his neck and paced in front of him. "Our plan is for you and Rebeka to return as soon as possible but to do that you'll need her strength as a sorceress. We must clear her mind. Do you agree?"

Arik nodded.

"Together," George said, "we can work to find the solution but to do that you need a battle plan." Arik started to respond. George raised his hand. "Hear me out. It may appear calm and peaceful on the outside but don't be misled. You're at war, with Bran. Rebeka is safe here. Other than on the manor property, she's never alone. I've made certain of that. Besides, the wards you set are still active and protect the manor against Bran."

He listened to what George had to say but it was his responsibility to see to Rebeka's safety.

"You need to learn about the past six months as well as the last four hundred years. Then we can plan your strategy to get her memory back and for you both to return home." Arik glanced at the library then the tower. George was right. He did need her strength to return. But leaving Rebeka now wasn't an option.

"Bring whatever I must see here. I'll not leave her."

"You can't be with her every minute." George leaned against the edge of the desk, his arms folded. "She has classes the rest of the day. Besides, the major is in her afternoon classes."

Arik peered into the library and saw the major sitting at the end of the table. The major may be a military man but he and his men had no purpose other than playing a part. He still doubted they could protect the manor and he was sure they weren't prepared to deal with Bran. No one here was.

"We can't tell people you're from the seventeenth century. They'll think you're insane. People don't travel through time. While Cora and I were trying to reach you we've given this a lot of thought. There are too many people here and if they ask you questions you…well, it will be easier if you had the answers. We need a few hours. We'll be back by nightfall. Arik, I've kept her safe for six months." The man sounded like his solicitor pleading his case.

"By nightfall. In one of your coaches without horses?"

George pushed away from the desk. "You won't regret this."

Arik returned his focus to the library. Rebeka waved to them. George held his fist to his ear. She nodded and returned her attention to her students.

"Does the gesture have some secret meaning?" he asked in an uncertain tone.

"What? Oh, this?" George mimicked the gesture. "It means I'll call her later. We have a lot of work to do. Come, Charles should have the car waiting."

He glanced at Rebeka. She was deep in conversation. He reluctantly followed George out of the room.

Charles stood in the drive next to an open black coach. He peeked inside. It didn't appear to be big enough for him, let alone him and George.

The touch of a familiar presence danced across his back and made him glance over his shoulder but all he saw was the light in the library window. He turned to the car. With more confidence than he felt, he slipped into the leather seats. Charles pulled on a long strap, gave it to him and closed the door.

George took the strap out of his hand and snapped it into place.

"Harnesses are for horses, Hughes." A wary tone crept into his voice.

George laughed. "This coach is driven by 350 horses."

"They must be very small indeed." His eyebrows arched at the notion. The idea of the machine had intrigued him when Rebeka told him about it. He couldn't comprehend how fast the machine traveled yet from what Rebeka said, people traveled this way all the time. Even she knew how to control it.

George burst out laughing. "This is only the beginning. There is so much more to show you."

He forced himself into a prebattle calm. Every druid bone in his body screamed George could be trusted. But some of the things he said made him wonder.

The coach began to roll forward, carrying them toward the gate. The ride was smoother than his best carriage. He had imagined the machine more a moving chair from Rebeka's description and was surprised to find it quite comfortable. He found himself relaxing.

George continued on and took his time driving through the abandoned village maneuvering around deep holes on the grassy roadway.

The village, even in difficult times, had been a lively, thriving place. It was difficult to see that only the stones survived.

Gathering speed, they climbed the road that led to the tree-lined drive. With the wind in his hair and the dappled sunlight in his face, he could easily be back in the seventeenth century. George stopped when they cleared the top of the rise. Arik peered over his shoulder at the valley and manor below. He scanned his domain and knew he would protect Fayne Manor and Rebeka with his last breath.

George turned to him. "Lord Arik. Your family welcomes you home."

"Ninoor nin ah ray. To hearth and home," he replied.

George pulled a lever and the coach sprang forward. They wound their way through the drive lined with ancient oak trees. Their branches swayed as if they danced and bowed for the Grand Master.

He kept his eyes straight ahead. "You've taken good care of them—both of them."

CHAPTER NINE

Rebeka stood in the shadows of the library window and watched Arik and George get ready to leave. Her heart pounded when she looked at Arik. She agreed with Helen. He did look like the man in the painting. But there was something else about him.

She hooked her hair behind her ear. How could she explain it? She hadn't been able to get him out of her mind all day. She saw him in the estate office behind the desk and she imagined he belonged there. That made no sense. And when the major saluted him, she knew it was right. Was it the aura of command and control that seemed to hug him like a second skin? She could predict the way he moved, the set of his shoulders, the tilt of his head.

And his smile. It was familiar.

She pressed herself against the wall to avoid Arik seeing her when he turned toward the window. At the sound of the car door shutting she stretched her neck and watched them drive off. The wake of dust was easy to follow through the village gate. Lost behind the trees, she caught sight of the small sports car again when it climbed the rise and entered the drive. She stayed rooted to the spot until the two red taillights faded out of sight but she still couldn't get the mysterious stranger out of her mind.

"What do you think, Dr. Tyler?"

Startled from her musings, she moved back from the window.

"Here's the last of them." Joan set a stack of black-and-white pictures on the table. "You were right. I needed to change the setting on the camera to get a clearer picture." Rebeka pulled herself away from the window and scanned the pictures, searching for pieces of the love song. She got to the last picture and was confused. Nothing was familiar.

"Were you able to photograph all the runes on the walls?" Rebeka asked. There must be more or some that Joan overlooked.

"No, that is everything. The major and I made sure we cataloged every glyph. I was amazed they went all the way to the ceiling. We had to get a ladder to get a good picture. Dr. Tyler, how old is this writing?"

"I'm not certain. Mr. Hughes seems to think about four hundred years." The others peered over Joan's shoulder to see the panoramic display. Rebeka started to go through the photos again. This was annoying. She was able to read them with Arik but now nothing made any sense. It must be the stress of the reopening. Yes, that's what it was.

But she worried. For the past six months pieces of her mind were vanishing—words, memories, things that had been important to her. One minute she knew them like the back of her hand, then they were fuzzy and then they were gone. Was this another "incident"? She put the pictures on the table, afraid of the answer. She'd look at them later.

"If you'll excuse me, Dr. Tyler, I wanted to work on my concept paper. It's due to the master's committee in a week and I need to get to bed at a decent time. I have an early start tomorrow. The Celtic

Stone Inscriptions class at Oxford is tomorrow morning. Thank you for making arrangements for me at the last minute. I would've hated to miss it. It may help us translate this," Joan said, pointing to the pictures.

"You'll enjoy Dr. Hamilton's lecture. He's an authority on Celtic history." She gathered her books and papers. "Everyone, that's all for today. Let's keep these runes between us until we have a better idea of what they are and can authenticate them. For all we know they say 'Kilroy was here.'" The students laughed, gathered their things and filed out of the room.

Cora had called and suggested a girls' night out but she had begged off. The scripts for the reenactment needed their finishing touches. The final rehearsal was tomorrow. A quick glance out the window confirmed that there was still enough daylight to meditate by the old house near the lake.

She stacked the books, a bit precariously, on the table to gather all the papers and folders. She wanted to neaten things for Helen. The woman liked to dust and clean early in the morning. A tug on a folder wobbled the stack. She saved them but lost the battle with the photos. They cascaded onto the floor.

Without looking at them she gathered the pictures into a pile but one group of symbols caught her eye. She pulled the picture off the floor. She was certain she knew this grouping. It was a small victory, but she'd take it.

Putting them all together, she bound them with a rubber band and set them in her backpack.

She glanced over her shoulder at the painting above the hearth. The expression on Arik's face when she told him the picture was hung for convenience made her smile. But that wasn't the truth—well, not the whole truth. Yes, it fit the space but it was more than that. How could she tell him she talked to the picture? Would he think she was crazy? At those times when she was lost, when she was alone, this picture soothed her. She had the same feeling about him, perhaps because there was a close resemblance. A soft chuckle escaped her lips. Her blatant ogling, that was an embarrassment, but he fit the picture so well. She shook her head. How strange the mind. Perhaps she was going mad.

With her backpack over her shoulder, her staff stowed in the leather strapping, she shut the light. "Good night, m'lord," she called over her shoulder as she did every night before she closed the door.

It was a quick walk to the old house. According to the grounds plan she read, this was Elfrida's cottage. Off-limits to the staff, between the manor house and the nearby lake, she tried to come here every evening to meditate. Today she was under the oak in the front yard. Once she was centered she began her exercises.

The drills were a part of her daily routine ever since she took a mandatory gym class in high school. Rebeka chose karate. She thrived on the mind-body connection and excelled in kata. An ancient discipline, the strict choreographed routines were made of prescribed movements. The goal was to perfect each technique, focusing on the central principles of maximum efficiency and minimum effort. While the training was directed at overcoming brute force by applying technique, balance, speed and timing, Rebeka found comfort in the strict discipline and repetitive movements. It trained her mind as well as her body and like everything else she tackled, she excelled at the sport.

She put on the headset to her MP3 player and selected strong, fast rock music that unlocked that place inside her where movement and sound fused. She took her staff and began. Her movements were fast and crisp. When the music played out and her routine was over, she left Elfrida's and took her time walking to her cottage in order to enjoy the sunset.

Ahead, she saw that lights were already on in her cottage and smoke spiraled from the chimney. Helen must have set a fire in the grate. The scene made an inviting picture.

Inside, all cozy and warm, she was more content than she'd been in months. Even the burden of the manor reopening seemed manageable. The aroma of baked chicken and grilled vegetables made her mouth water. She put her things down and washed for dinner.

Holding the towel, she came into the main room headed for the small kitchenette but her eyes were drawn to her staff. The group of symbols in Joan's photo nagged at her. She put the towel on the sink and pulled out the photos. She laid the photo on the table then put her staff next to it. Slowly she rotated the staff and searched for the matching set of runes. As the symbol rolled into view she pulled her hand away.

Okay, slow down. Her dad had carved each rune on the staff. She was certain this was a coincidence. The grouping must be significant but she couldn't translate it. She scanned more of Joan's pictures and tried to match them to her staff but she was overwhelmed.

These must be the runes that George matched to the tower wall earlier today. Her curiosity was piqued. There was one place she could look. The one place she had avoided for fifteen years—her father's journals and books.

She glanced at the old chest with the picture of her and her dad sitting on top. They had taken the picture the day she moved into the freshman dorm. Her chest tightened. It had been the two of them. They hiked, camped, did everything together. She held the picture, the last picture of them together. He died soon after in a car accident here in England. That year she spent her spring vacation emptying the house and packing away his books, papers and some small trinkets. She didn't look at anything. That would have been too painful. There were times when she had the notion to go through the chest but she just couldn't face it.

She set the photo aside, sprang the hasp on the chest's latch then pulled back the lid. The aroma of sage and mint, the scent she associated with her father, wafted up at her. She waited for the fragrance to fade before she peeked inside. Old parchments were the first layer.

This is where the old herbal had gone. A small snicker escaped as she remembered how frantic she had searched for it when she was working on her thesis. Well, found at last. She pulled out the bundled document and put it on the table. She'd take it to the library in the morning. Beneath the document was a cache of her dad's personal things. She took out his scarf, the one he liked to wear in the winter with his sports jacket. Her chest squeezed so tight that all she could take were small breaths. No, perhaps this was not the right time. She put the scarf back into the chest and closed the lid, the finality of the hasps closing locking away her grief. Not tonight. Tonight she didn't want to stir old pains. Tonight she wanted to enjoy her newfound peace.

Arik noted the familiar landmarks as they drove on. Other than their conveyance, he could imagine being with Logan and the others. "I know how Rebeka came to me, but how did she return?"

"We knew she disappeared at Avebury," George said as he maneuvered their way onto the road.

"Yes, she told me she had been standing by the

stones when the portal opened," he confirmed, "visiting the stones with a group of travelers. Doward found her by the trail on the other side of Oak Meadow." Arik let out a snort. He had closed that portal, too. No, the best way back was the way he came, through the scrying mirror.

"When the coach returned here, the guide, Agnes, told us Rebeka was missing. I headed to Avebury at once. There were enough remnants of the portal to piece together what had happened. Four months later, Agnes called again. This time she said she found a disoriented Rebeka by the stones. When I brought her back to Fayne Manor she was distraught. You do know that she thinks she saved you."

"Saved me." He grumbled. He suspected as much. If she had been patient, let him finish, he was certain she would have seen what he was doing.

"She said she heard your heartbeat. It was so fast she was afraid your heart would burst."

"She couldn't hear my heartbeat." He waved his hand, pushing the idea away. "Bran. He put that idea in her head. The enchantment was weakening and ready to fall. I was at the end of the chant but she…screamed." He wanted this nightmare over and his wife home. Instead he had delays and a woman who didn't even know his face. "There's no sense dwelling on that now. I've been doing that for six months. I'm here. We need to build a plan but not before we know what other traps Bran has set for us." George nodded his agreement.

They drove up Autumn Chase's drive. Arik got a good view of the estate. A new building stood where the large carriage house had been.

"That's our Autumn Retreat. It's a restaurant with a cellar that has an exclusive tavern. Cora manages it and does well." George stopped the motorcar by the front entrance and they got out.

"You haven't told me why she doesn't remember me. She seems to remember everything else," he said and glanced around as George brought him into the front foyer.

He searched the entrance hall for something familiar but found nothing he recognized. He might as well have been in a stranger's house. The idea caught him short. It was a stranger's house.

"George, when did you get home?" Arik turned at the sound of a woman's voice.

"Cora, come meet our guest." A pleasant-looking woman welcomed George with a kiss on the cheek. The two had a similar look in the shape of their faces, the set of their eyes and even the shape of their mouths. They were twins. Yes, now that he looked closely he was certain.

"Arik, this is my sister, Cora." George snaked his arm around her in a brotherly squeeze.

"An honor, m'lady." He gave her a formal bow.

She stared at him. Her mouth, without a sound coming out, flapped like a beached fish. "George," she looked at her brother and back to Arik, "you've done it. You've really done it."

"Yes, we have." The smile of accomplishment on George's face was catching. Arik smiled, too. "Cora and I have worked together. Locating and bringing you here was a family effort." George led them into a comfortable salon. To Arik the room appeared to be more a salon in the king's palace than Stuart's informal hall.

"Logan and I worked without rest, as well. I know the effort you put in on our behalf. I'm grateful." Grateful. That didn't say enough. They, too, took chances. He owed them a great deal.

"George was in the tower room after Lady Emily passed on. The walls were bare." Cora fidgeted with her skirt and took a seat near the fireplace. Arik lowered himself into the large master's seat—George's chair, he assumed. George hesitated and took the smaller one to the side.

"When Rebeka returned to us I remembered the scrying mirror and went to the tower room. I saw the writing. I was in the tower room the following week and there were more runes. That's when I knew you were trying to find her. When I saw the error—"

"We kept trying different formulas and chants. Nothing worked. We didn't know what to do until George considered using Rebeka's staff." Cora was all nerves. Her hands rubbed the arms of the chair. That was very telling. He kept watch.

"Yes, that's when I heard you and knew we would be successful," George said.

"Aye, and I'm glad you did. I don't think we could have done it without you both." He could feel the tension in the room dissipate. He had no idea anyone had been trying to help him all these months. He stopped himself from running his hand through his hair but, faith, he would never have found her if it wasn't for them. "But I never considered Rebeka wouldn't remember me."

"She did at first." He watched a silent message pass between George and Cora. George wasn't pleased. Arik kept his body relaxed and cloaked the wariness that was building.

"Rebeka was working hard to find you. No one knew where to start." Cora moved to the edge of her chair. "We knew Bran was involved. He tricked her into thinking you were at the meadow."

"Yes, George told me." He was cautious but waited for George's next move. It was obvious to him that Cora shouldered some responsibility. What had they done?

"Let me start at the beginning. You see, the sole information we had about you was from Doward's journal and your portrait. We found no mention or record of Bran in any of the manor papers or any other place." George covered Cora's shaking hands with his. The siblings obviously had a close relationship. George stood up and pushed his hands deep into his pockets.

"Whoever took the documents missed one in the library, the king's invitation to Bran and Caylyn's wedding." Cora's troubled expression didn't make him feel comfortable. "That led us to Orkney."

"She went to Orkney." Arik froze. Bran had gotten her to his seat of power. He closed his eyes. "Why did she go there?" He struggled to keep his temper under control.

"Her staff glowed when it was near the Orkney stone that was in your library. She said her staff only glowed when both of you touched it. That's why she was positive it was a message from you and just as positive there was a portal at Skara Brae." When Cora was finished she was almost in tears.

"We were in Orkney together." Arik turned to George, who was pacing in front of him as he spoke. He sounded detached and factual. He, too, believed he was responsible. "But she entered the estate house alone, drawn into an enchantment." He spoke with a quiet firmness. "While I tried to get through the enchantment, Bran ordered her to revive Caylyn. When she couldn't he…" George stopped in front of him and hesitated. "He touched her mind and took her memories of you." George's voice was a whisper when he finished. A tense silence filled the room. "I couldn't stop her." The man turned away from Arik, unable to face him.

Arik let out a long breath. An enchantment. At last some good news. There was a chance her memory loss was temporary. George and Cora waited in front of him like criminals expecting to hear a verdict. At the moment he had no compassion for the grief he saw on their faces. He pushed his emotions aside. He needed to find a solution. He had sensed some connection with her today. "She has a tendency to not see things from all angles."

"She was so certain she was returning to you." He had a hard time hearing Cora, her voice was so soft.

He had to return with her. Now. Before Bran did anything else. "I need your help to open the scrying mirror."

The silence continued for several heartbeats. "Is that wise if Bran still influences her? Here our magick is not very strong but in your time it is. If you return without curing Rebeka of the Dark Magick there is no telling what would happen." He felt the blood drain from his face. "I know this is difficult but you need those answers before you bring her back."

He studied them. For a moment George reminded him of Logan the way he laid things out. *Faith.* George and Cora were right. They couldn't return until she was cured. "I believed the hardest part of my quest would be finding her." He laughed at the irony. No, the hardest part would be getting her memories back, curing her of Dark Magick, maybe even finding their way home. But George was right, they'd have to stay.

"Helen believed you looked like Lord Arik in the picture in the library," George said.

"That's because I am." He spit out the words, exasperated.

"I've been giving that more consideration." George stepped in front of him. "We've been searching for someone to play Lord Arik for the reenactment. But what did she say when she saw you? Ah yes, the great lord himself returned all these centuries. That's when I had the idea of you playing yourself. It would keep you on the grounds and working near Rebeka."

He studied the brother and sister. The plan had merit. It would keep him close to her. Yes, this would serve his purpose. George had the same idea. He could feel the excitement rolling off him.

"The more I think about you playing the lord, the more the idea appeals to me. You'll give the reenactment the authenticity we need. Yes, this is perfect." George made it sound as if there was no other response for him but, yes.

"I'm not an actor." His skeptical tone appeared to go unnoticed.

"That's just it. I don't want you to act. I want you to be yourself. Cora and I can help you. We'll teach you what you need to know to get by. Your druid mind will be quick to absorb things and help you piece together the rest. That's a great advantage."

He didn't need to be convinced he saw the benefits, the only ones that mattered to him. He would be close to Rebeka and able to be himself. Still? His fingers drummed on the arm of the chair while he considered other alternatives. He saw none. How difficult could it be? George and Cora were eager for him to accept.

"Very well, yes." Their faces lit up like candles. He hoped he knew what he was doing.

It was Cora's turn to pace. "While George and I have been trying to reach you we've been gathering the information you'll need about this century to conform—" she glanced at him, "—fit in. You'll need a way to contact us when you have questions." She headed toward the door. "George, you call Charles and let him know that Arik will be staying at the manor. And I'll gather the materials." She walked back to Arik. "I know this will be hard work and I want you to know I'll do the best I can to prepare you. George." She looked past Arik to her brother. "You should take Arik to the Stelton estate. They have the best reenactment in the area. She turned back to Arik. "You can see what Rebeka is trying to do." She gave him a spontaneous hug. "Bye, George." She kissed her brother on the cheek. "And George, get some clothes for our guest. He's absolutely scrumptious looking but he'll need to fit in." Cora rushed out the door.

"Does she always take control?" Arik asked as they left the salon.

"Yes. It's one of her better qualities. She's a planner and an organizer. She's right. You can't walk around like Lord Arik, at least not yet. I'm sure I have some clothes that will fit you."

They were crossing the hall to the grand staircase when George stopped, guilt written on his face. Arik waited. It was obvious to him that the man needed to get something off his chest.

"I tried to protect her." Arik knew that expression. How many times had he seen it when he looked in the mirror?

"I'm certain you did but she's stubborn and at times unyielding." He paused. "You did protect her." He started up the stairs. "You got her out before Bran did more damage. For that I'm in your debt." So that was the big secret. George thought he failed when he risked his life to save her. He earned more than his trust. He earned his gratitude. He continued up the stairs. "Autumn Chase doesn't look as I remember it." He watched the relief work its way through George's body.

"Autumn Chase has gone through more enhancements than Fayne Manor. In the early 1900s it was converted into a world-class hotel. We've reclaimed it as our country house although we still have the restaurant. Cora does quite well planning parties."

"If her party planning is anything like what I just witnessed, her business must be very successful." They reached the second floor. There was still no semblance of Stuart's home.

"Let me show you where you can clean up. While

you do, I'll gather the things we need." They continued toward one of the chambers.

Thirty minutes later, George was at the worktable, books and papers strewn all over. The glow of the open tablet screen reflected on his face. Arik came out of the garderobe, a towel around his waist and another in his hand drying his hair.

"Cora stopped by with some clothes for you." George pointed to a neat stack on the bed. "She reminded me that there were papers you need to fill out for the position at the manor. She'll have them for you tomorrow. What did you think of the motorcar ride?"

"I understand how the motorcar, works. But I still like the feel of power between my legs."

George looked at him over the tablet's screen. "I'll show you something later that may be more to your liking." His hair dry, he slipped into his new clothes and slid his small dirk into his waistband. "I like the shower."

"Yes, I could tell. You were singing."

"Was I now?" He laughed and took a seat next to George.

"Yes, "Row, Row, Row Your Boat.""

"I'll tell you about that sometime." He could feel the grin on his face.

Even with her memory loss, finding Rebeka lifted a weight from his shoulders. Now that he knew how she'd lost her memories he could work on finding a solution. Bran wouldn't stop him. He'd make certain she shared the memory of the first time they sang together with George and Cora.

"We'll start with the necessities." George put a small square on the desk. Arik recognized it right away.

"Yes, this is like the device Rebeka had. It's for

talking to people when they aren't near you. I was interested in how it worked but she said it was out of...power." He picked it up. The one Rebeka showed him had been a dead black square. This one glowed. "Is it alive?" He kept examining it, trying to see how it was made.

"No, although it does have power, electricity. How to explain electricity?" George worried the problem. "Ah, lightning is a type of electricity." Lightning? Arik dropped the square, his gaze jerked toward George. His eyes narrowed.

"Bran's power comes from lightning." Was this some Dark Magick? A trap? His hand hovered near the hilt of his dirk. George raised his hands in defense.

"Arik, this has nothing to do with Bran. Nothing. It's a fact. Electricity is similar to lightning."

"I'm familiar with lightning strikes. Bran rained them down on Fayne Manor for months."

"Scientists found a way to re-create lightning. There are several ways: passing magnets closely along a metal wire or using specific chemicals and metals in a solution. None are magical."

"Alchemy." That he understood. Some of his "magick" was more "science" than other people in his time understood. The energy he got from the elements and the way this electricity worked was something he comprehended. "Next you'll tell me you can turn straw into gold." He took his hand away from his waist.

George smiled at his jest. "The Philosopher's Stone. Not even in this lifetime. But let me show you how this works." George held the device to his lips. "Call Charles." Arik was startled by the series of tones the device made.

"That's how you know it's working. When the phone rings, plays a song, you know someone wants to speak to you," George said while he waited.

"Good afternoon, Fayne Manor. How may I help

you?" Arik stared at the device, amazed to hear the steward's voice.

"Charles, George Hughes here. My cousin will be staying on at the manor for a while. Please have the captain's room in the garrison ready for him."

"Very good, sir." If Rebeka hadn't told him about this device he would have believed it was magick. He'd believed she had exaggerated when she explained her century, but if anything, she had made light of it.

By horseback it took him three hours to go between Fayne Manor and Autumn Chase. By motorcar it took twenty minutes. Now this, speaking to someone as if they were standing next to you. The adventure of this new time thrilled him. What else was there to learn?

"Thank you, Charles." George ended the call then handed him the phone.

"Amazing," was all he said as he took the device from George and examined it.

"It's not quite like mind-touching. You can only share spoken words. This," George tapped his finger on the device, "can't think but it can remember. I've put in information so you can contact the manor, me, Cora and Rebeka. How can I explain the concept?" George puzzled the question.

"It's quite simple." Cora walked in. "Arik, in your century druids can communicate by mind-touching over long distances. It's a gift, a magick that was developed with constant use over a long time. Now, in this century, we communicate over long distance with the telephone. We have no reason to use mind-touching." That sounded logical to him.

"Some of us continued the old ways," George said. "Some say twins have their own language. We had mind-touching. We used it all the time and were able to maintain much of our skill. But as for the others, they've lost their ability. We were concerned that other magick may have been lost. We had no idea if there was any magick left in the runes you put on the tower wall. This last time, when we reached you, I used Rebeka's staff. I hoped the staff would make the magick stronger. Lucky for us it did.

"This century has its own magick. If you're ready I'd like to show you how to use the tablet."

"Rebeka told me about her tablet. She used it to do her research and to write her documents." In that quiet, comfortable time at night, she'd told him of great things. "She told me about her time here and spoke of England's future and world wars. I laughed when she said she could hold my library in her hand." He watched George working the device. "I found it humorous that she had a hard time accepting my magick but none at all accepting hers."

George studied Arik's face. "I hadn't considered it from that perspective. I gather what's magick to some is normal to others. Here, let me show you how to use this magick and put your library in the palm of your hand."

He and George worked together for several hours and he learned how to command the tablet. "One last thing before we finish for today. You know how you opened your library to anyone who wanted to do research? People no longer have to travel for days or go hundreds of miles to your library. Now anyone can look at your library from here."

"Anyone? Are all the manor documents available?" His voice held a note of disapproval. There were some documents that were private and to be read by a select few.

George's eyes widened in surprise. "Well not everyone and yes, all the documents are available. We've been busy uploading them...making them available. Is something wrong?" Before he could say anything George's eyes flashed with recognition. "Not the druid documents, if that concerns you. They aren't in your library. I suspect they're untouched in the sanctuary."

Arik let his shoulders relax. So, the sanctuary hadn't been breached. Before his time the Romans had gone on a campaign against the druids. Much of his family's legacy had been destroyed.

"The sanctuary? I was certain it was a myth when I couldn't open it."

"It's not a myth, just well protected." There were many prized possessions in the sanctuary. He needed to see if there was anything that could help Rebeka.

"Before Rebeka lost her memory we tried to open the entrance but we weren't successful." He studied George and weighed his options.

"Clear the way to sanctuary and I'll open it." George nodded his agreement.

"The garrison will be empty tonight. The major and the men will be in Avebury. They have dinner and spend the evening talking to the veterans there. It's a special place for veterans blinded in combat." The men may have appeared too disorganized for his liking but their attention to their comrades raised their status in his eyes. "I have a little more I'd like to go over with you." Arik gave George his attention.

Arik stretched. They'd been working for hours. "That's enough for right now." George closed the tablet. "Come with me. There's something else I'd like to show you." George led him to the stairs. Arik had so many more questions he wanted to ask the tablet but they could wait. They went to the drive where one of George's men had something on wheels waiting for them. "You need a way to get between here and the manor."

"I had a fine breed of horses at Fayne Manor."
Now that he considered it, he hadn't seen any livestock
in the paddock and he hadn't visited the barn.

"You'll need something a bit faster. You said you
liked the feeling of power between your legs. This is a
Triumph Rocket III motorbike." George gave him a
helmet. "Put this on and I'll take you for a ride."

He straddled the machine in back of George as if
riding tandem with one of his men. They eased down
the drive and onto the black road. As soon as Arik got
comfortable with the balance George pushed the
machine faster. The wind in his face and the rumble of
the motor under him were more than exhilarating. It
was thrilling.

George eased to a stop at a flat area coated the
same way as the road. George called it *the strip*. They
both got off the machine and took off their helmets.

Arik spent the rest of the afternoon learning the
motorbike. By the time they were done he had driven
the strip dozens of times. Controlling the engine was
mechanical and took some practice, as did balancing on
the wheels. He was quick to learn after being tossed off
twice, and very much like a horse, the throttle and
brake took a gentle touch.

He was still smiling when they returned to Autumn
Chase.

"It appears his lordship enjoyed the outing," Cora
said as they entered the salon.

"Yes. It was outstanding. I would have believed
the machine was magick if you hadn't shown me how it
worked." George handed him a cold beer from the bar.

"Come, dinner's ready then George will take you
back to the manor."

George pulled in front to the private door that led to

the captain's room. After making certain all the men were gone, Arik stood in front of the large hearth and ran his hand along the inside of the firebox until he found the mechanism. He pushed with a steady pressure while he murmured the chant.

The click of the lock told him he was successful.

He pushed back the large hearth stone. The dank smell of dust brushed against his face. He caught the faint odor of sulfur, the remnants of the magick that protected the entry.

They walked along the corridor that traveled deep underground. Arik flicked his hand and one by one the torches that lined the walls sprang to life.

Gooseflesh covered their skin as they moved farther into the tunnel before it leveled off and opened into a large cavern. They stood at the entrance. One by one the torches ignited around the room. Even after centuries of abandonment, the room was alive with unspent energy.

Arik stood and soaked it in. George stood in awe.

"It's more than I imagined," George whispered with reverence. "I can feel the energy." He stared at Arik and sucked in his breath. The runes on Arik's chest gave off a soft glow.

"I'm not surprised." Arik nodded. George followed Arik's gaze. He threw his hands up in surprise. The runes on George's shoulder and chest glowed through his shirt.

Arik breathed a sigh of relief. The truth to George's loyalty was in the man's runes. They glowed clear and pure. As he had suspected, the man could be trusted.

"Let's finish here before the men come back." Several tunnels ran off the main room. "This way to the library."

George followed him. Other passages branched off the main path. "These lead to the armory and gathering rooms." They continued on until they entered a cavern filled with bookshelves that had been carved into the rock walls. In the middle of the room was an ornately carved hazelwood table with several chairs. A thick layer of dust covered everything.

"The books we want are on the other side of the room." Arik headed for the far corner with George a step or two behind. Arik's heart dropped. He knew before he reached the shelf that the documents weren't there.

They stood in front of the empty shelf. "Is there another place where the books would've been stored?" George asked.

"No." Arik took his time and scanned the room. He couldn't sense the magick used to lock them. "The books aren't here."

"Do you think…?"

Bran. "I don't know who else has need of them or knows how to find them." Would Logan move them somewhere to protect them? What better protection than here? He shook off the disappointment. "Come. We'd best leave before the major and his men return."

They started back through the tunnel. The torches snuffed out as they passed. They stepped through the hearth. George checked the door while Arik completed the chant and tripped the mechanism. The hearth slid into place. They stepped outside the garrison.

"I want to make certain the wards protecting the manor are intact. I'll do that first thing in the morning." After the disappointment of the missing books he wanted to make certain they were protected against any unwanted guests.

"I'll meet you in the Great Hall at breakfast. There's more to go over," George said.

Arik nodded in agreement. He retrieved a satchel from the back of George's car. It was filled with the clothes and grooming supplies Cora had given him. He stood back as George drove off.

He entered the captain's room. It had little furnishings in his time, and it was not much different now—a place to put his clothes, bed, table and chair. One day, and already the things he learned and witnessed were...startling and wonderful.

He gazed out the window. Here, in the darkness, he could imagine being home with Logan and the others. His chest eased. How many times had he looked out into the night and begged the Great Mother to show him the way?

Now, he was with her.

He looked over at her cottage. This would do for now.

Chapter Ten

Arik stood on the terrace in the early morning mist. The golden rim of the sun eased over the east hill. He removed his shirt and closed his eyes.

"Hail and welcome. As above, so below. As within, so without. May guidance and love mark our way. And bring success for our clan today. So mote it be." He opened his eyes. *Thank you, Great Mother, for showing me the way to Rebeka*, he added and shrugged back into his shirt.

The wards that guarded the manor had been placed in a strategic pattern. He wasn't taking any chances. If Bran was able to create an enchantment in this century he wanted to make certain the wards he created four centuries ago still held.

He walked the manor's perimeter and prodded the ground, pulling back the sod to unearth each of the four anchor stones. He cleansed each one until he saw his sigil and the elhaz rune—the warding sign.

The process took him longer without help, but knowing what happened to Rebeka at Orkney made this a priority. Warded, Bran wouldn't be able to enter the manor without a direct invitation, something he didn't plan on extending.

The four corners marked, he took the well-worn

path to the lake, the center of the manor complex. As he came round the bend where it branched toward the lake his pace slowed.

Elfrida's cottage stood behind some strange chain wall. The cottage was old in his time but well cared for and cozy.

Now it was a cold, abandoned building.

He forced himself to keep his eyes forward, chiding himself for thinking of the past. He couldn't tolerate any distractions. He needed to be focused and committed. It was deceptive how familiar things weren't the same at all. He stole a last glance at Elfrida's cottage and kept moving on. He took a breath to quell his anxiety. Logan had criticized him for his preparation.

Faith. He wasn't prepared at all. It was difficult seeing things he knew well gone to seed.

When he got to the boulder by the lake he closed his eyes and, in a soft voice, chanted his request. The energy of the wards hummed their response—they were in a delicate position and in danger of collapsing.

With his dirk in hand he drew a five-pointed star. He removed his shirt and shoes then took his place in the star's center. Standing firmly on the soft ground, the earth molded to his bare feet.

He breathed in the air and murmured the chant of thanksgiving as he exhaled. His arms opened wide and his eyes focused beyond the treetops as he sought the guidance and acceptance of the heavens. Feeling a familiar oneness with his surroundings, he began to chant.

The song on his lips was soft, steady and strong.

He visualized roots growing from the soles of his feet going deep into the earth. The drone of the chant hummed through his body and the roots deepened until they were at the very center of the earth. He lowered his arms, altered the chant, and the runes that covered his body pulsed with a soft glow. The energy he built raced through the ground to each of the ward stones and responded with the Grand Master's request.

Each one glowed with a soft light that brightened with each beat of his heart. When the light was at its fullest he lifted his hands and a radiant net, anchored from the ground, was revealed. It reached high into the air. Its large canopy covered the manor.

He was startled when he saw the damage. The trees that surrounded the manor bore the burden of holding the magick net in place. He bowed his head and with gratitude thanked the trees for bearing the load.

He focused on each point of the star and began the healing chant.

One by one the broken strands of the net stretched and repaired the gaping hole.

The trees sighed as the burden lifted and the canopy once again was firm and strong. When he was through he thanked the Great Mother, the source of all energy. He returned his energy to the ground then slipped on his shirt and shoes. He returned to each ward stone and replaced the sod. One last chant and he was finished.

The morning was getting old and George would be there soon. He started back to the manor.

As he gained the porch steps, the spray of gravel and the rumble of a motorcar drew his attention. He shaded his eyes from the sun as George and Cora drove through the gate and stopped by the porch. Behind the motorcar, in a small wagon, were two motorbikes.

"Good morning." George got out of the car. "I hope you had a good night's sleep." Arik trotted down the porch steps to greet George and Cora.

"I slept well." Last night was the first night in months he slept without worrying about where Rebeka was.

"I had the idea we could continue your lesson today." George motioned to the wagon.

"Riding is one of his passions." Cora leaned out the motorcar window. "He didn't stop talking last night. He found a new partner." Arik nodded and flashed George a broad smile.

"Now would be a good time to go for a ride," George said. Arik was hoping to continue the lesson, too.

"See what I mean," Cora said. "Any chance he gets. He's like a boy with a new toy." He didn't know what to make of Cora. He knew they had worked hard on his and Rebeka's behalf. It was obvious that Cora's devotion to the family was strong and to her brother, unwavering. She had not been at Skara Brae with George and Rebeka but she shared the responsibility. Loyalty was a precious commodity in his time and, he expected, here as well.

"Ready?" George had the motorbikes out of the wagon and was handing him his helmet. "How about a ride along the Stone River?" George asked.

Arik nodded, his helmet already on.

"Have a good ride. George, don't forget you have a meeting later with the National Trust. I'll see you back at Autumn Chase." Cora drove off.

He and George started their engines and rode through the gate. Hugging the motorbike with his knees, Arik reveled in the throbbing power beneath him. The deafening noise added to his exhilaration. The gears shifted smoothly as he commanded the machine and it leaped forward. It responded to his touch without hesitation, as if it was alive.

The terrain's natural long climb and graceful bend was as he remembered. In place of the rutted trail, he drove on a smooth black roadway. He and George followed the winding road, alongside the river, as it wove through the forest. The dabbled thoroughfare and the cool early spring weather were invigorating. He pushed the machine faster. George was right with him.

They stopped at the bridge.

"It was a wooden bridge the last time I was here," Arik said. This was the place he was ambushed and up the road Bran's men had ambushed Logan, Doward and Rebeka.

"It's one of the improvements that had to be made for heavier vehicles. I'd like to go on but I have to meet with the National Trust. I'll see you back to the manor—"

"That won't be necessary. You go on. Autumn Chase isn't far from here."

"Before I forget…" George took out papers from the leather bag that straddled the rear wheel. "Here are the papers you'll need for Rebeka."

Arik nodded and stowed the papers in his side bag. They revved up their engines and pulled out. George crossed the bridge on his way to Autumn Chase. Arik rode along the river to Oak Meadow.

He came around the bend and saw the giant oak tree in the distance. The large sentinel trees bordered the meadow and the graceful willow in the adjacent field still stood. He pulled off to the side not far from the stone signpost and waited on the bike while it idled.

"Logan, after all my careful planning I'm here without a plan," he said to the empty meadow. "I wish you were by my side not only for your help but to witness what I have. If all goes well, we'll be together soon." He gunned the motor.

Before he returned there was one more place he wanted to see. He pulled away and left the meadow behind.

He veered off the road and headed north along the narrow trail. Here, without the black roadway, he could imagine he was back in his time. He rode the worn path that threaded through the trees then came to the clearing where the old mill stood now long deserted.

He pulled into the mill yard, turned off the motor and lowered the kickstand. The energy around the building was as strong as it was when he'd set the wards. The structure itself, though, was another story. The stone-and-wood building appeared lifeless, its windows boarded, its roof patched. The large waterwheel was still, set low next to the building with most of its panels broken or gone. The flume, the water's route from the river to the wheel, was perched high on top. The large drop was made on purpose to create a good deal of water energy. He glanced at the dry flume and followed its path back to the rushing river where the sluice door was closed, diverting water passed the mill.

He climbed the outside of the building. The uppermost floor, the sack floor, was wood and worn. It couldn't be used. The remnant of the old sack hoist was unrecognizable. He peered between the boards on the window and saw that patches of the floor were missing. If he tried hard he could see past the stone wheel level all the way to the meal level three stories below. There was debris everywhere but the stone building was sound. He climbed down, dusted himself off and got back to his bike.

The mill, the village, the farms were all gone. Everything he worked for, everyone he cared about, it was all gone.

Rebeka had warned him the manor was different. He'd believed because he knew about the future he was prepared to live in it. He stood next to the mill door.

For him it was all about hearth and home, as it had been for Rebeka. That's what she craved when she had come to him. That's what was missing now. He slapped his hand against the stone mill. That was how he would rebuild their relationship.

Give her what she hungers for.

When they first met he had been stern. She would call it difficult. It didn't matter what she called it. That was the Arik he would be. It was the man she fell in love with. He hoped she would fall in love with him again. He returned to the motorbike, put on his helmet and started back to the manor.

"No, George. I haven't seen him this morning…" Rebeka closed the door to her cottage. The last thing she needed was to babysit one of George's relatives. As soon as the notion was out she knew it wasn't very gracious considering all George had done as a friend to help her.

She had been snapping at everyone since yesterday. She crossed the drive and stood on the porch.

"Well, if you think he can do it. But didn't you want the Renaissance Festival actor to play Arik…?" She considered the oversized man the agency had sent. He was more like King Henry VIII than Lord Arik. "No, I didn't like him much, either. Yes…I know you're right—we do need someone to play Arik…he volunteered? And you think he can do it…well, I have my doubts he'll fit in…I'll let him know as soon as he gets here…The others have been studying for months. How can he catch up?" Well, if he couldn't do the work at least she could tell George she'd tried. "Of course I'll watch for him. I have to go or I'll be late…Yes, I'm giving out the scripts today. I've got to go. The others are waiting for me."

The rumble of a motor and the clatter of flying gravel grabbed her attention. A large man got off a motorbike and stood staring at her through his sleek black helmet. The close-fitting clothes showed off his well-defined body, from the T-shirt that was stretched to its limit trying to cover his chest, to the sculpted jeans that showed off his trim hips and strong legs. A sense of familiarity washed over her.

His back to her, he took off his helmet and placed it on the brace. He retrieved papers from the bike's side bags. When he turned to face her she couldn't believe her eyes.

Arik.

He was so out of place on the motorbike, and so hot.

"Oh, George, sorry…Yes, he just arrived." She took the phone from her ear. "Yes, speak to you later," she said. She didn't bother to end the call. She put the phone in her pocket.

Arik headed toward the porch then stopped in front of her. "Good morning, Rebeka." She could feel the sexual magnetism that made him so self-confident and it registered with her in all the right places.

"Did you enjoy catching up with George and Cora?" she asked, trying to keep the overwhelming attraction from her face.

"Yes, it was very…educational."

"I was speaking to George. He said you volunteered to play Lord Arik. You do know this is a long-term commitment. I wouldn't want to interfere with any obligations you have at your estate." What was she doing? She was shamelessly fishing for information. She should be embarrassed, but she wasn't. She wanted to know more about him.

"Yes, he mentioned it and no, I don't have to return right away. I've left things in my brother's very capable hands."

Jeez, there were two of them. "Good, then let's go into the library. There's some paperwork you need to fill out."

"I reviewed it with George and Cora." He handed

her a folder.

She reviewed the forms. "This appears to be in order. You've put George as your next of kin." She gazed into his eyes. "Is there someone closer, a wife?"

A mild panic hit her when his smile saddened. "My wife is gone."

"Oh, Arik, I am so sorry." She put her hand on his arm. For a brief moment she saw a heart-stopping tenderness in his eyes. He must have loved her deeply. "I didn't mean to pry or touch on a difficult topic. I wanted to make certain—"

"George gave you the information you need to know." The tone of his voice told her the subject was closed. It served her right for asking.

She checked the time. "The others are waiting for me. I don't like being late. Let me take you to meet those you'll be working with." They went into the manor. "I'm giving out the scripts this morning. I'll have to give you yours after the meeting. I haven't got it with me."

"Scripts?" he asked. She tried to throttle the dizzying current that was racing through her faster than his motorbike. If he looked at her one more time with those blue-green eyes she was going to... He coughed. He was waiting for her answer. What the...was his question? Oh, scripts.

"Yes, I've written out all the interactions so everyone will know what to say."

She led the way to the ballroom. She scanned the room to make certain everyone was there. Rather than taking a seat, Arik stood by the wall as if he were overseeing the meeting. His apparent attitude, along with his smug expression—which was better than a bucket of cold water—had her clenching her teeth. She was furious.

"Okay, everyone. Let's get started. Here are your scripts. I've taken the scripts we've been working with and added the notes we've discussed. Joan, give these out, please. Study them, know your responses and be prepared to give them if a guest asks you a question. We want their experience to be as accurate as possible.

"Beginning today, we're in the seventeenth century. Everything we do and say will reflect that time. As we discussed yesterday, from now on we will be using your seventeenth-century names. So get used to them. And no, you cannot invent anything that wasn't available in the seventeenth century. So no breakthrough inventions, like computers or cell phones."

A rumble of laughter rolled through the room.

"We have a new addition to our staff. *Lord* Arik has arrived." She motioned to Arik leaning against the wall. Everyone in the room that wasn't already examining him turned in his direction. He dipped his head and gave them a pleasant, *lordly*, smile.

"If you have any historical questions or questions about protocol, feel free to ask me," Rebeka said. No hands went up. "Right. You all have my cell number if you need to reach me. Good. Please be dressed and ready by noon." The room began to empty.

"Dr. Tyler." Charles made his way through the exiting crowd. "Louise Richards and the staff from the National Trust have arrived. I've put them in the library."

"Thank you." She turned and found Arik surrounded by a group of students, all female. She tried to disguise her annoyance in front of the others. "Arik, come with me and I'll give you your script."

"If you'd like, join us," one of the women standing next to Arik said, "at the old garden house. We'll be rehearsing there."

"Thank you. Perhaps later. If you'll excuse me." Arik broke away from the group and joined Rebeka. She watched the students stare after him, salivating.

"You seemed to have made a good impression." There was a critical tone to her voice, with a vague hint of disapproval. Arik stood with an ease that made him approachable yet underneath the surface she imagined him a bit...dangerous. *Jeez, every woman will go crazy for him.*

"Did I?" He shrugged in mock confusion.

"I know you haven't had any time to study. I hope you can fit in. These people have been working at this for months, with good results. It wouldn't be a bad idea for you to practice with the group." They crossed the hall to the library.

He held the library door open, giving her just enough room to squeeze past him but before she was through, he lowered his arm and blocked her way.

Startled, she looked into his eyes for an explanation. He didn't have to trap her—he pinned her with his stare and took her breath away.

He bent close and whispered, "If I have any difficulty I'll come and see you." Her cheeks burned and from the gleam in his eyes he enjoyed her befuddled expression. Arik dropped his arm and let her pass. With a toss of her head she entered the room. He followed behind.

"Louise. How good to see you." She scanned the room. "Where are the others?"

"They've gone to the garden house to review the displays and make sure the exhibition labels are correct. By the way, that was a brilliant idea, turning the building into a museum. I was on my way back to London and when I found out they were coming to work on the collection today I took the opportunity to join them. Besides, I have news that is best given in person."

"It sounds serious." Rebeka took a seat next to the Trust's field representative.

When Lady Emily died, she willed Fayne Manor to

the National Trust with the exception of the small cottage across from the manor, the contents of the library and a necklace, a family heirloom. Those were destined for Rebeka. George worked with Louise to secure the property with the Trust.

"Rebeka, I don't know how to soften this," Louise said. "The papers provided for admission to the National Trust have come into question. They appear to be forged. I've spoken with the Trust until I'm pale from exhaustion but the Trust's attorney is sending a letter requesting that you provide the original proclamation for their evaluation. It should arrive tomorrow. You'll have until the first of May to provide the document. I told them I'd vouch for Fayne Manor but they wouldn't hear any of it. They were going to give you thirty days. I at least got you more."

Arik stepped out of the shadows where he had stationed himself, crossed the room and charged toward the table. "What question?" His voice demanded an answer. Throwing doubt on a family's legitimacy was an old trick to separate them from their land.

"Arik?" He didn't miss the stunned expression on Rebeka's face.

Louise spun to face him. "The establishment of the manor as a gift from the crown is in question. The papers appear to be altered. The Trust has launched an investigation."

He saw the flicker of interest intensify in Louise's eyes as he got closer. She did everything but lick her lips. Her appetite didn't interest him. However, Rebeka's burning glare directed at Louise did. "When Alfred the Great was routed out of Chippenham by the Danes in the Twelfth Night Attack, he consulted with

Mannis, the head of the family. He is in Rebeka's family line. Together they planned the Battle of Ethandun." He had Louise's rapt attention. He wasn't certain if it was because of his knowledge or his chest. She couldn't keep her eyes anywhere else.

"Alfred couldn't defeat the Danes in a siege battle." Thank goodness Rebeka found her voice. He believed he'd have to keep the conversation going with Louise by himself. Although he was certain she would seek other entertainment.

"You're quite correct. That's why Alfred sought out Mannis." He turned and gave Rebeka his full attention. "He and his garrison of men were well known for their battle abilities."

"Yes, but Alfred wasn't a supporter of Mannis," Rebeka said.

"Not on the surface. Together with Alfred, they planned to starve out the Danes and their men. Your ancestor's army, Mannis's army, strengthened Alfred's."

"Rebeka, who is this man?" Louise asked. They both stared at her. Arik had forgotten she was there he was so intent on his discussion with Rebeka. "We know about Alfred the Great but not about Mannis's connection with him or the event. If his information is correct there should be some proof." Louise turned to him. "Where is it?" Her voice was courteous but patronizing. Her arrogance didn't sit well with him. Perhaps it was a poor first impression, although he doubted it.

"The battle's well documented but the details about what happened have long been in question," Rebeka said, already pulling a book off one of the shelves.

"The battle is not in question—but if your family participated we need the records. Besides," Louise turned to him, still focused on his chest, "how does that prove the land grant?" Her eyes tracked up his torso and stopped at his eyes. He was used to seeing adoration, even lust, in a woman's eyes but her eyes held something more predatory.

"I'm sorry, Louise, this is Arik. He's George's cousin from the north. He'll be playing Lord Arik in the reenactment." Rebeka paged through the book. He assumed she searched for a reference. It wouldn't be there. History has the king the victor. His right-hand man barely mentioned. But there were other records.

"Do you have proof Rebeka's ancestors participated in the battle?" Louise asked.

"Alfred prevailed and won the battle, but only because Mannis gave him support. To honor him, Alfred gave him a special sword." Doward told this tale often. Usually tales of wars were embellished, not forgotten.

At least not for the winners.

"Yes," Louise exclaimed. "The great druid sword, the Sword of Rapture, but it's been lost for centuries. Is that why there's so much mystery around this event? Did Alfred call upon the druids for assistance?" He was startled on several fronts. That this woman knew Mannis was a druid. That had been a well-kept secret. That the sword was missing. Lost in battle? Or taken as spoils? Or locked away, forgotten? Or for safe keeping? He considered the sanctuary. He sniffed the air for any trace of lightning and found none. That wasn't proof Bran wasn't involved. He had to speak to George.

Rebeka turned and nodded at the picture over the hearth. "That's the only known picture of the sword."

"To answer your question, Louise, Mannis practiced the old ways. It's because he did that he had to become a competent defender. His life, his family and followers depended on it. Alfred the Great utilized Mannis's competency to his advantage." He gave Louise his best this-interview-is-over stare.

"Well, Rebeka, you have an excellent person for

your reenactment. He seems to be very well versed in folklore, if not history." Folklore indeed. He kept his temper at her quip.

There was a light tap on the door and Charles entered. "Excuse me, Ms. Rebeka. Ms. Richards's car is waiting."

"Thank you, Charles." Louise faced Rebeka. "We'll have to postpone our practice today. I have to get back to London for a meeting." Louise turned to Arik. "We need to document this story in some way to help with the authentication. And as you know we will need corroborating evidence."

"Of course." Rebeka hadn't taken her eyes off him. He understood her confused expression. He'd have to instruct her how to make her face unreadable. He didn't like that Louise could see her thoughts. It gave the Trust representative too much power. He moved next to Rebeka to silently declare his allegiance and, he hoped, give her strength.

"Call if you find anything," Rebeka said. She started to see Louise to the door.

"Oh don't bother. I'll see myself out. Nice meeting you, Arik." Her eyes ran up his body. "Very nice indeed." He gave a polite smile but underneath he seethed.

"How did you know about Mannis and the sword?" He noted her demand, ran his hand through his hair and came to a quick decision.

"I'm a sword master. Great swords are an interest of mine. It led me to the Sword of Rapture and your family story." His tone was matter-of-fact, as if everyone knew about his hobby. She made no objection so he assumed she accepted his ruse.

"Then you know there's no trace of the sword after that picture was painted. There's speculation the sword was already lost before the portrait was commissioned." She stood by the hearth. "Its significance is now coming to light and that information has not been made public." She turned and faced Arik. "And I'm not aware of Mannis's connection with the battle."

He had instructed her, when he taught her about her family line. He would have to teach her again. Right now there was a more pressing issue: they had forty days to find the evidence they needed to save the manor and the family name.

"That book," he pointed to the one she held, "won't help you." He moved along the library and went to the section with the more ancient documents.

Rebeka followed a step behind. "What are you searching for? How do you know about the documents?"

"This library has always been open to anyone seeking knowledge. In the past," he turned and pinned her with his stare, "I've been here often." He tried to stay as close to the truth as he could. He moved on. Was Bran involved in this new disaster? He moved along the row of books, searching the titles.

"Ah, good." He pulled a large book from the shelf and paged through the manuscript. Rebeka peered over his shoulder.

"These are from the seventeenth century. You want...?"

"The ninth century." He came to the end of the book.

"The older volumes are back here." She headed to another bookcase.

He closed the cover with a snap. "Yes, of course."

"Is something wrong?"

"No, no," he responded. He put the volume back in place and joined her at the other shelf. He scanned the spines and removed the book he wanted. He flipped through a few pages then closed it. "Hold this." He turned his attention to the drawers that held the older documents and searched the scroll.

He read a few lines and replaced them. There was nothing here. He moved to the documents pertaining to the soldiers.

"Tell me what you want. All these books and documents in this section have been reviewed and cataloged for the online library."

"Here it is." He took the document. "Bring the book." He unrolled the parchment on the table. "Here is your proof." He pointed to the text.

Rebeka, still holding the book, stood next to him and read the scroll. "I remember this document. I had difficulty with the translation and brought it to a colleague. It appears to be an order for household goods."

He was caught short by her words. "It's not an order for household goods. What makes you think it is?"

"Ropes and ladders, what else could it be? For the garden?"

He read through the document and came to a specific area. "Here." He pointed to a section. "It's a request sent by Alfred the Great to Mannis, demanding he come to his aid. He mentions the possible exchange of land. He's also provided a list of supplies Mannis is to bring him. Perhaps your expert didn't know this dialect. This should be the proof you need."

He saw the lines of concentration deepen on her face as she studied the document. "A possible exchange of land or a land grant?" She lowered herself onto a chair and studied the document.

He watched and waited. Would her mind clear? Would her heightened concentration break through Bran's enchantment?

"The Trust won't be satisfied with *possible*. Is there another source we can corroborate this with?"

"That." He motioned to the book she held. "In

the journal you'll find a reference to the exchange of land." He took the book from her and paged through it until he found a specific section.

"Yes. I'm familiar with this, too. It appears to be filled with stories. We concluded this man was a tinker and brought wares and news between the villages. He has a colorful way of documenting the events. I think of him much like the Roman Josephus and his documentation of biblical times. How can his writing help?"

His fingers tapped the table in frustration as he searched the document. She saw history from only one perspective. She needed to see the broader picture. "Here." He pointed to a particular page.

"These are runes. They're used for divination and…" she glanced at him with a small smile, "…love songs," she added and turned back to the document. "Not for documentation."

His face eased into a smile. Her playful quip pleased him. "Some would agree with you. Some would say this language was used to avoid being read by the uninitiated." He read through the entry, searching for a particular passage.

"A code?" Her question hung in the air, saturated with disbelief.

"The sword Alfred gave to your family held—"

"Magick. You're going to tell me you believe in that old tale." Her voice was filled with cold sarcasm. "I believed you were smarter than that."

He didn't miss the scornful expression on her face. He'd have to change her mind. He had before. "People in different times believe different things. To the ancient ones thunder and lightning were mystical. The more people learned, the more they could make sense of the world around them, but sometimes believing is as good as being true. You have to examine things—"

"From all angles," she completed his sentence, a

distant expression on her face.

A small thrill pulsed through him. When she first arrived in his time her impulsiveness to act on the first piece of information had driven him mad. How many times had he repeated those words to her? He waited a heartbeat to see if she remembered more. The memories were there. *That's it, Rebeka, one crack at a time. Little by little we'll tear down the barrier.* "Yes, I know. It's easy to get caught in one point of view." He kept his voice even and calm.

"If I believe what you're saying, what do you think these runes say?" He had her thinking. He was certain she would see he was right.

He placed his finger on the document to hold his place. "I know what they say. These runes tell of a ceremony where Alfred the Great awarded the Sword of Rapture to Mannis. It's right here." He tapped his finger on the papyrus. "They refer to Mannis's men here as mercenaries." Pointing to the runes, he had no trouble translating them.

"'Alfred the Great called all his soldiers and mercenaries to the center of his hall. He drew his sword, proclaiming it the Sword of Rapture. "Kneel," he commanded the mercenary leader. "Kneel before your king and receive his greatest honor." Mannis knelt before his king and spoke the words of fealty. "I shall maintain the honor and dignity of the most ancient rite and the new, most noble royal Order of the Rapture to the best of my power if God let me. I shall never bear treason about in my heart against our Sovereign the King. So defend me, God."'"

Her head popped up. "This is how the Order of the Rapture began." She returned her attention to the document. "What else does it say?"

"'The oath taken and fealty given, Alfred the Great and Mannis signed the oath and order of proclamation, giving Mannis the land between the valley and the

Stone River. He affixed a blue wax seal on the document, using the insignia on the sword hilt, a sigil combining Alfred's golden dragon with Mannis's sacred spiral. Thus they sealed the oath for all to see.' The entry is dated spring 879." He tapped the book with his finger. "It's all here."

"Why is it so secret? There is no other document about this event. Alfred documented everything. Why not this?" she asked, still looking at the scroll.

"It's an ancient order devised by Alfred and Mannis, the Grand Master of the druid Council and leader of your family. The royal order was a secret because Mannis was a druid. Politically, Alfred denounced the druids and outwardly sought to remove them." It was an old strategy. Remove those that are smarter than you then take their place.

She turned back to the table and scribbled notes. "You mean kill them. He feared their power."

"I know it's difficult to translate these ancient documents unless you know the writer's intent. Words have a variety of meanings and it can be confusing."

She raised her head in deep concentration. "Ian must not have read the entire document," she said, more to herself. She looked back at Arik. "But this is still circumstantial evidence. The National Trust wants the proclamation mentioned here."

"This may be enough to delay them from taking action and give us more time," he said.

"George can take care of that." She bent over her books. "I'll start the research. There are hundreds of older documents we have yet to review." She pointed to the ancient journal. She gave him a questioning stare. "I've learned more in the past few hours than I have in several months."

"It's part of the history of the area. I've made it my duty to know. How else can their knowledge and legacy be kept alive and passed on to others? If we don't, their story will die as if the people never existed."

"You know more than some of the world's top scholars." He caught the challenge in her voice.

"The family had been persecuted since the time of the Romans for their deep druid beliefs. No one was to be trusted. That's why some documents are protected from being read. What you see as odd strokes and lines have meanings for others. To them these are private papers."

"Yes, well, I'm still learning. Until last April, I didn't know I had a connection to the family. But I won't let the family die." With care, her hand touched the journal. "I've found them. I'd fight the devil himself to preserve Fayne Manor. This is my family, my home."

"As it should be, m'lady." A soft sigh escaped his lips. The shine of determination that lit her face excited him. This was the woman he remembered and searched for. "Well, I must practice with the others. I'll leave you to your research. The proclamation must still exist."

The fire in her eyes and determination to save their family made his chest swell with pride. And he fell in love with his warrior wife all over again.

CHAPTER ELEVEN

Arik entered the Great Hall. "Join me in an ale." He took the offered tankard from George. He needed something after the morning he had with "his" villagers. "Rebeka mentioned you were studying with the others." He glanced at George and knew the man was trying hard not to smile.

"I would have considered it amusing, too, if it wasn't so frustrating. I attended confident I knew the seventeenth-century lifestyle. It is obvious, I do not." He took a fortifying gulp. "The others were diligent and cordial." In truth, they were intimidated by him but he was used to that. He watched rather than interacted, although there were some things he just couldn't abide with and had to correct. "Some of the ideas about Lord Arik were absurd. I don't swagger." He sipped the ale then looked at the tankard. The brew was tart but smooth. He took a bigger swallow.

George laughed and choked on his beer. Arik was quick to pound him on his back. "Sorry," George said when he caught his breath. "You do swagger." Arik flashed him a stern glare then finished his ale.

"Rebeka showed me the document and journal entry you found yesterday. I agree, they may be enough to settle the issue. The Trust has taken lesser documents as proof. We gave them everything they requested three years ago when Fayne Manor was accepted into the Trust. The documents were all authenticated then. I can't imagine why they're now in question. Cora and I talked last night. Do you think Bran has anything to do with this?"

"I've had the same idea. No, I don't see how he could've managed it. Has anyone threatened the manor?"

"You mean buy it out? No, never. There was some discussion when Lady Emily died without an heir. But her will was quite clear. She made financial arrangements. With her endowment and the planned income from the estate, Fayne Manor was solvent. The National Trust · manages it." Arik nodded his understanding. Lady Emily's plan was a good one. So where did the threat come from?

"We should stay alert and try to piece this puzzle together. Someone has to benefit, or will, if we can't prove the family claim," Arik said.

"Yes, I agree. Emily had copies of all the papers we gave the Trust. I'll see if I can locate them. In the meantime, I'll be in Avebury today. I'll drop off the document and journal entry at Louise's office." George took a long pull on his ale.

"Other than telling you that you swagger, what else happened at your class?" Arik glanced at George. The man was enjoying his discomfort.

"I seem to have passed my seventeenth-century test." He raised one eyebrow and brought the ale to his lips. Assimilating into this new community was a challenge but well within his ability. As lord, well, he didn't have to worry about those duties here, although there were ways to enhance the reenactment.

"Did Rebeka give you the script we prepared for that actor?" George smirked. "It was somewhat overdramatic."

"They kept correcting me about what to say and how to act. They were not correct." Several times he had to stop himself from roaring at them. *Absurd* was an understatement. The lord, at least this one, didn't go around ordering his tenants and villagers.

"It will all work out in the end." Work out? Without taking action? The reenactment, Rebeka's memories, ownership of the manor. Things didn't simply work out. Didn't the man understand time was slipping by? May 1 wasn't that far away. Even if a wait-and-see attitude would work, they didn't have time.

"You can't leave it to fate. It takes more than a script for the reenactment to be successful. It takes a plan." He hammered each word against the table with the point of his finger.

"Once everyone knows their roles, how to act and what to say, it will be fine. Right now they're trying to live in two worlds." Arik studied George for a moment while he gathered his temper. He took in the growing flush on George's neck.

"Yes, I think I understand that all too well," he said half out loud with a distinct mocking tone as he rose from the chair. That was what happened at Orkney. Wait and see. Hadn't the man learned anything? He let George stew a bit longer.

"Arik."

Arik laid his hand on the druid's shoulder and relented. "There is no need to say anything. Everyone feels the stress."

"How are you getting along with Rebeka?" Ah, now there was a subject that was even more stressful for him.

"I believed she remembered. She mentioned something we spoke about often. I was certain. But it came to nothing." Will that work itself out, too? The spark was there—he just needed to find a way to burst it into a flame.

"You can't expect things to happen quickly. This is going to take time." He appreciated the genuine concern in George's voice but it didn't help. Going to take time? Everything was going to take time.

"Excuse me." Rebeka peeked into the estate room. "I thought you were in here." She looked from George to Arik. "Is something wrong?"

"Not at all; a family conundrum. I was getting ready to leave." George set the tankard on the table and rose to his feet. "Arik, I'll see you tonight." He passed Rebeka as she entered the room.

"Arik, Charles has your clothes for the reenactment." She placed her staff next to the table. "Please be dressed and at the village on time. But before you go there is something I wanted to discuss with you." She rummaged through her backpack and pulled out several papers.

"I see you changed the script. Why? I was very careful when I worked it out." She flashed the script in his face. Her voice reminded him of his boyhood tutor when the man was particularly annoyed. He silenced a biting response and continued his relaxed attitude. A swipe of his hand brushed aside the offending documents.

"When a dispute comes before me it's not settled with a sword fight. It's negotiated to the agreement of both parties. If everything was settled by the sword there would be no one left to carry on business." His voice was heavy with sarcasm. It was humiliating what she was turning Fayne Manor into with overdone scripts and sword fights.

"Listen, I'm well aware of how people conducted themselves in the seventeenth century. However, we need to attract more people to Fayne Manor. They love the drama. Every reenactment has a duel of some sort."

"If every reenactment has a duel what would drive them here to see another?" he roared and noted her startled expression. The men didn't even know how to manage the swords. Any one of the young boys at his manor could do better.

"Well, because…" she sputtered. It was obvious to him that she couldn't think of an answer.

"No one talks like that." He pointed to her papers that were still in her hand. "You of all people should know that the spoken language of the time wasn't stiff and formal. That was left to the legal documents and student manuscripts." He picked up his script.

"'As you like it, madam, that is much ado about nothing.'" He tossed the papers onto the table.

Her chin jutted out. "You're so smart, you come up with a better idea. Until you do," she got to her feet, "and I agree to it, it's my way. It's my ass on the line here."

She took her things and left the room.

He looked after her with a raised eyebrow. His eyes followed her out the door. "And a very pretty little ass indeed," he whispered.

By noon he was changed and ready for opening day.

He left the garrison and headed to the village. On his way he skimmed the script Rebeka had waved in his face. In the morning he was to be in the estate office carrying on business. Rebeka's note in the margin said to make himself look busy.

Midmorning he was to go into the Great Hall where he was to hear disputes from the vassals. Vassals. He let out a long breath. Here her note instructed him to appear attentive.

Late morning was weapons practice with the men—he found no note here—and the afternoon he was to inspect the estate. An additional note said if time permitted he could go hunting. Well, she'd gotten it right, more or less.

However, he preferred practicing with his troops in the early morning before going over the house accounts. As for disputes, he settled those when he and his men visited his farms, which was not on the list.

He kept on toward the village and reminded himself there were no farms. He tucked away the papers and continued on.

"Lord Arik." The group of costumed women walked beside him.

"Ladies." He nodded his greeting. He was surprised at how accurate their costumes were. Their enthusiasm was catching.

"Opening day. It's so exciting." He had to admit, there was a festival atmosphere in the air.

"Yes, it is. And what will you be doing today?" The women stared at him, a bit miffed. They searched their script. Didn't they understand him?

"Did she change the script?" one asked the other.

"No, I didn't get a new one." They fussed with the papers.

"Faith." He raised his eyes to the heavens. "I was being social. You won't find that in your script."

"Oh, of course. I guess I'm taking Rebeka a bit too literally." The women put away their scripts. "Some of us are scheduled to help the baker and the others to sell ribbons. Come stop by my stand and see what I have to offer." The ladies exploded into peals of laughter as they moved on ahead of him.

He gave a bit of a smile at their playfulness and continued on. Everyone was prepared and ready. Rebeka had been anxious about the opening. Perhaps now things would settle into place. She had classes in the morning and worked on the reenactment in the afternoon through the early evening. That left her little time, but she was in the library in the late evening going through   the   documents,   searching   for   the proclamation. It was a slow, painstaking task. She had refused his help. Had he been too hard on her? He let out a breath. No, she had to hear the truth. He put their discussion out of his mind.

He entered the village square crowded with tables and merchants but saw a very different scene: the houses appeared worn out, dark and empty.

He scanned the area knowing what he'd find. There were no women hanging laundry, no children playing in the garden or dogs running around. How he wanted to feel at home and see a familiar face. He didn't want to stay here longer than necessary. He hardened himself not to look or think about it. He'd be no help to anyone if his mind was elsewhere.

How had Rebeka managed? At least he had George and Cora to help him. She'd entered his century with no one to guide her.

"Everything appears to be ready. The first guests will be here soon," George said, coming alongside him with Rebeka. Despite his misgivings on how the reenactment was organized, he was eager for the reopening. It was one thing off his list.

"Major," George called out. Arik scanned the area. It wasn't like the man not to be at his post. He caught sight of the man hurrying out of one of the houses putting away his notebook and pencil. "Major, they've called everyone to order."

"Sorry, sir." The man took his place with his men.

Rebeka stepped forward. "Can I have everyone's attention?" The voices hushed. "You've all studied hard and I know you'll make our reopening a wonderful success. Enjoy the day and if you have any questions you can speak to Mr. Hughes or me. Good luck, everyone."

George stepped forward. "I know you'll do a terrific job. You're all well prepared thanks to Rebeka's fine research and instructions. To celebrate, there'll be a private party at The Autumn Retreat the end of the week. You're all invited. Good luck, everyone." George stepped aside and everyone took their places.

Arik took Rebeka's arm and threaded it through his. "M'lady. You look lovely today." Her hands shook like a nervous bird.

She turned to him. "Thank you." He gave her a dazzling smile, the one he saved only for her. She rewarded him with a tender gaze and was pleased. He'd take the small victory. They walked to the gate and waited to greet their guests.

A swell of excitement filtered through the group when a cloud of dust announced the arrival of the first coach.

"It's a disaster. It's been a week." Rebeka was at the library table with George, Cora and Arik. He was worried about Rebeka. Her spirits sank daily along with the attendance. "The receipts are much lower than we expected."

George read his notes. "The goods at the market didn't sell. Feedback indicates they were nothing special. Close to 35 percent of the visitors were family members of the staff and they had deep discounts. Attendance at the demonstrations did not meet expectations."

"You mean no one was there. That's because they were more interested in following Lord Arik." Rebeka gestured toward him. "There was always a crowd around him, even the students."

"He's built a great rapport with them and the staff." George kept focused on his notes while Arik bristled at being spoken about as if he wasn't in the room. He removed himself from the table and busied himself with a book on a shelf near the terrace door.

"I was hoping to give this project to the staff to manage. I haven't the time to rewrite the scripts or investigate souvenirs. I haven't had time to search for the proclamation and we have a little more than thirty days—thirty-two days, to be exact—to produce it. I need to get back to my research." Arik leaned against the bookcase. He watched and waited while the situation unfolded.

"Rebeka, it's the first week. Be patient. Everything looked good on paper." George was on the sofa going over the numbers. The man could review the numbers a hundred times. They wouldn't change. But Arik kept quiet and followed George's plan to wait—it would all work out.

"Cora did exit surveys with guests and tour guides," George said. "Do you have the results?" Cora opened a binder and thumbed through the pages. Arik had a good idea what the survey findings would be. But he would wait—it would all work out.

"Yes, I've been organizing them. The survey supports the comments I listened to when I walked the grounds. There was too much historical detail. The discussions were too long. Most people wanted more seating if they had to listen to long lectures." He watched Rebeka's frustration rise. She was a teacher and she was going to teach them whether they wanted to learn or not. What they wanted was to be entertained.

"One person said that for the time she was here she wanted to believe she was in the seventeenth century. When I told her this was the seventeenth century she was very clear. She told me not as she knew it. It seems people have their own ideas what the seventeenth century was like." Cora placed the report on the table. *Faith*. He waited—it would all work out.

George took the report. "Arik and I visited the Stelton estate to see how they're organized. Their shops and reenactment are more casual and, well, believable to the twenty-first-century imagination. Their market was filled. If I understand what our visitors have voiced and what I've seen at the Stelton's, people want the romance of the era, not necessarily reality. Perhaps we should rethink things a bit."

Arik pushed off the bookcase and stood staring out at the terrace. He sensed Rebeka's eyes on his back. He was still thinking about her comment. They had thirty-two days to find the proclamation. While they waited for it all to work out, he had searched all the places where he would've kept the proclamation. He hadn't found it.

Thirty-two days wasn't a long time. Maybe, if she had her memories back and they worked together... No, he couldn't take the chance of using the precious time they had without any guarantee that she would remember. He took a deep breath. He was concerned about her despair. It hung heavy in the air. This wasn't like her. He'd seen her face great odds and her determination never wavered—it grew stronger.

"Rethink things? When do we have time to do that?" Rebeka rose from her chair. "Here are our choices. We either spend time rethinking and reworking the reenactment to keep the manor running. If we fail, we lose the manor. Or we find the proclamation to keep the manor running. If we fail, we lose the manor. We can't do both, so we lose either way. But I'll think about it. Right now I'm too tired. I'll see you later at the party." She didn't bother to take her things. She passed Arik and continued out the terrace door. He watched as she trudged to her cottage.

Cora got up to follow her. He touched her shoulder and she stopped. "You needn't worry about her. She needs time to think. She'll decide on a solution." At least that's what he told them.

Cora gave him a weak smile. "I have to go back to

Autumn Chase to get everything ready for tonight's party. I'll stop by and see her. Make certain she's alright. A little girl talk before I leave. George, I'll meet you by the car." George nodded and she hurried out of the room.

"I'm also worried about the National Trust," George said. "I didn't want to say anything before but I spoke with Louise today. She hinted that if the Trust has any notion Rebeka can't manage the reenactment they may take action. They'd close the manor. That would compromise her program with Oxford." So much for *it will all work out*. He couldn't stand by and do nothing any longer.

"I won't let that happen," he said, more to himself, and turned to the man. "I've watched and been quiet long enough." He tugged on the bell pull and rang for Charles.

"Yes, sir?"

"Tell the major I'd like to see him." Charles nodded and left the room.

"With the loss of her memory I also see confusion, which I can understand. But I don't see her determination. I've tried it your way, letting it work its way out, but it's not been successful." He returned to the library table and read Cora's notes. He opened his tablet and started typing. "I think it's time she found out how Lord Arik runs his estate, whether she approves or not." He checked his tablet display. "I'll take care of the reenactment." He lifted his head and glanced at George. "You see to the National Trust."

"You may have been right. God knows I hope you are. See you tonight." George left to meet Cora at the car.

"Excuse me, sir." The major entered the room and saluted. "Charles said you wanted to see me."

"Stand easy, Major." The glow of the tablet vanished as he clicked off the device. He closed the folder with Cora's notes and came around the desk. The major let out a bit of the starch and struck a more casual stance.

"I saw you surveying the village buildings last week. What did you find interesting?"

"Not too long ago one of Dr. Tyler's staff gave a talk on old buildings. As a carpenter, before I served in Afghanistan, I renovated old buildings but never had an opportunity to see them in their original condition. While I was deployed I drew pictures of the old buildings and planned different ways to renovate them. It kept me occupied and gave me something normal to think about." Arik noted a momentary haunted look in the major's eyes. "It kept me sane in very insane circumstances." Arik could identify with that. He and his men had fought for the king in some insane situations.

"Come with me." Arik put his tablet and notes in the small bag and slung it over his shoulder. "We're going to inspect our old mill. I want to evaluate the structure." He led the way. "I examined it last week. I think we can get it running. The grinding stone is intact, the cog wheels need replacing and the water paddles need mending." The major had taken out a pad and pencil and was making notes. He liked the man's initiative. He wondered what skills the other men had.

"I have that, sir. We had a guest lecturer from the university who gave a talk about the construction of medieval mills. He called them water engines. Perhaps he can provide some guidance."

"Excellent suggestion." Some expert advice would be welcome. It would add to the educational experience. Arik led them through the forest on an almost impassable trail. It was the miller's son's shortcut.

The trees thickened the deeper they trekked into the forest. Dried twigs snapped and fallen leaves rustled as they traipsed on. The idea of restoring the mill appealed to him.

Building a business around it would be even better. He took a deep breath. The fragrance of an early spring renewed him. He tasted the sweetness of the fresh water on the air before he detected the rush of water off in the distance. They continued on further and came to the old stone wall, which had been there for centuries. As children he, Logan, Bran, Rebeka and Leticia had defended the manor from imaginary invaders. His hand dragged along the stone. He held onto the vision of his childhood a bit longer before he and the Major climbed to the other side.

They came along the path into the mill yard and conducted their preliminary review.

"Sir, the building appears to be sound." The two men stood outside the mill's boarded-up door.

Arik's black T-shirt clung to him. The dark stain that spread across his back was his badge of recognition for scaling the boarded-up mill's stone walls to see its condition inside. His knotted muscles ached pleasantly from the exertion.

The spiral of the major's pad peeked over the edge of his shirt's breast pocket. His pencil was tucked behind his ear. "The stones were well positioned." The major slapped the flat of his hand against the stone wall, as if to prove his point. "There are a few cracks but they're easy to repair."

Arik and the major pried the boards off the door. They dusted off their hands and entered the empty granary. The flagstone floor was covered with decades of neglect.

Arik peered into the room that housed the mechanism. The gears smiled back at him like an old man with missing teeth. The large running stone stood idle, propped against the wall. They climbed the ladder to the second floor. The damaged grain hopper, which would have to be replaced, hung poised over the bed stone waiting for the next bag of grain. Arik scanned the first floor of the mill and breathed in the familiar smell of earth and fallen leaves.

"The mill was in use until the 1940s," the major said, "when an unexploded bomb came through the roof." Both men looked overhead. "They repaired it and kept going for a while but over time the mill was closed."

"That explains the roof repair. It was fortunate the beams weren't damaged." Arik tested one, satisfied it was solid and sound.

"The local civil patrol and the fire warden removed the device. No one knows why the bomb didn't explode. They had no problem detonating it once it was removed. The people in the area think the tree branches somehow slowed the decent and caused a softer landing. It's in all the books about the area."

They climbed down the ladder. *Thank you, Great Mother*, he thought silently.

"The wheel needs repair but it appears sound." Arik agreed. Perhaps there was enough to work with to restart the mill? "The sluice doors are firmly boarded and will need some work, but the water level is good." The major continued his report. The men moved outside and put the boards back on the door.

"The forest has taken back the millrace but that should be easy to fix. We'll need to dig out the channel and reline it with stones." Arik glanced back at the building. Yes. This might work. "We can get it back in operation."

Encouraged by what he saw, he decided to move his plan forward, but he needed an ally. Rebeka wanted to manage every aspect of the manor. It was obvious to him that she didn't have time to add another project to her list. He didn't think she would support his plan. George was the more likely person. He'd see the plan's merit from a business perspective.

"I believe one of the men, Bill, has some experience with mills, sir."

There were more craftsmen among the men. "Major, arrange a meeting with the three of us. I read in the employment records that one of the men, Frank, was in the Corps of Royal Engineers. Ask him to attend also." The idea was encouraging. He was certain these men would make good captains for the project.

"Yes, sir. May I ask what you intend to do?"

"Isn't it obvious? We're going to restart the mill and grind our own grain." In his time he knew exactly what to do. He'd gather the miller, the mason and his men, and start the work. He suspected it didn't work that way here—or would it? The major put the pencil behind his ear and returned the small notebook to his pocket.

"Will you be attending the party at Autumn Chase this evening?" Arik asked as they started back to the manor.

"Yes, sir. We're all looking forward to the party. The Retreat is an exclusive tavern for an elite crowd. Mr. Hughes opens it to us from time to time. Will you be there?"

"Yes." Rebeka would be at the party and he didn't want to miss an opportunity to be with her. He started humming "Row, Row, Row Your Boat" as they continued back to the manor.

Arik stood against the wall by the bar holding an empty bottle of ale and stared across the room. Autumn Chase sported a five-star restaurant with a cellar that held one of the top nightspots in the area, The Autumn Retreat. Tonight the room was crowded, the music was loud, and there was plenty of food and drink—

compliments of George and Cora Hughes.

"You look…pensive." George took Arik's empty bottle and replaced it with a fresh one he grabbed from a passing waiter and took one for himself.

"Your retreat isn't very different than the king's court or a country house party. Music, people talking, drinking and trysts arranged for later in the evening. No, it's not very different at all. Scantily clothed women in a closed space with very hungry men. It doesn't leave much to the imagination. While the clothes are different, the intent is not." He took a long swallow of ale while he watched Rebeka on the other side of the room.

He'd avoided court and house parties. He had never liked the gossip or the backroom politics. As a single man with a title, every mother in England with an unwed daughter had tried to broker a marriage with him. Although being married didn't stop some women from pursuing him.

"Some things never change." George toasted with his bottle. "Have you seen Rebeka?"

"She's over on the other side of the room." He nodded in her direction. She was surrounded by her students. He waited for a better time to approach her.

A group of musicians entered and set up their equipment on the small stage.

"I have a surprise for everyone. I hope you enjoy it. Be right back." George stepped onto the platform and grabbed the microphone. "Good evening, everyone."

The room quieted quickly.

"I hope you're all having a good time. Cora and I would like to welcome you to The Autumn Retreat. We're pleased to celebrate the reopening of the Fayne Manor Experience. Dr. Tyler, Cora and I want to thank you for your hard work." Whistles and hollers, along with clapping and table pounding, filled the room like a bawdy London tavern.

George waited for quiet. "To get you in the seventeenth-century mood, I've asked Alf Lacey of the Midland Minstrels to play for us this evening. As you may know, Alf and his mates are renowned for their interpretation of Renaissance music. This evening we've arranged to simulate the entertainment of the period. That includes singing, dancing, drinking and eating, not so different than today. Anything else, you're on your own." A muffled laugh rolled through the crowd.

"So put your seventeenth-century dancing shoes on and get your voices ready. Our dance master tonight is Sir Kenneth Grayson. Sir Grayson is an Oxford medieval dance laureate. You will be happy to know Sir Grayson will not be grading you tonight."

George gave Alf the microphone and left the platform to another round of laughter and applause.

"Good evening, ladies and gentlemen. I'm Alf Lacey. Tonight you're attending a seventeenth-century party. So let's begin. The first dance will be a slow processional dance, the pavane. It's a sedate, dignified dance for couples. We'll then move quickly to the allemande, a more lively line dance. If you will, choose your partners and take your places, please. Ladies, feel free to ask anyone you like."

"Will you be joining the dance floor?" George asked Arik.

"I don't think so." He put the beer on the bar and stepped away from the wall. The way was clear to the other side of the room and Rebeka was alone at a table.

"Lord Arik." He turned to see Joan standing in front of him.

"Yes?" He quickly glanced at Rebeka and returned his attention to Joan.

"Want to dance?" She stood there shifting from one foot to the other. It wasn't a very eloquent request but there was determination in her eyes. Who was he to deny a determined woman?

"Oh, don't let me stop you." George backed away.

He believed he saw a twinkle in George's eye. "Of course, Joan. I'd be delighted," Arik lied. He accompanied her to the dance floor and they took their place on the line. Arik watched the smirk on George's face fade as a coed approached him. George and his partner took the floor behind him and Joan.

Sir and Lady Grayson, dressed in period costume, stood in the middle of the dance floor. They gave a modicum of instructions and a brief demonstration.

"Very well done. We're ready to begin. I will call out the steps for you. Lady Grayson and I will be available should you get lost along the way. Mr. Lacey, you can begin."

Alf started to play. The ebb and flow of the crescendos created elegant music. He had to steer Joan clear of some near disasters. Some of the students were confused and Arik swore they didn't know their right foot from their left. Others couldn't maintain the beat even though Alf and his minstrels played it heavily.

He easily led Joan through the forms, keeping her in step and in time. She followed his lead well. He caught Rebeka's eye but made no move. He wouldn't hurt Joan's feelings. He had to admit she was a good partner and found he enjoyed the dance.

"Well, Lord Arik, you seem to be the best on the dance floor," Lord Grayson said. "You not only look the part of the lord but you dance the part as well. My lady." Grayson nodded at him and Joan then moved on.

The music over, he escorted Joan off the dance floor toward the bar. "Thank you, m'lady." He brushed his lips across her knuckles. "You dance well."

Her eyes wide at his gesture, she stammered her response. "Thank you, m'lord." She bobbed a clumsy curtsy. "You made it very easy. You just put me where I was supposed to be." She turned at the sound of her name and waved to one of the other women. "I've got to go. Thanks again for the dance." She was gone before he could say another word. He glanced across the room but Rebeka's table was empty. He quickly scanned the room but didn't find her. He was annoyed he'd lost sight of her.

"A beer, please." Alf stood next to him at the bar. "You were better than the dance master." Alf lifted the bottle in a toast to Arik.

Arik nodded his thanks. He took a seat and stared out across the room.

"I'm Alf Lacey. You must be Lord Arik."

He looked at the man and saw more than a musician. "Any relation to Hughes, Swift and Lacey?"

"Guilty. I'm Alfred Lacey, barrister by day, minstrel leader by night. I've been helping George with the National Trust."

"I see you two have met." George returned from the dance floor and stood next to them. "We'll be starting the singing soon. It's great fun."

Arik rose from his stool when he saw his opportunity and spotted Rebeka across the room. "You'll excuse me." He took two glasses of wine from a passing tray and crossed the floor.

"Drink with me, m'lady." It was a command, not a question. He handed Rebeka a glass.

"Thank you." She took a sip.

"To hearth and home." He watched the shine of her eyes.

"To hearth and home." Her lips tipped up in a smile. "You dance well, m'lord."

He nodded his thanks. "I didn't see you on the dance floor." She seemed in better spirits than when she'd left the library. He speculated if it had anything to do with Cora's "girl talk" or the other empty wineglass on the table. "Do you dance?"

"I was watching you dance. I know Joan doesn't know the steps but she did them well. I have to think it was your leading. And," she said frankly, "you dance with grace."

The music started again. He took her glass and put it on the table with his then held out his hand in a silent request.

"This is an advanced dance." Lady Grayson stood in the center of the room. "The Volta. It scandalized Queen Elizabeth when she danced it with her Robert Dudley. It was the first dance where partners were close to each other. The pattern consists of intricate steps and lifts. Scandalous." A mild laugh rippled through the room.

"I should go back. We have such little time." Rebeka stared at his offered hand then at him. He said nothing, but he didn't have to. His eyes said it all. He held her gaze a bit longer and she took his hand. They made their way through the crowd to the empty dance floor. He rubbed his thumb over the soft skin of her wrist and felt her quickened pulse. The intimate touch soothed her as much as it enflamed him. He waited to see if she would pull her hand away, already determined not to let her go, but her hand didn't move and his spirits soared.

There were three other couples on the dance floor but as the music progressed they all gave way to Arik and Rebeka. He had danced the Volta with her at the harvest festival only a few months ago. The feel of her in his arms and the fragrance of lavender and rose that surrounded her were intoxicating.

With the next spin and lift, Rebeka broke the pattern and put her hands on both his shoulders. He took full advantage and easily lifted her higher into the air to everyone's gasp. He held her and slowly turned. Her head tilted toward him made her hair cascade around them like a dark veil.

It was only the two of them.

Slowly he lowered her to her feet, sliding her against his body, shivering from sweet torture. He brought her to the next position and continued the dance, keeping time with the music. *Faith*. He ached to put his arms around her, to crush her lips with his. His step almost faltered when he looked into her eyes and saw something vaguely sensuous.

With the dance finally over, they bowed to each other and left the dance floor. He led her directly to the terrace for some fresh air and closed the doors behind him to stop anyone from following them. The cool night was refreshing after the closeness of the room and exertion of the dance.

"Sometimes I feel I don't belong here. It's a strange but strong feeling." Her voice was a low whisper. His heart thundered. Did she remember?

Another crack in the enchantment. Soon, she would be back to him. Soon.

He took her to the far side of the terrace and would have gone father if the railing wasn't there, all the way to the seventeenth century.

Instead, he took her in his arms. Through his shirt her hands were warm on his chest. He tilted her face toward him. The passion in her eyes drove him on.

He covered her lips with his. His blood pounded and his body hardened. He brushed her hair away from her face and crushed its soft silkiness in his hand before he caressed her head. Her lips parted and he took full advantage, tenderly sweeping in and tasting the wine still on her breath.

You are mine, echoed in his head. *Do you hear me? You are mine as much as I am yours.* He knew she couldn't hear him but he needed to tell her.

Her hands snaked around him, holding him around his waist. She pulled her head away and looked at him.

"Arik?" she whispered. "Please don't be a dream. Please be real." Her haunted voice tore at him.

"Beka?" He searched her face, the spark of recognition bright in her eyes. "I'm here. I've come to take you home."

The terrace doors opened, startling them. She stepped out of his arms and shuddered.

Marle and John spilled out onto the terrace searching for a private spot. He wheeled around ready to pummel the intruders but was hit with a sweet, pungent metallic odor, a roll of thunder in the distance. He looked in her eyes and knew her memory was already retreating. A raw grief washed over him. She was gone before he could tell her he loved her.

In the distance he watched the lightning dance. Bran. He put his arm around her and drew her close. She shivered and snuggled closer.

"We better go back inside. You're cold." He took her hand and once again made soft circles on her wrist as they headed back into the room. Little by little he watched the confusion return and his heart ached for her and for him.

She entered the room by his side, light-headed and fuzzy. The loud music and the pungent aroma of food were familiar. Arik held her tenderly but close. The feel of him next to her—that, too, was familiar. She wondered if he knew that his strong arms were all that was holding her together as they circled the room greeting everyone.

The fuzziness faded and voices cleared. Her step faltered but he was there to steady her. He held her gently and she was content being with him.

She saw a different side of the man. He wasn't the

righteous, commanding man she'd believed he was. Here he was charming and playful. There was a magnetism about him that excited her. His witty comments made her laugh, his smile was inviting and his kisses made her heart stop.

But his touch, his taste, his voice were familiar, even dear to her, which made no sense. No sense at all.

CHAPTER TWELVE

"The plan is good. It's authentic to the seventeenth-century approach. We can use it as—what would Dr. Tyler call it?—an educational experience. Bill, can you, Frank and the men from the Corps of Engineers, manage the repairs?" Arik was wide awake last night. It took him hours to get to sleep. He kept reliving the brief moment she remembered him. He was certain it was because she was surrounded with the past.

Arik took a seat with the men at the gatehouse table. They were good men and had rallied to his request. They would be a strong team once they bonded. He was aware that would take time. They needed a common cause. The mill repair would serve multiple purposes.

"I'm pleased with the mill renovation work plan Bill and Frank presented. I'd like to get started."

"Yes, sir. But why do you want to fix the mill?" Bill asked.

"To grind grain; that's what the building is for." Arik leaned forward, making himself part of their circle. "Now visitors see the shell of a building and are lectured *to* about its use. Seeing the building in action will give them a finer understanding of the millworks and the manpower needed to run it, to say nothing of the quality of the flour it creates." Four hundred years ago, his miller's flour was highly sought after. People came from Avebury and beyond to buy it. Alfred's flour was one of the manor's best revenue sources. Merchandising the flour had been Bran's idea. It would work here, too.

Bill and Frank nodded to the major. "Instead of a lecture about the building, they'll experience it. Am I right?" the major asked.

"Yes, Major." Arik folded the papers and stacked them. "I'll let you know as soon as the materials arrive." He stood, a signal the meeting was over.

"Yes, sir." The men rose.

George entered the gatehouse and acknowledged the men as they left. "What will the visitors experience?"

"The major and I surveyed the old mill. Bill and Frank assure me with our backs to it we can repair it and have it functioning." George didn't flatly reject the idea. Arik was encouraged. The men had crafted a sturdy plan; all he had to do was convince George.

"The materials will be costly." George took a seat. Arik typed into his tablet.

"Here's what I propose. In order for the manor to make a profit, the reenactment needs to be authentic and exciting. Only the staff can drive that. I think we're in a unique position. I researched old mills—there are several in the area but none are functioning, or if they are, it's only minimally. We can mill the grain we grow and sell the food we make with it." He pointed to his tablet's screen and gave George the major's report.

"What?" On the screen was a map of the area that indicated the location of various mills. All had a red x through them. "None of these are functioning?" George asked.

"No. You can't enter most of the buildings, only look at them from behind a barrier." Arik laid out his strategy like a battle plan. "The parkland is rich soil for grain and produces a good yield. We plow the parkland and return it to farmland. We grow grain."

"For the mill." George's voice rose in surprise.

"Exactly. We bring the manor back to the way it functioned in the seventeenth century." He leaned back in his seat and watched the idea take hold in George's mind.

"Go on, I'm listening." With George's support he was certain Rebeka would agree to the plan.

"I want to make it a total experience for Rebeka…and the visitors."

"So, the mill plan is secondary to this primary objective." He was losing George.

"I hope immersing her in the seventeenth century will help break the enchantment, yes, but that's not the only reason. At my manor, the income came from the flour we milled and the herbs and vegetables we gathered."

"We have large stores that provide a wide variety of flour and baked goods. We can't compete with that," George said. Arik took a breath. The men had considered that and put it into their plan.

"No, but we tie the flour and herbs to an educational experience. The men have a list of items they think people would purchase, all related to the mill and herb garden instead of the meaningless items we're selling now."

"I see your reasoning but we've investigated restoring the mill. The cost is prohibitive."

He took coins from pocket. "Will this help?" He gave George three gold James I Unite coins. The coins were valuable in his time and if history was any indication, their value had only increased. He'd made a smart move bringing the coins with him. To think he was going to leave the pouch behind.

George took the gold pieces. "I should say so.

More than enough. Although I'm not a coin collector I do know the value of James I Unite coins and these are in excellent condition." George hefted the coins. "Have you mentioned restoring the mill to Rebeka?"

"No."

"I'm going to see her now. Let me mention this to her. We've spoken about the mill before and decided against it for cost reasons."

Arik leaned back, satisfied. Taking away the financial concerns, he hoped she'd see the merit to his plan.

"George, we came to the conclusion some time ago that restoring the mill was beyond our budget. You were the one who told me it would cost too much." She dug in her heels. What was Arik thinking? Had he any idea how much repairs would cost? "I can't talk about this now. Louise is due here any minute." The sound of laughter in the hall caught their attention.

"Thank you for the invitation, Louise. Perhaps another time," Arik said as he held the library door open for her, a long case in his hand.

"I think you can hold an audience's attention." She put her hand on his chest. "You can put the case anywhere." Louise reluctantly removed her hand. He gave her a dazzling smile and put the case on the table.

Puh-lease. Don't swell his head any more than it already is.

Rebeka did a slow burn watching the two. The man was already much too arrogant. She fixed what she hoped was a pleasant smile on her face. "Hello, Louise."

"Hello, Rebeka. George, you must convince Arik to attend the Trust's annual meeting. It would be wonderful for Lord Arik to give the Fayne Manor report. I'm certain he'd be a sensation." What was

Louise thinking? She was the lead contact for this project with the Trust, not the bulky brute playing Lord Arik. Louise hadn't asked her to do a presentation to the Trust.

Louise joined the others at the table and took a seat. "The documents George gave me are in the process of being authenticated. Even if we validate their legitimacy, without substantiating evidence there is a possibility that the Trust still may consider the story a legend. You know how tedious they can be. Cross every *t* and dot every *i*." Actually, she had worked with the Trust on other occasions and they had accepted much less in the line of substantiating evidence. They were quite aware that old documents can be lost over time.

"Yes, we're aware. We've put more resources to finding the proclamation." Rebeka knew what needed to be done. Louise didn't say that the documents weren't accepted but she'd best go on the assumption they weren't. That meant she had thirty days and counting.

She had her students help her organize the library and had gone through almost every document prior to the year 1200. So far there was no proclamation or any references to one. She'd have all the target documents done in another week and a half, two at the most. That would leave her about fifteen days. At least she didn't mention the reenactment—yet.

"I had planned this to be so much more exciting."

Rebeka had no idea what Louise was talking about and from the blank stares on George's and Arik's faces, neither did they.

"I commissioned this before there were any questions about the manor. It arrived yesterday." Louise turned to Arik. "I've brought Lord Arik a gift— to use in the reenactment." What was going on? She'd have to speak to Louise and remind her who she was to deal with. Arik was the hired help. Rebeka was the lady of the manor.

Louise's eyes were bright with excitement as she opened the case Arik had carried in. The Trust representative stood possessively close to Arik. He actually stepped closer to Louise. Rebeka was sure it was to see what was in the case but for heaven's sake, he was encouraging the woman. But from his smile that didn't quite reach his eyes, he wasn't enjoying it. Still, she was annoyed—with both of them.

"We had this made based on the portrait. If you're playing Lord Arik I felt…I mean *we* felt you should dress the part." Louise pulled a sword from the case and gave it to Arik.

Rebeka's irritation subsided once she noted the reverence on his face as he accepted the blade. His large hand easily managed the broad sword with respect, confidence and a gentle lover's touch.

He turned the weapon over and showed everyone the fine etching and metal work on the caged knuckle guard.

"The sword is the thing legends are made of." Louise's eyes moved from Arik to the weapon. "What do you know about it?" Louise asked.

"You're correct. The sword continues the story. It's the combination of Alfred the Great and Mannis's blades." Rebeka swore he looked at the sword as if it were an old friend.

"Alfred the Great wanted to commemorate the joining of their forces. He owed Mannis a great deal. Without him they wouldn't have won." Rebeka didn't know what to think. Either Arik was a very good actor or he believed that the story was true. It was a wonderful story of loyalty and heroism but there was nothing to corroborate it. She wanted to believe the tale was true, not only because of her family connection but because he believed it so strongly.

"A man's sword is very sacred to him. It's a symbol of his authority. He wears it for all to see. Mannis wanted to make certain everyone knew to whom he gave his allegiance." Arik held the sword high. "He gave his sword to Alfred. Mannis's intention was not lost on the king, who knew he needed to leave a leader everyone respected, one who had his endorsement. He had his sword smith combine the two swords to honor the joining of their forces and declared Mannis the hero of the battle. Then he gave Mannis the title Knight of Rapture. At the ceremony Alfred presented him with the new blade, the Sword of Rapture, explaining one blade represented strength and the other knowledge. After Mannis's death, the blade and the title were given to each successive Grand Master as a reminder of the covenant between Alfred and Mannis.

"Now there's only one blade." He turned the weapon over, exposing the empty place where the missing blade belonged. "It's been lost for centuries."

Louise handed Arik the scabbard and belt.

He slipped them on. "Thank you, Louise. You do me a great honor. I will take good care of them."

Louise's obvious excitement annoyed Rebeka. Arik was too enraptured with the sword. It was beautiful but totally out of place. The sword was a gift to Fayne Manor, not him. Rebeka didn't appreciate it.

She was horrified—no, she was scratch-your-eyes-out angry—when Louise tried to kiss Arik. At least he had the sense to give her his cheek.

But Louise boldly took hold of his face and kissed him on the lips.

"Really, Louise?" She didn't know what she had in her hand but it flew across the table.

"Oh please, Rebeka, don't tell me you didn't want to do the same thing," Louise whispered to her. "Every woman who comes to the manor leaves speaking of our Lord Arik." Louise straightened, patted Rebeka's hand and gave her a knowing smile. "I'll need to know about the proclamation as soon as possible. Now, where do you want to exercise today? In the ballroom or outside by the lake?"

"The ballroom will be fine." She and Louise rose to leave.

"Come, I've just the place to watch them. They're both quite good," George said to Arik.

Arik and George watched from the minstrel gallery. The two women, appearing comfortable in their exercise clothes, stood next to each other in the center of the empty ballroom. They easily flourished their six-foot staffs in front of them, progressed to a figure eight and finished by tucking their weapons under their arms.

They held their staffs in neutral in front of them with their feet comfortably apart. They raised their arms in salute and took their starting position.

Arik watched as they progressed through the set of basic moves, fighting an imaginary opponent in synchronized precision. They stepped forward with each pair of overhead strikes. They repositioned their hands and initiated the set of side moves, progressed from center to lower strikes and finally to lunges. They barely stopped before they repeated the forms from the beginning. The weapons flashed with increasing speed with each set. The room was quiet except for the whisper of their staffs as they whistled through the air.

From his high vantage point, images of her fighting imaginary enemies with him, Logan and Marcus came to mind. Her movements had been smooth then, but now she executed them with beauty and grace.

She was a fierce warrior. *Faith*, she had proven it

more than once. At the Stone River, when Doward delivered the unknown woman to him, they had been ambushed. He had been astounded when he watched her fight. She had more than held her own standing with Logan protecting Doward.

His warrior wife had been fearless.

"You're not surprised at how she fights?" George whispered.

"No. Rebeka instructed Logan, Marcus and me. We practiced together often." He itched to be next to her and in that quiet, controlled place where body and mind were one. Logan had insisted they continue their practice after she was gone but it had lost its meaning for him.

"She practices every day. She told me she imagined someone next to her." George continued watching the women. "I liked to think it was you. I'm glad I was right."

He glanced at George, who kept his eyes on the training below, and saw the man's satisfied smile. But his heart pounded at his words. She may not remember him, but he was a part of her.

The women finished with their warm-up. They faced each other and repeated the exercise, taking turns at being the aggressor. From there they progressed to free-form fighting.

The quiet room exploded with the sound of the staffs colliding against each other and the floor.

Louise held nothing back. He winced at the hard hits she landed. The woman set upon Rebeka with a barrage of strikes, advancing and moving Rebeka into a corner where she had little room to maneuver.

Rebeka appeared to pull up her staff. Louise spun with *her* staff and caught Rebeka in the shoulder.

The sound of the hit echoed in the room.

"Hold," Arik commanded. Both women stopped mid-strike.

Arik hurdled over the balcony railing, landing lightly on his feet. He closed in on Louise.

Like a stalking lion he approached her. Her shocked expression didn't faze him. Fear. He could smell it and it gave him satisfaction. She dropped her staff and peeled away the shoulder of Rebeka's exercise shirt, revealing a large red welt. "I didn't think I struck you so hard. This is going to bruise badly. You'd better get some ice on it right away." Rebeka tentatively touched the welt and grimaced. She grabbed her arm and cradled it close to her body.

George burst through the ballroom door. Arik's eyes locked on Rebeka's as she leaned against the wall. He pulled George back when George started to help her. Louise didn't make a move. He'd suspected Louise's friendship was false. He wanted to take Rebeka's staff and have a match with Louise she wouldn't soon forget.

Rebeka pushed herself off the wall and stood on her own. He relaxed.

"That's enough for today," Arik said, leaving no room for discussion.

"I'll go change and meet you in the library. I'll send Helen for some ice." Louise quickly left.

Arik took her staff. She didn't appear badly hurt. "Do you need help or can you manage on your own?"

"I can manage." She walked into the library between Arik and George. As she settled on the sofa Helen came in with an ice pack.

"Why did you stop?" He placed the ice pack on her shoulder as she tried to get more comfortable.

"I thought she said to hold. I must've been mistaken." He found that interesting. He had the same notion.

Louise, now in her business clothes, hurried into the room. "Before I leave I wanted you to know that at last night's Board meeting there was some mention of the Fayne Manor trust fund. I don't know anything about it." She held up her hand to ward off questions. "The Board isn't letting me in on this discussion, and I don't know what's driving it. But I would try to find the proclamation as soon as possible."

Rebeka's breath caught and she bolted up. "I…I don't understand."

"Why didn't you mention this before?" Arik's tone demanded a reply.

If Louise was surprised at his outburst she didn't show it. Instead she laid her hand on his arm and let it linger. "I didn't want to spoil practicing with Rebeka." She put on a sincere face but her lying words didn't pass his scrutiny. "This is out of my hands. All I can do is stall them from taking action, but not for long."

He put his hand over Louise's. "It takes time to methodically research in a library of this size." He softened his voice but not his determination.

Rebeka flashed him a cold stare. "Excuse me, Louise."

With a reluctant sigh Louise turned to Rebeka.

"I don't think Arik—"

"Louise." George stood behind Rebeka and put his hand on her good shoulder. "How long before the Trust will take action?" He was glad George understood that he didn't want any bickering. Louise had played Rebeka's friend but if he had his doubts before, they were confirmed now.

"I don't know, two weeks, three at the most." Louise stopped fussing with her things. "You know I'll do anything I can." The sincere expression on her face didn't match the oddly hollow tone in her voice.

"That's all we need." Arik gave Louise an encouraging smile. If she knew him better she would have known how dangerous it really was. Arik saw through her veneer. This was more than a flirtatious woman. This woman had a purpose and it was not in

Rebeka's best interest.

"Please, find the proclamation quickly. Thanks for the practice, Rebeka. I'll see myself out," she said as she left the room.

He and George relaxed as soon as the door closed.

"Two or three weeks. It will take that long to finish going through the library. No one I contacted about the missing estate papers has found any information. I'm beginning to think they were destroyed." She turned to George. "Why didn't you let me finish? Arik is not in control here."

"No, I'm not, but you had been through one battle already." It didn't take a seasoned warrior to identify a defensive fighter. He knew it wasn't Rebeka's style. "Is she always on the offensive when you spar?"

Her brows knit together. "She's upped her game. But I *know* she called a stop to the match." She hadn't answered his question but he decided not to press the issue.

George read the financial papers Louise had given him. "I'll have my office review these. We created the trust fund. I can't imagine what issues they're having. It's been running without any problems for three years."

"What if they hold our funds? We'll be ruined," Rebeka said.

Arik gave George a small nod.

"There's a new benefactor who's pledged money for the restoration of the mill and some of the other areas. With what he's provided, we'll be fine for a while."

She straightened quickly and winced. "Who?" She repositioned the ice pack. Standing behind Rebeka, Arik shook his head.

"The benefactor prefers to remain anonymous—at least for now. He's giving us the funds on the condition the mill is restored." He glanced at the papers. "After hearing what Louise said, I'll open a separate account for the restoration. I have funds I'll put into the account."

"Renovating the mill has great educational potential. I believed it was a good idea when we first discussed it. Please thank our benefactor. I have some funds. George, if you and Mr. Anonymous are investing in my dream, I should have some skin in the game, too." She repositioned the ice pack. "We should give our enterprise a name."

"How about Rapture Revived?" George said.

"Rebeka. Ian Sloan here."

"Ian. Good to hear your voice." She rummaged through the papers on her desk to find the folder with Ian's name. "Thank you for returning my call." It had been ages since she last spoke to him. He was a professor at Oxford's Centre for Medieval and Renaissance Studies. She first met Ian when they had collaborated on several papers while they were both working on their doctorates. She still got an occasional query from other scholars about their work.

"I'm sorry you had to cancel your trip to Oxford. I was looking forward to seeing you." Something in his voice made her stop. Did he think she wanted to rekindle their relationship? Or was he joking? Today was April first, April Fool's Day. Their relationship was years ago when they published together. It wasn't anything lasting, they both knew that. Still, she had an uncomfortable feeling.

"Yes, it would have been good to reconnect." She found the folder. It had the document clipped with Ian's and also Arik's translations. She took the clip off the papers and set the translations next to each other. "Thank you again for the translation. I know your expertise is medieval myths and folktales, not legal documents, but with your understanding of runes and old languages your name is at the top of my list."

"It wasn't any trouble. It did look promising. Too bad it turned out to be nothing." His offhanded manner irritated her.

"Yes, I read your report." She hesitated. Questioning and discussing nuances in translations was nothing new, but this was different. She was questioning his entire analysis. "I've been given another translation—a much different interpretation." She held her breath.

"Rebeka, I understand interpreting runes is more an art than science but I assure you what I've given you is sound." His I'm-right-you're-wrong tone set her teeth on edge. "Your letter that accompanied the document gave me a very clear picture of the document's importance. I know how much you want this all to work but trust me, there's nothing there." She concentrated on the paper clip, her forefinger jockeyed around the desktop.

There was a single tap on the door. She looked and saw Arik enter carrying some papers. She motioned for him to take a seat. She'd known Ian for years, worked with him, yet she was willing to bet her life on Arik's translation. Her nervousness eased.

Instead of taking a seat, Arik stood at her side and read the papers he had in his hand.

"Ian, I have a meeting. Before I go, I think you may have overlooked some important items—where and when the document was written. Please take another look at what I sent you." She worked the wire paperclip, bending it out of shape.

"Of course, but I really don't think my opinion will change." She had no trouble translating what he said.

He had no intention of reviewing his translation.

He was going to let it stand. There was no use continuing the call.

"Thanks, Ian. I'll speak to you later in the week." She ended the call and hoped she was wrong. If he reviewed it with an open mind...well, she didn't think that was going to happen.

She'd have to think of another resource—a greater authority.

She reclipped the page as best she could with the deformed metal wire and picked up another set of documents.

"I reviewed the plans for the mill. They're very complete." The tremor in her hand concerned Arik. Had she more bad news from the Trust? He didn't know how much more stress she could take.

He kept reading, immersed in the documents. "Yes, we have a man who was involved in an old mill renovation. We've gotten the benefit of his frustrations. He's provided us lists of tradesmen as well as where to go for supplies. Some of the tradesmen want to be part of the project. George is negotiating the contract." He put the papers aside.

"George told me you wanted to farm the parkland." He caught the irritation in her voice and speculated if it was spurred by her previous call or the plans.

He moved to the front of the desk. "We need something to mill. Rather than buy grain, we'll buy seed. Some of your students are interested in historic agriculture and agrarian economics. They're quite bright and have put together a well thought out proposal that will make the manor self-sufficient. Their plan starts with growing wheat and goes to baking bread. There's nothing like the smell of freshly baked bread. Wouldn't you agree?"

"The manor can't live on bread alone." That caught his attention. A brief smile brightened her face. So she was creative in quoting the Bible. It was good to see her smile.

"No, certainly not. The plan is to cultivate and sell herbs and vegetables. The income will supplement the receipts from the entrance fees and other souvenirs."

"You seem to have it all planned. Do you always take over?" Take over? *Lead*, he wanted to tell her. If she stopped worrying about him taking over she might remember that he and George had already discussed this with her.

Was she losing other memories? The idea made him uneasy. No, he was certain it was her drive to do it all herself that made her forgetful.

"The original idea to renovate the mill was yours. Your students developed the idea. Guests will participate wherever they can alongside instructors and tradesmen."

"A hands-on experience. I hadn't considered that. But you didn't answer my question. Do you always take over?" He remained silent. He walked behind her desk and lowered his mouth close to her ear. "I'm not taking over. I'm saving your ass." His words were deadly serious, his voice low and confident. He smiled when he saw the flush run up her neck and she stretched toward him ever so slightly. He didn't know who he teased more—himself or her. "Do you have a better idea?" He pulled away from her. He had made his point. Besides, being that close made him want her more.

"No. It's not that it's a bad idea—"

"It's about control. Each of us has our skills. Mine is running a manor such as this."

"Mine is teaching. I've built the project into our master's class curriculum. One of the architectural students will give a lecture on the mill and another will speak on the economics of the agrarian society prior to the Renaissance, the Age of Enlightenment." She paused briefly. "On a different subject, Dr. Sloan—the expert who read the document you translated—stands by his interpretation. The runes say nothing significant." Arik didn't outwardly flinch. So that's what got her so out of sorts.

Was she going to take someone else's word over his?

"Arik, you're an amateur at this. To you, it's simply a game. To me, it's my life." He knew exactly what was at stake. Better than she did. "You don't know anything about the scientific method for research." She leaned back in her chair, her hands resting on its arms. He swiveled her chair so she faced him and stood in front of her with his chest puffed out and his hands on his hips.

"It seems *you* are the one who is the amateur. You know nothing of history but odd facts, not their meaning or their impact. You see history through your time, your century, and apply your meaning."

He bent closer with both his hands grasping the arms of her chair, holding her captive and invading her space. He left her no room to see anything other than the purpose in his eyes. "It's a chess game, Rebeka. You have to examine it from—"

"All angles," she whispered. Her breath caught at the words. He felt the blood drain from his face. Would she remember him? Break through the enchantment completely?

"If you see it only from your perspective you will surely miss the meaning." He pulled himself away. He waited and watched but her eyes held no recognition. "If you'll excuse me."

Disappointed, he left by the terrace door. He trotted down the steps and into the garden. How much more could he stand of watching her almost remember or remembering a little, only to have it lost? He glanced back at the manor. Was this Bran's plan? *This is torture.* He told her he would find her. He meant mind and body.

She closed her eyes. The loss of his closeness left her bereft. *All angles* ricocheted in her head, along with the tap of his boots against the slate floor as he'd retreated across the terrace. From the expression in his face she was afraid he wouldn't come back.

Visions of large chess pieces flashed in front of her and a young girl's voice. Was it her own? No, it wasn't.

Angles—it was a lesson she'd learned a long time ago but couldn't place where or when.

She knew Arik was right. She hadn't examined the problem from every angle. She'd accepted the easy answer without investigating it further. She rested her head in her hands. The translation, the mill, Arik— everything was swimming together. Nothing made sense. Concentrate. She opened her eyes, hoping he was still there.

She hurt from disappointing him.

Another notion that made no sense.

She pulled herself out of her chair and collected her things. Arik was right. She hated blind acceptance in others. There was no way to condone it in herself. She had planned to search a few more places for the proclamation tonight but she was drained and needed some sleep.

She collected what she needed, but what she needed was a miracle, a proclamation. She glanced out the terrace door. She needed to tell him she was sorry. One step at a time, that's what she told herself. Everyone would have to settle for the best she could do. Before she walked out the door, she looked at the picture above the mantel.

"Forgive me," she whispered.

CHAPTER THIRTEEN

"Good afternoon, ladies," Arik acknowledged the female guests he passed across from the barn.

"Lord Arik, I have a question." He stopped and gave one of the women his attention. "Yes, m'lady?" He patiently answered their questions. Yes, it was a long and arduous task to become a knight. No, he hadn't killed anyone recently but he was looking forward to it. Yes, it was difficult to run a large household. Screw damsels? Some concepts defied the centuries. *No, I don't fuck damsels. Although one does come to mind that I have every intention of...*

"If you will excuse me." He gave them a short bow. They should be whipped for their wicked mouths. They wanted to embarrass him. He smirked; it was their faces that were red. He joined the men.

It had been three days since they'd discussed the restoring of the mill and the men had started cleaning it out. His coin appeared to move mountains, according to George, at least. The supplies started arriving yesterday thanks to Bill's contacts.

"That's great, Arik. You pass anything in a skirt and she's ready to raise it for you. I've been working on the one in the yellow sweater all morning. I almost had her." Jaxon, standing with three other soldiers, gestured at the bevy of beauties standing close by.

"Just about had her? You haven't even spoken to her." One of the others let out a well-timed snort. "Had her."

"The ladies want a little attention. You stand here ignoring them. If you changed places with them who would you speak to?" The men looked sheepishly at him.

"It's easier at a pub. You buy them an ale, you make conversation. Here, what do you do? What do you say?" The men nodded their agreement with Jaxon.

Arik glanced past them. The women had moved and were stretching their necks to see what the men were doing.

Arik pointed to one of the men. "Go tell the ladies to stand back a bit, by the water barrel. Tell them they've come in time to watch the wrestling match."

"What wrestling match? Who's wrestling?" They looked at each other in confusion.

He turned to Jaxon. "You and me."

"Quick, you've got to see this," one of the students yelled as he ran past the open classroom window. "At the barn," he shouted over his shoulder.

The garrison was empty within minutes. Rebeka grabbed her staff and followed the stampede. When she arrived at the barn, the crowd was so thick she had to force her way to the front. "What's going on?"

One of her students leaned toward her and pointed to the two men wrestling. "So far Jaxon hasn't been able to get Lord Arik on the ground, no matter what he tries. I'd have my money on Lord Arik, if I was betting." He focused his attention back on the wrestlers.

"Me, too," Rebeka said. She watched and shouted

her encouragement with the others before she retrieved Arik's things by the fence where she enjoyed a ringside seat. There was something familiar in the dance.

The startling déjà vu feeling tingled as it crept up her back.

She could predict Arik's graceful movements. They flowed from one hold to another. Had she seen this all before? That's wasn't possible.

Finally, without a winner, the men ended the match with a handshake. The crowd applauded and screamed their enthusiasm. Arik spoke to Jaxon, who gave him a wry smile. Jaxon ambled over to the water barrel.

The woman in the yellow sweater gave the overheated Jaxon a cup of water. He gave her a thankful nod and while his eyes held hers, he poured the cup over his head—to her delight. His T-shirt stuck to him and outlined his well-defined body. The soldier lazily took off the wet shirt, showing off his well-ripped abs and washboard stomach. His biceps, knotted from the exertion, rippled when the woman placed her hand tentatively on it. With her eyes focused on him she gave him another cup of water. This one he drank. She found herself breathing a bit heavily. Jaxon certainly gave the ladies a good show.

Rebeka saw all their guests were engaged with the soldiers. She pulled her attention back to Arik. His black T-shirt was wet with sweat and clung to him like a second skin.

"You could use a splash of water yourself." Rebeka came toward him and handed him his things. She bit her bottom lip, trying to quiet her body.

She wanted him—all over her.

"Yes, I could. The exercise felt good." He took his things from her.

"Perhaps a dip in the lake..." Her voice trailed off as she peered in the direction of Elfrida's cottage.

"Stuart, he wouldn't wrestle…" Her voice was soft and distant. There was a quizzical expression on her face.

"Who is Stuart?" She stared at him, disoriented. She knew the name but couldn't place the face. It was just out of sight.

"Stuart and his family owned Autumn Chase in this period. Perhaps you saw his name in some research." No, she didn't see it in any research. It was someone she knew. Dammit, she couldn't place who it was.

"Arik." Her voice was hesitant. She rested her hand on his chest and felt his pounding heart. He was real.

"Arik," she said confidently. The hard lines of his face softened. She was free, not locked in the room at Skara Brae. But already the mist was pulling her back.

"Don't give up on me." His face brightened. "I love—"

"Dr. Tyler. Dr. Tyler." She glanced past him. Marle was waving as she rushed toward them. A cold chill ran up her spine, ending in a quick, stabbing pain in her head.

Something had been familiar but the idea was lost.

She stared at Arik but couldn't put it together. "I'm sorry, I lost my train of thought," she said to him then stepped past him. "Yes, Marle?"

"Ms. Richards is waiting for you with her quarterstaff." She rolled her shoulder. The bruise was still there but not the pain.

She checked her watch. "I forgot." She sniffed the air. "Smells like we're in for a lightning storm." She left without another word.

"What was all the commotion about?" Louise pulled out her quarterstaff.

Rebeka entered the clearing by the lake. "The men had a spur-of-the-moment wrestling match. You should have been there. Arik and Jaxon put on a good show."

Louise swung around. "He did? I would have loved to see that. I could only imagine him all glistening and damp, and those arms of his. How they must look all knotted and strained. Did they strip down to their loincloths?" She laughed, fanning herself with her hand and letting out a deep breath. "Have you ever watched him from behind? He's got the tightest little—"

"Do you want to exercise or do you need a cold shower?" Louise was getting annoying with her Arik talk.

Louise smiled. "I don't know why you insist on denying you're attracted to him. Really, Rebeka, have you taken a good look at him? He's quite the man and he doesn't seem to be only brawn. He has brains, too. I like them smart to a point, then smart is the last thing I want. I prefer to set the pace." With a wink she left Rebeka where she stood and took her stance in the middle of the clearing.

Rebeka ignored her.

She had no intention of telling Louise how the man seemed to seep into all her thoughts, even her dreams. No, the less Louise knew about her and how she felt about Arik, the better. A deep breath and a shake of her shoulders loosened her muscles. Clearing her mind of the brawny brainy guy wasn't as easy. She took her place next to Louise and gave her head and shoulders another shake.

She was set and ready to go. They warmed up with their flourishes. Rebeka eased into the familiar routine and got into her stride.

"I haven't a lot of time today so let's get right to it." Louise set her stance. Rebeka didn't mind; she followed suit.

They held their staffs ready for freestyle and feigned engaging.

"Timid today?" Louise smirked. "Lord Arik doesn't like timid women. I have firsthand knowledge." Her voice dripped with sarcasm. "You would think he likes to be in control. Well, he does, sometimes."

Rebeka stiffened at the idea of Louise with Arik, but she let the comment roll off. She knew Louise's tactic.

The woman's moves were not elegant. Instead she relied on provoking her opponent to break the structured pattern. That was the easy way to fail.

But the image of Louise and Arik played over and over in her mind.

"If you're going to play defensively, then I'll have to start." Louise brought the tip of her staff down for a low attack at Rebeka's legs. Rebeka blocked her. They circled and parried, creating a steady rhythm of attack, block and set up to the beat of their wooden staffs.

Louise double-tapped Rebeka's staff. The break from the rhythm, along with her distracted mind, threw Rebeka off balance. Louise spun, took aim and hit her hard on the back. The strike sent her to the ground in the wet grass along the shore. She rolled a full circle before coming back onto her feet.

"You're not concentrating." Louise advanced. Rebeka blocked and set her staff vertically, with its tip on the ground wedged into her instep. Louise circled and swung at Rebeka's unprotected midsection. But Rebeka spun to the side. When Louise's staff hit hers she kicked up her staff, rotated it with a corkscrew motion and knocked Louise's staff away.

Louise was quick to counter with an overhead attack. Rebeka thrust her staff at Louise but missed.

Louise spun around and hit Rebeka full force in her side.

Rebeka held her staff across her body, her hands at

either end. Louise advanced, striking first from below, and then above. Rebeka blocked the repeated onslaught.

On a downward stroke Louise kicked up dirt.

"Hold," Rebeka called and stopped to clear her eyes.

Her eyes still closed, Rebeka turned in time to see that Louise had taken advantage of the distraction and was about to spear her foot with the end of the staff.

She blocked the attack. Louise knocked the staff from Rebeka's hands.

Rebeka took an aggressive stance and let her instincts take over. She didn't need to see. Her body told her where the threat came from. The dirt still in her eyes, she didn't have to wait long for Louise's next attack. She was ready. The woman charged her staff at waist level. As the staff came within her reach, Rebeka grabbed it and pulled it hard to her right.

The momentum and Rebeka's redirection caused Louise to lose her grip. Now in Rebeka's hand and her eyes still closed, Rebeka swung long and hard, catching Louise behind her knees. As she fell forward, Rebeka wound tight like a spring and released, hitting Louise in the chest. Louise flew backward into the lake, sitting in several inches of water.

At last the dirt cleared from her eyes. Rebeka, breathing hard, bent over with her hands on her thighs and gulped air.

"Louise, you seem to be all wet." Rebeka took her staff. Louise got out of the lake, a surprised expression on her face. "I've got to change for a class. You may need ice for that." She pointed to the bloodred welt that showed through the top of Louise's shirt. "You know the way out," she said over her shoulder as she made her way back toward the manor.

"She remembered. For a moment she remembered." He was with George and Cora at Autumn Chase staring across the sculpted gardens.

Cora put down her cocktail. "Are you certain?"

"I saw the recognition in her eyes. She spoke of Stuart. I'm certain she would have said more but Marle interrupted us and when I searched her eyes again they were vacant."

"You said there were small signs that she recognized you." George offered him a refill. Arik waved him off. "Perhaps you should be closer to her, stay in the manor rather than at the garrison. I'll think of a way to get her to move and have you both under the same roof."

The distant sound of heavy machinery caught Rebeka by surprise. She peered out the manor door and watched as the machines converged on the parkland. *What are they doing?* The noise added to her building headache. The longer she listened to the din the more she gnashed her teeth. Unable to sit still any longer, she charged toward the gate. She was going to get to the bottom of this one way or another.

It wasn't until she got to the tractors ripping up the parkland that she slowed and realized her headache was at full tilt.

Her students were clustered around Arik who seemed to be holding court, giving instructions. More than annoyed, she stomped up to him. "What do you think you're doing?" she shouted over the noise in front of everyone.

She pulled at his arm to turn him around. He didn't budge but rather stood solidly in place and glanced in her direction, giving her a scathing stare. The people around them dispersed quickly.

"I said," she shouted even louder. "What do you think you're doing?"

A long moment ticked past as his gaze seared hers. Three more heartbeats passed before he returned to watching the activity.

"We've harnessed the horses to plow the ground and help with the clearing." Rebeka's very excited historical agriculture student approached Arik holding some papers. "The plan is to plow straight over to the western edge." The student gestured to the far end of the field.

"No. That side of the field is lower than the rest and floods. The seeds will wash away. It's best to stop over there—the area marked by the cypress trees." Arik pointed to the stand of trees short of the western edge. The student nodded and trotted off to instruct the others.

"Who told you to plow this up?" Rebeka paced a small spot wearing out the short grass.

"We discussed it three days ago when you gave Bill and the mason the order for the mill." She rubbed her temples. Her headache cut between her eyes. She had to get a grip on this. Her mind was more jumbled than usual.

"We did not. I clearly remember discussing the parkland but I didn't decide whether to move this forward. I don't like this, Arik. You've come here like you own the place. You don't. I do. No decisions will be made without my direct orders. Do I make myself clear?" Her chin rose in a blatant challenge. She blanched at the dangerous glint that flashed in his eyes but stood her ground.

She'd certainly told him. Now he knew who was in charge.

He wheeled around to her. He made no attempt to hide the storm that brewed underneath. "We ordered the grain when we ordered the items for the millworks.

You placed the order yourself because you wanted to be in control. I am not one of your students, Dr. Tyler, and will not be treated as such. Do I make myself clear? I'm here to do a job and I will do it the best way I know how." He left without waiting for her to respond.

She pulled out her cell phone, dialed George then stomped back to her cottage.

"George, how long do you intend for Arik to stay under my roof?" He had charmed not only the women who visited the manor but now George.

She was breathing hard. She marched up the drive, frustrated and agitated.

"Rebeka, it's not your roof. Technically, it's still the National Trust's roof. At this moment, they can take the bloody roof down if they want." Startled by his verbal attack, she was rigid with shock. He had never spoken a harsh word to her.

When he continued, his voice was calmer. "We can speak about this later. I'm off to court."

She ended her call and shoved her phone into her pocket as she entered her cottage. Nothing seemed to calm her. Perhaps a run would get rid of this pent-up energy.

She jogged over toward the lake, stowed her towel and water bottle by the large boulder. Her eyes focused on the trail that was a natural track around the lake. She did her stretches and lunges. She jogged in place to get in the right frame of mind. The gentle lapping of the lake, the rustling of the trees all had a calming effect but she needed more. She started out with a slow, even gait and increased her pace until it was an all-out sprint, running as if the devil himself were chasing her. After a while her muscles were screaming. She pushed harder to the halfway point then eased back on her stride. She was calmer than she'd been in days.

She had a lot of work to do to prepare for Angus Hamilton, a guest lecturer, who was coming from Oxford tomorrow. That was a coup. He was a guest lecturer and an expert in linguistics. The Trust would recognize his translation. That would work very nicely. Louise was bringing John Blake, a member of the Trust Board to hear the lecture. Angus's work was great but in person he would be more compelling.

Blake. She was certain his primary mission was to see the manor. Receipts hadn't been as good as expected. She needed to put his mind at ease and it had to be something substantial and impressive.

Her mind wandered to the conversation about the seed order. She had ordered seeds rather than harvested grain. She should straighten that out with Arik. Why had she gone off like a madwoman? Was it to cover up the strong desire that drew her like a magnet? Or was it his outstanding knowledge of the seventeenth century?

She stopped. Could it work? She resumed at a trot. Everyone would be in costume when Angus and Blake arrived. She had wanted to show both of them the reenactment and the authenticity they had created. Arik was the most authentic and magnetic personality of the group. If she could get him involved… She needed to think this through.

She saw him ahead by the large boulder with one of the men and jogged over to them.

"It might work. We should be able to drain the water off that lower part of the field into the lake," the engineering student said.

"Good. Add that to the plans and give Mr. Hughes an estimate of the cost." The man made his notes. He and Arik started toward the manor.

She put her hand on his arm. He looked at it, then at her. "You go on ahead. I'll meet you at the field,"

Arik said. The student nodded and continued on the path.

He said nothing, just stood there. She removed her hand, opened her pouch and took out a bottle of water, trying to decide how to begin.

"That's a nasty scar on your leg."

She glanced at the deep scar on her thigh. She hadn't considered it in months. She agreed it was ugly.

"It must have been serious. How did you get it?" She bit the side of her cheek, trying to figure out what was so important about her scar.

"I don't like to speak about it." George and Cora had also questioned her about the mark. She would be more than happy to tell all of them but she had no idea how she got it. "You're right, I did order the seed." She paced in front of him. "I don't know what made me so angry."

He didn't say anything.

She stopped and let out a deep breath. "I'm not myself lately." He turned to leave.

"Wait. Please."

He glanced over his shoulder toward her, his eyes more blue than green, a sign he was in a temper. "For what?" he snapped. She deserved that after making a scene in front of the others. What had she been thinking?

"I don't know what's come over me. One minute I hate you and another I—"

"Yes, I'm quite aware of your feelings. They're of little concern. I'm here to make Fayne Manor as profitable as possible and I will do that whether you hate me or find me agreeable." He had the most compelling blue eyes when he was in a fit. They also pinned you in place. She wanted to look away but she deserved the scolding. She stood straighter and apologized with her eyes, hoping he saw her sincerity.

"Yes, I understand." She took a deep breath.

"I assure you I am not the enemy."

She had the notion his voice was gentler. "No, you're not, but something inside me fights you." Her voice was a whisper. "Perhaps we should start over."

"Perhaps." But she didn't think he meant it. Her head hurt with his indifference. She had no idea when his approval had become so important to her but it had. Without it she was drowning, searching for a safe haven when there was none. "Enjoy your run."

He took her staff and held it out to her. Her touch made the staff glow. She stared at it then at Arik. "The sun must have caught it just right. Or maybe it's a magical sign." Arik's gaze met hers. He remained silent but Rebeka saw the disappointment on his face.

"I was... I didn't mean to offend you," she hurried to add. Hadn't she made things bad enough? He gave her a curt nod and released her staff.

She watched him go back toward the manor.

When would she learn to keep her mouth shut?

CHAPTER FOURTEEN

Rebeka entered the library sipping her third cup of coffee. She was a little out of character. Coffee in a paper cup and a seventeenth-century lady of the manor was incongruous to say the least. She needed to gather the materials for this morning's lecture and the visit from the Trust. They'd be arriving any minute.

On top of her things was a note from George. "Left to get Angus. This came to my office. See you later."

Before she opened the envelope she knew it was Ian's letter about the document she'd asked him to translate.

"Your Pictish must be rusty. True, there isn't much use for the archaic language these days but I still insist you misinterpreted some of the significant words. Here's my translation."

Rebeka read what he sent and wanted to crush the paper. "He's wrong." She threw the paper onto her desk in disgust. She left to meet her students but she couldn't get her mind off the translation. Too much was riding on this document, especially if she couldn't find the proclamation.

Calm down. She spoke to Angus and he was more than happy to review the document and give his opinion. What if Angus's translation supported Ian's? No, that wasn't possible. Perhaps she could let George or Cora host this morning's lecture. They could introduce Angus and she could get back to searching for the proclamation.

Angus would understand her absence. No, she couldn't do that. She hadn't seen him in a long time and was eager to catch up with him. He used to visit with her father at the university in upstate New York. They were old friends.

She got to the gatehouse as Louise and John Blake arrived. She waited patiently as they got out of the car.

"Good morning," Louise said.

Louise slid out of the car with a catlike grace and gave Rebeka a warm welcome, as if their sparring at the lake had never happened. She wished she knew what was going on in Louise's head. She knew the woman hadn't forgotten their match. Time enough for that later.

"You look lovely, Lady Rebeka. You know John Blake. He's on the Trust's Advisory Panel for Learning and Engagement. We were speaking about Sloan's document on the way over." Sloan's document. When did it become Sloan's document? A quick glance at Louise's satisfied grin and she understood. It was payback for dumping her in the lake. That was fine with her. She'd do it to her again in a heartbeat. Excusing herself may be the better move. She didn't know if she could be civil to Louise today.

"Yes, Dr. Tyler. I'd like to speak to you about that but first," Blake said, "thank you for your invitation. I've been eager to see the progress you've made and hear Angus. I understand he'll be speaking today on druids." She was still trying to decide whether George or Cora could stand in for her. She could see Angus when the lecture was over. And as for Blake, she didn't have any time for the man. A cough behind her caught her attention. Arik put his hand on her shoulder. She let out a breath and the tension eased.

Another heartbeat and she was ready to begin.

"We're glad you're able to be with us today. Why don't we go into the garrison?" That wasn't so difficult. She ushered them through the door.

"I see everyone is dressed in period." Blake glanced around with a pleased expression. Two students ushered him and the others to their seats.

"Yes, consider the gate a time portal that transports you back to the seventeenth century," Joan said. "We've put together a presentation document for you with a map of the manor and how we're utilizing the buildings. It also lists the classes in which guests can participate. We're in the process of planning semester-long classes that will be available for both on-site and online students. It's all done in period."

"How clever." Blake's smile was genuine. Joan did an excellent job. Arik had been right to suggest that the students present. "I'd like to discuss Ian Sloan's translation with you," Blake said to Rebeka.

"Well, Mr. Blake, you've come at an opportune time." The idea came to her when Joan mentioned *in period*. She concentrated hard. *Arik, work with me on this.* "Today is Lord Arik's day for settling disputes."

Blake gave out a hearty laugh. "That's very good, Dr. Tyler, but Lord Arik is only an actor. How will he know?" She gave him her most dazzling smile then stood by Arik.

"M'lord, in your capacity as lord of the Fayne Manor we ask that you settle our dispute." She ended with a curtsy. She decided to act the lady with all the deference to her lord as she could. Submissive was not in her blood but if Arik played along, they could do it.

He gave her a smile and a nod of acceptance. "For the lady of the manor, of course. What is the issue?" His commanding tone got everyone's attention. "Dr.

Sloan and I have different interpretations of this Pictish text. We need it resolved."

Arik stood by the table, Mr. Blake in a nearby seat. "What is Dr. Sloan's interpretation?"

"Basically," Blake said, "he believes the document is a list of provisions. Nothing more." Blake held up the paper.

"To some extent he's correct and it wouldn't hold any significance. However, it's what the provisions are for that gives the document its meaning."

"How do you know what it's for? It doesn't say anything." Blake turned the document every which way, showing that there was nothing there. She observed Blake's amused expression become serious. She hoped Arik understood their predicament.

"Do you have a date for the writing?" Arik asked Blake as he examined the document.

"I believe Dr. Sloan estimated about 900 AD."

"I would think the year alone would make this very valuable. However, this is a list for the siege of Chippenham by Alfred the Great and Mannis."

The man looked at him, a dubious expression on his face. "That's absurd. How can you know that from this scrap?" Blake's astonished expression didn't faze Arik, nor did it faze her. She surveyed the room. He was a magician. He'd captured everyone's attention and held them spellbound, her included.

"Look at the items, the references, where it was found and the date."

Blake glanced from Arik, to Rebeka, then to Louise. Rebeka let herself relax. The issue wasn't settled but at least Blake was listening and hadn't dismissed it. She took a big chance bringing Arik in like this but her instincts were right. It was working.

"Let me clarify a few points," she added. "Dr. Sloan said it was from about 900 AD. That puts it around Alfred the Great. There is a notation, 'King's

Lodge,' in the upper-right corner. We found it among the estate papers."

"We know Chippenham is the location of Alfred the Great's hunting lodge," Blake added, a light of recognition in his eyes.

She wasn't certain if Arik maintained his serious attitude for effect but he studied the document carefully. "The items listed include arbalest, ladders, hooks, rope and timber. All these materials would be important for a siege."

Blake gave it serious consideration. She watched him weigh what Arik said. "Rope and timber? They could be used for anything." Blake's matter-of-fact voice challenged Arik's words.

Arik raised his head from the paper, a thoughtful expression on his face. "If the arbalest wasn't listed I would agree with you." He paused then leaned forward. "But it is and that's what changes everything." His finger tapped the document. "An arbalest is a crossbow specifically used for sieges. That puts the rest of the items into the perspective of a siege."

Another strategic pause. "Rope and timber are the materials for building siege engines. Ladders and hooks are devices used when scaling the wall and attacking. Put those facts together with the date and reference in the upper corner and I think it becomes very clear what this list represents." Finished, he laid his hands over each other on the table and waited for Blake to speak.

"It doesn't say siege hooks and siege ladder, if that is what they are," continued Blake.

In her opinion, Arik had already won this battle based on his hard facts. "Historians labeled them siege hooks and siege ladders for their own purposes," Rebeka said. "People of the time called them hooks and ladders. You must examine things in the context of their century and not with your twenty-first-century eye." She blatantly repeated the lesson she'd learned from Arik.

Blake glanced at both of them. "Your argument is very compelling." He smiled and got to his feet. "I see how you've managed this project, not with actors but rather with authorities. I like this approach." He turned to Rebeka. "Well done. But we'll need a third opinion for the document. One that's unbiased."

"I've asked Angus for his opinion," Rebeka said.

"Excellent."

"John, let me show you the museum until Angus arrives." Louise threaded her arm through Mr. Blake's and directed him to the other building.

Rebeka took the document. "That was an impressive piece of deduction."

Arik didn't say anything. He didn't have to. The outcome spoke for itself. But it was more than that. His presence gave her confidence, made her feel…safe.

And that made no sense.

"Ah, there you are. Dr. Hamilton will be here shortly." Cora hurried into the room.

Rebeka turned to Arik. "Angus is a guest lecturer and a good friend. He's a bit eccentric. He asked to hold the class at the large oak tree at Oak Meadow."

"Is that unusual?" Arik asked. "In the time of the druids the meadow was their classroom."

"That does fit well. His presentation is *Druids, Their Religion, Their Medicine, Their Time*. He's well known and we're very lucky he was available." She paused. She wanted to tell him something special, that few would know. Maybe then he'd forgive her. "He was also a good friend of my father."

Arik didn't say anything. She swallowed hard and bit back her tears. He wouldn't forgive her.

"My father was a historian. He specialized in Celtic history. Dad and Angus were good friends. Would you like to attend?" She found herself holding her breath, hoping he would.

"If you like." She doubted he knew that when he smiled at her that way it made her heart stop. She was certain he didn't.

By the time Arik arrived at Oak Meadow students were gathered under the great tree waiting for Dr. Hamilton. He could feel the anticipation in the air. He made his way through the crowd headed toward the roadway. Many shouted their greeting. He nodded to some, raised a hand to others. He took in the sweet smells of the flowers and trees and let the energy fill him.

It wasn't much different than when he took his instructions here as a druid novice, with Bran at his side. He wished he had those days back. Logan had been right. He shouldn't have avoided Bran. It was his obligation. He should've stayed with him when Cay died. Maybe he could've prevented... He pushed Bran out of his mind.

As he arrived, George, Cora, Rebeka and their guest were getting out of the large motorcar.

"Dr. Hamilton."

Angus turned at his name.

"How good it is to see you," Blake said as he and Louise approached, breaking into the small group.

"Mr. Blake, Ms. Richards. Good to see you. Thank you for coming to the lecture," Angus said.

"Angus, this is my cousin Arik from the north." George put a hand on Arik's back.

"Dr. Hamilton." He dipped his head in respect. At first glance, Angus reminded him of Doward—clever, wise and with a streak of good humor. Maybe it was the white hair, his height, or his eyes. Something ancient stared out at him.

Angus looked Arik up and down and gave him an acknowledging nod. Then he turned back to Rebeka, a paper in his hand. "Is this the document you called me about?"

"Yes. We've been having this debate—Arik's interpretation of the translation and its significance as opposed to Ian Sloan's. The National Trust hopes you can settle the issue."

"Of course. I'd be glad to." Angus examined the copy. "When did you say it was written?"

"Ian dated it circa 900 AD."

"And where was it found?" Angus stroked his beard and appeared absorbed in the document.

"Among the family's estate papers." Nervous energy radiated from Rebeka. Arik moved behind her and her shoulders relaxed and the air around her quieted.

"Walk with me?" Angus asked Arik. Steady on his feet but using a cane, he traipsed with the others through the meadow toward the oak tree.

Angus was a spry white-haired man with a close-clipped beard. His blue eyes, faded with age, hadn't lost their twinkle. He surveyed the area and took everything in.

The others were a few steps behind when he and Angus dipped their heads under the low-hanging oak branches. Arik caught the murmur of a prayer in reverence to the mighty tree.

"You're not from here." Angus faced him with an open smile.

"No, I'm from the north." Arik repeated what George had already told the scholar.

Angus hesitated then moved on. "That's not what I meant."

Arik studied the man.

The professor already knew, so why deny it? "No, Angus. I'm not."

"Beware, m'lord. There is more going on here than you know." Before he could ask for clarity, the others arrived. "Don't worry. We'll talk later," Angus said to him privately.

"This field is filled with energy," Angus said.

"It was the center of druid activity before Roman times. Folklore says when the druids were under attack many went underground, literally. They dug beneath the meadow and established the druid stronghold here," George said.

"Yes, during the day they held positions like any other. But during the night they came out into the meadow and practiced their craft. The air tingles with the excitement." Angus turned to Rebeka. "Your father loved this meadow."

"What?" she whispered.

"Why so startled?" Angus patted her hand.

"I didn't know my father knew about Oak Meadow. He never spoke of it." Arik let out a sigh. He had come here often with her father when Maximillian tutored him and Bran. He suspected Maximillian visited the meadow in this century after he came through the portal. He tossed that idea around.

"You shouldn't be surprised. Your father had a great deal of knowledge about and respect for the druids and the fae—how they worked together and even how they parted. Almost all documented folklore is based on his work. You know folklore begins with truth. It's in the telling that it gets elaborated. Max was trying to get to the truth of the stories. I had hoped he would succeed. There were those who were against him." He bent his head toward Rebeka. "There is always someone opposed to the truth." He straightened. "But, well, he left us too soon."

"Yes he did," she whispered.

"He seems to have passed his love of folktales and music on to you."

"Yes. When I think back on things I see how instrumental he was in my life. He spoke about historical people as if he knew them—how they thought, what they ate. He made them all seem real to me. When it was time for me to pick a career, there was never a question that it would be history, working for a school or a museum." He saw the sadness in her eyes as she spoke about her father. He wanted to take her in his arms and give her his strength to deal with her father's passing. *Faith*, he wanted her to do the same for him.

"And why medieval history?" Angus asked.

"He hooked me on the romance of the age, the chivalry and the inquisitiveness of the time, the age of discovery. So you see, I had no choice." Arik could see Maximillian's influence. She made good use of her skills. He would have been proud of what she'd accomplished.

"Your father was an excellent colleague and great teacher. Some of his findings are landmark discoveries in our understanding of the Ancients in this area. Well, that's a discussion for another day. Today we'll discuss the impact of druids on medicine and religion."

He started for the small platform but turned to Blake and Louise. "It appears to be a list of war items." He gave the paper back to Rebeka. "I'll send you a note for your records."

"Thank you, Angus," Blake said.

"Let me help you to the platform," Arik said. Of course it was a list of war items. Angus couldn't have come to any other conclusion. Rebeka walked with them.

"I had to come. I tried to deny the feeling but I knew I wouldn't rest easy until I came here myself." He surveyed the area.

"I don't understand." Rebeka sent Arik a questioning stare. The statement had raised Arik's interest as well.

"I've sensed this urgency for some time. It's not

constant, at least it wasn't until recently. Over the past few months it's become a compulsion. I was planning on a visit when I received your invitation."

"What type of feeling?" Arik stepped forward and didn't try to hide his concern. It was more important that he not get any surprises.

"Something's not right. The harmony is out of balance." He searched Arik's and Rebeka's faces. "You're both in great danger. Change is inevitable but this is not a small change." Angus brought them close so only they would hear. "I fear it's annihilation." A meaningful glance passed between them. Arik understood the warning. His observation before he left Logan had been right. What was Bran planning? Would it happen in this century or his? Maybe he shouldn't wait until Rebeka got her memories back. They could return and he could... What? He was helpless. Utterly helpless. Would he lose Rebeka, his home, his family?

"Thank you, Angus." The old scholar nodded. Rebeka and Angus headed to the platform.

"Good morning." The crowd quieted as soon as Rebeka spoke. "I'd like to thank you all for coming this morning. Today, we are honored to have as a guest speaker, Dr. Angus Hamilton. As many of you know, Dr. Hamilton is in charge of the Celtic Studies program at Oxford University. Dr. Hamilton." She retreated between Arik and Louise in the audience.

"Come closer so you can all hear me," Angus said. He waited as they all settled. "There are three components to the spiritual way of the ancient druids: being creative in their lives, communing deeply with nature and gaining access to the source of wisdom..."

CHAPTER FIFTEEN

Annihilation. Arik had mentioned Angus's words to George but it hadn't been the time or place for a discussion. If Arik were home he'd be organizing his defenses, seeing to his people and training his men with Marcus and Logan at his side.

He evaluated the makeshift quintain for lance practices and pell with its posts for swords practice that stood idle in the fields—the practice area overgrown in some places, wet bogs in others. He glanced at the buttes in the distance where a lone archery target stood abandoned. They weren't useable.

Disheartened, he started back to the village. He let his mind wander and could hear Marcus calling orders and putting the men through their paces. His battle-tested men would fight for their homes.

How he would like—

A jolt threw him out of his musing and he glanced about. Finding himself in the center of the village, he wheeled around and evaluated every building.

He considered the major and his men all hardworking. The files he read showed most of the men were displaced veterans, far from home. It was admirable that Rebeka had barracked them but— He rubbed the back of his neck. They were estranged from their families.

He pinched his lower lip while ideas fired off. But first things first—he needed to understand the condition of things, then he could make his plans.

All of these men were battle tested—like his men. The more he considered the idea the more he knew it was the right thing to do—not only for Fayne Manor but for these men.

He pulled out his cell phone. "George? Can you meet me at the gatehouse? Yes…I'm on my way there now." He put away his phone and hurried on.

"Major, assemble the men."

"Hear, hear, men. Lord Arik wants to talk to us. Fall in." He waited while the men gathered.

It took longer than Arik wanted but that meant there was room for improvement. "You've done a good job getting the fields ready and the wheat planted." George stepped into the room and stood by the door. "The work on the mill is going well, too, faster than we planned."

"Yes, sir," Bill said. "We were able to find ready-made parts. It cut the cost and time."

"Good. We have another project." He plowed ahead eager to judge their reaction. "We're going to restore the village."

"Why, is someone moving in?" one of the men asked. A rumble of laughter rolled around the room.

"I'm not certain if they'll be holding a lottery or assigning houses as people make requests. It depends on how many want free housing." The men looked at one another for an answer.

"Why would they do that?" A loud buzz erupted in the room.

"Do what, move people into the village?" He waited.

"That, but why give it away free?" He saw the interest on the men's faces. The buzz in the room was a low roar.

"The village needs people to make it appear real—women doing laundry, children at games. We'll need families. Those who are already living here would likely be chosen."

The low roar settled to whispers.

"Our families? We can bring our families?" Frank asked. When they all understood what he was offering the room was quiet.

"As long as they're willing to be part of the reenactment, I don't see why not. The pay will be worked out." These men who had fought so hard deserved more. That would be reason enough. He wasn't fooling himself. He was well aware this also suited his plan. He needed to protect Rebeka and the manor. Men fighting for their homes would fight longer and harder. They were both winners, which was the best solution of all.

"Where can I sign on? My wife and baby are alone. I'd feel much better having them here with me," called out one of the soldiers. The murmur of voices started again.

Arik nodded. "Is there anyone else interested?"

Every man raised his hand.

"Very well. I'll discuss it with Dr. Tyler. Restoring the village will take a great deal of effort. Stonework is difficult. To prepare, we'll begin training in the morning. The advantage is we'll train like warriors and we'll give the guests a good show."

"We've all been through training. We know what to expect." The soldiers all nodded their agreement.

He scrutinized the men—they wouldn't disappoint him.

"Frank, we'll need your expert opinion again and that student who worked with you. I want all the village houses evaluated." Frank nodded. "Good. We'll meet at the village in the morning. The rest of you will start removing the debris out of the houses. I'll see you in the morning. Major, you can dismiss the men."

The men filtered out past George. He joined Arik in the front room.

"I was able to sell your coins to a collector. He was very excited." He was certain the man was pleased. The coin was almost solid gold.

"We may be able to excite him even more," Arik said. He stared at the men from the gatehouse window.

"I was listening."

"We're going to restore the village." His tone was matter-of-fact. His decision was closed to discussion.

"Alright, why?" When they had visited the Stelton estate, only select buildings had been renovated and open to visitors. He would have the entire village reinhabited. Perhaps he could even get the tenant farms working once again. He brushed that notion aside. First things first.

"The village is empty and vacant. It creates an ominous mood. Besides—" he spun on his heel and faced George, "—do you believe Angus's prediction?" He held George's stare and let out a heavy sigh. The resignation in George's eyes was answer enough.

"Yes," George said quietly. "Unfortunately, I do."

"The way to build an army is to give the men something to fight for. Something that is important to them." The rightness of the project grew stronger. Nothing was going to persuade him against it. "These are all good men. They need something to bind them together as a team, to believe in and to protect. It's not so different than my time."

"It's a very good solution. I wish I had thought of it myself. I'll work with you on the supplies you need. I have some sources eager to help veterans." He started to leave. "Have you told Rebeka?"

"No, not yet. I think she'll see the benefit of the project." His mind was already thinking which buildings to renovate first. The bakery. Yes, that one would be their top priority.

"Training the men for war?" He hoped this preparation would prove unnecessary. That it would turn out to be building houses for the men and their families.

"No, giving her students another eco-socio research project."

Rebeka hurried along. By the time she turned onto the path to the lake she was at a trot. She jogged in place, removed her sweatshirt, turned on her MP3 player and set out on the trail. Each footfall marked the beat of the music. Her body relaxed. With each deep breath she cleared her mind. Her heart rate ratcheted up with renewed energy and strength. She reached the halfway point and was in her stride. She rounded the lake to the last strains of the newest pop artist singing one of her signature songs. She loved the way the songstress fused elements of pop, blues, disco and gospel.

Her day was planned. The mill project was going well. The latest report showed they had more visitors there than they'd predicted. Joan had put together a solid presentation showing how the mill worked and the engineers spoke about how they were renovating. They even devised a few projects for the guests.

The idea of restoring the village and bringing in the wives and children would keep families together. She'd have to figure out a way to fund the project. George and Cora could help there. Besides approaching some of the veteran organizations, The Retreat had an impressive clientele list. Many were former military and politicians. That would be a good place to start.

She came to the back part of the lake and the

music changed to one of her favorite chants. If she wasn't breathing so heavily she would have chanted along to the soothing sound of the cadence. Rather than turn off the trail and complete her usual circuit, she decided to go on. She could use another half mile and followed the path to Elfrida's cottage.

She sprinted off the trail toward the cottage's back door. Breathing hard, she stopped at the chain-link fence and examined the gaping hole. The flash of someone at the window caught her attention. "How many times have I told everyone this cottage is off-limits?"

Armed with nothing but her anger, she wiggled through the hole and marched up the overgrown path. Her hand ran over the holes in the doorjamb where the boards had been pried loose. The rear door stood ajar.

Maybe renovating the village houses was a good idea. Giving the staff a place of their own instead of a bed in the gatehouse may keep them out of places they didn't belong. "Who's in here?" She ground out the words between her teeth.

From the rear door she walked along the small hallway. Standing in the narrow corridor, her heart pounded from more than her run. *Wait until I find them. They'll wish they'd never stepped foot inside this cottage.* As she listened for intruders she was overcome by dizziness and flinched as the walls closed in on her. Someone was behind her. She needed to get out of the hall. She rushed into the middle of the large room at the end of the hall.

Empty.

The only thing there was dust and debris. She peered out the window through the tacked-up boards at the large oak tree in the front yard.

Strong arms encircled her and turned her away from the view. She stared into Arik's concerned eyes. His smell, all spicy and so unbearably male, tugged at her. He drew her close.

His even and steady breathing gave her strength. He didn't say a word. She didn't question the warmth of his body, the hardness of his muscles and the gentleness of his touch, which was all strangely familiar. Rather, she absorbed it. She snuggled close, glad for the silence and safety.

She drew back, took his face in her hands and searched it carefully. It was strong, filled with character and, most of all, tender. Her heart leaped into her throat. "Arik." She noted the desperation in her voice. She kissed his lips hard and pulled away. "Arik," she said less urgently. She remembered thinking he was a knight when she first saw him. That he vanquished her terror and she was safe in his arms. She was right. As outlandish as the idea was, she knew it was right.

He held her. His shaking hand caressed the back of her head. She didn't struggle.

He drew her close and she welcomed his warmth, his touch, his kiss.

"Beka," he murmured in her ear.

"I…"

"Shhh." He laid his index finger across her lips. Her head fit perfectly between the hollow of his shoulder and his neck.

Recovered from her fright, she slid out of his arms. "What are you doing here?" Her voice held a measure of surprise.

He gave her a questioning look. "I came to find you."

"How did you know I was here?"

She got a brief peek as disappointment crossed his face before he took control of his expression. She was certain there was more he wanted to say. But their connection was too new for her to ask questions. "I saw you crawl through the metal fence and knew—"

"I'd need help. When I came to the cottage the fence was broken. I assumed there were vandals in here…" Her brows wrinkled in deep concentration.

"Did you see anyone on the path while you ran?" he asked.

"I don't think so. Why?" Concern was in her voice.

"I saw two people coming from this direction. Marle and John." He stared at the door. "Stay here. I'll search the other rooms."

Rebeka stood with her arms wrapped around herself. She already missed his warmth and comfort.

He returned. "I found nothing in the other rooms except an empty bottle of wine and this." He dangled a bra from his index finger.

She shook her head and let out a soft laugh, then removed the pink lace confection from his hand. "It's expensive. She'll want it back. I'll talk to her about finding a more appropriate place for a rendezvous."

"I'll talk to him. I'd like to know if he saw anything or if he only had eyes for his lady."

She smiled at his stern face but she saw the laughter in his eyes. "I better get back," she said halfheartedly as she stood close to him.

How could she not have known she loved him?

Chapter Sixteen

He was seated at the table in the tower room with his tablet, a counterpoint to the ancient runes that clung to the walls.

His eyes tired, he pushed himself back and took a deep breath when the smell of smoky pine drifted through the window. He turned and looked out. The sky glowed orange in the distance—in the direction of the mill. He bolted out of his chair, knocking it over. He leaned over the window's ledge.

"Fire," he bellowed.

He ran from the tower and through the library terrace doors, the quickest route to the gatehouse and the barn. He got to the garrison where Marle and John were rousing the men. "Fire at the mill. Move," John shouted.

Frank was already backing out his Spitfire. "Sir," he called to him. "Get in."

They raced up the rise and through the drive. Continuing at a hell-bent speed, they crossed the river. The mill wasn't far ahead. Frank pulled into the clearing. Arik was out of the car before it came to a stop. The roof and upper level were fully ablaze.

"Frank, go to the river and open the sluice gate to the flume. I'll pull the flume to the open window on the top floor. We should be able to save the gears and other two floors." Frank grabbed a tire iron from the car and sprinted off. He had to move fast before the fire spread to the gear room.

Arik tore off his jacket and started climbing the outside of the building to the flume. It was scorched and still warm. Someone had moved the heavy chute but not quite enough. He tugged it inch by painstaking inch until he got it close enough to the building so most of the water would go through the window. The dousing would slow the advancing fire and protect the mechanism below.

He looked inside. Half the floor had been removed. From where he stood, it was a sheer three-floor drop to the lowest level of the mill. He didn't have to bother opening the flume gates on his side. The water would overflow it quickly.

A low moan echoed in the empty space.

"Who's there?" He peered into the darkness but knew he wouldn't be able to see anything. Did an animal get trapped inside?

Silence.

He sensed more than heard the water rushing down the flume. Another moan.

No. The sound was distinctly human.

With the force of the running water it would be a matter of minutes before the gates gave way. The bottom of the mill would flood quickly.

He climbed down the wall into the wheel trough and squeezed himself past the axle shaft. He jumped over the pit where the vertical gear would be placed. Right now it was in the gear room. A dark, dank, tight space, he ignored the pungent odor that permeated the air and found the door that led to the inside of the mill. He tried to open it but it wouldn't budge. If he was to survive he'd have to go back the way he came, through the wheel trough. Not an easy feat with tons of water pouring on him and the waterwheel threatening to turn.

Another loud moan led him back to the pit. Someone was lying at the bottom. He lowered himself into it and turned the body over.

Bill looked at him.

"Can you move?" How did the man get here? He didn't have time for questions now. He had to get them both out.

"I…I can't feel my hands," Bill moaned.

There was a loud rumbling. Arik was certain the water was hitting the locked sluice gates. Sprays began to pelt them from above. It was a matter of time before the sluice gate broke and the wheel would start.

If they stayed where they were the pit would flood—he and Bill would have no way out. Even a druid Grand Master wouldn't be able to save them.

The waterwheel lurched. There was no time. He hoisted Bill on his shoulder. The water spray turned into a cascade. The wheel strained and the axle vibrated erratically.

He concentrated and murmured the words of protection. The shaking axle eased. He climbed out of the pit and threw his leg through the opening into the trough. Carefully, he began to squeeze through. Bill moaned, breaking his concentration. He refocused but not quickly enough. The axle wobbled.

He pushed through as the wheel brake splintered and the waterwheel began to turn.

Rebeka jumped up. She sniffed the air and knew—fire. She grabbed her pouch and staff and raced to the gatehouse as the last soldier was getting ready to ride.

"Where's the fire?"

"The mill. We're following Lord Arik and Frank." His car filled with people, he left.

Rebeka was already on her cell phone. "There's a fire at the mill." She spoke to George as she rushed on. "Arik and the men have already gone there. I'm going now. Meet us there." She ended the call and headed to the garage. Her car was blocked in by a student's.

She didn't stop to think.

A moment later she had on a helmet and the Triumph wound up. She knew Arik would be in the thick of things and she needed to get to him. She raced across the fields and jumped the bogs instead of taking the longer route along the road. She was almost there when she came to the stone wall. It was too high to jump. Anxious, she rode alongside the wall for some time then stopped. It was taking her in the wrong direction.

She turned the Triumph and raced a good hundred yards perpendicular down a small depression. She took a wide turn and fishtailed the back of the motorbike around.

She revved the engine and headed for the wall at full speed. The bike caught the rise and sent her airborne.

The back tire brushed against the stone as the bike cleared the wall.

She landed hard. The bike wobbled and leaned to one side, nearly wiping out but it remained upright with her still on it. She knew staying upright wasn't her skill but dumb luck. She crossed the stream and continued on, hoping her luck held out. She could see the smoke and flames above the trees. She turned the bend, gave the engine more gas and skidded into the mill yard. Men were using anything to fight the fire. She set the bike down and threw off the helmet. She rushed from man to man searching for Arik.

He was nowhere to be found.

A shiver of panic rushed through her. *Where is he?* "Major," she shouted and grabbed the man's arm.

"Have you seen Arik?"

"Frank said he was by the waterwheel." He turned to a knot of men. "Jaxon, get some men. The wheel is turning. Get to the flume on top of the wheel and get a bucket line started." The major went with the men.

She ran to the mill door and with care put her palms on it. It wasn't warm. The fire wasn't here yet. She opened the door. With the top of her nightshirt covering her mouth she burst inside, but the smoke was too thick for her to get far. She came out coughing. Flashes of pictures bombarded her. She ignored them. Her head ached but she wouldn't acknowledge it.

She was determined to find him. She ran to the side of the mill, thinking to slip in through the window. Great puffs of steam filled the area. She couldn't see the window. Tracks of tears streamed down her sooty cheeks. She closed her eyes and used all her energy to concentrate on him. "My heart," she repeated under her breath over and over. She opened her eyes.

Steam gathered on the millrace coming from the large wheel. A thick vapor billowed and grew as more water hit the fire. The water coming down the millrace grew from a trickle to a fast-moving stream racing back to the river. She tilted her head and took in how the fire backlit the steam and gave it a flickering, soft orange otherworldly glow.

"My heart," she murmured. Swirls of steam roiled in the center. Slowly the silhouette of a man emerged.

"Arik," she muttered. She let out a breath she didn't know she was holding and felt the corners of her mouth tug in a relieved smile. His stride was strong and determined.

She ran to him.

"Major," she yelled over her shoulder. The man was all at once at their side. Together they eased the man off Arik's shoulder and got him to the ground. The major was already evaluating his soldier.

"What happened?" It didn't take much to see Arik was in better shape than the man he carried.

Arik, at least, was walking.

She looked at the major. "Who is it?"

"It's Bill," Arik said as he faced the major. "How is he?"

"He's been beaten pretty bad and his hands are burned." The major gave them a haunted expression. Arik put his hand on the major's shoulder.

"I'll take care of him." Rebeka examined Bill's pale skin and rapid breathing. Afraid he was going into shock, she elevated his feet and made him as comfortable as she could. More students arrived in a caravan with buckets and pails, leaving them strewn on the ground for anyone who needed them.

"You and the major go and help the others. I'll stay with Bill," Rebeka said.

"Where is the worst of it?" Arik asked the major.

"On the other side," was all he said. He gave Rebeka a curt nod and was gone.

"Rebeka." Cora ran to her. "We've called for help. They said there was a serious fire at the newspaper office in Avebury and would be here as soon as possible."

"Do you have a first-aid kit?" Rebeka asked.

"Yes, George keeps one in the car." She rushed to the car and came back with the kit.

Rebeka rummaged through the contents and picked out what she needed. "Cora, fill one of those buckets with water." Both of Bill's hands were blistered, a mix of second- and third-degree burns. She made certain he wasn't wearing any rings. "Bill, can you hear me?"

"Yes, ma'am," he said through clenched teeth. She knew he was in pain and was frustrated she had limited resources to help him.

Cora returned. "Here's the water."

"Help me wrap his hands with the gauze. We must keep his fingers separated then I can bathe them in the water." When they finished she poured cool water over the bandages to give him some relief.

"Can you spare some bandages?" Marle stood in front of them. "There are some men on the other side of the building that need help."

"I'll stay with Bill," she said to Cora. "Go with Marle." Cora took what she could and left to help the others.

Alone with Bill, Rebeka kept his bandages damp. There wasn't much more she could do. She peered down the path. Where was the ambulance? Bill fidgeted. With her back against a tree she chanted to soothe him—or was it to soothe herself?

She wasn't certain, but it didn't matter. Bill quieted and that's what counted.

The cadence of her chant marked time with her heartbeat that echoed in her ears. Light-headed, with a sense of weightlessness, she concentrated harder and dove deeper into her chant. Her father's voice mixed with hers was both familiar and encouraging. She knew he wasn't there but that didn't matter. She embraced it and followed his lead.

The sounds of the disaster around her quieted until they were indistinct. She concentrated hard and continued to chant, going deeper than she had ever gone before.

Distorted pictures moved through her mind. She kept her focus on the chant. They stretched and faded. Children running in a field, a mother's kiss, a father's pride, a husband's love.

The drone of the chant and rapt in concentration, took her to a place that swirled with darkness. Faster and faster she repeated the chant. Tighter and tighter her voice choked the darkness. She knew where she was. Skara Brae. Brighter and brighter the place became until in a burst of brilliance the darkness was gone. So was the vision of Skara Brae.

She was bombarded with an onslaught of memories and sensations as they came up from the depths of her mind.

She kept repeating the chant, not willing to lose what she'd fought so hard to gain.

As the sky lightened she saw that only small wisps of smoke remained. Now she watched the sun begin to peek over the hill, exposing the disaster. The stone walls of the first two floors were blackened and dripping with water. There was severe damage to the roof and walls of the third floor. She scooped the last of the water out of the bucket and sprinkled it on Bill's bandages. The sluice doors had been blocked. The millrace was almost dry. She'd have to go to the stream for more.

She didn't move. She wanted to go over the memories again. She wanted to see his smile, feel his touch and hear his voice. He wasn't a dream. He found her as he'd promised. Her lips moved as she repeated the chant.

"How's Bill?"

She glanced at Arik as he knelt next her. At last.

Exhausted, she let the sight of him wash over her.

He wasn't a dream. She wanted to cry, laugh, scream—but most of all she wanted him to hold her. He had come for her.

She examined him like a hungry person searching for a meal. His face was sooty and his eyes were bright if a bit tired. His T-shirt was torn and wet. He smelled of smoke but—she took a deep breath—under it all he smelled like Arik.

Her Arik.

"He seems to be resting comfortably, dozing on and off. I've been keeping the dressing wet with cool water. His breathing seems even and I don't think he has a fever." She let out a relieved sigh. She'd been waiting for hours to speak to him and now she didn't want to speak at all.

He was here with her. She was going to burst into a thousand pieces.

He signaled to a redheaded attendant who stood close by. "When the emergency team arrived they examined his hands and left you to tend to him," Arik said. The attendant removed Bill to the triage area.

Her brow wrinkled in confusion. So she had gone that deep. "It's amazing what you revert to."

"What do you mean?" He took a seat next her, his eyes closed, his back against the tree.

"My father used to sing a healing chant to me when I was sick. It calmed me so I chanted it to Bill. When I did it calmed him, too. When I stopped he got restless. So I went deeper and kept on chanting." She glanced at Arik from the corner of her eye. Her heart was pounding so loud she was surprised he didn't hear it. Her eyes shifted past him to the damaged mill.

"I'm glad Alfred can't see this." She kept watch to record the moment he realized she'd remembered his miller's name.

"Beka?" He turned and his warm breath brushed across her face, sending shivers across her back. She brushed his hair off his forehead.

"Yes?" She gazed into his eyes and hoped he saw she was there, all there.

"How—"

She couldn't wait any longer. She covered his mouth with her lips, leaving her mouth burning as if on fire. Her emotions whirled and skidded.

He pulled away to look at her. There it was. The moment it registered with him. He captured her lips with fierce, hot possession. She burned hotter and hotter, hungering for him. His moan was her undoing. She was lost to an all-consuming rush of heat.

He held her tenderly while her body calmed. She was in his arms. That's all that mattered.

"The chant. Of all the chants this one demands your full concentration. I wouldn't fail Bill. The deeper I concentrated, the clearer my mind became."

"You must be exhausted." He drew her closer.

"I wanted to speak to you, to tell you. I was afraid if I slept...I wouldn't remember." She reveled in his warmth and wanted him closer. "I love you." She stretched her neck and kissed him lightly. "At first I believed my dreams were just that, dreams, until I understood...you're here. That's when I refused to stop chanting even though Bill was asleep. If anything, I was more determined to keep it going. I needed to tell you I love you. I wanted to hold you and look at you one more time. Even if it was to say good-bye, I—"

"Shhh." He kissed her forehead. "Rest. I'm here with you. I've come a long way to bring you home, so it's not good-bye. It will never be that. If we have to, we'll both sing the chant, every day. I have no intention of losing you again. Do you understand? I love you. I won't let you go."

CHAPTER SEVENTEEN

"Arik." With his arm around Rebeka, he turned to see George rushing toward them with something in his hand. "One of the students found this among the supplies." A gasoline can, the letters *FM* stamped on the bottom, was in his hand. "Before you ask, we didn't bring this here." He held up the can and wiggled it. "We had no need for gasoline. I'm certain if we inventory the cans by the manor generator we'll find one missing."

Arik bit the inside of his cheek. "The mill room had a distinct odor. It wasn't until I got Bill out that I recognized that the smell came from his clothes." Yes, it was gasoline. There was no question that treachery was involved.

He held her close, not willing to let her go. He would've preferred to be alone with her, loving her, but now was not the time.

"I'll take this to the fire chief. He'll want to see it." Arik nodded as George left to find the man. He glanced around the mill yard littered with the remnants of burned wood and roof tiles. Patches of grass still smoked. The door to the mill stood open as firemen came out with axes over their shoulders. All was in order here.

"I want to ask Bill some questions. He may be able to give us some information." He and Rebeka picked their way through the debris and headed to the triage area.

They arrived at the emergency team's station. Firefighters were loading their trucks. His bedraggled men were gathered around Cora, who was giving out coffee and water.

He passed among his men, spoke to each one, thanking them for their help and asking about their injuries. He laughed with some and comforted others. But with each conversation his anger grew until he was furious. He hadn't seen this coming. He hadn't protected them.

George and Cora met him and Rebeka by the stocky redheaded attendant who was bandaging the last causality. "If you're trying to find Bill, he's waiting by the ambulance. We took the bandages off his hands and expected to see severe third-degree burns."

"You sound surprised." Arik was confused. He knew what he had seen. Bill would be lucky to ever use his hand again.

"His hands are burned, but not that bad. They're red and some areas are blistered. We downgraded the diagnosis to moderate second-degree burns." He turned toward his last patient. "We'll be taking you to the hospital as a precaution..."

The four of them left the medic and headed for the ambulance and found Bill. "You appear much better than you did the last time I saw you," Arik said. Bill's face brightened with a trace of a smile.

"How do you feel?" Rebeka asked.

"Lucky." He held up two mittened hands. "I didn't think I'd ever use my hands again. I'm glad I was wrong."

"You have any idea how the fire started?" Arik squatted next to him. He needed to get answers while things were still fresh in Bill's mind.

The other men gathered around them. Arik wasn't surprised they wanted to listen. Everyone wanted to hear how the fire started.

"I headed to the mill after dinner to check that we had everything we needed for tomorrow. The plan was to lay the rest of the floor in the morning. Once we were done we were going to set the pit wheel and connect the mechanism. There were noises coming from the second floor. A day or two ago the noises turned out to be two of Dr. Tyler's students, Marle and John, trying to find a private spot." Bill shook his head and chuckled. "I must have scared them. I saw their bare backsides running into the woods—carrying their clothes. Tonight I heard voices. I suspected they were back. I decided to scare them good.

"I snuck up on them, jumped out and yelled. When they spun around I flashed my light in their eyes. I got a clear enough look to see it wasn't Marle and John. It was two blokes I'd never seen before. That's when I smelled the gasoline. One of them was still spraying it." Arik caught a tight note of panic in Bill's voice. "We fought and wound up on the ground level. I wanted to maneuver them away from the mill but when we got outside one of them got behind me and held my arms while the other one had a field day." He stared at the ground, lines of concentration deepening along his brows. "All I could see were little ladders." He picked up his head. "He had them tattooed up his arm."

"Does that mean anything to you?" Arik asked Rebeka.

"No, not at all." She turned to Bill. "How'd your hands get burned?"

"They must've heard something or someone coming. They dropped me and torched the mill. As soon as they left I tried to put out the fire." Bill blew out a breath. "I knew it would take too long to get to the manor for help. The top floor was on fire." The words rushed out of Bill like the water cascading down the flume. "I climbed up, pulled off my jacket and beat out the flames. I tried, I tried," Bill rushed on, "to move the flume. It was the only thing I could think of to stop the fire." Bill leaned forward and struggled to get up. All his men stood and listened.

"It was a good plan." Arik helped him sit back. "You saved the mill." The two men locked eyes. Arik knew that stare. It was the haunted expression of a man who's been in battle and thinks he hasn't done enough. "You saved the mill," Arik repeated softly.

"I tugged on the flume," Bill whispered, "but my hands hurt so much. I lost my balance. I grabbed on to the bricks and I found a niche for my feet and started to work my way down but my hands stopped working. The last thing I remember was falling into the pit."

"It was a brave move, one not many would have made. You have my gratitude." Arik scanned the sooty, scratched faces of the men around them. "You all have my gratitude."

"Sir, I should be thanking you," Bill said, a certain determination in his voice. "I stumbled into this. Frank told me you went into that inferno and carried me out."

"As you would for me." His response was low and even. The men around him nodded their agreement.

"We're ready to take this man to hospital." He turned to the attendant who spoke. Together they helped Bill onto a gurney.

"We'll see you tomorrow," Arik said. Jaxon came out from the crowd and stationed himself next to Bill.

"I'll go with him." Jaxon followed the gurney and jumped into the back of the ambulance.

With the fire out, the firefighters packed their gear and returned to their home base. The Fayne Manor men helped each other to their cars and headed toward the manor.

"How bad is the damage?" Arik glanced at the mill, the question directed at George. The man reeked of smoke. George's bright white shirt was torn and black with soot. A lock of hair tumbled across his forehead and his eyes were red and irritated, all in contrast to his usually impeccable presence.

"The roof and all the wood on the upper level will have to be replaced. We were lucky the fire didn't get to the bottom floors where we stored the gears. They weren't touched. The waterwheel was damaged and we'll have to bail out the pit."

The major approached them and waited.

"Yes, Major?" Arik asked.

"Everyone is accounted for and has started back to the manor. I've put two men on watch here. I'll have a report on the necessary repairs for you tomorrow." The major saluted. Arik watched as the last of the men left the mill yard. There was a familiar spirit about the man who led his men and anticipated his needs—Marcus.

"Bill's burns were much worse than what we just saw." Arik returned his attention to George. The four of them started toward the waiting vehicles.

"I heard you chanting to him when I came by to see if you needed help." Cora's matter-of-fact expression softened and her voice trailed off into a whisper. She glanced at Rebeka. "You...you healed him." They stopped at the edge of the yard.

"Yes." Arik stood behind Rebeka. "I sang my father's healing chant and helped Bill..." She peered up at him.

"And remembered my husband."

Her words sent something right through him. The months of torment, the endless days and sleepless nights he researched and tried to find her. And when he finally found his way through time, the days and weeks he watched her and knew she didn't remember him. They all became unimportant.

George broke the silence. "It should never have happened. I was responsible." George's distraught voice was low and thin. "I should never have let her go into the estate alone." He saw the man's pain and said nothing. George would have to find his own peace of mind. "I failed my responsibility."

"You couldn't stop me. I would've gone without you one way or another. But I do know that I couldn't get away from Bran myself. You pulled me to safety. No, you didn't fail me. You saved me."

He was pleased with his wife's response. Rebeka stepped in front of George. "And my family." Rebeka glanced at Cora. "You both did. If it hadn't been for you, I never would've found them and Arik wouldn't be here. You must know that."

"George worked hard to find you and fulfill Lady Emily's request." Cora glanced from Rebeka to her brother.

"It hasn't gone unnoted." He was grateful to George. "We still need your help. We can't return until things are set right here. I don't think we've heard the last of Bran and we've got to find the proclamation."

"And don't forget who did this." Rebeka stood with her arms spread wide. She was right—there was more to resolve before they could return.

The crunch of gravel caught his attention as the major's patrol passed. Streams of sun filtered through the trees and filled the mill yard. "We'll meet back at the manor. Rebeka, ride with me." He was already halfway to the Triumph.

He threw his leg over the motorbike's seat as if he had been riding it for years and gave her the helmet. She slipped behind him as the engine rumbled into life. Her hands fanned out over his chest, her touch a familiar sensation. It was a sweet torture but at last he would have her to himself.

He followed the shortcut through the forest. The

trees flashed by in a blur. The fallen leaves billowed up around them. With her body warm against his back and her arms holding tight around him he was content.

They came out of the forest and crossed the small field with a weeping willow. They passed through the tall pines and into Oak Meadow.

She tapped him on the shoulder. He came to a stop.

Before he killed the motor, she was off the bike and on her way toward the oak tree. His long strides had him by her side quickly.

The early morning April air warmed as the sun rose. The oak tree welcomed them. He could almost hear the tree sigh. She pulled him along until they stood under the oak branches and the canopy of leaves that sheltered them.

His rough hand cupped her cheek and held her face tenderly. His heart pounded as he lifted her chin and drank in the passion he saw in her eyes. At last, after months of searching and weeks of wanting, she was his.

"Hold me. Don't let me go," she said as she nuzzled his neck and sank into his strong embrace. "Love me," she whispered in his ear and felt him shiver. She wanted to feel his arms around her, his lips touching hers—she wanted him to bury himself deep inside her and shout her passion to her world and to his.

They sank to the ground and held each other close. She was afraid to let him go, afraid the emptiness would find her, afraid of losing him, again. With an unending thirst, she focused on his mouth, the shape of his lips, the kisses that they promised.

His hand stroked the side of her body from her breast to her thigh, claiming it for himself. She stretched and molded her body to the contours of his, the way he liked. One stroke of her breast and she tugged on his shirt. He didn't hesitate. He obliged her and pulled it off. Her hand played down the familiar hard planes of his chest. Her eyes widened when she saw the marks. His back and chest were covered with intricate symbols. How hadn't she seen them before? "These weren't here." She traced them with her finger.

He stopped her hand and brought it to his lips. "For six months I tried to find you." He tilted her face to his. She closed her eyes and felt the tingling traces of Dark Magick that thrummed around him.

She moved away, a concerned expression on her face. "What have you done?"

He pulled her back into his arms. "I did whatever was necessary. Now be still and let me hold you." She settled against him.

"I've tried to remember holding you, feeling you before I love you, reliving every moment with you."

She put her head on his shoulder. He opened her nightshirt and stroked the top of her chest then, with trembling hands, touched her breasts. A low moan escaped her lips. She tipped her face to see his eyes.

"Why are your eyes closed?" she asked.

"I'm seeing if you are as I remember." He laughed softly.

"And?"

"Better," he said as he bent and kissed each breast.

She pulled his head away and kissed him. He ignited a flame inside her that set her on fire. A delicious shudder pulsed through her.

The muscles on his chest danced as her fingers lightly traced the runes. "This rune is for the Great Mother." Her finger poised over the sign. "Thank you, Great Mother," she said as her lips brushed against his skin. She watched it deckle in gooseflesh. Her finger moved on. "This is our sign." Encouraged by the hooded passion she saw in his eyes, she kissed the rune and moved on. The tips of her fingers traced down his chest. "Here it is again." The rune was below his navel. Another kiss. Her fingers trailed down further.

He pulled her up and rolled on top of her. Her body instinctively arched against his. "You are mine." His warm breath brushed against her face. Two heartbeats passed. "Do you hear me? You're mine," he said more urgently.

"Yes." Her voice was an intimate whisper. His lips tugged into a sideways grin.

It was the smile that made her bones go limp. It was his magick.

"Forever," was all he said as he settled between her legs. Every inch of him was hard and ready. She focused on his lips while her hands ran over his body. The insistent need to touch him consumed her.

"Love me, Arik. Now." She wanted to taste him, smell him, feel him.

He bent down and let his lips brush gently across hers. Arik soothed and calmed her with his touches and kisses only to build her heat and her passion. Tiny licks of pleasure shot through her while his erection pressed against her.

He slipped inside her and she let out a sigh of relief. "I please you," he said his voice rough with passion.

She answered him by wrapping her legs around his hips and pulling him closer. Heat rippled through her body as combustible desire ran through her with every stroke. As the last wave peaked, they both found their release.

He held himself on his elbows, his forehead touching hers. "You are my heart. I make love to you and want more. It's never enough."

She wrapped her arms around him. "I feel the same."

He rolled onto his back and took her with him. "I've never stopped wanting you."

"I wanted you when I saw you in the minstrel gallery," she said and he squeezed her close. "Could we go back now while I remember?" She pulled away from him. She could see in his face he wanted to go back as much as she did.

He let out a breath. "You know I want to go back, too. But the only way you can be safe, that the future can be safe, is to deal with Bran now."

The buzz of his cell phone interrupted. They ignored it.

"The portal is closed and Bran can't create a new one. He can't cross time. He was an enchantment at Skara Brae," she argued.

"Yes but almost as dangerous as if he was here." He didn't have to tell her. She knew he was right.

"If the portal is closed, how did you get here?"

He pulled her back against him. "It's a long story. I was fortunate. While Logan and I searched, George and Cora did, too. I came through the tower mirror." He kissed her forehead. "I'm concerned about you. Until we know who started the fire, and if they are working with Bran, we can't let anyone know your memory is back." She started to object but realized that Arik was right. What would Bran do if he knew she remembered after he took such pains to make her forget?

"Especially Louise."

"Louise?" She had suspected he didn't like her. Now that she considered it, Louise had been getting more aggressive when they practiced since Arik arrived.

"She's not all she seems. Fawning over me to anger you, and her aggressive sparring—no, we mustn't let her know until the time is right. I keep asking myself why anyone would want to set fire to the mill. I don't think Bill was the target. He wandered into the situation." The loss of the mill would put a strain on the staff and finances. None of this was compelling. It had to be something else.

"Maybe it's just kids and an accident."

"If gasoline wasn't involved I might agree with you. No, someone started the fire on purpose." Rebeka smothered a yawn. She was going to fall off her feet.

His cell phone rang again.

She took it from his pocket and gave it to him. He swiped the screen. "Yes?...We will be there shortly." He ended the call. "Come, it's time to go back."

"Now? This minute?" She pouted as he buttoned her nightdress.

"Come. It's been an exciting night for both of us." He helped her up. They put themselves together.

"Arik, what if my memory...?" She trailed off as she put on the helmet. "I'll be with you. I suspected you're free of the enchantment." His words were encouraging but she sensed his concern.

"I told you, in addition to waking you with kisses I plan to chant to you every morning and evening if I have to." He brushed his lips against hers. They got on the motorbike and rode to the manor. "Rebeka, I think you should move back into the manor."

Rebeka's back stiffened. "I assure you I can take care of myself."

"Yes, I know you can. But a good warrior knows there's strength in numbers. Until we know who is behind this, no one is to go anywhere outside the manor alone. Move into the manor. There is always someone nearby. The cottage is close but isolated. Once we catch who's responsible you can move back." They got on the motorbike in silence.

"You think it's that serious? It was the mill that was set on fire, not the manor," Rebeka said before he started the engine.

Arik said nothing. But she recognized his best

intimidating stare.

"I'll have Charles move my things later today." He started the engine and they started back.

Rebeka leaned on the doorjamb and peered past the red velvet ropes into the lady's chamber. Arik suggested she move into this room, but the suite with its soft colors and romantic decor was one of the main attractions of the house tour. Now she recognized the accuracy of the reproduction. She pushed off the wall and headed to the small room across the hall.

The door stood wide open. The warmth of the fire in the grate and the scent of lavender and rose brought back a rush of memories. This had been her room when Doward and Arik had first brought her to the manor.

The sight of Jeannie caring for the gash on her leg flashed in her head.

She had skidded down a mountain and cut it badly when she'd popped out of the portal into his century. That had been when she met the tinker, Doward. She let the memories settle before she entered the room.

"I still think you should be in the lady's chamber." Arik stood behind her, his hands gently on her shoulders. He kissed her neck.

Caught by surprise, she gasped as she leaned into his solid frame. She closed her eyes and stretched, hoping he would take advantage of the better access she was giving him. The warm breath of his deep chuckle on her neck made her melt. She tried to turn to him but he would have none of it. He held her in place and circled her with his arms, his hands across the top of her chest, his fingertips trailing over her delicate skin.

She felt his arousal and had no desire to move. His

hands were gentle as they caressed her breasts. His lips left a trail of kisses along her neck and pooled on her shoulders. He was driving her wonderfully wild. She broke free and faced him. He titled her face toward him with the crook of his index finger and lowered his mouth onto hers. Everything he did, every touch, made her body throb for him. He swept her into his arms and carried her up the tower steps. At the top, he kicked the door closed and set her in the middle of the room.

"The beautiful tapestries are gone." She was beginning to see what he had gone through for the past six months.

"I removed them for a good reason." She moved to the walls. The flickering light made the magick runes dance across the stones.

"You've tried to find me for—"

"Six months. You sound surprised." She stepped closer to the wall and with a tentative hand touched it.

"No, not surprised, fortunate." She faced him. "I'm surprised that you would use Dark Magick." She didn't hide her concern. "I've developed a new respect for it."

"I'd do it again to find you." He would. She was more than fortunate. It was an odd feeling to have two memories of the same place, one where you feel at home and the other where you're a stranger.

"George feels responsible for letting you go to Skara Brae. I'm as guilty for not teaching you about Dark Magick. If I had, perhaps you wouldn't have—" She kissed his lips to shift his mind to another course.

What's done was done. There would be plenty of time to go over it. Right now she didn't want to talk about Bran or Dark Magick. She held his face in her hands. "I love you. I can't find the words to tell you how much or how deep. You're a wizard."

The corner of his lips tugged in a boyish grin that

made her insides flutter. His eyes glistened with promised passion. She snuggled in his arms longing for his touch, licking her lips in anticipation.

"Then let me bewitch you, again." His voice was soft and seductive. She closed her eyes and surrendered to his magick.

CHAPTER EIGHTEEN

"Have you gone through the files of all the men?" George said as he sat across the table from Arik. They both worked on their tablets.

"Yes," Arik said. He could use Marcus right now to manage the training and patrol schedule. "A hundred and fifty men, six squadrons at most, aren't enough. I'd feel better with at least another hundred and fifty. We don't need to patrol the outlying countryside—only protect the manor and mill."

Arik leaned back and glanced at George. "In my time I could easily call on my neighbors for support. Here it's not so easy."

George had his eyes on his screen. "Do you have any ideas?"

"Training's a challenge. We need more equipment." Arik pushed his chair back and stared out the window. "The only way to stop Bran will be to fight, the old way—with swords." His hope for a settlement, a truce even, had faded.

"Our immediate need is to protect the manor. The training and maneuvers had an added benefit—the authenticity would draw more visitors." Arik and George had gone over every soldier's file in order to discuss them with the major. It would be difficult to protect the manor with one hundred fifty men but not impossible.

"We should take an inventory of the weapons as well," Arik said.

"We created a war room in the garden house museum. Let's see what's there." George turned off his tablet.

The grounds were empty and quiet when they left for the garden house. Exceptionally quiet. In the distance the sound of tramping feet reached Arik's ears. They both stopped and glanced over their shoulders. They focused on the sound's direction. It came from the road that led to the lake.

Two lines of men jogged toward them. The major gave the cadence and the men halted. Another beat and one hundred and fifty soldiers pivoted like a well-oiled machine. They faced Arik and George. Each man stood at attention while Arik reviewed the troop. Were these the same men he'd seen a day ago?

"Sir." The major gave Arik a crisp salute.

"Major."

"When we returned from the fire we realized the manor was, well, sir, under attack. It wasn't difficult to see it was sabotage. I took the liberty of establishing a perimeter around the mill. A chain-link fence is being installed and our men will patrol until further orders." He may not have Marcus but he had the major. He knew he had the men he needed.

"Very good, Major." He wouldn't have to encourage the men to train. They were already motivated.

"We also decided we've been sitting around too long. We were lucky last night but unprepared. We've upped our daily training. We're on our way to the practice fields."

"Thank you." He passed among them. "I know Dr. Tyler appreciates your dedication and so do I." He continued to address each man separately, thanking them for their help, asking them about their bruises and burns. When he was done he stood next to George and the major. "What's your plan?"

"Exercise in the morning. The men will rotate standing guard, working at the mill and restoring the village as planned. Yesterday we evaluated the wall around the manor. The person who built it did a good job of preparing it for defense. We've developed a watch schedule, should we need it. And, sir, we know of others who would be interested in signing on." Arik welcomed that news. Now he understood why they called this man Major. He was competent, forward-looking, intelligent and courageous, the qualities he demanded in a leader.

"Very good. We'll talk about the details of your plan later. Don't let me stop you." He started to leave but hesitated. "I might join you at the practice field when I'm done." He had always trained with Marcus and the men. It would feel good to get back into that routine.

The major's face lit with a wide smile.

It was good to know the men had taken the threat seriously. Very good. The major gave the order and the soldiers wheeled into position and started off at a jog. He watched the tight line disappear down the road.

"If the men are going to train, we better find them weapons," Arik said. He and George continued on.

"They'll need to be repaired. We had them all rebated," George said. *Faith*. He hadn't anticipated the points and edges would be filed flat. "They were all high-quality pieces. Once you review them we can decide what to do. I know a few artisans who can do the work." Arik nodded. Another obstacle.

They entered the museum and headed for the weapons room. Swords and claymores hung from the museum walls in a deadly mosaic pattern. There were battle-axes, throwing axes, long bows and halberds. Taking care, Arik hefted the claymore to judge its weight. He didn't have to touch the edges. He could see George was right, all the points and edges had been filed flat.

"As weapons, these are useless."

George made notes on his tablet. "I'll make a few calls when we're done."

"It will take a smithy months to restore all these." He gestured to the wall.

George flashed him a smile. "The first building we'll restore will be the smithy, then the bakery. We'll get a team together. There are techniques and machines that we can use behind the scenes to move this along. For the other weapons, we can put on demonstrations for our visitors."

He glanced at George. For a moment he saw Logan. He would have enjoyed this adventure. But as much as he enjoyed George, Cora, the major and the men he didn't waver in his desire to return home. But not until he and Rebeka were finished here.

"Done here," George said as he turned off his tablet.

"There is one other place where we'll find weapons." They left the garden house and headed toward the garrison. He hoped the weapons there hadn't been tampered with.

Arik opened the sanctuary. Once inside the cavern, with a nod, he indicated the correct tunnel and headed to the armory.

The gate stood solid and secure. He touched the lock, released the spring and entered. His eyes followed the light as it revealed the accumulation of weapons and chests. He cleared his mind and centered himself. Beneath his shirt his runes warmed and glowed. An envelope, with his name scrawled in his brother's hand, rested atop a velvet cloth that sat on the large table in the center of the room.

> *Brother,*
>
> *As I promised, Rapture will always belong to its rightful knight and leader, as will your ring. Doward and I sit a nightly vigil in your tower awaiting your return.*
>
> *Logan*

He removed the cloth. The sheen of oil on the blade made it gleam in the flickering light. He touched Rapture's hilt and sensed his brother's presence. He wiped the blade with his hand and knew Logan hadn't used it. He removed his hand and the visions faded. Now he understood Louise's words. The sword hadn't been lost. Logan had locked it away.

Its magick was intact.

He held his signet ring and he felt the connection to his past. He saw each Grand Master's face and heard each voice. "To hearth and home," he murmured to the shadows and detected their reply.

He handed the blade to George and watched his eyes widen with respect as he turned it over.

"Amazing." He turned to Arik. "I can feel the touch of each Grand Master." He examined the blade. "It's an honor."

Arik took the sword from him, returned Rapture to the table then covered it with the cloth. He and George turned to the racks of weapons that lined the walls. "These are battle ready. They've been oiled and preserved with care." George checked the edges of a nearby axe. Arik surveyed the bows as well as fletching and arrowheads on the cache of arrows. He thumbed the edges of the halberds, swords and claymores.

"You're right. They've been well preserved." He let out a sigh of relief. There were enough weapons for half a legion, twenty-four hundred men.

"Our men don't know how to fight with these weapons." George shook the halberd in his hand. "This is a large undertaking." He returned the long two-handed spear to its place.

"I know it takes men years to learn the blade but half the work is done. Each of these men are battle tested. What they don't have in years they'll make up in heart."

"You make it sound so simple." They left the armory. Arik locked the gate behind him.

"It's a simple solution but one that entails a lot of hard work," he said over his shoulder. "I didn't say it would be easy. Come, I want to see the men training." George followed him out of the sanctuary.

The grunts of the men on the practice field were a familiar sound. He joined the major and watched the men for several minutes as they practiced hand-to-hand combat. Any doubts he'd had vanished when he watched the exercise.

There wasn't one among them that wasn't working with a full heart.

"Do any of the men know how to use a sword?" Arik asked. He was already evaluating the men for which weapon would be best for them.

"Some have fencing experience." The major turned to him. "Will they be fighting with broadswords?"

"The men will be training during the day, with visitors watching. Dr. Tyler tells me that's what they want to see."

The major let out a snort and turned back to his men. "It'll be a good disguise." He added *straightforward* to the major's list of leadership qualities. He was more like Marcus than Arik first believed.

"I'd like to see who has the most promise. Put the men into groups of fifteen. Each will have a sword master to lead them." He was already planning the training sessions. They'd have to start with the basics but hoped they would excel quickly.

"Sword master? How will we find sword masters?" He wasn't surprised by the doubt in the major's voice. George told him it was a dying art.

"The same way Mr. Hughes and Dr. Tyler found the others for the reenactment—they'll audition." Arik smiled. "We'll show them a sword fight then see who has an interest."

It was a crisp and clear afternoon. Invigorating. The turf covered practice area was a flat open meadow next to the planted field. It was a patchwork of beaten down areas, some scrubbed down to the bare earth from the men's war games.

The ring of steel hitting steel echoed across the field. Arik rallied to George's aggressive attack as their blades flashed in the sun. He was impressed with George's ability and technique. In a well-planned maneuver, George had bested him sending him to the ground much to his surprise. For a few moments, Arik was himself, a seventeenth century knight and lord, filled with relief and satisfaction. He had his Rebeka and soon they would return home.

"It looks like we've got quite a crowd," Arik said to George as they continued to parry.

One barrage from Arik caught Hughes off guard and sent him on his ass. Arik immediately brought up his blade. "That makes us even." Arik extended his hand to George. "You fight well. I would have you on my side of an argument. Perhaps you should've been a knight instead of a barrister."

"That's high praise coming from you." George pounded Arik on the back. "Again? Tomorrow?"

"I look forward to it." George was better than he had anticipated. He'd enjoyed sparring with him.

George stood close to Arik. "Do you think this

worked?" he asked in a hushed tone.

Arik scanned the onlookers. "It seems to have piqued their interest."

"This was a good idea. Let the men want to learn how to use the sword. I'll teach them what I know. I'll meet you in the garrison. I think you've made a good decision. The major has handpicked each man. They are a loyal lot and trustworthy." George gave Arik his sword and left.

"Lord Arik?"

"Yes?" He turned to see Joan standing in front of him with a towel and bottle of water.

"I thought..." her voice was a whisper. "I thought you would need these." She laid her hand lightly on his knotted forearm then quickly pulled it away.

"Thank you, m'lady." He tilted his head in acknowledgment. He looped the towel around his neck and drank the water.

Several of the men gathered around him. Arik watched them and followed their eyes. They were glued to the two swords.

He reviewed the men and picked Steven, one of the men with the best potential. His movements during training reminded him of Logan.

Stamina was another issue.

He handed the man the sword.

"It's heavy. You and Mr. Hughes made them look light." The man hefted it—judging its weight, evaluating it. A man had to know his weapon in order to command it. This man showed a lot of promise.

"How does it feel?" his friend Jaxon asked.

"It's odd but it feels right."

"That's because of the balance. Most men have swords made for them. The weight and balance make all the difference." Arik gave the towel and bottle back to his admirer. "Take your position," he said to the soldier.

A broad smile spread over Steven's face. The others moved back to their circle. The crowd hushed and waited.

Arik took the defensive position. He let Steven lead the attack while he evaluated each step and move. Steven's movements were labored. He forced the sword through the air, putting unnecessary stress on his body. His movements weren't smooth and he hadn't found his rhythm, but that would come with practice. However, if he didn't change his tactic he would tire quickly.

"No, don't aim at my sword." Arik took the offensive. "Either block it or aim at me. I'm a much bigger target."

The immediate barrage ended. "But don't I want to stop your sword?" Steven asked, struggling for breath. He stood bent over, the sword across his thighs.

"There are two ways to fight. Both are correct and depend on your style. You can drive the initiative and keep your opponent on the defensive, or you can wait for an opportunity for a sound counterattack, fight defensively. Most good swordsmen strive to be skilled at both. In field fighting the strategy is offense. The objective is to hit your opponent fast and hard—disable or kill him—then move on to the next." Arik tapped his shoulder. "Now try again."

"That isn't much different than how we fight today." Arik caught what one of the onlookers said. Hundreds of years later and combat hadn't changed. The weapons may change but the intent is the same.

"Relax your shoulders. They're too tight." Arik continued the sparring. "Tension is your enemy. Staying flexible will allow you to keep a wide stance and that is where your strength is. Don't keep your feet parallel. Put one back and turn it out."

His student made the quick adjustment.

"Yes, that's right. Can you feel the difference?" Arik pushed forward but Steven didn't budge. "Good. I can't push you off balance."

"Hold," the major shouted.

Arik held up his sword. Steven was out of breath. Sweat covered his face. His shirt stuck to him as if he'd been out in a rainstorm. His sword arm appeared to have long gone limp but he had kept going.

Arik had continued the barrage to see how long he would stand. He didn't stop. Quite impressive. Exhausted, the soldier was clumsy and let his sword brush across his forearm, slicing it open. Steven ripped off his shirt.

Arik grabbed it from him and wrapped the arm tightly. "It appears worse than it is," he said. "Leave the cloth and have the major see to it." Arik didn't need to ask the man about the battles he'd been through. Arik had his share of battle wounds but he was humbled by the scars on Steven's chest and back.

"I didn't feel the cut." Steven looked astonished.

"When the edge is sharp you don't feel it." Arik sheathed his sword.

"These aren't practice blades," another soldier said. "He could've killed you," he said to Arik.

"It was my job to make certain that didn't happen." Arik turned to the others. "Tell me, when you were in service and practiced with your weapons, did you practice with real ones?"

"Well, yes we did," all the men responded.

"And we marched with real packs, too," called out another. The men rumbled in agreement.

"Of course. You must learn to respect your weapon. Work with it until it becomes part of you, an extension of your arm, before it will do what you want. In that way a sword is no different than any other weapon." Arik saw the respect in each man's eyes.

"Mr. Hughes and I will teach you to be

swordsmen once your bodies are ready. The principles of the sword require you to be strong, flexible and quick. The blade is large and heavy. You must command it. It can never command you. That's enough for today."

The men rushed around Steven.

"Jeez, he wasn't even breathing heavy. And after fighting with Mr. Hughes. Are you alright?" Frank asked.

"I'm fine," Steven panted. "The movies have it all wrong. No one can fight for any length of time with a broadsword."

"It seems Lord Arik and Mr. Hughes can."

Steven gathered his things and got into place. His exhaustion was evident but so was the satisfaction anyone could see on his face.

"Everyone to the garrison," the major commanded.

Steven learned quickly. Arik hoped the others would, too. There wasn't any time to lose. Enthusiasm ran through the men. That was encouraging. Training would be tiring and difficult but these were strong men. They would do well.

Arik greeted the men as they entered the garrison. The major was already taking care of Steven's injury.

"Stand easy, men," Arik instructed. George closed the door behind him.

"You all appear tired. Has the major been working you hard?"

A rumble ran through the crowed. "Nothing we can't handle," Brian, one of the engineers, shouted. The others agreed. "We're looking forward to our turn with the blade," he added.

Arik smiled. "It seems every boy wants to play the

knight. I remember playing knight, with my brothers and sister."

"Defending the manor?" Frank asked. A soft laugh filled the room.

"Yes, defending the manor. The manor has a long history. Eleven centuries, to be more precise. Much has happened during that time." He searched the men's faces. He held their interest. "People were born. Couples were wed. Wars were fought. People died. It's a long and illustrious history. I'm pleased you're proud to be a part of it." The men stood straighter.

"In the seventeenth century, the land was in conflict and our manor survived but only through the hard work and efforts of their men at arms." Arik stepped to the hearth then turned to the men. "There are many hidden secrets in old manors and castles. Fayne Manor has its own, as well. This is between each of you and me. No one else. Do I have you word? Your honor?"

The men looked at each other.

"Sir, on my honor whatever you have to say or show me is between you and me," the major said, standing at attention.

"Thank you, Major." One by one each man in the room made the same pledge.

Arik faced the hearth. He had already tripped the mechanism and left the large stone ajar. Now he pushed it open, exposing the tunnel.

A gasp rolled through the men along with various curses.

"There is something I'd like to show you. Who will come with me?" The men gathered around him. Within minutes, every man stood with him. He led them into the tunnel deep into the ground. The torches flared to life as they passed. He never doubted George when he said these men were loyal and trustworthy. He was surprised when George suggested bringing them to the sanctuary. But he was right. He needed to demonstrate his loyalty and trust to them.

"This is like a theme park," muttered one of the men. The others around him shook their heads. Finally, they arrived in a large cavern. The torches ignited around the room.

"How'd he do that?"

"It must be by remote control or by sensors when you enter the area," assured another. "Pretty cool."

Arik and George made certain there were no stragglers. "Fayne Manor was successful. Its very success made it a target. Some men wanted to ruin it and others wanted to own it. But each time the master of the manor rallied his men. He defended and protected all who lived here. His men and their kinfolk were as important to him as his own family. They worked, drank, played games and fought side by side. All a man had to do is see the talisman to come to the aid of his comrades."

"A talisman?" A soft buzzed echoed in the cavern.

"Yes, a trinket that identified the men of Fayne Manor," Arik said.

"Ah, like the patch on our uniform. That would be nice. Something to hold on to," someone said quietly.

Arik scanned the men. These were men who wanted to belong to something bigger than themselves. That was something he could give them. "Follow me."

He took them into the tunnel. He stood in front of the weaponry gate, silently worked the lock then opened the door. The men entered and stood at the edge of the darkness and waited. One torch, lit against the wall, revealed a chest. Arik knelt by the chest and pulled out a handful of medallions. "This is the Fayne talisman. Each man believed it protected him." He didn't tell them that it was a magical druid symbol. There was plenty of time for that later.

Jaxon investigated the disk. "Did the men carry

it?"

"When they joined the ranks, each man received the disk. Before they went into their first battle the symbol was marked on their arm." Arik raised the edge of his sleeve to reveal his Fayne mark.

"There is one more thing." He stepped to the far end of the long table. The torches on that side of the room flared into life. In front of him was the real Sword of Rapture. It glistened in the torchlight and held each man's attention.

"This is the symbol and the strength of Fayne Manor. No one has seen the true sword for hundreds of years. Let it be a beacon for you as it was for the men who preceded you.

"Last night I fought to save the mill next to loyal and courageous men. Those are ideals I treasure highly. They are ideals that not all men have. It's what separates you from others." He let that idea stew for a few seconds. This is between you and me," he said, his voice deep and resonant. "No other. I pledge I will protect and defend you and your families to the best of my ability. So let it be."

The major was the first to come forward. "I swear I will protect and defend you and your family to the best of my ability. So let it be."

Arik extended his hand to the major. "So let it be." The major stared at Arik's hand and clasped it soundly then received one of the disks. The man took off the chain he wore around his neck. He added his new talisman then put the chain back on.

George was next then one by one each man came forward and pledged themselves to Lord Arik and received the Fayne talisman.

"I am proud to be one of you. Each of you has proven your valor and strength to your country. I am honored you are now of Fayne Manor." He stood in the midst of George and his soldiers, their eyes shining with pride and brotherhood.

George led the men back through the tunnel and into the garrison.

Arik followed behind the men, closing and securing the sanctuary. He wasn't surprised by their reaction but he was proud that to a man they all stood with him.

"Thank you, Major, for stepping forward," Arik said.

"Two nights ago I saw how you took care of the men. You made certain everyone was accounted for, consoled the injured, lighten their spirits and, at your own risk, saved Bill. You are a principled, fair leader who cares about his men. How could I not serve you?"

"Thank you," he said as they stood in front of the gatehouse.

"About the sword demonstration, what do you think of Steven?" the major asked.

"I watched his eyes as we fought. He was thinking and learning with each step. He used my own tactics against me. He's a good student and learns fast. Once he increases his stamina he'll be an excellent swordsman. Yes, mark him for one of the sword master positions. And make certain you include deep breathing exercises, push-ups, sit-ups and plenty of stretching in tomorrow's training. They need to work on their shoulders, back and arm muscles to sustain a sword fight."

"The restoration of the village should help with the body building. Fixing those stone houses will have the men lifting blocks all day." The Major started off for the village.

CHAPTER NINETEEN

The lights of several cars parked at odd angles in the manor drive flashed through the library windows at syncopated intervals, giving the room a harsh blue glow. "This way, sir." Charles showed their guest into the library.

"Dr. Tyler, Mr. Hughes, I'm Detective Chief Inspector Bardsley." He gave an envelope to George. "I spoke with the fire warden about the incident at your mill. The evidence was all there. It took less than a week to come to a conclusion. He has confirmed it was arson. There is the final report." Arik joined Rebeka.

George read through the documents. "Yes, he sent a copy to my office."

Arik and George had agreed with the fire warden's findings. It wasn't a huge leap of faith. The accelerant was proof enough.

"Dr. Tyler." Rebeka gave the man her attention. "Your student..." He read through his small spiral notebook. "Yes, Marle. She gave us a description of the two who attacked your man." He thumbed through his pad. "Bill. We have them in custody. Caught them in a minor traffic accident. The young lady is quite perceptive. She gave us a good description of the men and the tattoo. It supports Bill's statement. She'll have to identify them but that is only a formality."

"Marle? "Arik asked as he stepped forward.

"Yes, when we questioned the students, she and her friend…" more rummaging through his notebook, "…John, said they had been at the mill. It was 'their place,' she said. Anyway, when they heard people coming they rushed into the woods then Bill arrived. A few minutes later the suspects pulled Bill out of the building. The men rolled up their sleeves. That's when Marle and John smelled gasoline and saw the tats on one of them. She called it a heta. They took off through the woods, ran back here and woke everyone."

So that's how Marle and John knew about the fire. Arik had assumed they saw the fire or smelled the smoke as he had and roused the men.

"Heta? Are you sure that's what she said?" Arik asked.

"She drew it for me." Bardsley showed Arik and Rebeka his pad. "Bill confirmed this is what he saw."

"Thank you, Chief Inspector. We're glad this is closed," Rebeka said.

"I wouldn't call this closed just yet. Why did they torch the mill? These men do things for money. I want to know who is behind this and what else they plan. We can assign some guards—"

"That won't be necessary," George said. "We have our own men on it. But let's keep communications open. As legal representative for Dr. Tyler you can forward everything to me. I'd like to be at the interrogation."

"I'll contact your office as soon as those arrangements have been made. Well, that's all for now. Dr. Tyler, Mr. Hughes. I'll find my own way out."

They watched the blue lights fade as the cars left the drive.

"Heta is a Latin *H*. It must be Bran's mark," Rebeka said as Arik looked out the window.

"It's similar. The mill is warded. Bran or his men couldn't get past them."

"Are you certain?" Rebeka asked.

"Yes." The thought that there was another threat was…uncomfortable but he was certain it came from this century, not his.

"Then who's behind setting the fire and why?"

"We should be back by midafternoon," Rebeka told Arik and George as she got into the waiting car with Cora. "The archivist at the Overbury Estate found a document containing a reference to Mannis. It's not the proclamation but it's worth reviewing. The photo she sent had runes in the margins that no one could decipher."

Arik hoped she was right. He had been helping her and her senior students search through the old documents. It was a tedious process. Written in a variety of languages, each document had to be scrutinized for any reference that might lead them to information. They had several dead ends but this one appeared promising. They had only fifteen days until the Trust's deadline. While he helped Rebeka, George and Cora were digging into the financial questions the Trust raised.

"I know the connection between Alfred and Mannis was hidden but it appears to be nonexistent." She gave him a worried glance.

"They're well hidden but they exist. We found Doward's account. There'll be others. We'll find it." He stepped away from the car. She gave him a watery smile and pulled away.

"Are you as certain as you sound?" George asked as they started for the garden house to take an inventory of the weapons. Arik brought his attention back to George.

"I'll stay positive until we've exhaust all our options." He was baffled that everything from 1570 to 1670 was missing. Either the documents were truly lost or they contained information that someone wanted hidden. Deep in his bones he knew they still existed. With luck, Rebeka would have some success. He and George entered the garden house and made their way to the weapons room to determine which weapons to use for demonstrating the smithy's work.

"What about these?" Arik focused on the swords.

"I've contacted my father's former colleague." George cataloged the swords and noted what repairs needed to be made. "He asked for an inventory of what needed to be restored." He held up the list. "Other than their dulled edges and points, the quality of these weapons is excellent. Your idea of having the guests watch the repairs is a good one."

Someone knocked on the door frame. "Excuse me."

Arik put down the sword. "Yes?" He spun around. Joan stood inside the doorway.

"Is Dr. Tyler here?" Joan surveyed the room.

"She's gone to Overbury. Is it something urgent?" Joan was one of the students going through the library documents searching for the proclamation.

"I found this parchment in one of the codices. It doesn't belong with the information on herbal remedies I'm reviewing."

"Are you certain?" Arik asked. She gave him the document.

"It's part of a scroll and appears out of place— much older. If you read the text you'll see it's written by several people and there's a variety of languages. I'm pretty good with many of the Celtic dialects but I can only read a phrase or two of these."

The touch of the document set the hairs on the

back of Arik's neck on end. The document was papyrus and well preserved. "May I keep this, Joan? As soon as I am finished here I can give this my full attention."

"Sure. I'll check back with you later. Thanks." Arik handed the text to George and waited until Joan left the room.

"It seems Joan has found one of the druid texts." George scanned the document.

"I'm surprised she could read past the enchantment. She's right about it being written by several different people. See, each author has their sigil at the end of their line." He pointed to one of the symbols. Arik rolled it up with care. "I'll see to this after we've finished here."

Three hours later George got into his motorcar and rolled down the window. "Let me know what that's all about." He nodded toward the rolled-up document. "You're pocket's ringing." George nodded to Arik's shirt.

Arik pulled his cell phone and read the display.

"I'll get the inventory out. The sooner we begin the repairs, the better," George said and drove out the gate.

"Rebeka."

"Cora and I are on our way back. There were runes in the margin of one of their documents. I had to chant to read it. The document was from Chippenham and mentions Mannis assisting Alfred the Great. We reviewed the entire document but it only had the one reference. We're going to go out to dinner. I'll see you later." It wasn't enough. Her voice was filled with disappointment. Perhaps the evening out with Cora would boost her spirits.

"I've a call coming in from Louise. I'm sure it's to remind us the Trust expects the document in twenty days. See you later." She ended the call. He was as disappointed as she sounded. However, if they found this reference there was bound to be more.

Arik went to the tower. Like the writing on his walls, the words in the document were locked away from prying eyes. He muttered the words to release the enchantment. A few of the symbols unlocked. The shock of his inability to unchain the others sobered him. "Faith." He should've known when he touched the document and sensed the presence of the former Grand Masters that the protection was deep.

He closed his eyes and quieted his mind as he took a deep breath. Calmly he exhaled and visualized all his turbulent and worried thoughts forced out of his mind when he exhaled. Two more breaths and he was ready. His mind free and the tension gone, he went deeper until he found that quiet place. At ease, he visualized his intent and whispered the chant that would summon the golden key. It resisted him.

This protection was deeper still. Although he knew it was possible, he had never come across a document with protection this intense. He concentrated harder and continued his chant.

His eyelids fluttered and a plain brass key took form suspended in front of him. The first part done, he moved on to the next chant. The key turned slowly at first, in time with the cadence of his chant. Faster and faster he chanted until the key was a spinning golden oval of light. He spoke the final verse and the whirling orb brightened and burst into a million pieces. He opened his eyes and watched as sparks of light dance across the document, revealing the text as it passed along. Another deep breath followed by a silent thank-you. He took his pen and was ready to begin.

The text held crucial information about the portal and its workings. The various sigils adorning the margins of the text were a testament to the number of ancient Grand Masters who provided their opinions and enhancements to the portal's evolution over the past thousand years. Some spoke of warding the area and others anchored the portal to the great standing stones. There was mention of the scrying mirror's magick.

Arik continued on for several more hours. Even though he unlocked the document, he researched and cross-referenced his translation using the books in his library. The day had turned cool and overcast. The threat of a heavy rainstorm hung in the air. The tower room was dark. The lamp on the table lit a small section of it. The rest of the room glowed from the light in the hearth. Arik was two-thirds down the page. He read over his notes and froze.

He struck out the last three lines and translated them again. But by the time he reached the second group of symbols he knew he would get the same answer—there was no other meaning.

No, he wouldn't accept the answer. For the past five days between working with the men on the mill, village repairs and with Rebeka searching for the proclamation, Arik worked on the druid document. He found a few differences in the translation but they all ended the same.

Finally, he threw down the pen and rose from the table. With one hand on his hip and the other rubbing the back of his neck, he paced the small room like a caged animal. He reread the translation, searching for any little nuance that would change the meaning.

On one hand the document gave the key for using the scrying mirror to return while on the other hand, she could never return home. And it was his fault. He stood at the wall for hours and traced the runes he put there so many centuries ago. He searched for a more agreeable translation but deep in his heart he knew he wouldn't find one. At sunrise he was still at his table. His hand, resting on the pad with his notes, fisted and crumpled the paper into a ball. He stood and threw it into the hearth. It flared as the paper went up in smoke along with all his dreams.

He marched to the pells holding the heaviest practice sword he could find. The storm that was building in the sky couldn't compete with the tempest that raged inside him. By the time he got to the practice field with its wooden posts, the light mist had turned into a steady drizzle.

He took hold of the weapon's grip and circled around the first post, tapping it with the flat of his blade. He never took his eyes off the round pumpkin someone had impaled on the top of the post. The strength of his taps increased as if he were evaluating his opponent, until he stood in front of the post and let loose a barrage of strikes that cut into the hard wood.

The rain came down in sheets but he didn't stop. The sound of his sword against the wood filled the pell and echoed in his ears until all he heard were his grunts and splintering wood. He punished the post, first slicing off the bark then moving on to downward and upward strokes, whittling it away until it was a mere stump.

The pumpkin, made into mash at his onset, littered the area. Splinters of wood were everywhere. He stood soaked and panting, holding his sword ready to attack the next post.

"There are easier ways to make toothpicks," Rebeka said.

He washed the expression off his face before he turned to face her. "You're drenched." He pushed his hair out of his eyes and came out of his daze. "How long have you been standing there?" He had attacked the wooden post as if he were a berserker. Now his arms were limp and his energy spent but it didn't change anything.

She had her shawl over her head but she was as wet as he was.

"Long enough. I came to see what was happening. It sounded as though there was an army out here. I didn't expect to see you taking on the pells by yourself."

The tension in his shoulders eased. What to tell her? He put his arm around her and they started back toward the manor. He needed a plan. His misery hung around his neck like an ox's yoke. He'd lose them all— Logan, Skylar, Aubrey. Raw grief tore at him as he realized he'd never see them again.

"Do you want to talk about it?"

He kept his eyes forward. "There is nothing to talk about. I needed to—"

"Kill something, obviously." They continued on until they got to the manor kitchen where Helen and Charles were having a cup of tea. "Oh dear, you have been strolling in the rain. Wait right there." Helen rose and left the room.

"Here, let me take that." Charles relieved Arik of the sword. "I'll bring it to the garrison."

Helen returned and handed them each towels. "Now upstairs with you both. I'll have some hot soup for you when you're ready."

They entered the tower room. He got out of his clothes, toweled off and tucked the cloth around his waist.

Rebeka wasn't quite into her towel when he pulled her into his arms. She didn't resist. He ran his hand over her back. She was already warm to his touch. His gaze traveled from her warm, tender eyes, to her strong shoulders, to her tempting breasts.

He took her face in his hands and drew her to him. Passion turned her violet eyes a dark purple that smoldered and sent heat coursing through his veins. He kissed her lips as if he was a sinner in need of redemption.

Her answering moan fueled his hunger for her.

With care he placed her on the bed and lay next to her. He nibbled and kissed her neck, taking in the scent of her skin.

She worked her way to his earlobe, nipped then bathed his ear with her soft breath. Her husky voice whispered she loved him. The velvet sound thrilled him as much as the softness of her skin. He couldn't get enough of her. Without her—without her wasn't an option.

He moved but she stopped him and he settled back. She set him on fire with her tentative touch as it traced down his chest to his groin. He covered her hand with his as she stroked him and he gasped in sweet agony. He was at the breaking point.

He wanted to sink deep inside her to chase...no, not to chase anything. He wanted to be deep inside her because without her the world, his world, would spin out of control.

He traced his fingertip across her full lower lip. It was slick and wet as he expected she was. He lowered his mouth to hers but stopped a breath away. The tip of her tongue invited him in and he swept inside. He raised his mouth from her lips and searched her eyes. His tongue made a path from her mouth to her throat then flicked between her breasts. Tenderly he kissed each one. He glanced at her eyes and saw her passion heighten. He pampered her breasts with kisses and tiny nips. His lips teased each nipple and he hardened with each gasp she took.

His hand slid from her firm stomach to the swell of her hips and drew her close to him. Already well aroused, the sound of her throaty voice made him harder still. He needed more than touching. He moved on top of her, nudged her legs apart with his knee and settled between them. His heart pounded and every part of him throbbed with anticipation.

He let her take command, positioning his member at her cleft. Even from there he could feel her warm and wet. He placed his forehead on hers and fought to keep control.

"Love me," she commanded softly.

He buried himself deep inside her, greedily taking her.

Her arms were tight around him, her hips tipped up to take in all of him. She urged him on, his plan of slow and steady morphed to hard and fast.

"Arik," she called out urgently.

He increased the pace.

"Arik," she cried as shudder after shudder pulsed around his member and he climaxed.

His every nerve was filled with wanting. Her every move was rapture. He held her close and rolled over, taking her with him. He settled her on top of him, stroking her back while they both calmed. His world was filled with her.

As he drifted off to sleep he had one thought.

Forever.

"Have you been up long?" Rebeka stretched to get rid of the morning haze. A smile touched her lips as the memory of their evening played over in her mind.

Arik, stretched out next to her, had his hands behind his head and stared at the rafters. "For a while."

She rested her head on his chest. "We never did have our hot soup."

The warmth of his smile echoed in his voice. "No, we didn't. I don't think Helen was surprised."

"Are you going to tell me what's bothering you?"

He started to get out of bed but she would have

none of that. She straddled him and pushed him back onto the bed. "That will keep you down."

"Down. Not exactly, if you insist on sitting there." A sensual smile lit up his face as he ran his hands up her bare sides and across her bare breasts.

She grabbed his hands and held them still. "Not until you tell me. I've recently come out of the dark. Please don't put me back there." She was certain he was taking great pains to keep something from her. She let go of his hands as he rose and pushed him away. She didn't want to be close to him, not until he told her what concerned him.

"Joan gave me a parchment to translate." He stroked her back.

She cuddled next to him. Joan had told her. So, what was the big deal? "Yes, she told me. She didn't think it belonged with the herbal codex."

"She was right. It's from a druid text." His hand, running up and down her back, stopped.

She forced herself to be patient. "I wonder why it was with my father's papers. I gave it to Joan. She needed some information about herbs for her thesis."

"Max. Of course. No wonder I had difficulty getting through the enchantment."

She leaned over, grabbed the sheet and tucked it in around herself. "What did it say?"

"The document is an accounting of the portal." He stared across the room at the runes. "There are consequences to time travel. I knew there would be but they didn't matter." He held her close. "All that mattered was finding you."

She touched his chest. Under her hand the steady beat of his heart sped up. It didn't soothe her anxiety. "We'll face the consequences together," she told him gently. "We're both affected."

"The portal holds the travel information. It knows where you started and where you need to be returned.

But it must be the same portal. No other."

"Yes, I understand."

She started to say something but he raised his hand.

"Let me finish. I adjusted the last portal to leave a special passage for you. I wanted you to be able to return here." He held her close. "That's the portal you were in. When the enchantment shattered it closed the portal forever. Even I can't open it. I didn't anticipate this."

"You said you came through the scrying mirror. What else did you find?" she demanded quietly.

"Yes, I used the scrying mirror and I planned to use it for us to return. But that way back is no longer open." He was quiet. "We can't go back," he said, his voice hushed with little emotion.

She pulled away from him. Her heart was pounding. "But, Arik, if you came through the mirror you can go back." Her mind tumbled with a hundred ideas.

"Didn't you hear me?" he snapped at her then regretted his outburst. He held her to his chest. "The way is closed." His voice was a choked whisper.

She pulled off the sheet and rummaged for her clothes, desperate to do something, anything.

He hurried out of bed and held her by her shoulders. "Where are you going?"

"You shouldn't have come for me. Now, you can't return." Tears ran down her cheeks. "What have I done?" She couldn't look at him knowing the pain she'd caused.

He lifted her chin but she pulled her face away. "I'm not sorry to be here. Look at me." He lifted her face. "Nothing is more important to me than you. Nothing." He dropped his hands.

"You say that now but will you feel the same when you realize that you can never go back, never see Logan and the others." She scanned around the small room searching for something, anything to change the situation. She saw the runes and whipped around at him. "You wrote me a love song," she said, grabbing his arms. "Together we'll write another. We'll keep searching." Her voice was firm and final. They stood in silence staring at the runes.

Reworking the formula wouldn't work. He had used his magick to adjust the portal for her to return here. There was no way for her to go back without either dying or being lost between times forever.

Her heart squeezed tight. What then? "You'll grow to hate me," she whispered.

"I could never—"

"I've taken you from everything you've loved and worked for—"

"No." He held her chin with the crook of his forefinger. "You've given me everything I've ever wanted. I came after you by choice. And I would do it again knowing the outcome."

She wished she could believe him. Maybe he would love her now, maybe even for the next few years, but would he still love her when he realized what she had cost him?

He wiped her tears away with a softness that comforted her. Comforted her? He was the one who'd lost everything. No, they both had. She was beaten and defeated. How could she ever forgive herself?

"We have a lifetime together. Besides, I would miss the hot shower and the motorbike." His voice was a hoarse whisper. She let out a forced laugh.

She searched for her clothes and found them in a pile on the floor, still damp. She pulled a towel around her. "I better go to my room before anyone sees me like this. Towels are not in fashion this year."

"I want you in my bed."

"Right now?" She chuckled and stretched on her

tiptoes and gave him a kiss. "Later, definitely later." His slow smile took her breath away.

"You're my wife and I want you in every sense of the word. But I won't compromise your position or your reputation. We'll marry."

She blinked, stunned by his statement. "That's not necessary. In this century many couples live together and don't get married."

He stroked her face with his knuckles. "Beka," he whispered. "In my century I married you. I love you and will marry you again in this one. You are my heart. Marry me."

She gave him kisses—soft, gentle ones at first that gathered in urgency. They were on the bed and she didn't remember how she got there. "We won't get to breakfast."

"I certainly hope not." He kissed each bare space as inch by inch he pulled her towel off.

CHAPTER TWENTY

"A toast." George and Arik raised a glass of wine at Autumn Chase. "To the bridegroom." He sipped champagne. "I'm certain the bride looks radiant," he continued over his lunch. "Does this have anything to do with the document Joan asked you to translate five days ago?"

Arik picked at his salmon. "The document is an accounting of the portal." He rested his elbows on the table and clasped his hands. He had reconciled that they both would be staying. It hadn't been a hard decision.

There had been no decision. He wouldn't leave her. But if he had known he would never return he would have... It wasn't worth thinking about that now. He had to move forward. They had to move forward.

"I told Rebeka when I sealed the portal I left one opportunity for her to return here. That part is true. I told her there was one other way, the scrying mirror, and that I had used it to find her." He unclasped his hands, took his fork and picked at the salmon. "I also told her that way was no longer open to us."

George's fork clattered onto the plate. "That's not true."

"No, it's not." He pushed a piece of potato around

his plate. He wasn't at all hungry. *Faith.* He was still trying to grasp what had happened. "But as far as Rebeka is to know, there is no way back." He put his fork on his plate. "The papyrus documents the portal magick." He stared at his plate not wanting to give voice to the truth. "When I adjusted the portal, it was for one trip." He glanced at George. "The magick is tied to her. If she tries to move through time again she…won't survive."

"She's a great sorceress. She *will* not survive or *may* not survive? There's a big difference."

"Sorceress or not, the magick is tied to her. I won't take that risk." He took a large swallow of champagne, the only thing on the table that tempted him.

"You're the Grand Master. You can conjure something." Did George think he hadn't considered that? *Breathe.* He relaxed his viselike grip on the wine goblet before he snapped the crystal.

"Don't you think I've gone over the document, taken apart each Grand Master's writings and tried to find a solution?" He ran his hand through his hair. He had tried everything.

George stared at him. "Isn't this Rebeka's decision?" The question hung in the air unanswered.

Arik took the napkin on his lap and placed it on the table. "What do you expect me to do? Let her be lost in oblivion forever? Or worse, torn to shreds? I won't let that happen. I will protect her." He pounded his fist on the table. He leaned back and regained his composure. "I told her I wasn't willing to give up my motorbike or hot shower. She said I was quite amusing." His tight expression relaxed into a weak smile. "Bran must've known about the portal's restrictions. At first I assumed he gained nothing, but I see I'm his target. I either lose Logan and the others, or I lose Rebeka. No solution is…ideal."

"We can search for a solution," George said. Arik

stared at his plate. George played his sounding board, his conscience and his second. There wasn't anyone else he could trust with this information. "I know this isn't easy for you."

"No, it's not." Arik's strong, commanding voice turned into a whisper in defeat. He and Rebeka would mourn not returning but they would help each other adjust. "But we're looking forward to our wedding."

"You'd better not tell Cora. She plans all the events for The Retreat. She'll have your wedding planned before the day is out." George gave Arik a smile.

"What shouldn't you tell me?" Cora came in and kissed her brother on the forehead. "What are you two up to?" She poured herself a cup of coffee and took a seat.

"The portal was destroyed and cannot be repaired. There's no way for Rebeka and I to return." Arik kept eating as if he had given Cora the weather report, sunny with no chance of returning.

A bewildered Cora stared back at him. She glanced at her brother. "George, is that possible? I mean, there must be some way." She faced Arik. "Have you told Rebeka?"

"Yes, we've discussed it at length." He raised his wineglass and tried to smile. "We've both reconciled with staying."

"What will you do?" He'd never seen Cora flustered. Her head kept swiveling from him to George.

"Do? We'll continue on as we have been these past weeks, making the manor self-sufficient. Rebeka has her teaching." He glanced over the rim of his glass at Cora. "I've asked her to marry me." He took a sip of his wine.

Cora stared at the two men, tongue-tied.

"Aren't you interested in her response?" George teased.

"George, stop tormenting the woman." He faced Cora. Disbelief, that's what he saw on her face. "She said yes. We want to get married as soon as possible. I planned we'd get married next weekend before she changed her mind. A seventeenth-century wedding would be appropriate." He saw the emotion in Cora's tear-filled eyes.

"We're grateful to you and George for all that you've done. No one foresaw this. But Cora, we're not unhappy with the outcome." Cora gave him a forced smile and a tense nod. He hoped he was convincing.

"Regarding the proclamation," George said. Arik nodded and cast an eye at Cora. She was speechless. It was a lot to absorb at one time and they shouldn't tease her but she was a good sport.

"Have you gotten any closer to finding it? I'm surprised Louise hasn't been more vocal about it." Cora was sputtering. George tried to hide his smile behind his luncheon napkin.

"We're still searching. We've almost exhausted all the old documents we have in the library and estate office. Rebeka thinks it may be wise to search in the historical records in Chippenham." Arik was certain Cora would burst any moment.

"Next weekend. You want to get married next weekend. That isn't much time. George, you'll have to arrange for a special license. I've got to speak to Rebeka." Cora got up from the table.

"No, it's not much time. To the Fayne Manor guests it will appear like a part of the reenactment. The staff, you and George will of course know." She looked from Arik to her brother.

"Men—what do you know? You think it just happens." He believed she was about to stamp her foot in protest. Instead she left the room mumbling.

"Cora?" Rebeka answered her cell phone. "Thank you...Yes, I'm very happy...Arik is quite certain...Well, additional research wouldn't hurt...I'm telling Louise before I let anyone else know...Don't be silly, Cora. Why would she be upset?...Someone has to tell her...No, not Arik...She'll be here in an hour...Bye." Rebeka ended the call and put the phone on the library table.

She read the herbal document for the third...or was it the fourth time? Concentration escaped her. She didn't take defeat easily. Perhaps after they dealt with Bran they could search for a way back.

Arik had been gone when she woke this morning. They had decided that he should tell George and Cora right away.

What was she thinking when she volunteered to tell Louise? The sole reason she was telling the woman was because of the tenuous situation with the Trust. Nobody wanted to jeopardize that. She'd called and had to leave a message. She looked at the document and for the fifth time—yes, it was definitely the fifth time—she cleared her mind and continued to translate the herbal codex Joan had been working on.

"Rebeka?"

Louise entered the room and hooked her thigh on the edge of the desk.

"Yes?" Had it been an hour already? She'd have to give this back to Joan to translate. Her mind was elsewhere.

"I'm on my way to London and can't stay long. Your message sounded urgent." Louise managed a smile.

"I wanted to tell you that Arik and I are getting married. We didn't want you to hear it from anyone else." Rebeka searched the woman's eyes for any hint of emotion.

Louise's smile broadened but it didn't reach her eyes. "What wonderful news. I knew you were interested in him. And here I assumed you were calling about the proclamation."

She decided to ignore her comment. They had fifteen days.

"We've decided to have the wedding here at the manor."

"What a wonderful idea. Let me know if you need anything." Louise got up to leave. "No hard feelings, my toying with him."

"Not at all." She saw Louise to her car.

"I expect an invitation to the wedding." The olive branch offering registered with Rebeka but there were other things on her mind right now.

"Of course." Rebeka stepped away and Louise drove off.

She had gotten as far as the manor door when the roar of the Triumph's engine and the spatter of the gravel on the manor drive interrupted the quiet morning. She stopped and watched Arik get off the motorbike.

The smooth jeans over his trim hips and the tight T-shirt thrilled her. She considered it his bad-boy look.

But he would look wonderful in soft slacks and a silk shirt.

On second thought, she wasn't willing to make him that civilized or give up her medieval knight, not yet. She grew warm at the idea.

"Like a good wife, waiting for me at the castle door." He came up the porch steps and kissed her forehead.

"Hard day at the office?" They went into the Great Hall arm in arm.

"I have good news."

"I'll wait like a dutiful wife."

"As you should." His gave her a secret smile, the one that curled her toes. "George is taking care of everything and getting us a special license. We'll be married by next weekend. I think you should be prepared for Cora. She's already making plans."

She gave him a devilish grin. "I know. I spoke to her earlier. There's a lot to do. Did you pass Louise on your way here? She left a few minutes ago. Don't look so disappointed."

"I didn't say anything." He took her in his arms and kissed her.

"Lovely. The color is perfect with your eyes. Where did you find the gown?" Cora put the finishing touches on Rebeka's dress.

"I bought it in New York when I attended the Society for Medieval Studies symposium three years ago. It was an extravagance but I fell in love with it." Excited as if she were a new bride, she primped in front of the full-length mirror. Cora and Helen had taken care of every detail. The manor was buzzing with anticipation.

The long mauve silk dress had a plunging neckline that was framed with small crystals. The long sleeves tapered to a point over the top of her hand, giving it a medieval styling. The bodice was a snug fit to her hips where the skirt fell in a natural drape close to her legs and finished in a tulip flare at the floor. The skirt was sprinkled with small crystals that swept down the front and swirled to the right into a trail along the hem. It was enough to make the dress glitter as she walked. She wore strappy silk heels that made it appear as if she had no shoes on at all.

A twisted rope of silver and crystals banded across

the top of her head appeared like a crown. Her long hair was swept up and held in place with two large, well-hidden combs.

"I hope he likes it," she said quietly. She was excited now as she was last August when she dressed for her wedding reception. Logan had walked her down the stairs, Arik waiting for her at the bottom.

They could be happy here. He would run the manor, she would have her teaching. It would work. It had to work.

Oh, Great Mother, make it work.

Cora's face, from over her shoulder, stared back at her in the mirror. "He'll see no one else, I assure you. You're a beautiful bride." Finally, Cora put a fine net veil in place.

"There, you're all ready." She turned to Cora and saw the tears in her eyes. "You look like a princess but I knew you would. Where's George? He said he would be here to take you downstairs."

"I'm right here," George said from the other side of the door that was ajar. Cora pulled open the door. "I was about to knock."

"Good, then I'll go downstairs." Cora stepped out of the way.

Rebeka stood in the center of the room ready to leave.

"Lovely. I can't wait to see his face." He gave her one last look and hesitated. "You are as dear to me as Cora. I'm honored you asked me to give you away. If ever you need me, know that I'm here for you, for both of you." He led her down the stairs.

"I don't know what to say…"

"We each have our duties. Mine was to see you safe with Arik. I assumed my reward would be the completion of that mission but it has been much more. It's the deep friendship that we've made. I would miss you both if you returned. Selfishly, I'm glad you're staying."

"You and Cora are more than good friends.
You've both been like family to me. You must know I
feel the same." She squeezed his hand.

They were at the doorway to the Great Room.

The room was filled with the manor students, staff
and members of the National Trust. Angus came from
Oxford, as did other scholars who were her father's
friends. Guests enjoying a day at the manor were also
there.

She scanned the room and breathed a sigh of
relief—Louise was missing.

At the far end of the room, Arik stood on the
raised platform with the major. Alf Lacey and some of
his friends stood to the side. A small drum started the
beat and a mandolin played softly in the background.
The murmur of voices stilled and the crush of people
parted as she came in on George's arm.

She caught muffled comments but her eyes were
focused on him. Arik stood there tall and solid. He
dressed more or less in period with a contemporary
touch. He wore smooth black breeches that hugged his
powerful legs. His soft leather boots fit snugly around
his calf. He wore a gray silk shirt with a large open
collar, exposing a silver torque that fit around his
throat. His black coat emphasized his broad shoulders
and was tapered to the waist then into a gentle flare at
his hips. Slits in the full sleeves gave a view of the
billowy silk sleeves underneath. He had a ruggedness
and vital power that drew her like a magnet.

He was hers.

She gazed into his eyes and her heart skipped a
beat. His extraordinary eyes twinkled with excitement
and smoldered with passion at the same time. Whispers
of good luck and good fortune filled the room as she
and George proceeded. Halfway to Arik everyone else
in the room seemed to fade. At last she stood in front

of him.

"Who giveth this woman to this man?"

"I do." George removed her veil and placed her hand in Arik's.

Her heart was racing. Arik held her hand gently, his thumb making small circles on her wrist, soothing her.

Somewhere she caught snippets from the minister. "Love is the force that allows us to face fears and uncertainty with courage. Base your marriage not only on the joyous days but the hard days. Remember that devotion, joy and love can grow only if you both care for them. Build yourselves a partnership based on strength and respect and it will sustain you all the days of your lives."

"Rebeka," the minister said. "Do you take this man to be your husband..."

She was marrying him because it was important to him. Well, that's what she had believed. She understood it was important to her, too, and for much the same reason. Family. Belonging to one, starting their own—all things she had wanted. Over the past months, when things seemed at their darkest, he was the one in her dreams. He was the one that gave her the strength to go forward. He was the one who fought to find her.

Her soul mate.

Her husband.

"...as long as you both shall live?"

"I will," she said.

"Arik, do you take this woman to be your wife..."

Wife. Maybe soon a mother. The very idea excited her. She watched his lips as he repeated the minister's words.

They commanded men. They planned the future. They teased.

They loved.

They were hers.

"...as long as you both shall live?"

"I will," he said.

"Arik, your vows, please."

Arik held her hand and spoke his vows in a strong yet tender voice only to her. "In your eyes, I have found my home. In your heart, I have found my love. In your soul, I have found my mate. With you, I am whole, full, alive. You make me laugh. And aye, try my patience. You are my breath, my very heartbeat. I am yours. You are mine. Of this we are certain. You are in my heart and you must stay there forever."

He had selected each word and phrase with care. She knew they came from his heart.

"Rebeka, your vows."

She'd crafted her vows the same way. "You are my inspiration and my passion. You are the magick of my days. You help me laugh, you taught me to love. You provide a safe place for me, unlike anything I've ever known. You support me to be myself. Every day I love you more. I am yours. You are mine. Of this we are certain. You are in my heart and you must stay there forever."

Arik took the combs out of her hair. It tumbled around her shoulders and down her back. She gave her head a shake to help it along. He ran his fingers through it and she imagined she would die from his touch. The smirk on his face told her he knew he was driving her wild. She lowered her eyes and when she glanced at him under her thick fan of eyelashes she swore he moaned.

The minister coughed to cover his laugh. He held the two rings. "From the earliest times, the circle has been the symbol of completeness. It represents a commitment of love that is never ending. When you see these rings on your fingers may it remind you of the commitment you made to each other today."

They repeated the minister's words and exchanged rings.

"You have made your promises, exchanged vows and wear each other's ring as a sign of that commitment and you have done so before this gathering of your family and friends. Therefore I declare you husband and wife. Arik, you may kiss your bride."

She'd floated toward him on a cloud. No one else mattered in the room. The minister was mumbling something to him but he didn't hear.

She stood next to him now, her fragrance so familiar, lavender with a hint of rose. George put her hand in his. Her pulse fluttered like a nervous bird. He drew small circles on her wrist to help soothe her. He said his vows gazing into her eyes, into her soul, telling her how he loved her and would always be with her.

Forever.

When he took the combs out of her hair and it tumbled down, the soft, silky feel made it difficult to not pull her up the stairs. How they teased each other. His heart squeezed even tighter, if that was possible. The exchange of rings complete, he waited for the minister's final words. He took her in his arms and kissed her slowly and thoroughly. When they moved apart someone was pounding his back with congratulations.

The rest of the evening was a blur as they moved from one group to another, one more toast and more good wishes. Glasses of wine mysteriously appeared in their hands, food on their plates. The students helped the household staff, played music and sang songs. The manor staff kept the platters and glasses filled.

A soft melancholy came over him as he imagined

Logan and his nieces among the crowd. He buried the notion and as the night wore on someone started their MP3 player and moved the party to the twenty-first century.

Hours later, their guests gone, he relaxed with Rebeka by the hearth in the tower room, a mug of wine in hand. Rebeka's gown was draped over a chair along with his coat and shirt. She was next to him in her nightshirt, yawning.

"Tired?" He took another sip of wine and shared the glass with her.

"It's been a long day. I hadn't expected everyone to come nor stay so late." He pulled her close. "It was a wonderful wedding. Joan seems to be taking our marriage well. She's infatuated with you. It was good of you to dance with her."

"Yes, it was, m'lady. She asked if I had a brother." He smiled.

Rebeka leaned forward. "She didn't."

"Yes, she did. I told her he was taken but I would keep watch for someone else for her." Him, a matchmaker? He shook his head at the idea.

"Actually, the major may be a good match." She took a sip of his wine. He watched the ideas race across her face.

"Let nature take its course. They're close enough here to get to know each other. Right now I prefer to think about other natural things, like taking my bride to bed." He got to his feet and held out his hand.

"Helen said she would have breakfast for us in the morning." She walked into his arms.

He gave her a devilish grin he knew would send her heart racing. "I told her maybe by lunch."

CHAPTER TWENTY-ONE

Rebeka was at her computer searching online archives for any information concerning the proclamation. Five days. Five days was all they had left. She had exhausted all the manor documents and royal archives. George and Angus had managed to get permission for her to access several private archives that were promising. She had a team of her students researching online. Nothing.

"Excuse me, Dr. Tyler."

Rebeka raised her head from her computer. "Yes?"

Joan entered the library.

"I wanted to drop this off on my way to class. I found this at the bottom of one of the document drawers. It's a photo." Joan placed an envelope on the library table. Rebeka peeked inside the envelope then pulled out a picture.

Rebeka blinked. She couldn't believe her eyes. She was staring at a photo of an old woman at a ceremony, smiling cheerfully, holding a framed parchment with a distinctive blue seal. The shock of discovery stunned her.

She turned the envelope over and a neatly cut newspaper article with the same photo fluttered to the table.

"Were there any other stray items?" She read the

article and felt the corners of her mouth tug into a smile.

"No. I did a thorough review and made certain there weren't any other surprises." Joan looked at her cell phone. "I'll be late for class."

"Go ahead. Thanks for dropping this off." Joan left and closed the door behind her.

The newspaper article was dated May 1, 2008. The caption on the photo didn't say anything about the document. It mentioned that Lady Emily stood in front of the hearth in the Great Hall and that the unique tapestry over the hearth dated back to the early 1600s.

She scanned the article, skipping the guest list of scholars and politicians, anxiously searching for information. The blue seal was too coincidental. This had to be about the proclamation.

"Lady Emily Parsons, heir to the Parsons family fortune, celebrated her ninetieth birthday today at her beloved home, Fayne Manor…"

She wasn't interested in the luncheon that was served or the royals that sent her good wishes. She was almost at the end of the article when her heart skipped a beat.

"Lady Emily's birthday coincides with the 1,130th anniversary of the establishment of Fayne Manor by her ancestor Mannis and Alfred the Great. She was kind enough to show this reporter a copy of the royal proclamation recently authorized by the Royal Society following the authentication of her claim. The proclamation was found among the papers she turned over to the National Trust for review."

Rebeka let out a nervous laugh. There was enough information here for George to use with the National Trust. She wanted to kiss Lady Emily for so many reasons. Once again she had saved the day.

She pulled out her cell phone, took a picture of the photo and the news article and sent it to Arik.

She examined Lady Emily's picture and tried to find the family resemblance. Staring back at her were violet eyes. "How can I ever thank you for searching for me? Giving me a family? Giving me Arik?" She was still studying the picture when Arik came through the terrace door.

"I sent your message on to George. He didn't remember the picture." She gave him the photo. When he finished studying it he turned to her. "She's a handsome woman. You have her eyes." He handed her back the photo and took the envelope.

"I sent the pictures to Louise. I think this is enough to prove the manor's authenticity."

"What's this?" Arik pulled a small newspaper article out of the envelope. "This is dated November 30, 2010."

"That's two weeks after Lady Emily's death." She glanced over Arik's shoulder as he read.

"Following the recent death of Lady Emily Parsons, a claim has been made against the estate as to the legitimacy of the family's title based on information dating back to the early 1600s."

"We need to find the family records to prove the line of succession. Someone must have the records from 1570 to 1670."

Her cell phone rang. "Hello, this is Rebeka Tyler...Oh, Louise." She put the photo and the first article back into the envelope. She pressed the phone against her thigh. "That was quick," she said to Arik and put the phone against her ear. "Yes, among other documents...Sure, I don't mind bringing it over..." She slipped the envelope into her backpack. "With traffic at this time of day, if I left now it would take me about an hour to get to your Avebury office...Okay...See you then." She clicked off her phone and put on her backpack.

"While you're there you might want to stop at the

architect's office and get the final plans for the village. They should be ready today." He gave her a light kiss on her lips. She scooted out of his grasp when he tried to pull her into his arms.

"No," she laughed. "I'll never get to Avebury." She planted a big, wet kiss on his cheek and danced out of the room carrying her staff.

Rebeka passed through the dimly lit lobby of the National Trust's annex, a combination warehouse and offices. She climbed the stairs and rounded the corner to Louise's outer office. The secretary, her coat on and keys in hand, was in the process of closing her desk light and looked up. "May I help you? Oh, Dr. Tyler."

"Is it that late?" Rebeka glanced at the large wall clock surprised the office was closing before 1:00 p.m.

"Oh, no. With everyone else gone Ms. Richards told me to take the rest of the day. She's in her office. You can go right in."

Rebeka opened the solid mahogany door and stepped inside. She waited for her eyes to adjust to the dim light cast by the single brass desk lamp. The large wood-paneled room had high ceilings. A variety of bookcases lined two walls. A sideboard stocked with glasses and a liter bottle of soda was on the third wall. Across from her was a pedestal desk situated between two floor-to-ceiling windows. The drapes, tied back with a thick decorative rope, exposed closed shutters that threw the room into total darkness. In front of the desk were two chairs and a small table. Open packing boxes stood on the desk and table waiting to be filled.

"Louise?" Rebeka glanced around the room.

The desk chair swiveled. "You made it here in record time."

"The traffic gods were with me," Rebeka said.

"You going someplace?" She motioned to the boxes. She peered at the woman. "Are you alright? You appear flushed." She came closer to the desk to get a better look.

"I'm fine. I wanted to tell you in person that I'm leaving the Trust. I've recently come into some money—you know how that is—and I'm tying up some loose ends."

"How wonderful for you." This was sudden, but she could understand not being one of the "in" crowd—at least she could understand intellectually.

"Did you bring it with you?" The chilled tone in Louise's voice made her hesitant.

"I think the article has enough information regarding the proclamation for the Trust." The hairs on the back of her neck stood up in warning. Louise's quarterstaff leaned against the wall. She never kept her staff in her office. She was adamant about never mixing that part of her life with her office persona.

Rebeka removed her staff from the leather straps and propped it against the chair next to her. "Would you like to see it?" She had a feeling Louise was playing a game of cat and mouse and Louise had not cast her as the cat.

Louise came from behind the desk. "Show me." Her features were a stone mask.

Arik was at the library table with his tablet. Perhaps the documents were scanned and the original boxes misplaced. He browsed the manor library index. Rebeka's students had done a fine job of organizing and building the references. They even created links to documents in other libraries. Would he ever get used to the advances of this era? He knew and almost understood the technology, but his seventeenth-century mind still found it…magical.

He searched through the findings. It included the research commissioned by Lady Emily. He read through copies of the county and church records searching for any mention of the family name or reference to family members.

Again nothing between 1570 and 1670.

He needed to find milestone events—births, christenings, deaths, marriages…

Skylar and Robert. Of course. George said his niece married Stuart's nephew. If he couldn't find evidence of his line, perhaps he could through Stuart's. He picked up the phone and dialed Cora.

"Cora. I need to confirm Skylar and Robert's marriage. I can't find any records at the manor. I hope you have something there among Stuart's papers."

"Of course I'll help you if I can." He could hear the click of her high heels as she crossed the marble floor. "What's the urgency?"

"The document should give—"

"—her lineage, of course, and name the manor. Brilliant. Give me a minute. I'm in the library."

"Arik." George knocked on the library door. Arik waved him in.

"Cora, George just came in. Let me put you on speaker." He turned to George. "I think we can substantiate the manor using Skylar and Robert's marriage papers. Where would we find them?"

"Stuart's journals are in the bookcase next to the fireplace, in chronological order."

"I'm in the library," Cora said. "We should look after 1610."

"No, look for 1606," directed Arik with a firm voice.

"But that's the year you left. You would have known if Skylar was getting married," Cora said.

"I have my reasons," was all he would offer.

"Wait a minute while I get the book." He heard some shuffling. Couldn't the woman move any faster? He calmed himself; they'd waited this long and a few more minutes wouldn't change anything.

"Here it is." He caught the sound of shuffling papers.

"Oh." Cora sniffled. "I'll…I'll read it to you. 'April 15. This day did not bode well for my Logan. Bran has gathered his forces and threatens Fayne Manor. Logan brought Aubrey and Skylar here for Father's safekeeping several days ago.'"

"This must be Holly's writing," Arik said.

"'Father and Mother have taken them to London for their protection. Word has been sent for them to make haste and return. I'm certain Father will bring much-needed troops. Logan and Robert will not let me deplete the garrison here.

"'A new priest arrived for his monthly visit before they left. Skylar begged Logan to let her and Robert marry before Robert returned to the manor. The sweet man can deny her nothing. He is so much like Arik. He granted her wish. They were married before Father left for London. Although the priest was ill prepared with the appropriate papers, Logan made sure he wrote everything out. The good priest said he would make everything right when he returned to the church in Avebury.'"

Arik slapped the desk. "That's where we go, Avebury."

"You knew about Bran's attack on the manor." He wasn't surprised at George's concern. The two worlds were as real to George and Cora as they were to him and Rebeka.

"I wasn't certain but I had my suspicions." He was confident he had the information he needed. "Cora, read through the journals there and see if you can find more about what's happened."

"Yes, Avebury is where we'll find Skylar and Robert's documents. I'll go with you." A low, incessant buzz distracted George. He pulled his cell phone from his pocket. "George Hughes here. Yes, Detective…What…Yes…Thank you." He ended the call.

"You're not going to believe this. Those thugs who beat Bill and set fire to the mill, they identified who hired them. Louise Richards. Scotland Yard is getting a warrant for her arrest."

Arik froze. "Louise called Rebeka and asked her to come to the Avebury annex." He pushed her speed-dial number on his phone. He glanced at the time. "She should be there by now." He tapped his fingers on the desk while the call went through.

"Hello, you've reached Dr. Rebeka Tyler. I can't come to the phone right now—"

He dialed again. Someone picked up but no one answered.

"I'm on with Scotland Yard," George said. "They'll meet us there. But they're not close."

"Cora, you stay where you are. If Rebeka calls, contact me at once. George and I are on our way to Avebury."

"I will. Be careful," she said. The call ended.

Rebeka reached into her backpack. The blue light on her cell phone pulsed, announcing an incoming call. She fumbled to send it to voice mail. The blinking stopped. She took out the envelope and gave it to Louise and set her backpack on the chair.

Louise glanced at the photo and the news article.

"I can bring this to the Board for their review. It does appear promising," Louise said, lifting her head.

"We missed you at the wedding."

"Under the circumstances I decided it best to remain home. Besides, I informed the Trust of my intentions and I was busy making plans. I'm certain you understand." Louise's lips twisted into a cynical smile.

There was a defiant tone in Louise's voice. "Of course. Will I be meeting your replacement?" She shot a look around the room.

"No, not today. Since today is my last day I thought we would have one more go at it before I left." She picked up her quarterstaff. "For old time's sake, as you Americans like to say. Besides, wouldn't you like to know which of us is the best?"

Rebeka tilted her head to the side and wrinkled her brows. Louise's low, guttural voice had the menacing quality of a tiger ready to strike. "I didn't know that was important."

"The question grew on me. You have your staff. You always have your staff. Are you ready?"

"Here? Now?" The center of the large room was empty but still.

"It may not be the manor ballroom or the lake but it will do." Louise twirled her staff and took aim at Rebeka's right hand.

Rebeka spun out of the way and stepped on the edge of her staff, sending it flying into her hand. She completed the spin and faced Louise.

"Yes, here. I've always wanted to beat you soundly. I never believed it quite appropriate at the manor. See, I do care, Rebeka. I don't need others to see you defeated. It's enough that you and I know." Louise advanced, poking Rebeka with her staff.

Rebeka stepped back, trying to figure out a way to put an end to this. But the woman was serious and pressed on maneuvering toward the center of the room, every so often landing a glancing blow.

"Arik said you were phenomenal with the staff. He told me, several times, that he believed you were special but I don't see it." There was no talking Louise out of this match. She realized that the woman had been building up to this moment for some time.

Louise stopped when they reached the center of the room. Louise would use the next few seconds to prepare. So did Rebeka. She heard and saw nothing. She perceived and felt everything. She was focused, ready and totally committed.

Louise stepped forward with her opening gambit. She brought the point of her staff down and aimed at Rebeka's legs. Rebeka blocked the low attack. She stepped forward and swung her staff up, tapping Louise hard on her chest with the tip of her staff.

She hoped that would give the woman incentive to stop.

"Ah, the aggressor. Now it's getting interesting." Louise's eyes glowed with delight.

Rebeka stepped back, anticipating the counterattack, and blocked Louise's strike.

Louise came at her again. Again Rebeka pulled away, avoiding Louise's thrust. Holding her staff in the sweet spot where the balance was just right, she directed her staff under Louise's and again targeted the woman's chest.

"Come, these are basic strikes. You can do better than this." Louise knocked Rebeka's staff away.

She let the momentum caused by Louise's deflecting strike bring her staff around full circle. With a small correction, she redirected the staff and struck Louise on her left side.

Louise recovered and came at her, the smile on her face replaced with a glowing mask of rage.

Rebeka stepped forward and narrowed the space between them. She brought the middle of her staff underneath Louise's. The tip of her staff caught Louise in her soft, fleshy armpit. Taking advantage of the closeness of their hands, Rebeka covered Louise's wrist and staff with her hand, immobilizing her. Rebeka twisted to the side and, using her staff as a lever, raised Louise up and over. She fell hard on her back.

Rebeka gave Louise her hand to help her up but Louise pushed it away and got to her feet.

"All I need to do is wait. Soon enough you'll fade away. You shouldn't have come back. You should have stayed where you were."

"Why, Louise?" Fade? What was she talking about?

"Why? I saw an opportunity to get what I wanted. Lady Emily had done the research. I put the plan together. George Hughes isn't the only brilliant schemer. When he found you I was certain it was all a swindle. I even had the Trust check the financial records. Two can play his game. I needed the manor to fail and you to be gone to keep people from suspecting anything. A few changes to the documents and the new heir is found. Just like George found you, someone would find me."

"Your plan won't work now. You can walk away and no one would be the wiser."

"It's gone much too far for that." She raised her staff.

Rebeka was ready for her. She kept her eyes on Louise's face and waited for the small tell that would announce Louise's change from her pattern. They blocked and lunged across the room. The small flare of Louise's nostrils alerted her. She was ready.

Louise's strike came at her midsection. She stepped to the side, deflected the staff and struck Louise's neck with a well-placed thrust. "Enough, Louise," she demanded.

Louise fell back onto the desk. She rolled to the side, sending everything but the lamp shattering onto the floor.

Louise recovered and with quick strikes

maneuvered Rebeka against the wall. It would be difficult for her to defend herself in this spot.

Rebeka took a defensive position, holding her staff vertically in front of her and moving it from side to side, blocking Louise's strikes that rained down on her.

Louise grabbed the drapes and, with a firm tug, pulled them off the wall. Rebeka pushed herself forward. The drapery rod crashed to the floor behind her. The heavy rope ties that held them in place pulled free and flew against the adjacent wall.

The distraction was enough to allow Rebeka to plant her staff on the floor and vault over Louise, away from the wall and the heap of material.

Louise lunged at her with the point of her staff. Rebeka turned to the side, out of her line of attack, and fired off blow after blow, forcing Louise to step back.

With Louise off balance for the moment, Rebeka had only seconds to respond. She set her foot behind her and coiled like a spring. She tucked her staff under her arm and unwound, striking Louise full across her back and shoulders and sending her to the floor.

Louise spun and fell hard on her back, losing her staff. She clawed her way backward and scurried away from Rebeka amid the smashed glass from her desk all over the floor. She struggled to her feet holding a large shard of broken glass in her bloody hand.

Rebeka brought her staff up and over, snapping the point down hard on Louise's thumb. The crack of the staff and the sound of breaking bone were a second ahead of Louise's scream as she dropped the makeshift weapon.

Rebeka used the momentum of the staff to bring it full circle. She stepped forward and struck Louise on the side of the head. She pulled her staff back, then, putting her entire body behind her effort, stepped forward and thrust her staff into Louise's chest, throwing her against the sideboard.

"Louise, enough," she demanded and stepped back.

Louise grabbed the bottle of soda and squeezed the soft plastic, spraying the soda into Rebeka's face.

Rebeka stepped back to avoid the spray. She bumped into the desk and sent the already unsteady lamp flying to the floor, plunging the room into darkness. Her staff clattered to floor.

It was anyone's guess where it had gone.

She needed to get away from the desk before Louise trapped her there. Remembering there was nothing left on the desktop, she slid onto it and off the other side. She stood on the drapery, careful not to trip. She crouched low and crept toward the wall. The wall would give her some sense of where she was.

The sound of Louise's staff hitting the desk full force broke the silence.

"Dammit, Rebeka. Where are you? Why don't you let me get this over with? Make it easier on yourself."

The debris on the floor announced Louise's location as she crossed the room. A loud thump and the crash of falling books were close by.

"Shit."

Rebeka, squatting with her back against the wall, reviewed her options and discarded them as quickly as they came to mind. There was one that appeared more possible than the others. She needed to get to the door halfway around the room. She'd hug the wall and to cover any sound she might make she synchronized her movements with Louise's.

It was slow going on her hands and knees but she was close to the adjacent wall—one, maybe two, more moves. The door was within her grasp. Her hand touched something and she froze. Her fingers explored it. Relief rushed through her. It was the thick rope that had held back the drapes. She ran her hand along the rope. It was knotted at intervals. She looped it around her waist and waited for Louise to move again. Her hand in front of her like a blind man, she move forward and touched the adjacent wall. The sound of Louise's soft curses and the staff whipping through the air told her Louise had changed direction and was closing in. She stood and flattened herself against the wall. She didn't move a muscle. She focused on the sounds.

Louise wasn't even attempting to be quiet now. She kicked obstacles aside and swept the room with her staff, smashing anything that got in her way. Her hard breathing got closer. Louise's staff hit the wall a few feet from her, cracking the plaster board.

"Damn."

Louise slammed her back against the wall. "Blind man's bluff is not my favorite game. You'll find out how much I like it when I tag you."

Louise was inches to her right. She sensed Louise push herself away from the wall and sidestepped in front of her. Again Louise swung her staff.

Rebeka had no idea where her staff was. She needed a weapon. She removed the rope from her waist and hefted it in her hand. The heavy cotton braid had weight. She would have to make a move soon.

The slight movement in the air signaled Louise's overhead attack. Rebeka stepped away from the wall for a better position.

She held the rope taut in front of her as if it were as solid as her staff. Her hands between two knots, the final knot dangled at the end, about eight inches below her hand.

Rebeka blocked the strike.

A surprised gasp echoed in the room. Louise hesitated.

Rebeka snapped her wrist. The tail end of the rope whipped around and caught Louise in the face.

Louise let out a scream and dropped her staff.

"Rebeka," someone shouted from the other side of the door as it was thrown open.

The sound of feet running across the hall reached her ears. Louise clutched at her face. Rebeka looped the rope around Louise's hands. "It's over, Louise."

Blaring light poured in and Arik stood silhouetted in the doorway. For a moment everything stopped. Even in the darkness she felt his eyes on her, his silent assessment that she was all right and his rage that he had not been at her side. Her champion, her knight. The moment passed. George came up behind Arik and they rushed into the room with Detective Chief Inspector Bardsley and his men close behind.

Louise tugged at the rope, trying to raise her hands to her eyes. Rebeka didn't give her an inch.

Someone found the switch to the overhead light and clicked it on.

Rebeka squinted, trying to accustom her eyes to the light. Arik stood in front of her solid and safe.

The room looked like the aftereffects of a drunken teenage brawl. Papers were everywhere, mountains of drapes were piled next to the desk, and the floor was littered with broken glass, books and other debris.

Someone righted a chair then put Louise in it. The rope was still looped around her wrists.

The detective relieved her of Louise. "I have so much to tell you." She picked up her staff.

"You already have," Arik said.

She gave him a quizzical stare.

He grabbed her backpack from where it landed undisturbed, took out her cell phone and handed it to her.

She glanced at it and smiled. "I got a call and sent it to voice mail."

George came up to them. "No, you answered it and left the connection open," he said. "We overheard everything. I made certain it was recorded."

"Louise Richards, I have a warrant for your arrest," the detective chief inspector said.

"Arrest?" She glanced at Arik.

"The men who beat Bill and set fire to the mill were paid by Louise," he said.

George picked through documents he found undisturbed against the wall.

"I'm sorry, Mr. Hughes, but we will need this all as evidence," the detective chief inspector said.

"Of course. I will represent Dr. Tyler in the case. Please make certain your office provides me with a complete accounting of the evidence." George put the papers back.

"Dr. Tyler, would you happen to know how Ms. Richards cut her hand?" the detective asked.

"She picked up a shard of broken glass and attacked me," Rebeka answered.

"The evidence is adding up. Accomplice to arson and battery is one thing but attempted murder takes this to a different level. Do you have anything to say, Ms. Richards?"

CHAPTER TWENTY-TWO

"George should be here any minute." Cora poured herself a second cup of tea. "What do you think Louise will say?" She stirred her cup and took a seat at the library table.

With Rebeka safe, Arik shifted his concern to Louise and her attack. If she was responsible and the arsonists wore Bran's tattoo, how was this all connected? He was eager to hear what George had found out.

"Hello, everyone. I've brought a guest." George came through the library door followed by Detective Chief Inspector Bardsley.

"Tea, Detective?" Rebeka held the pot poised to pour another cup. She, too, was eager to hear the results of the interrogation. George took the pot out of her hand and poured his own cup.

"No thank you, Dr. Tyler. I'll be quick. I've come with Mr. Hughes to give you an unofficial report."

"Then the interrogation is over," Cora said.

"Yes. It was quite interesting. Almost bizarre, if you ask me."

Charles came in with a trolley carrying six boxes of documents. "Put them over here, please." George pointed to one of the bookcases. Charles made quick work of it and left the room, closing the door behind him.

"I wanted to return these to you. They're from Louise's office. Mr. Hughes has verified they're the missing Fayne Manor documents," Bardsley said.

Arik could almost hear a collective sigh of relief from around the table. The detective was nice enough but he hoped he'd leave soon. He wanted to see what was in the boxes.

"It seems Lady Emily had given the documents to the Trust's researcher, as they requested, before she asked me to assist her in finding Rebeka." George took a sip of his tea. "When the Trust confirmed her claim they ordered the documents returned to Lady Emily. Their *researcher* had other ideas."

"Don't tell me. Louise was the researcher." Cora put her cup down hard on the saucer. "She always had that I-know-something-you-don't attitude about her." Arik considered that for a moment. Cora was right.

What did Louise know that they didn't? He glanced at the boxes stacked by the bookcase. He was more eager to go through them.

"According to Ms. Richards's statement, it was obvious that when Lady Emily approached the Trust an heir didn't exist," Bardsley said as he took an offered scone. "Her plan was to forge a new proclamation giving the land to one of her ancestors and eventually make her claim to Fayne Manor and all proceeds." Arik listened, his rage boiling beneath the surface. That anyone was attempting to take his domain… Rebeka's touch got his attention. His temper cooled, a bit.

"One of her ancestors?" Cora asked. "How is that possible?"

"Proclamations include mother's and father's family names for land rights," Rebeka said. "We use legal documents all the time for following family lines." Arik threaded his fingers in hers and noted that she was as agitated as he was.

"Yes, she altered Mannis's mother's name to point to her family. Her plan was to have someone present her forged proclamation after May the first," Bardsley said as he raised the cake slightly. "Very good scones." He took another bite.

"May the first. That was the deadline she said the Trust gave us." Rebeka had a quizzical look on her face. "I understand all that but why the fire?" Magick is at its strongest several times a year—Beltane is one of them. Arik half expected to see the Shade. He had a strong feeling that Louise had a specific reason for picking May 1.

"Someone at the Trust found the old newspaper article. She panicked. She had our friends that are in custody torch the newspaper to cover up the theft of the file they had on the Lady Emily. That's what they burned at the mill," Bardsley said. "She must've believed she had everything under control and panicked when Rebeka sent her the picture and article."

"In the meantime," George said, "the Trust was experiencing some financial differences with Trust accounts Louise managed. She needed to make certain we didn't make any requests. That would draw attention to her. She contrived a story we were being investigated. I confirmed with Mr. Blake that they've been suspicious of Louise all along."

"That's when the Trust called us in to investigate." Bardsley leaned back in his chair. "Louise has been suspected of fraud for some time. When we found the arsonists we showed them her picture and things started to fall into place." Arik still had unanswered questions, ones Bardsley couldn't answer. He was still concerned about the tattoos on the arsonist's arm and the May 1 date.

"Your man Bill was right. He did hear a woman's voice. She hid in the shadows while her men took care of the documents and Bill. Before she left she told them to burn down the mill." Bardsley got to his feet. "I'm happy to tell you that this case is closed. And I'm glad of it. The woman has this self-satisfied grin that has the Trust concerned she may have compromised other properties. They're reviewing that now."

"Yes, she's a bit unnerving. She sees me and nearly breaks out laughing. They've ordered a psychiatric evaluation," George said.

"Well, if you'll excuse me," Bardsley said. George started to get up. "Please, sir. That won't be necessary. I'll find my way out."

Bardsley left the room.

"That was interesting," Rebeka said. Arik wouldn't call it interesting.

"George, did you speak to the men in custody?" Arik wanted to make sure Bran wasn't involved. "About the tattoos."

"Yes. He said Louise took him to a tattoo artist in Avebury. She gave the artist the design and paid the fee. I got a good look at the tattoo." He took out his phone and thumbed through his pictures. "Here." He showed them a photo.

Arik and Rebeka moved to see what he had. "It's a heta as Marle described," Rebeka said. She glanced at Arik. "It's not Bran's mark."

"But it's close enough. Louise knows more than she's saying." He looked at the boxes again.

"I've got to get over to the garden house. I see you're eager to get to the boxes. Call me if you find anything interesting." She kissed him and started to leave.

"Wait for me," George said. "I have to get back to the office. I want to finish up this business with the Trust. We can touch base later. Come, Cora. I'll drop you off at home." The three left. Arik didn't want to be ungracious but he was glad they were gone. Rebeka was right. He wanted to read these documents. He was certain the secret Louise held was in them.

He took one of the boxes to the table and settled himself in the chair. It was going to be a long day. The manor journals were the first to tackle. They were stacked in chronological order. He located the 1606 journal and pulled it out. His heart pounded as he opened the final pages dated April 29, 1606, and read Logan's entry.

> For a fortnight, Bran's forces have been gathering at the western edge of the field. I've taken every precaution and had the farmers and villagers move behind the wall. Marcus and Doward agree the attack will come soon. It is clear Bran intends to leave no one alive.
>
> At Doward's insistence Robert and I took Skylar and Aubrey to Autumn Chase to protect the family line. Skylar begged to marry Robert. I could not deny her. He has sworn if we do not succeed he will return to Autumn Chase and care for them both.
>
> I fear I have failed. I promised to defend Fayne Manor and keep it safe. I had no idea Rebeka's life depended on Fayne Manor's survival. I will keep searching for Maximillian's writings hoping to find a solution. It is our last hope. We make our final stand tomorrow on Beltane and pray the gods are with us.

He read the words over and over until he could recite them from memory. The book fell from his hand.

Something clicked. Something Louise had said.

He pulled out his cell phone and replayed the

conversation Louise had with Rebeka at her office.
Louise may not be all that crazy.

"…All I need to do is wait. Soon enough you'll
fade away."

Fade away.

He reread Logan's words. "I had no idea Rebeka's
life depended on Fayne Manor's survival."

He pulled everything out of the boxes. There were
books and documents before 1606 but he found only
minor papers without any family information after
1606. The next journal was dated 1670. The farms were
not doing well and he recognized only a few of the
villagers' names.

He raked a trembling hand through his hair. He
couldn't keep the information from her. Hiding it
would not change the outcome. *Think*. He needed to
find something, anything that showed him the manor
survived after 1606. Anything.

"Where're you taking that box?" Rebeka was entering
the museum when one of the new Trust interns
fumbled with a box at the door.

"The men who are doing the renovation at the
blacksmith's came across more artifacts. I'm putting
them in the workroom behind the garden house with
the other items being processed. It's really exciting.
Like our own archeological dig," the intern said.

"Yes, very exciting but it's not surprising. This area
is rich with artifacts. We've found objects and
documents about the estate that date back to 1086,"
Rebeka said.

"It's very humbling to find something that old.
I've got to hurry back. We're going to Avebury. There's
a lecture on the energy emitted by the standing stones.
Afterward we're going to measure it. All very magical, if

you ask me."

"The magick is greater at the stone's middle but if that's hard to find try the base. Here, let me hold the door for you." The intern sidestepped through the doorway.

The memories and excitement of new discoveries, regardless of their importance, brought a smile to her lips. She still tapped in to that elation and satisfaction when she unlocked a translation or pieced together the mysteries of the past. All very romantic for sure but as a teacher it was rewarding when she saw the discovery on her students' faces. It was like an initiation of sorts into some special society that only they understood. Staying here with them would not be difficult.

She came out of her daydream and moved on to the area with the new exhibits. This area focused on village life. The last of the items had been put in place and was ready to be displayed for May 1.

The cases were arranged by occupation. She compared the items in each case to their picture on her tablet, its description and how it was to be displayed.

Item 050106, in the case with miscellaneous items, held her attention. She took out her cell phone and dialed. "Come to the garden room, the village exhibit. There's something here you should see." She clicked off her phone and checked the item number on her tablet.

Her head came up at the staccato sound of Arik's long, purposeful strides across the wooden floor as he entered the room. He stood next to her.

"What is it?"

"I don't remember this item when we planned the displays. I looked it up in our catalog. Louise marked it specifically for the May 1 display." She pointed to the object in the case.

"I checked the description. Miscellaneous piece of metal," Rebeka said. "Why Louise would put it into the exhibit is beyond me. I don't see the merit when we have so many other, more identifiable items. Did she discuss this with you?"

An agonizing moment ticked by as it registered. "No, I've never seen it before."

"Is it important? I think we'll get questions and we won't have any answers."

"It could be anything," he said, struggling to keep his voice calm, wanting to tear the item from the case and heave it into the seventeenth century. If only he could.

"I assume you're right." She opened the case and removed the object.

"I'll take that. I'd like to take a better look at it."

She gave him the piece of metal. "I'm sorry I bothered you." She closed the case and turned off her tablet.

"It's not a bother. I'm glad you showed it to me."

"I have a few more things to finish here then I'm going over to the mill to review those exhibits before they test the waterwheel. Want to join me?"

"Not right now. Perhaps later. I have things that need my attention." He took her in his arms and kissed her deeply. She snuggled against his chest.

"I won't get finished if you keep doing that. But after seeing this," she gestured to the case, "I want to review all of Louise's work. There are a lot of decisions that need to be made."

"Yes, there are." He went to the garage with his arm around her. He turned her around and held her by her shoulders. "I love you, Beka. More than life itself. I love you."

She slipped her arms around him. "I love you, too, and I thank the day I fell into your arms. I wouldn't change any of it. Now," she said, stepping back, "I have to get this finished. I'll see you later. Then you can show me how much you love me." She got in her car and pulled away.

He watched the red taillights fade as the car drove off. He returned to the manor and went to his tower room. He reviewed the metal piece. The cleaved marking, the shape of the fragment, the embedded bits of stone and angle of the break told him it was a piece from a broken siege hook.

May 1. Louise knew what this was and its significance. That was why she had grinned at George during the interrogation.

He stood in the center of the tower room and stared at the now dim runes and searched them for an answer but found nothing. He paged through the books that were strewn on the table and slammed each closed, tossing it aside when he didn't find what he needed. He picked up the next book with the same results. He pulled out parchments. His finger traced the words and symbols as he searched for an answer. He tossed them on the pile on the floor.

"Nothing." With a sweep of his hand he tossed everything off the table.

"Give me the answer."

He stood at the wall, his hands fisted at his sides. "Give me the answer." His demand turned to pleading. He slammed his fists against the wall. "Give me the answer." Again the wall accepted his fury. Over and over he made his demand and tried to beat the runes into submission. But the stones were cold.

"Great Mother, give me the answer."

His forehead rested on the wall as he considered his options. Did he have any? He let out a groan. Leave her. The idea tore out his heart.

He stood back from the wall. He knew what he had to do and what it would cost him—no, both of them.

"Give me strength." He closed his eyes and chanted to the Great Mother.

CHAPTER TWENTY-THREE

Arik, dressed in the clothes he had arrived in all those weeks ago, entered Autumn Chase with his duffel bag and climbed the stairs. He took his clothes out of the duffel and put them on the bed. He placed his tablet and cell phone on the desk. He twisted his wedding band on his finger and hesitated. He couldn't part with it. He left the room and didn't look back.

He was so focused on his next task that he was startled to see Cora standing next to his motorbike.

"I got back from the caterer about Sunday's brunch. I didn't know you were here. Is Rebeka with you?" Fayne Manor was everything he fought for, everything he loved. No, not everything. His everything was at the mill, reviewing the exhibit.

"No, she's busy getting the new exhibits ready." He would miss Cora and the way she took control. "I came to return some things. I left them in the suite."

"You didn't need to make a special trip. I'm sure it could've waited until Sunday. But I'm glad you're here. Everyone has accepted for Sunday brunch. They're all looking forward to spending time with you and Rebeka."

He took her hand. "Thank you for everything, Cora. I need to go back."

"No need to thank me. You go on. Hope the mill test goes well." He got on the motorbike. "I'll see you at brunch." She stepped back and he rode off.

He pulled the motorbike into the garage and, like a man going to the gallows, he entered the gatehouse. The garrison was empty. Relieved, he stood by the hearth and opened the druid sanctuary. The deeper he got into the tunnel, the more he shed the twenty-first century and became the knight and warrior he had been. He crossed the main chamber, trudged down to the druid weaponry and opened the gate. The prize he was after was under the cloth on the long table.

He hesitated but buried his emotion deep where it wouldn't interfere with what he had to do. He took his sword and scabbard and buckled them on then left the sanctuary. He tripped the mechanism and slid the stone back in place.

"I saw you go into the sanctuary." Arik turned at the familiar voice. "I made certain no one disturbed you," the major said.

"Thanks. Are the men gathered for this week's meeting?" He needed to assure the chain of command.

"They're outside." Arik and the major left the gatehouse and stood in front of the men.

"Good afternoon." He studied each man, determined to remember them and their stories.

"Good afternoon, Lord Arik," they replied in unison.

"I see the work goes well. The mill stone has been set and is ready for the first milling test. The fields are planted. And work has started on the houses. You've all worked hard and you have my thanks. Unfortunately, I have not had good news from home and I must return."

A rumble of concern rolled through the men like a tidal wave.

"Is Dr. Tyler going with you?" someone asked.

Arik took a deep breath. "No, not this time. She's needed here. There is a lot that needs to be done." He let the men settle before he continued. "The major will be in command. Treat him as you would me. That will be all."

"Sir," Jaxon called out. "We hope your troubles are few and resolved quickly." The others voiced their alarm.

He was startled by the men's words. "Thank you. Your concern is appreciated." Each man came forward and shook his hand and hoped he would be back soon.

"Lord Arik, you can count on me for anything, anytime. Just say the word," the major said.

Arik knew what the man was offering and he was humbled by it. "Major, there is one thing you can do for me. Keep my wife safe."

The major started to salute but stopped midway and took a step closer. "I will defend and protect her with my last breath if necessary."

Arik put his hand on the major's shoulder. "I know you will and that makes my leaving easier." He would miss the man.

Arik returned to the tower room. He lit the hearth and cleared the pentagram. He tried to craft a message to Rebeka. Instead he fed the hearth with his false starts and empty words until he knew that only the truth would do.

"Beka, your life is in my safekeeping. Fayne Manor is destined to fall on May 1. I will not let that happen. I've returned to ensure its survival and yours. For now this is what I must do."

He reread the message. He told her the truth and knew that by making the decision on his own it would anger her. Maybe it would make her hate him. Would it be enough for her to stop loving him? He hoped so.

She'd have to move on.

He would never forget her.

His message complete, he set the wards. The Sword of Rapture lay on the pentagram with its hilt pointed to the hearth and its tip pointed at the mirror. The firelight danced on the sword's polished blade, making its runes come to life with a soft glow. He spoke the prescribed words slow and soft and increased its tempo, building the chant's power and intensity.

A flare in the hearth played across the blade; its reflection flashed in the scrying mirror. The swirl on the mirror's surface settled and the portal opened. He gazed at the drawn, eager faces of Logan and Doward. He stepped through the portal and didn't look back.

"Hello…?"

"George?" Rebeka stared at her cell phone checking the number she dialed. "I'm sure I called Arik."

There was silence on the other end.

"George? Where are you?" A knot swelled in her throat.

"I'm at Autumn Chase. Cora said Arik was here and I, well…" He hesitated.

Fear roiled through her. She was breathing hard, trying to keep the panic under control. It wasn't working.

"He's left all his clothes, his tablet and his cell phone. Cora said he was going back."

Confused, she climbed down the mill ladder. "Going back? Where?" She knew where. *Why* was the question. She bit her lip so hard to stop it from quivering that it throbbed with her heartbeat.

"Rebeka, where are you?" George asked.

"I'm at the mill." She heard him running down the stairs.

"One minute. Cora, he's gone...don't ask questions...get in the car. Rebeka, Cora and I will meet you at the manor."

Rebeka careened along the road, urging the car to go faster. She glanced at the forest and wished she had the motorbike so she could take the shortcut. She slammed her palm into the steering wheel then urged the car on.

"What is he doing?" She brought back the conversation to see if there was any hint. None. Her stomach knotted as she kept getting the same answer. He was going back. Without her.

She pulled onto the manor drive and saw George's car in the rearview mirror. They both skidded to a halt by the garage. They jumped out of their cars and stood there. George and Cora appeared as bewildered as she was.

She searched the area and tried to determine where to go first. A flash from the tower window grabbed her attention. She took off running for the tower stairs. George and Cora weren't far behind.

She exploded through the tower door and took in the sight. The fire was still overly bright in the hearth. His sword on the floor was within the warded pentagram.

No Arik.

She rushed to the mirror and faced Logan and Doward. And Arik's back.

Logan grabbed Arik's shoulder and turned him around.

She saw his crisp frame falter and his face harden. She moved closer to the mirror and searched his eyes. The fire in the hearth began to die and the vapor in the mirror began to cloud. Her heart pounded. She pushed on the mirror but the portal was closing. The idea of him leaving her tore at her insides. She glanced at her staff and saw the soft glow of the runes. She stared at Arik.

Testing the portal, she stretched her staff through the gathering mist.

"Grab it. Pull me through," she yelled.

With the palm of his hand he pushed the end of her staff back, sending her away from the mirror. Shocked, she searched his face for an explanation. She saw none. All she saw was the thickening mist and the sound of the mirror as it shattered into a hundred pieces.

Arik stood in front of the mirror and saw more than the shattered glass. The disbelief and pain on her face was forever fixed in his mind. He straightened and turned away from the empty frame.

"Rebeka?" Logan asked as he moved to go past Arik.

Arik grabbed his arm and held him back. "She is not coming back."

Logan gave him a questioning stare.

"I'll tell you about it later." His cold words hung like icicles on the battlements.

"I'm glad you've returned. We've much to tell you," Doward said.

"Brief me on our way to the sanctuary. Tell me everything." He tried to blot out her face from his mind but it kept reappearing.

"The women and children are safe in Avebury. As for the men, to a man, they wouldn't leave. They defend Fayne Manor," Logan said. "They'll be glad to see you." The three men burst out of the manor door.

"Lord Arik." The cry rolled through the manor grounds. He acknowledged them as he raced toward the garrison. The way to the druid sanctuary open, Arik, Logan and Doward entered.

"We've kept Bran's army to the northwest," Logan said as they traveled into the tunnel to the main chamber. An array of maps littered the table. Marcus stood when he entered, relief on his face.

"Lord Arik." Arik put his arm around the man's shoulder. "It's good to have you back."

"Thank you, Marcus."

"Rebeka?" Marcus asked.

"She's not here," was all he said. He kept his eyes on the maps. He didn't think he could stand their scrutiny.

Logan rummaged through the parchments until he came to the one he wanted. "Here." He pointed to an area. "We've been able to maneuver them over to the western section. We've had three days of rain."

"Good work. I knew that area of the field would be of good use. They can't move fast from that boggy area," Arik said. "But this can't be his main force. Bran's smarter than that."

"He's sent small detachments. Our patrols report his main force will arrive here tomorrow or the day after." Logan pointed to a section of the map.

Arik glanced at his brother. "You've done well."

"We've held them back. We're able to subdue them but I'm certain it's another ruse to make us feel safe before his larger, more aggressive assault. Every day I wait, saying today it will come. The men prepare only to be told to stand down." Logan broke away from his brother.

"That's what he's doing. He wants to strike when you don't expect him to."

"Arik, where is Rebeka? Why didn't you let her come with you?" Doward stood next to him. Logan was not far behind.

He stepped back from the table. He straightened his shoulders and put a tranquil mask on his face.

"She will not survive another trip through the portal." He glanced at the disbelief painted on their faces. "And you know," he said quietly, "her existence is tied to the life of the manor. If the manor falls she'll never have existed. I couldn't let that happen. I knew no matter what action I took I would lose her. If I stayed she could disappear. If I came back I would be without her but at least she would be alive." He chuckled humorlessly. "Mother told me over and over the manor must never fall." He glanced at Logan. "She knew and said nothing."

"When did you start to believe you would not succeed? You weren't supposed to be able to travel through the portal but you found a way. Have you given up all hope?" Logan demanded. "How many times did you tell me, once you doubt your ability you have already lost?"

When had his brother gotten so smart? He saw the fire in his eyes and for a moment he believed him.

"I, for one, will not give up. I'll keep the goal in mind. Mother gave us both those instructions. Besides…" Logan's face broke out in his warm smile. "Now that we're together who could stop us. And when we win this battle we'll start to work on a way to bring her home," Logan said. "I'll not leave my sister behind." His index finger poked at Arik's chest.

"I didn't doubt that we would work to find a way but I couldn't make a guarantee. I'll spend the rest of my life trying to find her again. For now she's safe. If we fail here—"

"We will not fail," Doward said.

Arik let out a heavy sigh. "What's the situation?"

"Bran's men watch the manor at all times. So we give him what he expects to see, the patrol leaving and returning as planned," Marcus said.

"We also have men in raiding parties. They fight on foot for mobility and concealment. They use a strike-and-withdraw tactic. Hit them hard and retreat," Doward said.

"Arik, I can feel something big building. This is becoming too predictable. We've put together a plan for when Bran starts his major offensive," Logan said.

"Show me." So far, Logan, Marcus and Doward had done well. But they were right. This was all a prelude to a bigger assault.

"There are several areas that are good for a confrontation. All are on one of the two roads in and out of the manor valley. If it comes to that, we'll maneuver Bran's forces to one of those spots. But there are weaknesses," Marcus said.

"We're waiting for reinforcements," Logan said. "We've sent word to Stuart. He is on his way from London with troops. I'm certain Bran will strike before he arrives. We need a plan that would work with our small forces. Both roads to the manor are wide and go through the dense woods. The woods are too thick for fighting. The action must stay on the road. It's limited space." Logan pointed to the two roads and surrounding forest.

"Our men would be on foot. It makes us maneuverable. We take our position across the road. A line of pike handlers, archers and crossbowmen," Doward said.

"It's a good plan, if you can get Bran onto either of the roads. Put archers in the trees that line the fighting ground. They can pick off the enemy and also alert us to Stuart's arrival and Bran's reinforcements," Arik said. A more terrifying realization washed over him.

"You have that look on your face. What do you see that we didn't?" Logan stood alongside his brother and stared at the map.

"It's his boldness. He won't care about death or injury to his men. There's little loyalty there. They're hired mercenaries. He wants to show his superiority. So if you were him where would you attack?" Arik leaned over the map and rested his palms on the table.

"If I wanted to humiliate you I would do it in front of your people and your family... Do you think he would attack in front of the manor?" Marcus asked.

"I think he would choose our own practice fields, which are close enough to the manor for everyone to see. And I also agree with you that it will be before Stuart arrives with any help. It's three days until Beltane. I'm certain that's the day he's waiting for." Arik rose.

"Will the wards hold?" Marcus asked.

"They won't be able to ransack the manor for a while. If we don't win the day," he said to his captain, "will it matter?"

"We'll have to win the day." Logan slapped his hand on the map.

"Yes we will. I want to go to the tower room and study the field. Are you with me?" Arik started for the tunnel.

"Of course." They followed behind.

Arik tripped the mechanism to move the stone back into place and they left the gatehouse.

"Wait, you'll need these." Logan offered Arik his ring and sword.

"Before you say anything, they're yours. They always have been." Logan stood there and waited.

Arik put them on. He pounded his brother's back. "Thank you for keeping them for me."

"Rider approaching. Open the gate," the sentry called. The gate opened wide enough to let the horse and rider through. The man stopped in front of them, dismounted and saluted.

"Lord Arik." The man's face lit with excitement. "Welcome back, m'lord."

"It is good to see you, Willem. Walk with us to the tower," Arik said. "What news do you have for me?"

CHAPTER TWENTY-FOUR

Present Day

Rebeka stood in front of the shattered mirror. Her heart hammered as she tried to make sense of what had happened. "I don't understand," she whispered. George was by her side, his hand on her shoulder.

"There's an explanation. I'm certain," he said.

She glanced at him but her mind was frozen. All she saw was the hardened features on Arik's face. All she knew was he was gone.

"He's left you a message." Her breath burned in her throat. But she swallowed hard and brushed away the hot tear that ran down her cheek. She took the paper, read it and reread it. Her anger grew each time. His betrayal cut her deep. The fact that he believed he was protecting them didn't count.

"He thinks the manor will fall on May first." For a brief moment, sifting through the mirror's debris, she toyed with putting the puzzle back together but that was ridiculous. There were thousands of slivers of glass sprinkled on top of the pentagram.

George and Cora rummaged through the papers on the table. "There must be something here that explains why he left."

"How dare he." She fisted her hands, her cheeks burning in anger. "If the manor is in jeopardy it's as much my fight—more my fight—than his. The inheritance is through me." She stood at his desk. "What books and documents has he been using? He hasn't just picked up and left. He thinks he's protecting us."

"Why wouldn't he tell us the truth about traveling back? It's not like him." Cora peered at her brother for an answer. "There's something more here."

"I don't know, but I'm certain that's part of this puzzle, too." Rebeka helped pick through the documents.

"I don't see anything relevant here. It's three days until Beltane. That's when he says the manor will fall. And it's happening in his time, not ours. We need to see the older journals." They left the tower room and rushed into the library.

"He's organized the papers. I left Arik reading through them this morning." Each of them focused on a different stack and went through them looking for anything that would explain Arik's actions.

Rebeka found the 1606 journal. She turned to the last pages and gasped when she read Logan's entry. "You were right, George." George and Cora read the entry over her shoulder.

"Logan wrote this the night before Beltane. That's why Arik traveled back, to ensure your safety," Cora said.

"There's something we're missing." She rested her hand. "Why would he tell me we couldn't go back when it's clear that he could?"

"Yes, I know." George's voice was low.

Cora and Rebeka stared at him. "Don't just stand there. What do you know?" Cora demanded.

Rebeka watched as George's face crumbled. She knew that Arik had sworn him to secrecy. It wasn't a good sign.

"George, what do you know?" Cora was insistent.

"Joan gave Arik a piece of parchment to translate." He turned to Rebeka. "It was from a druid text and it was about the portal. Among other things, it included information about the consequences of using the portal." He turned to the fireplace, his discomfort obvious.

"If Rebeka attempted the portal again she either would not survive or be lost between times forever. Arik had one more passage." He dropped in the nearby chair, tired and spent. "The last thing he mentioned was he wouldn't leave without you." His voice was almost too low for her to hear. She read Logan's entry again.

"Logan mentions my father's books. I've avoided going through them." She wrapped her arms around herself.

"Avoided them? Why?" Cora asked.

A wisp of calm quieted her pounding heart. Yes, her father's books. "I always knew my father was 'special,' not like other dads. And that's more than a child's viewpoint. He was so much more than an eccentric scholar. But after he died, something—I can't tell you what—stopped me every time I tried to touch his books. I couldn't read them and I couldn't toss them out. I needed to keep them close. After a while I locked them away in the steamer chest and took them with me wherever I lived. I believed my inability to go through his things had to do with his death. Now I'm not so sure." She stared at Arik's picture over the hearth. "This is a turning point, one that has to be handled carefully. There's too much at stake." Arik's words echoed in her head. Yes, and that started with investigating what was in her father's chest.

"Do you need any help?" Cora asked. She let out a breath. They had done a good job of protecting her and the manor. It was time for her to pay them back.

"No. This is something I need to do myself."

She stood in her room, the old steamer trunk against the wall. It was just a chest filled with books and things. Why was she so apprehensive? She stood in front of it and ran her hand over the top. Building up her courage, she opened the hasp and pulled back the lid. Once again she was met with the aroma of sage and mint. She took his scarf and crushed it to her chest. "Help me, Dad. I can use it now." She wrapped it around her neck.

She pulled out his books, mostly Celtic reference, and read through his notes. Portions of lectures and even some student assignments that had never been returned were in a bundle. She pulled out a box tied with string and opened it. Inside she found her school report cards and some of the small gifts she had given or made for him. She burst with excitement that he had kept them all.

She put the box aside and let out a deep breath that had a hard time getting around the knot in her throat.

The last item startled her. It was a manila envelope addressed to her in her father's hand. Her finger ran across his bold, masculine writing. The familiar script comforted her. A piece of him was with her.

She opened the package and took out two journals. Nothing else.

Her breath caught when she opened the first worn brown journal. It was filled with Arik's handwriting. The last entry was March 1606.

She was propped up in bed and began to read page after page of his attempts to find her.

Working with Logan, they had tried to open the

portal at the standing stones. He even tried to contact the Ancients in the Otherworld.

Magick herbs were mixed, chants were recited and enchantments investigated—nothing worked. He developed an enchantment but he had ruled that out. It would provide only a temporary solution. Formula after formula he wrote and finessed but they all led to failure.

Her breath caught at the mention of Dark Magick. Her heart ached for him as she sensed the pain and longing in his writing. It soared when she read his excitement at finding that someone else, George, she supposed, was helping.

Hours later she closed the book, her heart warm. His last entry was made the day he arrived. He had never stopped. He had tried to move heaven and earth and he had.

She opened the second journal. This one was filled with runes. She flipped through the pages and found a note pressed between two sheets. It was written by her father.

"Rebeka, keep this book well hidden. It is for your eyes only. I remain, your father."

She read the odd wording that was so unlike him. She couldn't reconcile the urgent tone of his message. The runes that filled the pages of the book were unrecognizable to her, except for the one sigil that combined her name and Arik's. It seemed to be sprinkled throughout the text.

She closed the book and rested her hand on its leather cover. Her father was telling her something, but what?

She decided to attack the problem the best way she knew how, like it was any other research project. The idea made her light-headed. Had her father known all along? Was he preparing her for today? She was certain of it. While she considered what to do next, her finger followed the outline of the rune embossed on the book's cover. Over and over she traced the figure. The pattern was familiar.

Her eyes opened wide when she realized what it was—the tower.

She pulled out her cell phone and punched speed dial. "George, I need you and Cora in the tower room."

She clicked off the phone. Taking her staff and the two journals, she climbed the stairs to the tower. She stood by the window while she waited for George and Cora.

It was a beautiful view. She wondered if she would ever see it again standing next to him. She took in a deep breath and watched the sun slip below the horizon.

Three days. She had three days to figure out a lifetime of secrets.

"Rebeka, we came as fast as we could," Cora said as she and George rushed into the room.

"My father left information hidden in the runes. I need to unlock them. He pointed me here." She held up his journal and placed it on the table. "You helped Arik with the runes using Arik's sword and my staff. Now, I need your help with the ritual."

"We'll have to make a new pentagram. That one is corrupt with the mirror's shards." They cleared as much off the floor as they could. The new design would cover as much of the room as possible. "Here's chalk and candles," Cora said. George drew the form with Cora's help.

Ready to begin, Rebeka stood in the center of the pentagram with her staff in hand and the Sword of Rapture at her feet.

"Hail, Guardians of the East. I summon the power of air," Rebeka said.

"By the air that is in her breath, be with us now," George and Cora responded. Cora lit a candle on the eastern point of the pentagram.

"Hail, Guardians of the South. I summon the power of fire," Rebeka said.

"By the fire in her spirit, be with us now," George and Cora responded. George lit the candle on the southern point of the pentagram.

"Hail, Guardians of the West. I summon the power of water," Rebeka said.

"By the waters of her womb, be with us now." Cora lit the western point on the design.

"Hail, Guardians of the North. I summon the power of the earth," Rebeka said.

"By the earth that is her body, be with us now." George lit the final point.

"As above, so below. As within, so without. Four lights in this place be, to open the meaning of the runes to me. So mote it be." They waited and watched the tower walls long into the night. But they remained dark and cold. They chanted until the first rays of day lightened the sky.

"Why won't they answer?" she said under her breath. "Two days, that's all we have left," she murmured.

"Give me the knowledge," she demanded and tapped her staff on the tower floor. "Give me the strength." She tapped the floor again. "Give me the knowledge." Her voice stronger, her demand more urgent. Another tap.

"Give me the strength." She repeated the phrases over and over, punctuating each with a loud tap of her staff. "Give me knowledge... Give me strength."

She wouldn't take no for an answer. She demanded the Great Mother to respond. And she wouldn't give up. Arik never had. She kept making her demand well into the late afternoon.

A spark to the right of her line of vision caught her attention. With renewed strength she continued. The sparks grew brighter. More and more runes pulsated in time with her tapping.

She didn't see a pattern. She quickened the cadence and the flashes on the wall kept pace. Quicker and quicker she made her plea.

"Give me the knowledge, give me the strength, give me the knowledge, give me the strength." She was silent but the beat of her staff echoed through the room.

Faster and faster she pounded her staff on the floor. Faster and faster the flashes responded until the sound of her staff and the pulses of light were steady.

In the midst of the frenzy she raised her hands high. "Show me the way." She shouted her demand and stabbed her staff into the center of the pentagram.

Light and sound stopped.

One by one select phrases on the wall sent streams of light to her staff and the Sword of Rapture, illuminating select runes.

One by one the pulsing runes on the wall faded until they were all extinguished.

Rebeka lowered her arms. Her staff and the sword were surrounded by an aura.

She approached the walls. Several runes were burnished into them. Their meaning was clear. "Thank you, Great Mother, for the knowledge…and the strength to use it."

It was Arik's writing, for certain, but with another interpretation. And here he believed the writing was to find her. He should've examined it from all angles. She smiled at the idea. "Thank you, my love," she murmured.

"It's the prophecy," Cora said, staring at a section of the wall.

"Knowledge destroyed is Knowledge that never existed. But when the purity of Knowledge is combined with the heart of Strength none can tear it apart."

"It must be the key to unlock your father's writing," George said. "We can—"

She placed her hand on his arm. "I'll see you when I'm finished."

George and Cora nodded and left.

She picked up her father's journal and pen and paper. She was at Arik's desk and began the difficult task of transcribing the pages.

There was a hush over the manor as the day lengthened into evening. Several times she gathered a book or two from the library and returned to the tower.

She worked through the night. The following afternoon she was done with the first draft. She reread the transcription. "I wasn't expecting this," she said to the empty room. Fine-tuning the draft wouldn't change its meaning.

"Hello, George...Yes, I'm done...Meet me in the library." She reviewed the translation one more time then went to speak to George and Cora.

"You've been up there for hours." George lowered the newspaper he'd been reading.

She placed the book, her staff and the sword on the table and handed George the translation. She took a seat next to Cora at the library table.

Tired, she put her elbows on the table and pressed her fingers to her temples and waited to hear George's remarks.

"This talks of a battle at the manor and that the family line ends." George put the paper on the table and moved it away. She didn't blame him. She'd distance herself from it, too, if she could.

"Yes. When Angus gave his lecture at Oak Meadow he told us the same thing, except he used the word *annihilation*. But I don't think Angus saw this." She pointed to a portion of the text. "Did you read the part that says if the manor falls I will never have existed?"

She understood why Arik returned. That didn't make her any less angry with him.

"No," Cora said as she read the document for the first time and fidgeted with the paper. "Where does it say that?"

"Only knowledge is burnished into the tower wall. It's a leap of faith, but if the manor falls—"

"Knowledge will be lost." Cora's voice was low. She picked up the translation and read it again. "You don't seem to be upset." No, she wasn't. Her reasoning was simple. Arik would succeed and that meant she'd be with him. "We've known the prophecy but not how to fulfill it."

"The heart of knowledge combined with the purity of strength cannot be torn apart," George added.

Rebeka took her staff and unwound the leather strap around the top. "One of the burnished runes goes under the strapping." She pointed to the rune. "I wasn't certain what it was so I removed the leather. That's when I detected the circular marking." She twisted the top of her staff. "It took a few tries but it gave way." She pulled off the top of her staff and drew out a long metal sword.

"The Sword of Knowledge," George murmured, sitting straight in his chair. "No, the *heart* of knowledge. I believed the blade was a story and didn't exist." Rebeka put the thin blade back in the staff. She wouldn't risk setting it in place until it was necessary.

Cora glanced at her with sympathy. "It says the sword will survive—"

"All along we've known that I am knowledge and Arik is strength. Together we will both survive." She left no room for discussion.

"But you can't travel back," Cora said.

"What have I got to lose? If I stay here and Fayne Manor falls I'm lost forever. But if I succeed…" She closed her eyes to calm down. "I won't fail. I'm his only hope. I won't sit by and do nothing."

"We'll figure this out," George said. She detected the confidence in George's voice.

"It's two days to Beltane. We have very little time. What do we know about the portal?" Cora asked.

"There was one at the stones but that's closed, and the other was the scrying mirror…it's shattered. I don't know of any others," George said.

"Arik told us passage was a round trip except for Rebeka's. This last one was a special one-way ticket?" Cora asked. "Arik used the scrying mirror for his travel. Rebeka used the stones."

There must be something in Arik's journal that he'd overlooked. She reached for his book, knocking her father's journal to the floor. When she picked it up her father's note fluttered out.

"Rebeka, keep this well hidden. It is for your eyes only. I remain, your father." She put the note aside but the comma caught her attention. "I remain."

A large smile spread across her face. "He didn't go back. He didn't use his return passage." She smiled and was more alive than she had been in days. She was close, so close. She wouldn't give up now.

"Who?" George asked.

"My father. He knew. Why else would he leave me this message? I'm more convinced than ever that there's a way back. There must be another portal." She racked her brain. She pulled Arik's book over and searched for any information about a location.

"If Max knew he must have given you some information. He wouldn't leave it to chance. He must have told you, indicated it to you in some way," George said.

"George, I didn't even know he was a druid Grand Master," she said.

"Precisely. So he couldn't come out and tell you. He had to do it subtly." George paced the room, running his hand through his hair. "I'll go through the druid documents and see what I can find."

"I'll go through his things again. Maybe I've missed something."

She took her father's journal, put on her MP3 player and chose one of the chants he recorded for her. More than anything, she wanted to hear his voice.

Soon she was yawning. She was no closer to solving her problem but she was a lot closer to her father. The anger, sorrow and pain of losing him had faded. Now she had memories of their time together. She laid the book on her chest, listened to the droning chant and nodded off.

In her dream she saw herself standing by the tower window watching a battle unfold on the practice fields. The Fayne Manor soldiers fought on but were outnumbered. For every foot of ground they gained, they lost two. But no one gave up. In the thick of it, men stood bloody but determined. Her eyes snapped to the distant cliff where the flash of blades caught her attention. Bran and Arik were having their private war.

Together, she must be with him. The dream shimmered at the sound of her father's chant. She turned from the window and found herself standing at the edge of Oak Meadow, her staff in hand. A warm breeze tousled her long hair. Her nose sniffed the sweet aroma of wildflowers. The grass and splash of colorful flowers covered the field and gathered around the stone signpost. The carving on the post was crisp and clear, as if it had been recently cut. Under the spreading oak branches, a lone faceless figure emerged. His black coat flared around him. The fallen leaves in front of him scattered, clearing a path as he walked toward her.

Dad.

She'd had this dream before and knew the routine. He'd stop at the signpost, she'd turn away and when she glanced back the air would be swirling faster and faster. He'd call out…

She jolted upright, wide awake. Breathing heavily, she forced herself to remember every aspect of the dream and put it on paper. With the paper in hand she ran down the stairs.

"George, Cora." She rushed into the library. Empty. Startled, she stood in the room to gather her wits. She hurried to the garage and pulled out the motorcar. The sun was setting and she needed to get there quickly. Minutes later she was at Oak Meadow. She examined the stone signpost. It appeared like any other, etched with directions. Why was the signpost in the middle of the estate grounds? Directions weren't needed here. She pulled the grass and flowers away from the base. Short of pulling it out of the ground, she needed to make certain. She put her palm flat on the stone surface. A wave of panic rolled through her.

She didn't feel anything.

The energy wasn't through the entire stone but rather in bands. She placed her palm at the base of the stone and pulled it away. It tingled. The stone wasn't placed there as a marker. It was an ancient standing stone.

She sat on the ground with her back against the stone and watched the sunset color the sky. One day. Now all she needed to do was open the portal. George had done it with Arik. She hoped he could do it again.

"Can you think of anything else before we leave?" Rebeka wanted to put the druid documents back into the sanctuary.

"No. We have your staff and Arik's sword and you've replaced the documents. Have you reconsidered an enchantment? It may be safer." George closed the gate to the armory.

"You know that's only temporary. I'll be ready to go tomorrow. It'll be cutting it close but I have no other choice. Besides, magick is strongest at Beltane." She and George entered the large cavern. Apprehension tried to wiggle its way into her mind but she squashed it. Failure was not an option.

"Who's here? Oh, Dr. Tyler, Mr. Hughes. I was concerned when I saw the way open." The major entered with the rest of the men behind him.

"You know about the sanctuary?" She glanced at each man, startled to see them.

"Lord Arik brought us here often. He told us about his life with his men in his time." The men filtered around the room, relaxed and comfortable.

"You know he's..." Truth and honesty was what Arik demanded from his soldiers. A soft chuckle caught in her throat. He wouldn't have it any other way.

"From the past." Jaxon's matter-of-fact attitude made her search the faces of the others.

Loyalty and *courage* were the words that came to mind, and *dedication*. That Arik was a leader didn't surprise her. That these men were a team—Arik's team—made her proud.

"Yes. He knew our stories fighting for England and to raise our families. Every detail of them and he didn't judge us. He told us his, about his battles for the king and his struggles to keep his family safe. Some of it was hard to believe at first but he brought us here and taught us about his time and his ways. There isn't a man here who wouldn't stand with him," the major said.

A rumble of agreement rolled through the room.

"He told us he needed to take care of his family. We volunteered to go with him but he needed us here to protect you." The major appeared disappointed. A quick glance and she knew the rest of the men felt the same.

"Then you know I, too, am from his time." The tone in the room was one of belief and support.

"Yes. He told us your story, too," Bill said.

"Lord Arik returned to protect the manor. It will be under siege shortly. He's gone back to be with his brother, Logan, and their soldiers." She scanned the men. Concern was on each man's face. Encouraged, she continued on. "If the manor falls my life will be forfeited. He's outnumbered."

A thundering protest punctuated by curses echoed in the cavern. "We can't stay here and let that happen." She glanced at Jaxon.

"Do you have any idea—"

How she would love to give Arik one hundred and fifty loyal men.

"I'll go with you." The major stood next to her. "I didn't give my pledge lightly. They weren't empty words."

"Mine, either." Jaxon stood next to the major. One by one, each man stood and renewed his pledge. In the sea of faces in front of her, everyone agreed.

"There may be a way," she said more to herself. The major quieted the men. "It's going to sound wild but I think..." Was she strong enough to bring one hundred and fifty men across time? They would have to follow instructions to the letter or they could all be lost.

Arik's well-disciplined troop stood and waited. "I don't know what to say. But you must know the risks before you decide. There's a way, using a druid enchantment, that will let you fight alongside Lord Arik." The idea crumbled before it was fully formed, leaving her defeated. So close but not close enough. "No, it won't work." She shook her head. There wasn't enough time.

"Why won't it work?" George stood by her.

"Arik's journal goes into detail about enchantment. He considered using it to bring him and another—Logan or Doward, he didn't say who—with him. But the design of the enchantment requires something to bind the men. We haven't got time to make or find something for everyone. If anyone loses it before you all return, the enchantment will break and all the men will be lost between times." She faced reality and knew she would be going alone. "No, it won't work." She wouldn't let defeat take hold. Magick required intent, focus and determination. She had to remain positive.

"Lord Arik gave each of us this. Will this work?" Bill handed her the metal disk.

A wild tremble rolled through her. "I know this. Each of Arik's soldiers wears one."

"He said before a man's first battle they have it tattooed on their arm. He showed us his. I'll have it marked on my arm so it can't be lost," the major said.

"Unless you lose your arm," someone in the group said, setting them all laughing. She watched as each man rolled up his sleeve. All the men were in agreement.

"There's not enough time to tattoo each man," she said to the major.

"I'll take care of getting the mark on everyone. Is there anything else you need?" he asked.

"You need to know what you're walking into. The men you'll face are mercenaries. They are fighting outside our front gate." The major didn't ask her how she knew. He accepted her information as fact, which was fine with her.

"We have the advantage. Men fighting for their homes have much more at stake. We'll fight to the end. How do we approach the field?" he asked.

"We'll be coming from Oak Meadow. There's a way to the manor that avoids being seen. It's a bit longer but worth it." She was almost giddy with excitement when she realized that this was going to work.

"You get us there by first light and we'll do the rest. Now if you'll excuse me." He turned to the men. "I want all the weapons inspected and the edges honed."

"I can help with that." George followed the major.

"Jaxon, see if you can use the gunpowder from the fireworks and have some of the men make grenades to bring with us. The British started making gunpowder in the fourteenth century. I don't want to underestimate the enemy." Jaxon nodded and gathered some other men.

She was so excited she almost danced up the road from the garrison to the manor. There was a chance, a very good chance, that this was going to work. She entered the library to get her pouch and gather what she needed. She saw Arik's and her father's journal on the table. As an afterthought, she slipped them into her pouch. She spent the rest of the day finishing what she could. By nightfall she had drafted her recommendations for the university, explaining she had an urgent family issue that would take her away for an extended period of time. She nominated Joan to take her place. Cora and George were there to help her.

Satisfied that she had done all she could, she went to her room. In the wardrobe she rummaged for the clothes she'd arrived in. She laid them out for the morning. She slipped into bed and turned off the light. Tomorrow it would all be over. She closed her eyes and made herself comfortable.

There was so much riding on her. Could she? Intent, focus, determination. It was Arik's voice she heard in her head. Tomorrow she would be with him. Her brow wrinkled. Of course she'd give him a good talking to about leaving her. She reviewed the ritual again as well as her list… Tomorrow. Arik was her last thought as she fell asleep.

CHAPTER TWENTY-FIVE

"Good morning. It's a beautiful sunrise," George said to Rebeka as she waited at the signpost in Oak Meadow.

"Yes." She glanced at George and Cora. "There is so much I want to say but all of a sudden there isn't time."

"You needn't say anything." Cora wrapped an arm around her. The touch was warm but it wasn't enough. She didn't know how to say good-bye forever. "It's not good-bye. When the history books are written, I'll read all about you and Arik," Cora whispered in her ear, setting them both to laugh.

The men trickled in from the manor. Within minutes the meadow was filled with the soldiers and their weapons, their cars abandoned on the roadway.

"Everyone's here, Dr. Tyler."

"Thank you, Major. Their tattoos?"

The major gave her a big smile and motioned to the men to raise their sleeves.

She laughed at their creativity. Each man wore the design made with a waterproof marker. "Very good, Major." She turned to George and Cora and asked them to begin.

The men hushed. The whisper of the light

morning breeze as George and Cora called on the four directions was all that could be detected. Their chant completed, George and Cora stationed themselves by the standing stone.

Rebeka stood before the men. They were on one knee. "You know where we go. Do you come with me willingly?" she asked.

"Yes, we come willingly," was their answer.

"Then clear you minds of everything. In all things today, intent, focus and determination are key. Think of being with Lord Arik to help him protect our homes and repeat after me.

"Guardians of the earth, hear my plea. Come now and help me. Protect my spirit as I go resigned. To be among those who wear Arik's design. So mote it be."

Rebeka waved her staff over their heads as they repeated her words in unison. She pointed her staff to the sky. Small sparks descended and brushed against each man's mark, making them glow.

"Thank you, Guardians. Keep them all safe and return them here when their work is done. So mote it be."

She took her place by the signpost. She raised her staff. George raised the Sword of Rapture.

"As above, so below. As within, so without. Four points in this place be to open the door of the past to me. So mote it be."

A flash of light made the men flinch; some covered their face. They all held Rebeka in awe when they saw the gap between the staff and sword shimmer. Rebeka and George walked on either side of the group, passing them through the glow. When the last man passed beneath the sword and staff, Rebeka nodded to George and passed through as well. The shimmer was gone.

The men gawked at one another. "When do we go?" one man asked.

"I think we've gone," another man answered.

"Oh yeah, how do you know?"

The man pointed to the roadway. Their cars were gone and so was the smooth blacktop. It had been replaced with a rutted dirt road.

May 1, 1606

Rebeka walked among the men as she'd seen Arik do many times. Satisfied that everyone had come through the shimmer safely, she took her place with the major at the head of the group.

"You all have walked this field hundreds of times," the major said. "Keep your eyes open. No one knows us or expects us. Okay, break into your groups and proceed to your objective as planned. I want to know where that supply train is and I want it taken out. The rest of you, Dr. Tyler and I are on point. Keep your eyes on us."

They moved out through the forest, staying off the trail. When they were close to the manor, Rebeka tapped the major on the shoulder. He gave the signal for the men to stop.

"Ours?" he asked, pointing to men stealing through the forest.

She shook her head. She knew all of Arik's men and those in the area he would call on. These must be Bran's men attempting to get behind Arik's defenses.

The major sent in a unit.

The men moved through the forest and followed the intruders without making a sound. The unit leader signaled his men with his fingertips across his throat.

The message was received.

The men waited for the mercenaries to get closer. When the moment was right the unit made their move. Each man grabbed a mercenary by the hair, pulled his head back and quickly drew his knife across his throat. They helped the bodies to the ground and rolled them under a bush then the unit returned to the group.

"It went fine, Major. They bleed and die like we do," the man said.

"We should be coming to the edge of the forest soon." Rebeka started forward.

The major pulled her back and unsheathed his knife. Two men on the road turned and faced them. They froze. Rebeka caught the major's arm and stopped him.

"Lady Rebeka?" one of them whispered.

"Yes, it's me," she answered and came away from the tree so she could see them clearly. "Major, this is Doward, a friend of Arik's, and Luke, the miller's boy." The major put his knife away.

"What are you doing here? Shouldn't you be…" her words trailed off. It was dangerous for an old man and young boy to be in the woods with Bran's men so close. She would be angry with them but all she wanted to do was hug them both.

"Luke went to Lord Stuart to see when reinforcement would arrive while I waited here," Doward said. "Stuart hasn't returned from the king. We need him today." Doward appeared older. His face was lined with concern.

"I can't believe you're here. Lord Arik said you weren't coming back. I knew you would." Luke threw his arms around her and gave her a big greeting then stepped back. He'd grown taller and bigger in the months she'd been away.

"How are your parents and the others?" As relieved as she was to see them, she was eager to find Arik. He couldn't face Bran alone and survive.

"Everyone is waiting for the attack. Logan and Marcus told the others they expect it at any time." His excitement was catching. "I'm glad you're here." He glanced over her shoulder. "Who are they?" He nodded toward the major and the others.

She stood to the side and motioned for the major to join her. "This is the major. He and the other men trained with Lord Arik. They've come to help."

"You've brought the men across time." The awe on Luke's face made her uncomfortable. She did what had to be done to save him, the others, Fayne Manor and Arik.

"You're a great sorceress, like your mother," Doward said. "I knew you would act on what needed to be done." He scanned the forest. Rebeka had never seen Doward so anxious. "I wish you hadn't waited so long. But I never doubted you."

Luke was unable to control his excitement. "How many?" he asked the major.

"One hundred and fifty," the major answered.

"We'll take you to Logan. You and these men may have saved us all," Doward said. "Luke, go ahead and tell the others I bring Lady Rebeka and an army." Luke charged ahead.

Rebeka stood at the edge of the forest well hidden from view. The sun would clear the east hills soon and the battle would start.

A rustling of leaves startled her out of her musing. She flattened herself against the tree. A large hand slid over her mouth.

"No screams of joy at seeing your brother-in-law after all this time," he whispered in her ear. He loosened his hand.

She swung around and held him tight. "Logan." She couldn't get another word out. She glanced at him again. He appeared tired. He was badly bruised with a gash across his chest.

"We can talk freely here. It's safe. And get that worried expression off your face. I think I look quite dashing." His fingers touched the gash.

"Come with me. There are some men I want you to meet." She took his hand and led him to where the men waited.

The men stood and sized up Logan as she walked with him into the clearing. "Major, this is Logan, Lord Arik's brother." She watched Logan evaluate the army she'd brought.

The major saluted him. "It's a pleasure to meet you, sir. Lord Arik has spoken of you often."

"Major. My brother has not been home long but he has told me much about you and your men. We're glad you've joined us," Logan said. "Rebeka, how did you bring them all here? There must be—"

"One hundred and fifty men. I told you," Luke said. "We don't have to wait for Lord Stuart."

"I can tell you all about how I got them here later." Rebeka stared at Logan. She was happy to see him but she couldn't lose sight of the problem.

"We pledged ourselves to Lord Arik and Dr. Tyl… Lady Rebeka. We're ready to serve. Tell us what you want us to do," the major said.

Logan stepped out among the men. "Yes, I know, Major. Arik has told us of your battles for England. As one soldier to another, I am honored to count you as one of us. Come with me to meet the others and I'll go over our battle plan." He took Rebeka's hand and led the way. The major and his men followed.

"You don't have to hold my hand," she said. Logan gave her a smirk that made her smile.

"The last time you were in these woods you walked four hundred years into the future. No, I'm not about to let go you." He laughed. "Rebeka, I feared we had lost you forever. So has Arik. He has no idea you're here, does he?"

"No. He didn't examine things from all angles," she said.

He stopped and stared at her. "My brother didn't study things from every conceivable angle before taking action. You must be mistaken."

"The writing on the tower walls had all the information." They continued on. "He used the runes to find me. I used sections of the writing and was able to understand the prophecy and come home. With a little help from my father."

Logan stopped. "Your father?"

"His journal. He left me information." She pulled him on.

Rebeka stopped at the edge of the woods and stared at Logan's men at arms. The men waited in a double line. They stood silent and alert as she and those with her passed between them. When everyone had gone through, Marcus came forward.

"Lady Rebeka, your men welcome you home."

A great cheer rose. She waited for quiet.

"Thank you, Marcus."

"M'lady. It is good to have you back with us," shouted one of the men.

"It's good to be home. I know the urgent task we face. I've brought you support. These are the men who have served Lord Arik. They are battle-tested soldiers who have served England in another time. Their war stories are ones of bravery and devotion. Very much like yours. Meet them as brothers in arms and know they've declared themselves for Lord Arik, as you have."

"Luke was not exaggerating. You did bring us—"

"One hundred and fifty men," Luke said with a wide smile on his face.

"Marcus, this is the major," Rebeka said.

"Lord Arik has told me about the bravery of you and your men. It's an honor to meet you," Marcus said.

"Sir, we seem to have much in common. My men and I are ready to help any way we can," the major said.

"Let's go over our plans and brief the men." Logan brought him to the war table.

Rebeka passed among the men but knew before she had gone far that he wasn't here.

"M'lady, if you're searching for Lord Arik, he's not here. He left earlier," Luke said.

Rebeka whipped around. "Where did he go?" she asked urgently.

"M'lady, they didn't tell me but I suspect he's gone to the other side of the field. Last night he and Logan spoke about cutting off the head of the serpent," Luke said.

"Rebeka, the men are briefed and ready," Logan said. "The enemy is beginning to move." He nodded toward the battlefield.

"He'll be alone," Rebeka said.

"Yes. It was a risk he wanted to take. I couldn't stop him. I've arranged for Luke to go with you to Autumn Chase. You'll be safe there."

Rebeka gave him a glare that said she didn't want to be anywhere that was safe. "Logan, if I wanted to be somewhere safe I would be back in the twenty-first century teaching my class. No, I know where I'm going to be." Together they could defeat Bran. She had to get to him.

Logan rubbed his neck with his hand. "At least when Arik yells at me for you being on the battlefield I can tell him I tried. If Bran finds you he will not play fair. He is out to destroy you and Arik. Keep that in mind." He nodded across the field. "They're on the northwest side on the high ground."

"Logan," called one of the men.

"Coming. When I see you later I want to hear all about this shower Arik told us about." He kissed her on the forehead. "It is good to see you again." He squeezed her hand and left to meet with his men.

She watched him as he blended in with the soldiers. She couldn't separate the two fighting forces. But unless she got to Arik it would all be for naught. She moved up the trail to cut across to the northwest side. The path climbed the rise. Halfway there, she got a good view of the battlefield from the enemy's perspective.

This wasn't the way for the manor to spend Beltane. She remembered happier times. She could see the woodpile for the Beltane bonfire neglected at the side of the field.

Intent and focus. She was already determined.

The ground rumbled with the pounding hooves of the advancing army as they spread across the field from the west. In the distance she could make out Fayne Manor men standing behind a wide wooden barrier made of sharp pikes. The first line of men were on their knees with their poles; behind them were archers and behind them the crossbowmen. The men stood ready. Soon they would receive the order to attack.

Rebeka was discouraged when she saw the manor's left flank in disarray. Would they lose the day so soon? She needed to get to Arik. She refocused her attention and pushed on to the top.

"You know there is no hope for you or your men. I've already seen to your witch," Bran said.

Arik and Bran stood watching the battlefield below. He gripped his sword tighter at Bran's reference to Rebeka but said nothing.

"I don't have to fight you, you know. I could let

you live knowing I've taken everything from you. You'll die a little more each day," Bran preened.

Arik watched the field and knew the tactic. Logan was drawing the men to his left flank. Arik scanned the far ridge. Had Stuart arrived with reinforcements? He stayed calm and watched.

"You seem to be having some difficulty with your left flank. Pity. Well, it will make this a shorter day. For all of us," Bran said.

Arik waited for the battle to begin.

A. Little. Further.

As he assumed, an arrow was let loose, trailing a purple cloth. The left flank broke.

The riders swerved and aimed for the weakened area. Horsemen swept up and clashed with foot soldiers who fought hard before the line broke. Men and horses thundered past them, over the top and into the dry stream bed.

Bran shook his head. "The outcome is apparent, is it not?"

Arik remained quiet and watched Logan and Marcus's men reform their lines on the west and north sides. As Bran's men raced up the other side of the bank one hundred and fifty men appeared on the east and south sides of the ridge.

All was quiet.

"For honor!" came the call from the east side. "For honor!" came the call from the west side. Bran's men raced up the slope. The battle had begun.

"It seems you are a little premature, Bran. But then you always seem to be a step behind," Arik taunted. He watched the different moods cross Bran's face. And waited.

A large explosion behind Bran's advancing forces made both men flinch.

Bran turned his back to Arik and drew his sword.

A gentleman's fight? Arik didn't think so but went

through the motions. He, too, turned and prepared but was distracted by a movement in the brush. Was there someone in the nearby woods sneaking up behind him?

Bran turned and brought his sword down in an overhead blow. Arik barely blocked the attack.

Bran took advantage and moved in while Arik was still off balance and made a sweeping move at Arik's midsection. Arik backed out of the way but slipped and fell.

A smile crossed Bran's face as he kept up his advance. Bran's thrust gave Arik a glancing blow to the thigh then he came in to do more damage. Arik tumbled free and got to his feet. Clashes of metal rang through the clearing as the two men set a rhythm of strike, block and prepare.

Waiting for his moment, Arik took advantage of Bran's labored response. The tip of his sword slashed Bran's cheek.

Bran touched the wound with his fingertips and stared at the blood. Curses fell from his mouth while his expression clouded in anger. He was like a madman and marched forward, throwing strike after strike. Arik blocked each attempt. On a downward cross-body block, Arik let the momentum of his sword carry him around full circle and came face-to-face with Bran, their blades locked at the hilt.

"Fight all you want but we both know you are destined not to leave this field," Bran said through clenched teeth. He pushed Arik off with more force than Arik anticipated.

Arik stumbled and fell. Bran lunged at him but missed his mark. Arik sprang to his feet, hitting Bran hard in his face with his fist.

Bran stumbled back but regained his balance. The two brothers fought on.

Arik moved in for an overhead strike but Bran punched him hard in the stomach, forcing Arik to fall forward onto his knees. Bran brought his sword down in an overhead strike. In desperation, Arik grabbed Bran's hands to block the blow. Bran's mouth spread into a sour smile before he kicked him in the chest. Arik fell backward, his sword falling out of his hand.

Bran kicked the blade away.

"On the ground before me—that's where you belong," Bran said, his voice vengeful. He attacked with an overhead killing strike but Arik rolled to the right out of the way. Bran came at him again. This time Arik reversed and rolled to the left, the momentum of his movement bringing him to his feet.

Bran held his sword with both hands, raised it high and aimed at Arik. Arik grabbed Bran's hands. He struggled to keep the sword up but Bran had the advantage. With great determination, Bran pushed the sword down and Arik to his knees. Bran kicked Arik and sent him flying. He landed on his back, spread eagle.

Rebeka scampered over the edge and into the woods, keeping out of sight. Farther down the rise, Bran and Arik watched the battlefield. She skirted the woods and worked her way to the clearing, closer to Arik.

"For honor!" erupted from below.

Moments later the sound of the explosion filled the air—the men had destroyed Bran's supply wagons. Staying well hidden, she maneuvered to get closer to Arik. A misstep and he turned. She dropped where she was. She wanted to scream at him for leaving her, hit him for not telling her what he was doing. But those ideas faded when Bran attacked him. There was nothing she could do, not yet. She'd wait and find the right moment.

Careful to be as quiet as possible, she pulled the

Sword of Knowledge from her staff. She had no idea how she would get it to him but she would.

She had to.

She watched Arik's movements flow from one to another. She steeled herself to stay quiet and keep still. Impulse after impulse fired, driving her to take action. But she stayed where she was.

Her heart leaped into her throat when she saw Arik on the ground and watched Bran kick Arik's sword away. The men fought on. Bran rained down one brutal blow after another. She held herself back but would be ready when her opportunity came.

"This is almost too easy," Bran said, his sword high in the air and Arik on his knees in front of him.

Rebeka smashed him hard in his temple with the end of her staff. Not waiting for him to recover, she struck him hard behind his knees and brought him down then pivoted away out of his reach.

Arik rolled to the right, grabbed his sword and got to his feet. He stood next to Rebeka.

She handed him a long, thin blade.

If Arik was surprised to see her or the Sword of Knowledge, he didn't let on.

She watched Bran's disbelief as Arik set Knowledge within Rapture. With the final click the etched runes on the blade came alive with a golden glow.

"That's only a story. It won't save you. I've planned and waited too long. I will succeed," Bran said. Arik cocked his head to the side.

She detected it also—two voices, Bran's and another.

It gave her an idea. She hoped Arik would understand what she was doing.

Bran lunged at Rebeka but she blocked his attack. Her mouth moved and she mumbled the healing chant. She closed her eyes and centered. For her the clash of steel, the noise of the battle, all faded.

Arik and Bran fought on but all she heard was the chant, over and over again.

Arik stepped in and pressed forward with a flurry of blows. Sparks flew with each strike as he hammered at Bran. Arik watched Bran's face and saw a glimmer of someone else and only traces of his brother. With each strike Arik bellowed the cleansing chant.

The glimmer on Bran's face distorted in all directions but he fought on. Arik and Rebeka kept repeating the chant. Arik punctuated the cadence with sword strokes as he battered away at Bran, tiring him out.

Their swords locked, Bran pulled his free arm back. Arik saw the grimace on his brother's face.

Bran threw his punch. Arik caught his fist in his hand, twisted Bran's arm behind him and brought him to his knees.

"Fight it, Bran. Don't give in. Let me help you. Let us help you."

The voice that roared wasn't Bran's. Rebeka put her hand on top of Arik's, the one that held Bran. Bran writhed from their touch as if it were a hot brand.

She repeated the healing chant over and over. It wouldn't cure him but maybe, just maybe, it would give him a chance to fight the demon himself.

"If you let me up I'll kill you and your precious wife." But it wasn't Bran's voice they heard.

"How can I kill my brother?" Arik whispered in his ear. He released Bran, throwing him forward.

Bran got to his feet, cocked his arm and stopped.

He stood staring at Arik and began to shake.

"Fight it," Arik demanded.

Bran, worn out and empty, let his raised arm fall to his side. "Kill me." His voice was clear but tired. "Put an end to this. I have nothing to live for. Cay's gone. I know nothing can bring her back." He straightened, eye to eye with Arik. "I've done terrible things."

Bran was a beaten man. But Arik wasn't willing to lose him. "Bran, do you trust me?" His voice was strong. His brother nodded. "I can save you, but at a cost."

"Why save me? After all I've done. Do you have any idea what it's like to be unable to control things, horrible things? No, don't save me. Punish me."

"You still don't know? The blame is not all yours. I saw your pain, lived it with you when Cay was ill. I let you convince me." Arik hesitated. "I should never have taught you Dark Magick. I have my portion of blame and have paid a heavy price." He glanced at Rebeka.

"Thank you for that. You are the knight who is loyal and trustworthy. I'm not made as you are." He paused. "Is there hope for me?"

Arik reached out his mind to Bran's. His mind was clear but heavy with guilt. Yes, he could save him but would he agree to the cost? He withdrew from Bran's mind.

Bran took a deep breath. "What do I need to do?"

"It's not that easy. Everything has two sides—even magick—good and dark. We must keep it balanced, especially the magick. Magick is part of our world here. If you stay here, I can't guarantee it will not take you again. You're a willing host."

"You mean I'm weak." Bran's chin jutted up.

"No, you were desperate. I know how that feels. I was desperate for Rebeka."

"How will you save me?"

Arik took a deep breath. "You have to be

someplace where there isn't any magick. You can't stay here." Bran's head didn't move. His eyes told Arik another story. He knew this was the only way to keep Bran safe. "You'll have to make a new life for yourself."

"This is worse than death." Bran's choked sob tore at him but he had no choice. Bran hadn't left him any.

"I'll send you where you'll succeed but it's a place where they don't have magick, any magick."

"Send me? Not Orkney?" Bran grasped at Arik, fear written on the man's face.

Arik ached at the sound of desperation in his brother's voice. "No, not Orkney." He stood tall, not wavering or giving comfort to Bran. It wouldn't help him. Bran had to do this alone. "As Grand Master I can give you an opportunity to make things right."

Bran stood facing Arik. "You were always the knight."

"And you'll forever be my brother. Remember that always. You. Are. My. Brother."

"I'll never forget." A resigned Bran stood before him, the man he had been all those years ago.

Before he lost his courage, Arik started the ritual. He tapped the glowing Sword of Rapture once on each of Bran's shoulders. Rebeka stood close and chanted along with him.

The druid runes on Bran's body glowed. But he paled in agony as they dimmed and died. Rebeka sang the healing chant louder and faster.

Bran's body slumped to the ground. Dark patches appeared where the runes had been. They would heal but he'd always feel their loss.

Rebeka helped Bran to his feet. "Rebeka, I'm…"

"I know, Bran. I knew when you tried to save me at Skara Brae."

Bran nodded he was ready. Arik passed the Sword of Rapture over him. A shimmer of golden light cascaded down and surrounded Bran. When it faded into nothing Bran was gone.

"As above, so below. As within, so without. Bring Bran from darkness into the light. Restore our brother, the manor knight. So mote it be." How could others understand? He loved his brother. He knew him better than anyone. The horrible things he'd done were unforgivable but there had to be a place for him.

"Will the Dark Magick go with him?" Rebeka asked.

"No, the physical cleansing is complete. Now he must heal his soul." He knew Bran had the strength. But he would have to be patient.

"All he ever wanted was to belong to Fayne Manor." Rebeka stood next to Arik.

"Perhaps one day it will be his." He took her into his arms. She was here and he was thankful. He fought Bran not caring if he died. Death was better if he had to live without her. He crushed her to him.

"I believed I had lost you," she whispered.

"The hardest thing I ever did was leave you. But I would have found you."

He peered past the edge of the cliff. "The battle's over. We should see to the men." He squeezed her close and they went to their men.

"I told you there was no cause for worry," Logan said to the others.

"It's good to see you, Lord Arik," the major said.

Arik's jaw gaped open. "How? How did you get here?" Arik turned from the major to Rebeka. "Stuart didn't arrive. You did. With the major and his men." He should have known she wouldn't be stopped.

She couldn't be stopped.

"I was being a dutiful wife and following your wise

instructions. I examined the problem from all angles and found my answer in the writings on the tower walls. Luckily, the major and the others take their pledge seriously, as I take my vows. They knew you needed them and they came."

"I saw the glimmer. Bran is gone?" Logan asked.

"Yes. With Rebeka's help we did what we could. The rest is up to him." They stood by the village gate. "I was surprised when you gave me this plan, to save Bran."

"Doward explained how the Dark Magick used him as a tool as I would use my sword. If there was a chance of getting him back then there was no question. I love him, too."

Arik, with Logan, Marcus, the major and Rebeka, walked toward the manor. "But he couldn't stay with us. He had a price to pay." For Bran, the solution was harsh. Fayne Manor was everything to him. His journey wouldn't be easy but he was sure he had the strength.

"All the men are waiting for you." Logan motioned ahead.

"Here they come." A shout went up as they passed through the manor gate.

Marcus's and the major's men waited. "You've met one another. Good. I find it difficult to determine whether you fight under Marcus or the major," Arik said.

"That's because we all fight for Lord Arik." The soldier's remark was followed by shouts and hollers.

Arik searched their faces and swelled with pride. He waited for the men to quiet. "You have all done yourselves proud. Logan, you commanded the men and held off all major attacks. Your strategy won the day. Marcus, you and your men held your ground against overwhelming odds. Your tenacity won the day. Major, you and your men came to us in our hour of need, requiring a leap of faith. Your honor won the day. I am proud to count each of you as my man and I thank you."

"Lord Arik and Lady Rebeka." Everyone cheered.

"It seems this morning's event got in the way of our celebration of Beltane. The women have been cooking for days and there's plenty of ale. Enjoy your celebration—you all worked hard for it," Arik said. He watched the two armies blend, each helping the other with bruises and wounds. It was difficult to tell them apart. He laughed when he heard Bill trying to explain how a shower worked.

Arik searched the crowd. "Logan, a word." He indicated a secluded spot.

Logan excused himself from the major's men and joined his brother. "Yes?"

"You let her near the battlefield."

"Arik, she crossed time not certain if she would live, created an enchantment to bring one hundred and fifty men with her. She unraveled the puzzle of the prophecy and found the Sword of Knowledge. I didn't have a chance of stopping her from getting to you." Logan's arm was around his brother's shoulder. "When are you going to understand she is as stubborn as you? Frankly, I would thank all the gods for her. I know I do." Logan smiled and returned to the celebration.

"What was that all about?" Rebeka carried a wrapped package. "No, don't tell me. You were questioning him as to why I was near the battlefield. He told me you would. Before you say anything, don't you ever make a decision like that and not involve me. Do you hear?" She jabbed his chest with her forefinger.

He stared at her, speechless. He covered her hand with his and at last found his voice. "He was telling me what a fortunate man I am to have such an extraordinary and brave wife and I agreed with him."

"Oh." Now she was speechless.

"What do you have there?"

"Mary couldn't wait to give it to me. She said it's a gift from the women. They had planned to give it to me at the Spring Festival." She removed the string, pulled back the cloth and unwrapped a tapestry. It was Fayne Manor. Two people stood on the porch and the tower room glowed with a yellow light.

"Where will you put it?"

There was only one place it could go. "Over the hearth in the Great Hall."

"Arik, Major, what are you doing in the library? It's time to bring the men to Oak Meadow," Rebeka said.

"One minute, Rebeka," Arik said.

He unrolled a parchment, its prominent blue seal evident. He read down the scroll and tapped the signatures: Alfred the Great and Mannis.

"Major, this is the proclamation granting the Fayne Manor land to our family," Arik said.

He unrolled a second document with illuminated script and a large red seal.

"This is the original Royal Charter granting our title. George needs both these documents for the National Trust. I don't want to risk them being carried through the portal. When you get back, tell George to dig up the large stone in front of the garden house. Underneath it is a vault. They'll be inside."

"I'll tell Mr. Hughes as soon as I return."

Everyone marched with the men to Oak Meadow and said their good-byes.

Both groups of soldiers mingled and wished each other well. The major and his men were going back with gifts and tokens and the gratitude of everyone. Arik and Rebeka spoke with each man, thanked them and wished them well.

Marcus and his soldiers stood on the trail. Arik stood with the Sword of Rapture on one side of the signpost, Rebeka with her staff on the other.

She raised her staff over their heads. "Clear your mind and think of home. Now repeat after me. Guardians of the earth, hear my plea. Come now and help me. Protect my spirits as I return and tell the others of the freedom we have earned."

The men repeated the words.

"Thank you, Guardians. Keep them all safe. I send them back for their work is done. So mote it be."

Arik raised the Sword of Rapture.

"As above, so below. As within, so without. Four points in this place be, to open the door of the future to me. So mote it be."

The air between the staff and sword shimmered. Rebeka and Arik walked on either side of the men. When all the men had passed through, the shimmer was gone. So were the major and his men.

EPILOGUE

Present Day

"We've found the vault. It's right where the major said it would be," Jaxon said.

A large group gathered in front of the garden house and the deep hole in the lawn. Angus joined them from Oxford. Rebeka's students, Helen and Charles, and of course George and Cora, all watched.

"Can you pry it open?" George asked.

There was a bit of banging and lot of groaning. "It's open," someone shouted.

Jaxon gave George an oil cloth bundle and a heavy wooden box. The major helped him up. Everyone crowded around the small table they'd placed next to the hole.

Cora unrolled the oil cloth and took out a note in Arik's hand. It was dated May 2, 1606.

> *George, we trust the major and the men returned safely. We can't thank them enough for what they risked to help us. We are forever in their debt. Enclosed is the original proclamation granting the Fayne Manor land to the family. The second document is the original Royal Charter granting the family*

> *title. Angus should be able to authenticate them for the National Trust.*
>
> *Arik and Rebeka*

"Here's another note. It's dated May first, 1607." Cora opened the note carefully.

> *It is hard to believe a year has gone by. Life here has gotten back to a routine. There are no more wars to fight, only crops to harvest and affairs to manage. Logan and I set a goal and I'm happy to say we have met it sooner than expected. In the box you will find James I Unite coins. Use them to keep the manor self-sufficient and to protect our descendants. I write also to tell our good news. Rebeka is expecting a child in the fall. To hearth and home, my friends. Until we meet again.*
>
> *Arik*

*****

If you enjoyed *Knight of Rapture*, please spread the word by leaving a review on the site where you purchased your copy, or a reader site such as Goodreads or Shelfari! I love to hear from readers, too, so drop me a line at Ruth@RuthACasie.com or visit me on Facebook at www.facebook.com/RuthACasie. I'm also on Twitter: @RuthACasie. If you'd like to receive my occasional newsletter, please sign up at www.RuthACasie.com.

Thanks so much!

Turn the page to see how Rebeka fell out of the twenty-first century and into Arik's seventeenth-century arms the first time in an excerpt from *Knight of Runes* by Ruth A. Casie—available now.

Druid Knights Stories

She was his witch, his warrior and his wife.

He was her greatest love.

Four hundred years couldn't keep them apart.

Now Available from Carina Press and Ruth A. Casie

Read on for an excerpt from

KNIGHT OF RUNES

PROLOGUE

England
May, 1605

I should not have stayed away from the Manor so long.
Something stirs. Lord Arik's eyes swept the surrounding
area as he and his three riders escorted the wagon with
the old tinker and the woman. They sped through the
forest as fast as the rain-slicked trail would allow.
Unable to shake the ominous feeling of being watched,
Arik remained alert. At length, the horses winded, he
slowed the pace as they neared the Stone River.

"The forest is flooded. I suspect the Stone will be
as well. Willem, ride on ahead and let me know what

we face at the crossing."

Willem did his lord's bidding and quickly returned with his report. "The river ahead runs fast, m'lord. The bridge is in disrepair and cannot be crossed."

Arik raised his hand and brought the group to a halt. "Doward," he said to the old tinker. "We must make repairs. There's no room for the wagon at the river's edge. You and the woman stay here and set up camp. Be ready to join us at the bridge when I send word."

Logan, Arik's brother, spoke up. "I'll keep watch here and help Doward and Rebeka."

Arik nodded and, with the others, continued the half mile to the bridge.

"I am not pleased with this new delay."

"It can't be helped, m'lord. We would make better time without the wagon," said Simon.

"I'll not leave Doward and the woman unescorted through the forest, not with what we've heard lately. We'll have to drive hard to make up the lost time."

The frame of the bridge stood solid, the planks scattered everywhere, clogging the banks and shallows. Arik leaped from his horse onto the frame to begin the repairs.

"Hand me that planking." Arik pointed to the nearest board.

Simon grabbed the plank and examined it. "Sir, these boards have been deliberately removed."

Arik took the board and lifted it before him. An arrow whooshed out of the trees, and slammed into the plank's edge. Willem pulled his axe from his belt as Arik and Simon drew their swords. In a fluid, practiced movement, Willem spun and found his mark. He sent his axe flying. The archer fell into the river and was swept downstream, Willem's axe still lodged in his forehead. A dozen or more attackers broke through the stand of trees.

Arik tossed the board into the river and readied his

sword. The enemy was poorly dressed carrying clubs and knives. There was only one sword among them. The leader. Arik's target.

"They plan to pin us here at the river's edge. Come, we'll take the offensive before they form up." They moved forward, driving a wedge through the enemy's ragged line, forcing what little formation they had to scatter and fight, each man for himself.

A man, club in hand, rushed at Arik. Before the attacker could bring his weapon into play, Arik pivoted around him. He raised his sword high, and slammed the hilt's steel pommel squarely on the man's head. Arik moved on before the man's lifeless body dropped to the ground.

Willem and Simon, on either side of Arik, advanced through the melee. Their swift continuous swordplay moved smoothly from one stroke to the next, whipping through the air. They slashed on the downswing and again on the backswing, sweeping their weapons back into position to repeat the killing sequence. The knight and his soldiers steadily advanced, punishing any man who dared to come near them.

"For Honor!" Logan's war cry carried from the small camp to Arik's ears.

Arik stiffened. Both camps were now under attack. He pulled his blade from an attacker's chest. The body crumpled to the blood-soaked ground. Arik breathed deeply, the coppery taste of blood in the air. "For Honor!" he bellowed in answer. His men echoed his call, arms thrown wide, muscles quivering, the berserker's rage overtaking them.

The remaining attackers paled and fled headlong into the forest.

Motioning to his men to follow, Arik raced toward the camp. He could hear the shouts, and cursed himself for not seeing the danger. He crested the hill and came to an abrupt halt.

Logan's sword ripped through the air as he protected Doward. The tinker drew his short blade and did as much damage as he could. But it was the woman Arik noticed. Her skirt hiked up, she twirled her walking stick like a weapon with an expertise that left him slack-jawed. She dispatched the attackers, one by one, in a deadly well-practiced dance. A man rushed toward her, knife in hand. The sneer on his face didn't match the fear in his eyes. She stepped out of his line of attack, extended her stick to her side, and holding it with both hands swept the weapon forward, striking the attacker across the bridge of his nose. Blood exploded from his face in an arc of fine spray as his head snapped back. Droplets dusted her face creating an illusion of bright red freckles. As he fell, she reversed her swing and caught him hard behind his knees. He went down on his back, spread-eagled. She swung her stick over her head and landed a precise and disabling blow to his forehead that knocked him unconscious.

As she spun to face the next threat her eyes captured Arik's and held. In the space of an instant, time slowed to a crawl. Her hair slowly loosened from its pins and swirled out around her. His breath caught and his heartbeat quickened as a rapturous surge raced through his body. Something eternal and familiar, with a sense of longing, unsettled him. In the next heartbeat, she tore her eyes away, leaving him empty. Time resumed its normal pace. Another attacker lay at her feet.

Arik joined the fight.

England
2008

"Lady Emily, time for your tea." Ninety-year-old Lady Emily Parsons sat in the old solar at Fayne Manor, now a grand and comfortable drawing room, resting in the wingback chair that faced the large window. She removed her glasses and looked up. *Lord Arik's Journal Chronicled by Doward* lay open in her lap.

Helen, Lady Emily's housekeeper and companion, brought in the steaming Earl Grey tea with warm scones and clotted cream. The tangy citrus aroma of the tea and sweet fresh baked fragrance of the cakes filled the room. She set the tea service on the table.

"Tea already?" Emily closed the journal and put the book on the table. Her hand lingered. She stroked the old leather binding, her finger tracing the strange embossed letters on the cover. "He must have been a driven man." She straightened up and accepted the offered cup, enjoying the mild orange aroma.

"Who, m'lady?"

"Lord Arik. From everything I've read, someone was out to ruin him." Emily stirred her tea with a shaky hand and let out a heavy sigh. "If only we knew where to find his sister Leticia's journal I'm certain we would have the complete story."

"You've been working too hard these last few months. First, organizing your family papers and now finding this," said Helen, gesturing to the book by Emily's side. "Perhaps Mr. George can take your mind off things. He arrived a few minutes ago."

"Are those Helen's scones I smell?" George Hughes entered the room, his bold strides making fast work of the distance from the door to Emily's chair.

Emily watched as he took a deep breath, inhaling the sweet buttery aroma.

"Ah, there they are. Emily, you're not keeping those scones all for yourself. What need I do to get one?" He took her hand, kissed it, winking at Helen as she left the room.

"You, young man, can have one just for the asking," Emily said as she poured his tea.

He sat across from Emily, politely spooning cream

onto the small cake. She smiled, remembering a younger George sitting in the same chair scooping all the cream out of the saucer and onto his scone leaving the dish empty, his resulting mustache the only sign there had been any cream at all. She looked now at a fine young man in his late thirties, tall with a muscular build and dark loosely waved rich brown hair with a slight touch of grey at the temples.

There was mischief in his blue eyes as he wiped the last of the crumbs from his mouth using the large damask napkin. "I've brought you a birthday present."

"A birthday present? Is it my birthday already?" Emily teased him innocently.

He put the napkin down, went to her and took her hand. "Come. Let me give you your present before dinner." He helped her up from the chair, tucked her arm in the crook of his and led her downstairs.

"What've you been up to?"

"You'll see." He opened the door to the library. An easel holding a large wrapped frame stood next to the fireplace flanked by Helen and Charles, the butler. Charles stood at attention holding a tray of glasses filled with her favorite champagne.

"What is this? I stopped counting birthdays years ago." She was girlishly excited that her closest confidants had not let the day go by unnoticed.

"I think you'll be pleased. I took the old painting you found in the attic and had it cleaned and repaired. The restoration proved challenging for the art historian. He couldn't identify the picture's subject, it was mucked up so badly."

He gently sat her in a chair. With a brisk step, he walked to the easel. Standing in front of the painting, he removed the wrapping and stepped to the side for Emily to see the full picture all at once.

She gasped and brought her trembling hand to her throat. "George, the picture is exactly like the description in the journal."

"Yes. Here we thought all the family portraits were hanging upstairs in the Grand Gallery. I've no idea why there were any tossed in the attic. The historian dated this portrait to the late 1500s or early 1600s, making the time correct. Your research appears to substantiate that this portrait is Lord Arik with his brother and two nieces."

Emily sat without moving for some time mesmerized by the picture. No, by Lord Arik. "For months I've been studying him, trying to imagine what he looked like. George, this is a wonderful gift. Thank you so much."

"I'm glad you like it." George took two glasses of champagne and handed one to Emily. He turned to Helen and Charles. "Please join us." He faced the painting, lifted his glass in salute. "Lord Arik has returned!" George gave a respectful nod and lifted his glass higher. "M'lord."

Emily sat in silence her eyes drinking in the painting.

"If there is nothing else, Lady Emily, Helen and I will see to dinner."

"Thank you, Charles." Finishing her champagne, she turned to George. "Did you bring the papers? I'd like to sign them before dinner."

"Yes, I have them here."

"You have everything documented. There will be no doubt. You will find her, George." Lady Emily sat forward, concern fixed on her face. "Promise me, you will find her."

George took her hand and patted it gently. "Everything is as we discussed. There will be no doubt. Locating her won't be easy and may take some time. We've so little to go on. But yes, I promise I'll find her and personally see to your wishes." He placed her hand on the arm of the chair and took the papers out of his briefcase that stood nearby.

She noticed how easily he slipped into his business

persona. He would do his father proud. She relaxed and for the next hour reviewed her will with her solicitor. They completed their business just as Charles knocked on the library door.

"Lady Emily, dinner is served."

"Very good, Charles. Come, George. I can't wait to see what Helen has planned for my birthday." She turned to her butler. "Charles, in the morning please have Lord Arik's portrait hung in the Grand Gallery."

She looked at the picture. Was his lordship looking directly at her, his blue-green eyes twinkling? She smiled, gave a gracious nod and addressed the picture in a quiet tone. "Good eve, m'lord. 'Tis good to have you home."

Don't miss

KNIGHT OF RUNES by Ruth A. Casie

There's more to their story!

Now Available from Timeless Scribes Publishing

and Ruth A. Casie

THE DRUID KNIGHT TALES,
A DRUID KNIGHT short story

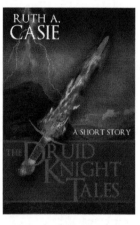

Maximilian, the druid Grand Master, was given a year to find his soul mate. On the final day, the sacred mistletoe has shriveled and died—proclaiming his failure. He must do what no other Grand Master has done before and journey to meet with the Ancestors formally relinquish his title.

Ellyn of Brodgar has the gift of healing. But each use of her magick, through a kiss, depletes her energy and brings her closer to death. Time is running out as she searches for a way to continue saving lives—especially her own.

Max and Ellyn are tossed into the Otherworld together—a place filled with magick and wonder, it's also fraught with danger, traps, and death. They have only until the third sunset to find the Ancestors, or be lost to the world forever. The domineering druid must work with the stubborn healer, not only for survival, but for the promise of the future—a future together.

Included, an epilogue fifteen years later. See how the man destined for Max and Ellyn's daughter takes the first steps in becoming a druid knight.

Arik, son of Fendrel and Dimia, prepares for training with his adopted brother, Bran, setting into motion a ripple effect that will carry love, betrayal, and death across the centuries.

Don't miss

THE DRUID KNIGHT TALES,

A Short Story

by Ruth A. Casie

Coming the Winter of 2015

KNIGHT OF REDEMPTION
by Ruth A. Casie

ABOUT...

Ruth writes contemporary and historical fantasy romance for Carina Press, Harlequin and Timeless Scribes Publishing. Formerly from Brooklyn, New York, she lives in New Jersey with her very supportive husband Paul.

When not writing you can find Ruth reading, cooking, doing Sudoku, or counted cross stitch. Ruth and Paul have three grown children and two grandchildren. They all thrive on spending time together. It's certainly a lively dinner table and they wouldn't change it for the world.

She loves to hear from readers, so drop her a line at Ruth@RuthACasie.com OR visit her on Facebook: www.facebook.com/RuthACasie or on Twitter: @RuthACasie. If you'd like to receive her occasional newsletter, please sign up at www.RuthACasie.com.For more information about Ruth's books, please visit www.RuthACasie.com.

42341065R00221

Made in the USA
Middletown, DE
09 April 2017